P9-BVH-037

Also by Allison Brennan

POISONOUS

Allison Brennan

St. Martin's Paperbacks

This is a work of fiction. All of the characters, organizations, and events portrayed in this novel are either products of the author's imagination or are used fictitiously.

POISONOUS

Copyright © 2016 by Allison Brennan.
Excerpt from *Shattered* copyright © 2017 by Allison Brennan.

For information address St. Martin's Press, 175 Fifth Avenue, New York, NY 10010.

ISBN: 978-1-250-06685-5

Our books may be purchased in bulk for promotional, educational, or business use. Please contact your local bookseller or the Macmillan Corporate and Premium Sales Department at 1-800-221-7945, ext. 5442, or by e-mail at MacmillanSpecialMarkets@macmillan.com.

Printed in the United States of America

St. Martin's Press hardcover edition / April 2016
St. Martin's Paperbacks edition / August 2017

St. Martin's Paperbacks are published by St. Martin's Press, 175 Fifth Avenue, New York, NY 10010.

10 9 8 7 6 5 4 3 2 1

Shortly after my first book was published in 2006, I met two amazing women at the first-ever ThrillerFest, both new writers. Now, ten years later, I've come to depend on them for advice, trust them with secrets, and most of all, love them like sisters. Cheers, Toni McGee Causey and J. T. Ellison. Your friendship means the world to me.

ACKNOWLEDGMENTS

As always, I have several people to thank for their help in making this book the best it can be.

While I'm savvy with social media, I didn't know how much I didn't know . . . until I talked to my two teenagers, Luke and Mary, who helped me navigate through SnapChat and Instagram and other social media apps that I've since forgotten. They also showed me examples they've seen of cyberbullying, which helped me understand better what our youth face today.

As always, Dr. Doug Lyle, fellow author and all-around good guy, helped with the forensic details for this book. If I got anything wrong, trust me—it's not Doug's fault!

The wonderful author Catherine Coulter, unbeknownst to her, inspired this book a year ago when she hosted a spring lunch for fellow authors at her house. I drove through the town of Sausalito and pictured Max chasing a kid on a skateboard. I wondered why. Thanks, Catherine, for giving me more opportunities to travel to Marin County for research . . . and of course our champagne lunches.

And because writers are truly amazing, a special thanks to the dually amazing Karin Slaughter and Lisa Unger. This fan girl was thrilled when you both read an early galley and endorsed this book. Thank you, thank you, thank you.

Zaneta Feleo, the administrative assistant to the Chief of the Central Marin Police Authority, helped me navigate their Web site, learn how the CMPA is organized, and answered numerous trivia questions. Because I write fiction, I took some liberties, but Zaneta helped me ground myself not only in the CMPA but in Marin County.

Last but not least, thanks always to: my agent, Dan Conaway—the calm, mellow fellow in our partnership who keeps me grounded; my editor, Kelley Ragland—the calm, smart voice of reason when my story goes off the rails; and everyone at Writers House and Minotaur who make it all happen.

Dear Ms. Revere,

My name is Tommy Wallace and I live in Corte Madera, California. Last summer my stepsister Ivy Lake was killed. Even after all this time no one knows who did it.

The police detective was nice but she wouldn't talk to me about what happened. She told me to talk to my dad. I thought maybe she didn't talk to me then because I was too young, so when I turned eighteen last week I went back to the police station but Detective Martin still wouldn't talk to me about what happened to Ivy.

I'm writing to you because you help people. I watched your show and you find out what happened to people who died. I went to your Web site and read how you found out what happened to that architect killed last year. That was in Atherton—not far from where I live! You said his family deserved to know the truth and have closure. I don't really get what closure means, but if it means knowing who hurt Ivy that is what I want.

Everything is different since Ivy died. My dad says that the police don't know who killed her or why. My stepmom gets mad all the time because the police haven't arrested anyone. My dad thinks Ivy's boyfriend killed her. My sister thinks Ivy's best friend killed her. My stepmother Paula thinks I killed her.

I would never ever hurt anyone, no matter what they did. But now Paula won't even let me come to the house to visit unless my dad is there and he works so much he's not home hardly at all. Austin says his mom is scared of me. He called her stupid. I told him it was not nice to call people stupid. I don't like being called stupid. I miss Bella and Austin so much sometimes I cry. My mom says it's okay if boys cry sometimes but Dad says I'm too old. I don't know why Paula thinks I hurt Ivy. She wouldn't let me come to Bella's birthday party because Dad was out of town. I don't want my little sister Bella to think I don't like her anymore. My mom tried to make me feel better by taking me out for ice cream. I thought she was mad at me, but when my dad came back from his trip he came over and my mom yelled at him the same way she yelled back when they were getting divorced. Dad left and did not say goodbye. Now I think he's mad at me, too.

I want everything to go back to the way it was before Ivy died, but Austin says that can't happen. He told me the only thing that will fix everything is if the police find out who killed Ivy and then Paula will know it was not me. But the police don't seem to be trying. Dad says we pay their salaries and they should be working harder. I don't have a job so I don't pay their salaries.

Maybe that's why Detective Martin won't talk to me.

I don't want anyone to think I hurt Ivy. I don't want Austin to get in trouble for coming to see me when he's not supposed to. I want to go to Bella's birthday party next April when she turns six and give her a present. If you can tell my stepmother I did not do anything wrong, she will have to believe you.

Thank you for reading my letter.

Sincerely, Tommy

Thomas Andrew Wallace

CHAPTER ONE

Maxine Revere and her right-hand everything, David Kane, flew into SFO on Labor Day. Max didn't like traveling on holidays, but with her hectic schedule she didn't have much of a choice. They took a shuttle to the car rental lot and David handled the paperwork while Max scanned her e-mail. A dozen messages down the inbox was a message from her lover, Detective Nick Santini.

I know you're angry that I canceled our plans this weekend. I'll find time later this week to come up for a day. Let me know when you land.

Max didn't know why she was still so irritated at Nick. She'd planned on flying in a few days before her scheduled meeting with the detective in charge of the Ivy Lake homicide—thus avoiding flying on a holiday. But Nick called her Thursday night and canceled. He said he had to swap shifts at the last minute. Something about his excuse didn't ring true, so she'd pressed him for the reason. Maybe what bothered Max the most was that she'd had to push him before he told her the truth. His ex-wife was fighting for sole custody of their son Logan and Nick had a critical meeting with his lawyer. Max hadn't met Nancy Santini, but she doubted she'd like the woman who was attempting to prevent a good father like Nick from spending time with his own child. Based on everything Max had been told, Nancy Santini was manipulative and vindictive, and why Nick couldn't see it, she didn't know.

She dropped her smartphone into her purse without responding to Nick's message. What could she say? That she understood? She didn't, and she wasn't going to lie to Nick about how she felt. He didn't want her opinion on the matter, and she certainly wasn't going to tell him she would be eagerly awaiting his unconfirmed arrival. If he drove the hour to Sausalito to see her, great. If not . . . well, she really didn't have much say in what he did or didn't do. Nick had made that perfectly clear when she started asking questions about his custody battle.

David approached her, rental keys in hand. "Whose head did you bite off?"

She looked at him and raised an eyebrow. When she wore heels, she and David were eye to eye. "Excuse me?"

"When you're angry, your eyes narrow and the lines in your forehead crease."

"You're telling me I have wrinkles. Terrific."

"It's Nick."

"If you already know, why ask?"

David led the way to the rental car. Max wished he wouldn't act as if she were on the verge of dumping Nick. She was the first to admit she didn't do long-term—or long-distance—relationships well.

Nick was different, and she wasn't being overly romantic to think so; she wasn't a romantic at heart. Yet when he'd canceled their weekend plans, her gut had twisted. She didn't want it to be over.

David popped the trunk of the luxury sedan and maneuvered his lone suitcase into the trunk alongside Max's two large bags. Her laptop and overnight bag went into the backseat. She sat in the passenger seat and slid back the seat for comfort. After five and a half hours on a plane, she needed to stretch her long legs.

If she had to she could travel light, but she didn't know how long she'd be investigating this case. She'd told Ben she wanted ten days for the Ivy Lake investigation. He'd *scowled* at her—that was the only word that fit his irritated-with-Maxine expression. Then she told Laura, his admin, not to schedule anything for two weeks. Max had almost managed to skip town before Ben found out she'd blocked off so much time. He called her in a tizzy on the way to the airport and whined. She'd already recorded the October show—early, she reminded him—it wasn't like she had to rush back. If she needed to do retakes, they had a sister studio in San Francisco.

"You took a week off in Lake Tahoe, and now for an investigation that shouldn't take more than a few days you're taking two weeks?"

She knew what needed to be done to keep her show running smoothly, and she'd do it. She wasn't going to explain herself. "Goodbye, Ben." *She hung up.*

Pulling out of the parking space, David merged the rental into the dense traffic that would take them through San Francisco and across the Golden Gate Bridge. Max stared out the window. She liked San Francisco, but didn't feel the passion for it like she did for New York City. She'd never once considered living here, though she'd grown up only forty minutes south of the city. She couldn't put her finger on why—maybe it was that San Francisco was too close to her family.

"Why does he let her get away with it?" Max asked after several minutes of silence.

"What are you talking about?"

"Nick's ex. The games she's playing."

"Nick is not letting Nancy get away with anything," David said. "There's a process."

"She's trying to deny Nick the right to see Logan."

"No," David corrected. "She's seeking full custody so she can leave the state without violating the joint custody agreement."

"Why do you know more about this than I do?" Max had mixed feelings about David's relationship with Nick. While it made her life easier that her closest friend actually liked the man she was sleeping with, she didn't particularly appreciate that Nick and David had conversations she wasn't privy to. Lately it seemed like Nick had been talking to David more than her.

"This is an area I have more experience in than you," said David.

"Maybe instead of a journalist I should have studied law and become a judge," she said.

David's spontaneous laughter didn't improve her mood.

"I would be a good judge," she said defensively. "I'm exceptionally adept at weeding through fact and fiction."

"Maybe in criminal court," he said, clearing his throat. "Not so, in family court."

"I'd certainly put a stop to her blatant manipulation tactics. She's changed her mind three times about where she and her boyfriend are moving. And who is this guy, anyway? First they're getting married, then they aren't, but are planning on moving in together. With Logan in the house? And doesn't Nick have a say in who his minor son shares a house with? The whole situation stinks."

"You need to stay out of it, Max. Nick knows what he's doing."

"I don't get it," she said.

"That's a first."

Max didn't respond. She wondered if there something else going on with Nick and his ex that David knew about that she didn't. But why would Nick hold back from telling her? They'd had a wonderful vacation together in

Lake Tahoe six weeks ago—all of them. David and his daughter Emma had joined her, Nick, and Logan. At least it was wonderful until Nick's vacation was cut short by his ex-wife. Still, Max had been understanding. Sort of. At first.

Okay, maybe she had been a bitch after the fourth call from Nancy Santini demanding that Nick bring Logan back to town. Nick never told Max the nature of his disagreement with his ex-wife but something Nancy said had Nick packing their bags and leaving the same day.

Max hated these sort of games, especially when kids were involved. She had no children of her own and doubted she ever would. But she'd interviewed enough kids over the years and learned one important fact: young people picked up on lies faster than most adults. Even if their parents tried to shelter them, they knew what was going on in their family.

Nick refused to say a negative word about Nancy in front of his son, and while Max could respect his position on the one hand, telling the truth was not being negative. The truth was neither good nor bad, it simply *was*, and Logan was smart enough to come to his own conclusions.

"You're thinking quite loudly," David said.

"I haven't said a word."

"Sometimes you don't need to."

"Speaking of kids, will you be *allowed* to see Emma?" She winced at her tone. David didn't deserve her anger, though he seemed to be trying to irritate her. "I didn't mean it like that."

"Yes, you did," David said. "I'm going to Brittney's tonight. She said we'd play it by ear."

"Another manipulative bitch," Max said under her breath.

"She is," David concurred, "but I want to see my

daughter, so I deal with it. I have fewer rights than Nick because Brittney and I never got married. I will not risk my time with Emma." He paused, then added, "Stay away from Brittney, Max."

In one sentence, David's tone had gone from normal to threatening. A few months ago, Max would have pushed the conversation, but she'd realized over this last summer how deeply she valued David's friendship. She wasn't risking her relationship with her best friend and business partner by arguing with him about the mother of his daughter. So, as difficult as it was for Max to shut up, she shut up.

Brittney treated David like garbage. She insulted him in front of Emma and refused to let David have more time with his daughter than the court mandated. The one consolation was that Emma was a smart and completely wonderful girl. She'd be thirteen next week and adored her father. Considering her parents didn't get along, she was surprisingly well-adjusted. Brittney might be a bitch, but David got along with his ex-girlfriend's parents and apparently they had a lot of clout over her. If it weren't for them, David once said, he couldn't have been a part of Emma's life.

Max put David and Nick and their respective children out of her mind and spent the remainder of the drive responding to messages from her producer, Ben Lawson, and staff. Ben had wanted to send a small crew with Max because he sensed this case was going to be good— meaning good for "Maximum Exposure" ratings. Max axed the idea of traveling with anyone but David. She needed time in the field without a cameraman. The interpersonal connections she made were key to her investigative success. Nuances in tone, expression, and body language could be lost when a camera was involved. Before agreeing to host "Maximum Exposure" for the cable network NET, Max had been a freelance reporter for years and she still preferred to work a case alone, asking questions, pushing people to be truthful, proving or disproving evidence.

She'd be the first to admit she was happy to let the competent NET research team take over much of the grunt work. They'd compiled all the public information on the Ivy Lake investigation, including news clippings, profiles of Ivy's friends and family, and television coverage. Having a staff saved her hundreds of research hours.

After going back and forth with Ben on the news crew until her irritation overflowed, she sent back a message: *I'll call in the crew when I see fit. TTYL.*

Ben just didn't know when to drop a subject, or how to give up control.

She could relate.

While Ivy's stepbrother's letter had affected Max and prompted her to act, she'd grown even more curious about the case after actually speaking on the phone to Tommy Wallace. Or trying to; Tommy barely spoke. She'd tried to get him to talk about why he wrote the letter, and his responses were simple and brief. Any other case and she would have been suspicious and likely dropped the matter altogether, but after reading the Ivy Lake media reports, she realized Tommy was mentally handicapped.

Which made her wonder if he wrote the letter himself or if someone helped him. And if so, why?

After talking to Tommy Wallace, Max had spoken to Grace Martin, the detective in charge of the Ivy Lake investigation. Max wanted to feel out whether law enforcement was inclined to help or hinder her investigation, and then specifically to ask about Tommy.

"I spoke to Tommy Wallace several times," Grace had said. *"He's slow, not stupid."*

Grace seemed amenable to Max's involvement when

they talked on the phone—the case was fourteen months cold with no leads. She agreed to meet with Max in person, which was a big win for Max—too often she had to fight with the local police for access.

Max read Tommy's letter multiple times. What really hit her was the lack of anger or grief. Maybe Tommy's "slowness" made him less emotional. Generally, when people wrote to Max of tragic events, there was pain and anger. Rage on the page, Ben called it. But Tommy's plea was unlike any she'd read before. And while he may have had help writing the letter, there was no doubt its sentiments were all his. There was a truth in the words that pulled her in immediately.

Tommy's letter got her looking at Ivy Lake's death, but the circumstances themselves propelled Max to action. Ivy had been seventeen when she'd been killed—pushed off a cliff, according to the forensics report. The police had interviewed dozens of individuals, mostly teenagers, and it seemed many had reason to hate Ivy.

If the pen is mightier than the sword, the keyboard is mightier than the pen. Perhaps unwisely, Ivy had used her keyboard to expose the secrets of her schoolmates through social media—including one girl who'd committed suicide after bearing the brunt of Ivy's attacks.

Ivy's dramatic death from being pushed or thrown off a cliff had spun a web of coverage in the media about cyberbullying, but in the end, the news stories stopped, the investigation hit a dead end, and life went on. With no killer in custody. No answers for the family.

No justice for Ivy.

CHAPTER TWO

Max had reserved two suites in the Mansion at Casa Madrona, one for her and one for David. The facility was less than an hour from the airport and had amazing views of the San Francisco Bay. She'd stayed at the Sausalito luxury hotel and spa several times before. Once, during a particularly contentious meeting of the Sterling Trust, the multimillion dollar fund that had been established by her great-grandparents, her family had reserved the entire Mansion at $25,000 a night for three days.

This week, she'd reserved two deluxe suites on the second floor of the Mansion, each with a living room, bedroom, and spectacular views. Max found the sight of water soothing, comforting in a way she didn't fully understand. She'd picked her penthouse in New York because of the view of and its proximity to the Hudson River; most of her vacations—rare though they were—centered around an ocean, lake, or river.

"You should take a nap before your meeting," David told Max after they checked in.

"I don't nap," she said.

"Start."

She ignored him. "Go see Emma's mother and try to

get into her good graces for the week. If you're not back by five, I'll take a taxi to my meeting with Detective Martin."

He glanced at his watch, then turned and left her suite without further comment.

You need to stay out of it, Max. She suspected David's advice was not only directed toward her relationship with Nick.

While Max had three hours, she had no time to take it easy—for a soak in the Jacuzzi bath or for a nap. First, she unpacked. She hated living out of suitcases. She'd done that for the first ten years of her life. She took the time to put away her clothes in drawers or hang them up in her closet. She unpacked her toiletries into the bathroom drawers, then frowned. There was no bathtub. The shower was large and wide, but no Jacuzzi. Dammit.

She caught a glance of herself in the mirror. David was right; she looked tired. A cross-country flight would do that, and she hadn't slept well last night. Insomnia was par for the course—when Max did sleep, she slept deep, but when she woke up, whether it was 2:00 A.M. or four or six, she could never get back to sleep. Last night she went to bed at eleven and woke up at two. And that was it.

Once she stowed her suitcases, she went to the living room and opened the doors that led to the balcony. The salty air of the San Francisco Bay refreshed her and the mild headache that had followed her from New York faded. The bright blue sky crystallized the bay, jewels of light sparkling as far as she could see, the water dotted with boats. She loved Sausalito, a community nestled on the edge of the bay, with unique shops, delicious restaurants, and numerous bike trails.

Sitting on a chair on the balcony, she kicked off her shoes. She could take a minute before getting to work. The last time she'd stayed at the Madrona had been solely for pleasure. Was it really three years ago? Before she'd started hosting "Maximum Exposure," she'd had a major argument with her then-lover, FBI Agent Marco Lopez, and Max had traveled almost as far from Miami as she could get while remaining in the continental United States. Still, Marco had followed her. They'd argued and made up, basically the cycle of their on-again/off-again relationship. After a weekend of hot sex, good food, and invigorating sailing she'd talked herself into the false idea that everything would work out between them.

The peace didn't last. Marco wanted to change her. Max didn't want to change, and resented that Marco thought he could mold her into his perfect woman. And how many times had he interfered with her job?

She didn't want to change—and Marco couldn't change. That it took her so long to realize the truth was a testament to how much she cared for him and had wanted their tumultuous relationship to work.

If Nancy Santini had been Marco's ex-wife, he would never have put up with her bullshit. Max instantly regretted the thought. Comparing Nick to Marco—she didn't want to go down that path.

Nick wasn't weak. He more than held his own against Max, and she knew she wasn't the easiest woman to be involved with. Nick was methodical and cool-headed and extremely intelligent. She had a thing for smart guys. Nick went above and beyond not to make waves or disrupt his son Logan's life in any way. She loved how Nick was with his son. How he played baseball with him. How he talked to him daily about schoolwork or sports or movies or whatever Logan was interested in. Yet Max could see, as clear as this beautiful late summer afternoon, that Nancy Santini used Nick's love for and desire to protect his son as a weapon against him.

"Stay out of it," she whispered, trying to take David's advice to heart.

Maybe it was best that Nick had canceled this weekend. Max didn't know if she could have kept her mouth shut for that long about Nancy.

Her stomach growled and she considered ordering room service, but Max didn't like eating in her hotel room. Back inside, she unpacked her carry-on—her laptop and all the files related to the Ivy Lake investigation. She unrolled a long piece of butcher paper and affixed it to the wall next to the desk. At home she'd created the timeline based on the facts: when Ivy was killed was the midpoint. Prior to that event was the suicide of Heather Brock, the girl who'd allegedly been bullied by Ivy so severely that she'd killed herself. "Allegedly," only because Max had seen none of the evidence—Ivy's social media accounts had been taken down, Heather's family hadn't returned Max's call, and no police charges had been filed against Ivy or her family.

There had been a civil case filed by the Brock family, but the filing wasn't yet online. Max had read a copy that had been sent to her, but it was poor quality and names had been redacted because they were minors. None of the exhibits had been attached. Still, the allegations had been serious.

It wasn't that Max necessarily assumed Heather's suicide had anything to do with Ivy's murder . . . but two teenage deaths in six months in a town as small as Corte Madera? Her staff was putting together an archive of all of Ivy Lake's deleted social media pages. Most people thought once something was deleted from the Internet it was gone forever, but that was rarely the case. Time, skill, and sometimes bribery could retrieve almost everything. Heather Brock's family would likely have documentation to prove their civil case.

Max changed into a sundress that, with a light jacket, would work for her meeting with Grace Martin, then she grabbed her oversized purse and left the hotel in search of a light meal. Later tonight she and David had reservations at Scoma's, one of her favorite seafood restaurants, but a salad or sandwich would tide her over until then.

The streets were crowded, and while Max thrived in the pace of New York City, the crowds in California didn't move. They crept along, stopping without warning or care, meandering and blocking the way, unmindful of anyone possibly in a hurry right behind them. East Coast, West Coast . . . two completely different mentalities.

She crossed the street and as she stepped up on the curb noticed a kid who looked familiar. Odd, considering she didn't know anyone here . . . she looked again. He was about thirteen and carried a skateboard. It took her a second, but she thought she'd seen him earlier, outside the hotel when she and David had first arrived.

Max never forgot a face. This kid had been at her hotel and was watching her. Dark hair in need of a haircut weeks ago, dark eyes following her. When she caught his eye, he immediately turned away.

Max could ignore him, but that wasn't in her nature. She strode toward him, brushing past lazy tourists window-shopping. As soon as the kid saw her approach, he hopped on his skateboard and tried to speed up, but he had the same problem that she did—people—so he stepped off the sidewalk and into the street.

Signs everywhere stated that skateboarding was prohibited, but he didn't care. He took off in the bike lane with a glance back to her, a half grin on his face.

Max was irritated, but curious. Who knew she was in town? Nick. Detective Grace Martin. Tommy Wallace. The kid wasn't eighteen, so couldn't be Tommy. And the Wallaces lived in Corte Madera, ten miles north.

Max gave up. She couldn't keep up with the kid. Frustrated, she entered a nearby café and ordered a salad and

a glass of white wine. She pulled her iPad out of her purse
and started reviewing the Ivy Lake files sent by her staff.
She skimmed the file names and descriptions, looking for
photos. She spotted the Wallaces' wedding announcement
from seven years ago.

She tapped on the screen to open the pdf file. It was
a page from the local paper, saved from their online
archive. Bill Wallace had married Paula Alden Lake.
They'd included their wedding picture—a bit elaborate, Max thought, considering it was a second marriage
for both of them—as well as an engagement picture that
showed their entire blended family sitting around a park
bench, with San Francisco Bay behind them. Bill's two
children, Tommy and Amanda, then eleven and nine,
stood behind the couple; Paula's two children, Ivy and
Austin, then ten and six, sat on either side of the couple.
Boys on the left, girls on the right. Artistically, the photo
was perfect. White shirts and jeans—trendy for family
photos—contrasted well with the red bench, blue sky,
and darker water. Green grass around the edges. It was
the kind of picture families framed and hung above the
fireplace.

The only one of the six with a genuine smile was
Tommy. The engaged couple looked as if they were made
of plastic, heads tilted toward each other just so, too perfect smiles on attractive faces. Amanda had forced a
smile; Ivy had a closed-mouth I-have-a-secret grin; and
Austin . . . he wasn't smiling or frowning.

It was Austin who'd been on his skateboard following
Max from the hotel.

Here in the photograph, he seemed contemplative,
looking older than his years. His eyes—sharp. The kind of
eyes that her great-grandmother would call "an old soul."

She'd often told Max that she was an old soul.

Max surprisingly felt a kick of nostalgia and grief

thinking about her great-grandmother Genie who'd died twelve years ago, when Max was nineteen. She should have had more time with her.

Thinking more about Austin, Max drained her wine and closed her iPad.

Max had e-mailed Tommy on Thursday to tell him she'd decided to look into his stepsister's death and would be in town "next week." She hadn't been specific because she hadn't finalized her arrangements with Nick. She rarely gave anyone outside of the people she worked with her entire itinerary. She usually wanted a day or two to immerse herself in the community, talk to people before they found out she was a reporter, visit the crime scene without anyone waiting for her or pushing her to think one way or the other. In her head, Max started with a pencil sketch about each cold case she investigated, faint lines that gave her a direction based on the information she knew and the research she'd done. She fleshed the picture out with her own impressions, then added detail and color by talking to the individuals involved. Family. Friends. Law enforcement. Suspects.

Max had planned to talk to Austin. She'd prefer to get his mother's permission, but she wasn't sure yet how she was going to handle the investigation and wouldn't know until after she'd spoken to Detective Martin. According to Tommy, his stepmother thought he'd killed his stepsister, so Max couldn't know if Paula Wallace would support her involvement.

Max would have to tread carefully. She'd let it go for now. Austin was long gone, and this time alone gave her the chance to review her notes and maybe even dig around a little more on Tommy's stepbrother.

Max's instincts twitched. She sent a note off to Ben to find out if anyone on staff had fielded a call about her today. As a reporter, she had to be accessible, but her staff would not give anyone her exact location. Could a thirteen-year-old boy have conned one of them into giving out her hotel information? Possibly.

Just because he was a kid didn't mean he wasn't a seasoned liar.

Before hopping a bus back to Corte Madera, Austin made sure that the reporter wasn't following him.

He'd almost blown it.

He probably shouldn't have sat outside the hotel, waiting for her to arrive. What had he expected? Well, he knew what he expected—he expected her *not* to show up. It wasn't that he didn't believe she would . . . but most people disappointed him. And she'd never told Tommy *when* she'd get here. If she sent that e-mail, then changed her mind, Tommy would be distraught. He was already nervous about sending her the letter.

But then Emma had called him last night.

"I can't talk long, my mom is in one of those moods," Emma said.

"You can come over," Austin said, both hopeful and nervous at once.

"I don't dare leave my room. But I overheard her talking to my dad. Max will be here tomorrow. I don't know what time, but my dad is coming over tomorrow afternoon."

"That's cool." Austin was cautiously optimistic. He didn't want to tell Tommy, just in case.

"Not really," said Emma.

"I thought you liked your dad."

"Of course I do! I just hate how my mom is when he's around."

"Divorce sucks."

"Yeah, well, maybe—anyway, I gotta go."

"Wait—where's she staying?"

"Why?"

"I don't know—I guess I'm just surprised she's really coming."

"I told you she would. I'll find out and text you. I really gotta go."

Austin considered going to Emma's and waiting until her mom went to bed, then texting her to meet him at the park. It's not like anyone would miss them for an hour or two, or that they'd be doing anything wrong. Emma's mom was ultrastrict, but Austin's mom mostly didn't give a shit what he did. All he wanted to do was talk with Emma. Try to figure out what was going to happen when the reporter came and what he should say to her.

But Austin didn't want to get Emma in trouble, so he didn't go. He was jumpy. He didn't know what to expect, and that kinda scared him. He really didn't think a famous reporter with her own TV show would actually come here to Corte Madera all the way from New York just to find out who killed Ivy. Why? Ivy wasn't anyone special. Truthfully, she was a total bitch and Austin hated her.

Guilt washed over him as he turned his face against the bus window. Ivy was dead. She wasn't coming back. He must be an awful person not to miss his own sister. He'd never wanted her dead, he just wanted her gone. And now she was, but things were even worse than before. Tommy was banned from the house and Austin's mom wanted to keep Bella too busy to be sad. She had to make sure Bella was entertained 100 percent of the time. Ballet. Gymnastics. Playdates. Bella was starting kindergarten tomorrow and you'd think it was the first day of college with all the supplies and clothes his mother had bought for the kid. Austin knew his mother missed Ivy, but she didn't really know Ivy. She didn't even want to. She ignored everything that didn't fit into her pretty box. Now Ivy was on this pedestal, all perfect and glowing like an angel, and if anyone said one word that wasn't about how perfect and beautiful Ivy was, his mom would lose it. Austin steered clear of home whenever possible, and no one missed him. He had baseball in the spring, and in the summer he just rode his bike and hung out with Tommy.

Of course, he couldn't tell his mom he saw Tommy nearly every day. She'd have a shit fit.

The bus ride was short, but Austin was antsy and couldn't wait for the doors to open. Hopping off, he walked to the bike rack, stowed his skateboard on his bike, and unlocked it. Today was his first day not being grounded in two weeks. He supposed he had his stepdad to thank for it, but he didn't like thanking Bill for anything. It was just as much Bill's fault as his mother's for Tommy not being at the house. Ivy had once said Bill was pussy-whipped. At the time, Austin had no idea what it meant, so he asked someone at school. He wished he hadn't. He knew all about sex, but he sure didn't want to think about his mom that way.

Still, it fit Bill Wallace. He'd do anything Paula said, even if that meant kicking his own son Tommy out of the house for no good reason.

Jerk.

Austin rode his bike the two miles from the bus stop to Tommy's house. It was a trek he made all the time.

Maxine Revere had better do what she promised. Emma thought she was some sort of superwoman, but Austin was skeptical. Why did she care what happened to Ivy? No one else did. His mom said she did, but she already had her mind made up. She didn't care about the truth, she only wanted to hurt Tommy.

Tommy, who used to be a happy guy, wasn't happy anymore. Before Ivy was killed, Austin and Tommy would bike to his house after school because Tommy's mom Jenny Wallace often worked late and Tommy's sister was either out or in her room talking on the phone or doing homework. Tommy didn't like being alone. They'd play video games, or go to the park, or watch cartoons. Tommy loved cartoons. "SpongeBob SquarePants," "the Fairly OddParents," and his favorite—"Jimmy Neutron." Bill had an old collection of "Looney Tunes," which he would let them watch, and Tommy could watch Bugs Bunny for hours. He didn't like the Road Runner because he said the Road Runner made Wile E. Coyote feel stupid. They'd take Bella to the park down the street and Tommy never got tired of pushing her on the swing or spinning her on the merry-go-round. He'd play as long as Bella wanted, or until it was time to go home for dinner.

All that ended last year. Now Austin lied about where he was going so he could hang with Tommy. Sometimes he snuck out of the house. His mom didn't care, so Austin grew careless. Two weeks ago she'd caught him sneaking back into the house—someone had ratted him out, probably Tommy's old fart neighbor. Austin didn't mind so much being grounded, but now Tommy thought it was his fault that Austin got in trouble.

Ever since Paula wouldn't let Tommy come to Bella's birthday party, Austin had known they had to do something. Paula had even told Bill that all the other mothers were scared of Tommy, that they didn't trust him around their little girls. Paula said no one would come to Bella's party if Tommy was there and she would be heartbroken. Austin didn't believe his mother—but Bill did.

Tommy had cried. Austin didn't know what to do. He went to his mom and pleaded with her to let Tommy come to the party. When she said no, Austin found her favorite earrings in the bathroom and pushed them down the drain. She would never find them.

Tommy still talked about the party.

"Did you give Bella my present? The baby doll with the pretty blue eyes and the pink dress? Pink is Bella's favorite color."

"She loves the doll, Tommy. She sleeps with her every night." That was the truth.

"Did you tell her thank you for the piece of cake? I love cake almost as much as ice cream."

"I told her." That was a lie. Tommy was so sad the day of Bella's party that Austin brought over a piece of cake and told him that Bella saved it just for him. In truth, Bella had missed Tommy for about five minutes until all her little friends showed up and the man with the ponies came.

Tommy had said one thing that got Austin thinking. "I wish we knew who hurt Ivy so Paula will let me be in the family again."

Austin told everything to Emma earlier that summer. It came out in a rush the night the police wouldn't talk to him and Tommy a year after Ivy was murdered. They were sitting in the park late at night down the street from Emma's house. She'd snuck out, but they weren't doing anything wrong. Just talking.

"I don't know what to do," Austin said. "I want to help, but I can't force my mom to stop being a stupid bitch. I can't force Bill to see how sad Tommy is all the time."

"I know," Emma said. "Max would help. I know it."

"Who's Max?"

"Maxine Revere. My dad works for her. She's a reporter, and this is what she does—solves cold cases. She has a television show where she talks about crime and stuff. She's like a private investigator, sort of, but not really. She's a reporter, but not like the newspaper or anything. She's written four books about murder and stuff."

"Your dad works for her? Can you see if she'll help us?"

Emma frowned. "It's just—my mom and dad don't get

along, and my mom and Max had a big fight last summer when I visited my dad in New York. I don't want my mom finding out that I'm doing this. Does that make sense?"

In a twisted way, yeah, Austin understood. "You think your mom will get mad at your dad or something."

"She hates that I like spending time with him, and one time I told her that Max took me shopping and she had a total meltdown. I really don't know why—she knows Max and my dad aren't together or anything."

"Maybe you can get her phone number and I can call her?" He had no idea what he would say.

"I know what I can do—my dad and I are going up to visit Max and her boyfriend in Lake Tahoe next week. I'll ask her a bunch of questions about her cases, she likes talking about them. I'll find out how she picks which cold cases she investigates, and then we'll know how to get her here."

"You think that would work?"

"My dad says that Max has a compulsive need to solve puzzles, and she looks at unsolved murders as puzzles. I just have to figure out how she decides which unsolved murders she investigates."

"You'd do that for me?"

"Of course. Tommy didn't hurt anyone."

"I wish everyone else believed that."

When Emma came back from Lake Tahoe, she said she'd figured out what Max looked for in the cases she wanted to investigate, and thought the best way to get her to come was if Tommy asked because he was eighteen. At first, Tommy was skeptical, but he sat down and wrote the letter. Austin and Emma helped—Emma had some great advice on what to say, insisting that if Max was curious, she'd definitely come—and they mailed it the next day. Austin asked why not e-mail, and Emma said that

Max got hundreds of e-mails every day, but only a few letters in the mail.

"She said she's supposed to see everything that comes in that doesn't fit into specific categories, but that her staff sometimes makes decisions for her. And e-mails often get lost or misdirected. So we need to send a real letter."

That was August first.

Two weeks later, Max called Tommy. And now she was here.

Austin parked his bike around the side of Tommy's house because he didn't want the nosy neighbor down the street to rat him out again. Corte Madera wasn't a big town, and everyone knew everyone else and stuck their big fat noses in everyone else's business.

He ran through the backyard and called up into the tree house. "Tommy! You up there?"

Tommy's blond head poked through the window. He grinned and waved. "Hi, Austin! What's the code?"

Austin sometimes tired of Tommy's games, but Tommy would sulk if he didn't give him the code. "SpongePants SquareBob."

Tommy laughed. Even though only Tommy and Austin used the tree house, Tommy changed the code the first of every month.

Austin climbed up the ladder and pushed open the door. The tree house was pretty cool and large enough for both him and Tommy to haul up sleeping bags and a portable DVD player and watch movies until midnight. Jenny never allowed Tommy to sleep in the tree house overnight; she was afraid he'd wake up and not know where he was and fall out. Austin promised he'd sleep over the door so Tommy couldn't fall out, but Jenny still said no. She worried too much.

Bill had made the tree house for Tommy just before the divorce. Austin thought that Bill had built it out of guilt. Based on the timing, Bill had started construction on it about the same time he started screwing Austin's mom up in Seattle. When Bill started dating his mother, Austin didn't know he was still married to someone else; a year later, Bill and Jenny filed for divorce. Paula moved the family to Corte Madera and she and Bill got married.

"When do you have to be home?" Tommy asked.

"Six."

Tommy looked carefully at his watch. He set the timer. "I don't want you to get in trouble again because of me so I set my alarm to go off in one hour."

Austin's fists clenched. "It's not your fault, Tommy. I told you that!"

Tommy didn't say anything. He just looked out the tree house window.

Austin took a deep breath. "I'm sorry I yelled." He was trying hard not to get mad at Tommy. He *wasn't* mad at Tommy, he was mad at everyone else. His stepfather for letting his mother banish Tommy from the house; his mother for being a snobby bitch; Tommy's mother for being such a worrier and treating Tommy like he'd never grow up; and Ivy. Ivy, his dead sister. He'd always hated her, and he felt like shit because she was dead and he *still* hated her.

"I saw the reporter today," Austin said.

Tommy's eyes widened. "She's here? For real?"

"Yes. She told you she was coming."

"I know, but people say a lot of things and sometimes they aren't true."

"She's here. I saw her. And Emma's dad."

Tommy leaned forward, his pale blue eyes wide and inquisitive. "What's she like? Did she—"

"I didn't talk to her."

Tommy frowned again. "Why not?"

"She said she'd contact you when she arrived. Did you check your e-mail today?"

"Yes, just like you told me to. And I have my phone with me, I'm not going to forget it. And I'm going to try not to answer my phone if my mom is around." His brow furrowed. "Why will my mom get mad about the letter? I think my mom will be very happy if Ms. Revere finds out who killed Ivy. Everyone will be happy."

Everyone except the person who killed her, Austin thought. The scary thing was that it had to be someone they knew. Austin had been thinking about it for more than a year, and that was the only logical conclusion. Everyone hated Ivy, but who hated her enough to kill her?

"Do you really think Ms. Revere will find out what happened?" Tommy asked.

"Yes." She had to. Tommy had been so sad since Austin's mom kicked him out of the house. Austin missed him. Bella missed him. But more than anything, Tommy was regressing back to his simple ways. Austin had known him since his mother married Tommy's dad, when Tommy was eleven and Austin was six. Tommy's mom did everything for him. She didn't want him to get his driver's license, she didn't want him to go away to college—didn't even want him to go to community college. But Tommy wasn't stupid. Sure, he learned slower than most people, but he *wanted* to learn. He wouldn't be a doctor or lawyer or work on Wall Street, but he *could* do something he liked. Tommy wanted to be a teacher—and Austin would do anything he could to help make that happen. He wasn't sure if Tommy would be able to teach in a school, but maybe he could be an assistant. Tommy loved kids, especially little kids like Bella. He had patience and he liked the structure of school. He'd once said if he couldn't be a teacher, he wanted to work at AT&T Park so he could see every baseball game.

"I'd do anything, Austin. I can clean the seats and mow the field and help people find their seats. I memo-

rized the whole stadium. It's on the computer, a map of every seat! I know where all of them are. But I won't clean the bathrooms. Remember when we went to that game two years ago? And we went to the bathroom? And someone had peed on the floor? And I almost got sick? I don't want to clean up someone else's pee."

Tommy had his own ideas and dreams and he wanted to take care of himself. But it would never happen if Austin couldn't get him out from under Jenny's thumb. When Tommy had come to visit and live at Austin's house, two weekends a month—and more often during the summer—he'd become more independent. More capable of doing things on his own. Austin had been working with Tommy on learning to read better. He was really good with numbers and basic math but his reading was slow and labored. Austin found an online test and in one year Tommy went from reading twenty-five words a minute to forty words a minute. Why didn't his own mother see that he was smart and he could learn, it just took him longer than most people?

Austin would never understand adults. He definitely didn't want to be one. Not that he liked being a kid, either.

He and Tommy played Crazy Eights. Austin didn't want to go home a minute before he had to, but five minutes into the game, his phone vibrated with a message from Emma.

Can you meet?

Austin looked at the time. It was nearly five. Emma lived in Larkspur, the small town next to Corte Madera. It'd take him twenty minutes to bike there. He'd be late getting home.

Screw his mother.

Sure. Now?

Emma responded: *Anytime. I have to get out of the house. I'm so mad at my mom.*

Join the club, he thought. He wrote, *I can meet right now, or later tonight.*

"Who is it?" Tommy asked.

"Emma. Her parents don't get along."

Tommy nodded sadly. "Like mine."

"Exactly."

It took Emma a minute, but then she sent him back a message.

I have to be in by seven. How about the bookstore at five thirty? That's like halfway between you and me.

I'll be there.

Austin got up. "I'm going to see Emma."

"You'll be late getting home."

"I'll tell my mom I'm going to the bookstore. I'll come home with a book. It's cool."

"Are you sure?" Tommy was worried. "Do you want me to come? I like Emma. She's nice."

"Maybe it's better if you stay here. Check your e-mail every hour."

"Okay, I'll do that." Tommy hugged Austin. "I'll see you tomorrow."

Austin climbed down the ladder and sent his mom a text message.

I'm meeting Emma at the bookstore in Corte Madera. She needs help with her homework. I might be a little late, is that okay?

He didn't wait for a response, or even care if his mom said yes or no. He'd found that if he asked her—even if she didn't respond—she was more willing to overlook anything he did. Another thing he'd learned was that the best lies were shrouded in truth. His mother knew Emma because they went to the same school. Emma's mother came from a wealthy family so Paula Wallace was just fine with Austin hanging out with her. As if having money made Emma better than other people. Paula would have a shit fit if she knew that Emma's dad was gay and her mother never got married, but she didn't need to know everything.

If Emma hadn't helped them write the letter, Austin didn't think they'd have captured the attention of a New York reporter. But Emma had made Austin swear that he wouldn't tell anyone that she'd helped because her mother hated her dad and therefore hated everyone associated with her dad, including Max Revere. Once, when they were at the library, he'd asked her why.

"Is your dad a jerk or something?"

Emma shook her head. She was pretty, with blond hair and big green eyes. And she wasn't stuck on herself like other middle-school girls. "He was an Army Ranger. A real hero—my granddad told me how he saved a whole bunch of people when he was in Afghanistan. A school of girls. They don't let girls learn anything over there."

"That's fucked."

She frowned.

"Sorry," he muttered.

She touched his hand. A little jolt rushed to his stomach. He really liked Emma. She listened to him. She got it.

"My mom doesn't like my dad because he's gay."

The librarian shushed them and Emma leaned forward so she could whisper. "Well, not because he's gay, but because he didn't tell anyone and they dated in high school. He told me once that he wanted to prove that he was, like, normal so he tried to act like all the other guys." She paused, looking at him but not really seeing him.

"You like your dad?"

"Yeah. I love him. Sometimes he's sad and won't talk to me about it because I'm a kid. I wish my mom wasn't so mean to him. She's not like that most of the time . . . well, she has her moments, I guess. She dates jerks. It's like she thinks she has to have a boyfriend or she's not

pretty or something. I don't get it." She frowned, then continued. "I just think she's more hurt than anything because she really loved my dad and was surprised when he told her the truth. And that was after she got pregnant—after they were engaged—and he said he couldn't go through with getting married and everything because it wouldn't be fair to her. They'd just graduated from high school. My mom is super emotional about everything. She goes up and down, that's what my nana says—my mom's mom. My mom loved my dad, but he couldn't love her back and she's never forgiven him."

"I'm sorry."

"Me, too."

"Is it weird that he's gay?"

She shrugged. "I don't really think about it. I mean, he's my dad first, you know?"

He nodded. He did know, because that's how he felt about Tommy. Tommy was technically retarded, but Austin didn't think about him like that, he was his brother—stepbrother, but Tommy always called him his brother.

Emma said, "I just wish my mom could forget about my dad and find someone who's nice to her, because she always dates assholes." She put her hand over her mouth. "You're a bad influence on me! Nana would wash my mouth out with soap."

Austin locked his bike outside the bookstore and went inside. When he saw Emma, all the frustration and anger he'd been holding inside all day just disappeared and he smiled.

CHAPTER THREE

Max's working relationship with cops was unusual. Since she only looked at missing persons and cold cases, she wasn't a traditional reporter. Her goal in any investigation was never to dig up dirt on law enforcement but too often they stymied her pursuit for the truth, and that's when she dug deeper, to determine if there was another reason for their hostility. Some cops simply didn't like outsiders, reporter or not. Some cops actually despised reporters. Others were indifferent. A few were friendly, and usually only after having worked with Max. And some were bad cops. She told the truth, always. And law enforcement never liked it when one of their own was proven to be incompetent—or worse.

Detective Grace Martin of the Central Marin Police Authority didn't fit any mold. Even cops who were willing to talk to Max rarely invited her to meet at the police station, but Grace told her to stop in near the end of her shift. And when the desk sergeant informed Martin that Max had arrived, she promptly came out and extended her hand.

"Grace Martin." Her handshake was brief but firm. The fifty-year-old detective had short gray hair and gray eyes. She wore dark slacks with a crisp white polo shirt, a little loose on her as if she'd recently lost weight, though she was sturdy. Max always looked at shoes—she had a thing for footwear. Grace wore high-end black Nike tennis shoes. Comfortable, practical. "I reserved a conference room so we will have a bit of privacy."

"I appreciate your time," Max said.

While Max towered over the cop, she suspected Grace could take her down without much effort. She very much looked like a woman who could take care of herself. Max immediately liked her. Even though she was usually right, Max's snap judgments about people sometimes got her in trouble. And liking the cop on sight wouldn't benefit her if Grace decided not to help Max.

Grace led her through the police station. The two-story building looked and smelled new. Its interior was bright and airy, with functional workstations and some private offices.

"Didn't you say you were bringing a colleague?"

"He'll meet me here. He had a personal matter to attend to. His family is from Mill Valley and his daughter lives in Larkspur."

"Local boy."

"Um-hmm." Max didn't say more. When David called her to say he'd meet her at the station, he didn't say anything about his meeting with Brittney. David rarely showed his emotions, but he sounded more than a little irritable on the phone.

Grace had a cubicle in the far back corner of the building. While she spoke to another officer in a low voice, Max casually looked around her space. It was devoid of clutter, with files neatly labeled. The only photos were framed—a young man and woman with two young kids. It appeared that Grace was a grandmother. It also looked like she wasn't married—she wore no ring and had no photos of a spouse. Divorced? Possibly.

"I'm on call," Grace said when the cop walked away, "so if I have to leave, I have to leave."

"Of course."

Grace led Max upstairs to a small windowed room. A clean whiteboard covered one wall and a round table could comfortably seat four. She motioned for Max to take a seat. "Coffee? Water?"

"I'm good, thank you," she said.

Grace walked over to a small minifridge in the corner and pulled out a Diet Coke. She sat across from Max, opened the soda, and sipped.

"I won't take too much of your time," Max said. She slid over one of her business cards even though she'd e-mailed Grace all her contact information. "The information you sent me helped tremendously. I have only a few follow-up questions."

Grace glanced at the card but didn't pick it up. "I need to make this clear—you may not quote me without written permission from my chief."

"You made that clear in your e-mail."

"He wasn't too keen on granting you any access, or even letting me talk to you, but I can be persuasive."

"I appreciate that." Max eyed the detective. "Not all law enforcement officers are so accommodating." She was hoping to prompt Grace to explain her motives, but she continued as if Max hadn't spoken.

"The second issue relates to the computer archives for the victim. The county prosecutor didn't want to grant you access to the information, but as I pointed out, the information we have was all public at one point in time. There are Internet archives that also contain the same information—as you mentioned when we first spoke.

Corte Madera is a small community and this case is especially sensitive. Because of our proximity to San Francisco, outsiders think we're a suburb of the city, but we have a long-standing community. Basically, everyone knows everyone. The victim's social media profiles were exploited by the local press, which was one reason we asked to pull them down. The information would simply continue to hurt people with no benefit to our investigation. Ivy's parents cooperated. Another key reason to freeze the information was to prevent potential tampering—most of our leads were generated off information we found on the victim's cell phone and her public accounts."

"Yet, you never had a viable suspect."

"We had multiple suspects," Grace corrected, "but every one of them had an alibi for time of death. Ivy was killed between ten thirty and two in the morning per forensics, but she used her phone to access social media at one ten, so we're confident T.O.D. was between then and two. Half of the alibis were claims to be home sleeping. Most of the suspects were teenagers—and sneaking out of the house is certainly not impossible. Still, we couldn't find proof that any of our key suspects did so."

"One reporter—Lance Lorenzo—suggested that Ivy committed suicide out of guilt for her complicity in the suicide of another student earlier in the year."

Grace's lip twitched just a bit. "Lorenzo took partial information and came up with a theory that I refused to confirm or deny because we were in the middle of an investigation. Probably half the people involved think Ivy killed herself, including her stepfather once we verified Ivy's ex-boyfriend's alibi."

"But not you."

"I don't know what happened to Ivy. Whether she was intentionally murdered or not I can't say. If someone accidentally pushed her off the cliff that individual committed a crime by not reporting the death. And if that was someone we interviewed, that person is guilty of lying to the police and impeding an investigation."

"An accident." Max jotted that information down in her notepad.

"I'm not saying that I believe it was an accident; I do not have enough evidence to make that determination. I agreed to provide you information because your reputation tells me you won't go off half-cocked like Lorenzo. That you're not going to print or broadcast anything that you cannot verify."

"That's correct. I don't publicly issue a report until I have all the facts. I have never been asked to retract anything I have said or written because it was false. What I'm hearing from you is that while some people think Ivy killed herself and others think her death was an accident, you think she was murdered."

Grace leaned back, her stubby, unadorned fingers steepled in front of her. "I've been a cop for coming up on thirty years. Yes, I believe that Ivy Lake was murdered, but I explored every angle. She showed no signs of contemplating suicide. Her grades didn't change. Her weight hadn't changed. She showed no signs of depression, wrote no suicide note, no cutting, no drugs, no drinking. They did a full tox screen and there were no narcotics or alcohol in her system, and no sign that she'd used drugs in the recent past. She didn't tell anyone she was thinking of killing herself, or use any of the references or catchphrases of someone contemplating suicide on social media.

"The coroner found injuries consistent with being cut prior to falling—or being pushed—into the ravine. There were three distinct cuts on her forearms that were caused by a small, sharp blade, thicker than a scalpel but thinner than a standard switchblade. We tested every knife found in her residence and none matched."

"That information wasn't released to the press," Max said.

"Correct. Because we had so little evidence at the scene, we needed something to hold back, something we could use against a potential suspect. Her cuts were consistent with defensive wounds, but they didn't kill her. She fell the equivalent of three stories—survivable, perhaps, if she'd rolled down the ravine. But based on where Ivy's body was found at the base of the cliff, we believe she was either running away from her attacker, or pushed by such a person. She landed on her back on a boulder. Her skull was fractured from the fall. Based on the limited evidence—and from my gut—Ivy *was* attacked."

Max believed in gut instincts. She often had them herself when she was investigating a case, particularly when she sensed someone was lying. But she never reported her theories as fact based on mere impressions, just like cops couldn't arrest someone just because their gut said they committed a crime.

She asked, "Was there evidence at the top of the cliff to indicate a struggle?"

"The ground was hard and yielded no usable footprints. It's an area popular during the day—joggers, bikers—and we collected evidence within a large radius. Nothing was useful, at least at this point. She had no forensic evidence under her fingernails. We considered possible sexual assault, but there were no signs of recent sex, forced or consensual. She'd split with her boyfriend, Travis Whitman, at the end of the school year—a month before the murder—and we looked at him hard. She'd posted some negative comments about him on social media. But it was more than that. It was his attitude and confirmation from his peers that he was angry with Ivy. He was lying to me about something, though I still don't know what."

"Would he be at the top of your suspect list?"

"Two people vie for that honor—Travis Whitman, first, because he's a jerk and a liar, and I don't like him."

Max smiled. "Honesty. I like that."

"Just because I don't like someone doesn't make them a killer."

"Except that he lied, but again, that's your gut."

"Exactly. And my gut can't convict anyone. After your call two weeks ago, I made another pass at him. Following up, basically just to annoy him. The night Ivy died he was home alone until eleven fifteen when his parents returned from a night out and found him watching television. They stayed up together until about one in the morning. I spoke with both parents, and they wouldn't lie to protect their son—I don't see it, at any rate. They were concerned, helpful, forthcoming. Unlike their son." She almost smiled. "It was fun shaking him up. Since Ivy's death fourteen months ago, we've had two murders in my jurisdiction. One a domestic violence situation, and one a drug-related homicide. Both I closed. It bothers me that I haven't closed Ivy Lake's murder."

"I will be talking to Travis," Max said. "Because I'm a reporter sometimes I have success getting people to open up to me. They want to look good on the news or in the paper, so they talk too much. Liars tend to trip themselves up. Who's your other primary suspect?"

"Justin Brock."

Max raised her eyebrow. "Heather's brother?"

According to what Max had read in the local newspaper, Heather Brock's family had filed a civil case accusing Ivy of using social media to bully and ostracize

Heather until she became so depressed she killed herself on New Year's Eve with alcohol and pills. The family's civil suit was dropped several months after Ivy's death.

"Justin is the opposite of Travis. I don't *want* him to be guilty. His family has been through hell with the suicide of his sister, and then dragged through the mud when they filed the civil suit against Ivy and her parents. When Ivy was killed, it all came up again about Heather's suicide. Justin certainly had the rage to kill her, and he's the only one without a solid alibi. He was home from college for the summer and his parents were out of town. He was alone, claimed to be sleeping. He could have been. No one can say, no one saw him after he left a party with his girlfriend at nine that night; his girlfriend said Justin was with her until nearly midnight, when they had an argument and he went home. With no physical evidence and no witnesses and a strong motive, I pressed him hard, but he said he didn't kill her. He said he didn't care that she was dead, either. Very blunt, very angry." She paused. "The day before Ivy's murder, Justin had confronted her at a street fair downtown. According to witnesses, their meeting was a chance encounter but his verbal assault was witnessed by a dozen people. He has a temper and knocked over a display when he left. He paid triple damages to avoid charges—now he's in prelaw at Stanford."

"But you think he's capable of pushing Ivy off the cliff."

"I hope he didn't, because I have empathy with him. Also, I can see him getting verbal with Ivy at the street fair, spontaneous and in the heat of the moment. But luring her up to the cliffs? I don't see that. He doesn't have a solid alibi—but we have no physical evidence tying him to the crime."

"Maybe he followed her there," said Max. "You don't know why she was at the preserve in the first place?"

"No. According to her brother, Austin, she left the house just before ten thirty and told him not to tell their parents she'd left, or she'd tell them he did something. I think it was something like going into the city with friends when his mom thought he was at the movies. I'd have to check my notes."

"Did she tell Austin who she was meeting?"

"She didn't tell him she was meeting anyone. According to Austin, Ivy was on her phone using Snapchat or some similar program. One that doesn't archive any of the photos or texts unless you request it. We got a subpoena, but the company doesn't retain the data on their servers. All we could learn was the cell service provider of the individuals she was chatting with, and that she was chatting with three different people."

"Could you subpoena the records of your suspects?"

"Tried, failed. We didn't have probable cause, according to the DA. Said we were fishing. Though I suspect if the DA had pushed for the records, the judge would have ruled in our favor."

"So your two primary suspects have weak alibis, both have motive, but there's no evidence to tie them to the crime and they didn't break during interrogation."

"In a nutshell. The next group of suspects have motive, but the motives are weak. One we dismissed because she was in San Diego—Ivy's former best friend, Bailey Fairstein. They had a falling-out that spread onto the Internet." Grace shook her head. "I feel damn lucky my son was out of high school before there was Facebook and Twitter and Instagram and all those other apps. Have you read the civil suit filed by the Brocks? Bailey is the girl who gave a deposition that Ivy purposefully posted sexually explicit photos of Heather Brock as retribution for Heather allegedly stealing Bailey's boyfriend, among other things. Those explicit photos not only showed

Heather in bed with her boyfriend, but Ivy allegedly uploaded a sex video on to a porn site. You can't get those things down. The FBI got involved and sent notices to the sites that Heather Brock was a minor and to remove the content. Some of the more . . . reputable, for lack of a better word . . . porn sites removed the video, but it's still out there."

Max leaned forward. "If I understand the law on the matter, it would seem to me that Ivy could have been charged with child pornography."

Grace nodded. "She might have been. But Heather's parents didn't know about the video until after her suicide. My office didn't investigate that matter, it's federal, but after Ivy's murder the FBI shared files from their investigation. Frankly, it wasn't much. Because Ivy was a sixteen-year-old girl who wasn't producing, selling, or buying pornographic material, prosecuting her wasn't a priority. The feds spoke with Ivy and her parents." Grace paused. "I don't know that there was any real punishment. I heard from one of Ivy's schoolmates during the murder investigation that Ivy was grounded for a month with no cell phone or computer. I think the lack of serious punishment, followed by Ivy going back to her old habits, led to Justin Brock's frustration."

"Who sent Ivy the video in the first place?"

Grace raised an eyebrow, a half smile on her lips. "You caught that, too. It was recorded on Heather's phone and e-mailed by Heather. Based on what happened in the weeks prior to her suicide, it appears that Heather may have recorded the video, but someone else with access to her phone sent it to Ivy."

"Anyone at school. Kids keep their phones in their lockers or backpacks."

"Exactly."

"Who else did you look at as a possible suspect in Ivy's murder?"

"Anyone she had posted something negative about. Frankly, there were a lot of them and nothing came from that endeavor. Most of the people involved were in high school or had just graduated. They were Ivy's peers. It came out during our investigation that many of these kids sent Ivy private information—gossip, photos, video clips—knowing that Ivy would put it all up on the Internet. So while on the one hand, some of these kids had cause to be angry with her, they were also culpable in her online shenanigans. But none of these individuals had the spark. I might have looked harder at Christopher Holbrook . . . he was the male in the sex video with Heather. He's now in college—he was a year older than the girls. Fortunately for him, he was also a minor at the time the video was made. But as you know, when these things get out they have more repercussions for girls than boys. Christopher wasn't in town the weekend of Ivy's death, either. He and his family were in Europe for five weeks. July third was smack in the middle of that."

Grace got up and stretched. Max hoped that didn't mean she was calling the interview off—she still had several questions.

However, Grace simply walked around the small room rubbing the small of her back. "My back gets to me—all the years I was a beat cop wearing that damn utility belt. You know how much they weigh? Mine was eighteen pounds. Ruined my back." She sat back down on the edge of the table and continued. "What I really fear is that the person responsible is a teenager with sociopathic tendencies. Most of the time when a young person faces questioning, they give something away. They may not confess right away, but they trip themselves up. Or the guilt pushes them to confess. Or they tell someone, who comes to the police or tells someone else. These are teenagers. Secrets are hard to keep in the age of the Internet."

Max knew that was true. "Or it's someone you haven't interviewed."

"Could be."

"I told you over the phone that Ivy's stepbrother wrote to me about the murder," Max said. "Tommy Wallace."

"Yeah."

"Is that out of character?"

"I couldn't say. But he came by a couple months ago asking about the investigation. I told him to talk to his parents."

"Did you consider him a suspect?"

"Not for long. His mother swears he was in bed, asleep. I told you he's a bit slow, I think they now call it intelligence disabled. Very polite, nice kid. Answered all my questions without hesitation, I don't know if he even has the capacity to lie or manipulate. He certainly has the physical strength to push someone off a cliff, and several witnesses recounted how cruel Ivy was to Tommy. He's been in a few fights. Nothing that the police were called into, but when we spoke to the high school, we got a copy of his disciplinary record. In each case there were conflicting statements about how the fights started, but after interviewing several students and teachers, I determined that each time Tommy had been intentionally provoked or was defending his stepbrother. He never struck first. But because he was the biggest kid involved, he got the blame."

"Could Ivy have provoked him?"

Grace considered. "I suppose. But he hasn't been in a fight in over two years. His teacher told me he's a gentle kid." She paused, as if remembering something. "After the fights, his mother said Tommy wouldn't speak for days."

"Why does his stepmother think he killed Ivy?"

"Honestly? She wants someone to blame, and Tommy is different. He's a large young man, tall and broad-shouldered. Not overweight, but not lean, either. He looks intimidating, until you talk to him."

"There must be a specific reason that Paula Wallace thinks her stepson is capable of murder."

Grace's expression hardened a little, and she shifted away slightly. Defensive and prepared to argue. "You're not going to use Tommy for target practice, are you?"

"I have no idea what you mean."

"The kid is simple. Stutters when he's nervous. People tend to go for the easy target."

"I won't take that comment as an insult," Max snapped.

"Take it any way you want," Grace said.

"I'm looking for the truth. Whatever the truth is." Max retrieved a copy of the letter Tommy had written her and slid it over to Grace. The detective took a moment to read it, then handed it back.

"I see," she said. "I didn't realize Tommy wasn't allowed at his father's house."

"I ask again," Max said, more formal than necessary because she *had* been insulted, "did Mrs. Wallace have a specific reason to believe Tommy was guilty?"

"She said Ivy had been scared of Tommy, that Ivy had told her mother he looked at her funny."

"Funny how?"

"Mrs. Wallace took that to mean sexual, but there was no evidence or any other statements that Tommy had a sexual interest in Ivy." Grace lost her edge and relaxed, as much as a cop could relax. "He's a simple kid, Ms. Revere."

Max's anger fell away as well. Grace was protective, a cop, suspicious of everyone. "Call me Max."

"If I may ask, Max, what do you plan to do that you think we didn't? Because I investigated this case fully. There is no evidence pointing to any one person." She was still defensive. Subtle, but worried she might have missed something. If Grace hadn't been so helpful and open, Max would have pushed that card and used it to her advantage; however, Grace had been more than accommodating and Max decided being direct would benefit her investigation.

"I will talk to Tommy first, then go from there. I'll interview the Brock family, Bailey Fairstein, Travis Whitman, Ivy's mother, and Tommy's parents. I will speak with Austin and Tommy's sister, Amanda. Sometimes, all it takes is a fresh pair of eyes—and a different slant on the questions. Plus, fourteen months have passed. This isn't a priority for you." Max instantly realized that was the wrong thing to say.

"Corte Madera isn't a large community, Ms. Revere. Every crime is a priority."

"I'm sorry," she said quickly. "I didn't mean to imply you didn't care."

Grace nodded that she accepted the apology. Damn, Max really hated feeling like she had to walk on eggshells, but having Grace's cooperation would make her investigation easier.

"I'd also like to bring in a private forensic investigator," she said. "Former deputy sheriff, licensed by the state, who I've worked with a few times on cold cases. The firm has an outstanding reputation and is funded by a grant, so there is often no cost to local law enforcement. They have a lab at UC Davis and have access to the most advanced equipment, including computer modeling."

"UC Davis? Are you talking about Nor-Cal Forensic Institute?"

"Yes—Graham Jones. He and his wife, Dr. Julia Mendoza, run it."

"I don't know them, but I've heard of the institute. I'll talk to my boss. I don't see that there would be a problem going to the crime scene and allowing them access to our records and photos, but there is minimal evidence. Everything we had was analyzed by the state lab."

"If you grant permission, the state will share their findings and methodology."

"Again, I need to talk to my boss." Grace leaned against the table. "It's after seven. I'm beat, and my son is having a barbecue tonight. Do you need anything else?"

Max stood. She had a few more questions, but they weren't critical now. She extended her hand. "Thank you for your time. I may have some follow-up questions, but I'll e-mail them. Let me know about NCFI. Graham said he could clear Wednesday to come down."

Grace looked surprised. "I've heard hiring NCFI is competitive. It can take weeks or months before they can take a case."

"They're definitely not looking for work, but we've been friends for years." That was only partly true. Max didn't see the need to explain that she partly funded their grant after investigating a cold case in Sacramento when Graham was still a deputy, or that Julia had become one of her closest friends. Graham would do almost anything for her. Within reason.

CHAPTER FOUR

Max and David sat down at Scoma's at eight thirty that evening. She was famished and immediately ordered both the calamari calabrese and oysters appetizer for her and David to share, as well as a bottle of an Italian red that was pricey but she knew to be delicious. "You'll have a glass with me, won't you? You're not here as a bodyguard, so you're off duty."

"With you, I'm never off duty."

"You've been grumpy ever since you picked me up at the police station."

"I really don't want to discuss it."

"I didn't ask. I figured Brittney treated you like crap and you took it."

His scarred face hardened. "Stop."

She sipped her wine and leaned back. "I'm sorry." She didn't mean it and David knew it. She loathed the way Brittney treated David, and she wanted him to stand up to her. She wondered if Emma ever looked at her father and thought, *wimp*. Max almost smiled at the idea—no one would use the word *wimp* or *weak* for the ex–Army Ranger. Yet Max hoped Emma understood what David sacrificed in order to spend time with her.

Maybe a few months ago she would have pushed David harder, resulting in him walking out by her clearly making her point; now she didn't want to risk their friendship. Her growing dependency on him made her uneasy. Intellectually she understood that her nearly dying at the hands of a psychopath had forged a connection between her and the person hired to protect and assist her. What she hadn't expected was that with it came an emotional need for her to continually smooth things over with David, to avoid confrontation. Max had never been dependent on anyone, and she rarely avoided confrontations.

Instead, she changed the subject. "Did you see your dad?"

"I'm having lunch with him tomorrow."

"Good. I was hoping to meet him before we go back to New York."

She'd never met David's father or anyone in his family. David didn't talk much about his childhood, which was marked by the death of his mother when David was fourteen. She didn't know how close David was with his father, though he made a point to visit him every time a trip brought them west.

"We'll see," David said. He wasn't looking at Max, and she wondered if there was a problem with him and his dad—or with her and David. Was she overthinking this? Why didn't she just ask him? When had she started second-guessing herself?

"I did get one concession out of Brittney," David continued. "Emma's birthday is next Monday; she agreed to let me take her to dinner Sunday night. I'll take her to my dad's house. If you're not still working the case, you can join us."

She smiled and relaxed. Max was reading far too much into every conversation she had these days. "And that's okay with Brittney?"

"Brittney and my dad get along. I have Evelyn to thank for that."

"Evelyn?"

"Brittney's mother. If it weren't for Evelyn, Brittney wouldn't have even put my name on Emma's birth certificate. I wouldn't have had a chance to know her. Brittney has a lot of anger towards me, some of it justified."

"Hardly," Max said.

He stared at her. "I've never told you what happened."

"I know you."

David was about to respond when the waiter delivered their appetizers.

Max started in on the oysters. "You'd better eat half. Otherwise, I'll eat everything and not my lobster."

David put them on to his plate. They ate in silence for a moment, then David said, "I've told you some of my history with Brittney. What I never said was that originally, when I found out she was pregnant, I offered to marry her. She was eighteen, I'd just turned nineteen, we were both about to graduate from high school. Brittney knew I didn't love her, but she wanted to get married. Maybe it was partly being pregnant, maybe she really did have feelings for me, I don't know. But the closer the wedding day came, the more I realized I couldn't do it. I'd been living a lie for so long, I couldn't ruin her life, too. I came out, told her I was gay, and that was it. She swore I'd never see the baby. Evelyn stepped in and helped craft the custody agreement. Evelyn's the one that makes sure my dad's included in their family events. Emma has a great relationship with all three of her grandparents. Brittney's father still won't have anything to do with me, but he and my dad are cordial." He paused. "I know I hurt Brittney. I didn't intend to, but that was the result."

Max was not only stunned that David had shared so much of himself, but that he used so many words to do it.

She said, "While I could see a teenager harboring such vengeful anger, that still doesn't justify how Brittney treats you now and tries to damage your relationship with your daughter." David's mouth drew into a thin line, and she quickly added, "But, like your advice to me about Nick, I'll stay out of it."

"If you only meant that," he muttered.

She moved on to the calamari. She would try her hardest to support David, but she had a difficult time doing it when she didn't fully understand his decisions.

"I'll try," she said quietly.

She took a bite of the spicy calamari and sipped more wine. She turned the conversation back to the case, where her confidence was warranted.

"I want to interview Travis Whitman first. He was one of two main suspects but had an alibi. According to his social media, he's out of school every day at lunch, then returns at three fifteen for football practice."

"How do you want to approach him?"

"I thought I'd wait at his car when he gets out of class."

"Confrontational."

"After my conversation with Grace, I think direct is the best approach. I don't want Travis to know I'm here or have a chance to prepare for the meeting. Catching him off guard will help me assess his honesty. I tried to reach Bailey Fairstein, Ivy's best friend—former best friend, according to the gossip—but she didn't answer and hasn't called me back. I'll give her a day, then I'll try again."

"Going to show up at her school unannounced as well?"

"Bailey transferred to an all-girls' parochial school after Heather killed herself. I don't think that's a coincidence—changing schools, cutting off ties to Ivy, distancing herself from her former life. At least, that's what I gathered through research. Bailey doesn't have a digital footprint."

"How old is she?"

"Seventeen—a senior, like Ivy would have been."

"I thought all teenagers these days lived on social media."

"Very interesting that she doesn't, right? Makes research harder of course, but I would prefer to talk to her anyway. And I can't help but assume that her lack of Facebook and Instagram is because of what Ivy had been doing." She took the last bite of calamari and washed it down with the wine. "I'll need to talk to the Brocks as well, and that's going to be sensitive. I also need to reach out to each family: Ivy's mother and Tommy's mother. Ben is contacting Ivy's mother about interviewing her for a segment on 'Crime NET'. I suspect she'll be more open to the idea if the show's producer calls her."

"I should be there when you speak to the Brocks."

It took her a second to catch David's tone. She was exhausted, she realized. It was after midnight in New York. "Why?"

"I have some insight into the situation that may be useful."

She wanted to ask him what he meant, but David's body language said he didn't want to talk about it further. Until she finalized the details, she decided not to bring up her plan to drive to Stanford for a sit-down with Heather Brock's brother, Justin.

David added, "You're cutting it close if you expect to get the segment on the show this Thursday. You don't even have a crew."

"I don't need one right now. And later Ben can send Charlie Morelli; he's the best and has a relationship with the San Francisco people. He can work through all the satellite and tech and editing stuff."

POISONOUS   53

"Stuff?" David's lips curved up. "For a writer, that's a vague word."

"Half a glass of wine and you think you can tease me? Sheesh, I should get you drunk and see what you really think."

"I'm not a nice drunk."

She didn't know what to say to that, so continued along her train of thought. "I'll be brief. I don't need much to run something powerful. A short segment, seven minutes. Two-minute lead-in, then four minutes of interviews with Ivy's mother, her stepfather, Detective Martin, NCFI if they can get me anything good, and B-roll. If I can get Bailey, the Brocks, or Travis it would help."

"The Brocks aren't going on camera to help find Ivy's killer when they hold her responsible for their daughter's depression and suicide."

"I can ask."

"Tread lightly on this one."

"Since when are you my director?" she snapped, irritable. She was tired, dammit, and David was in an odd mood. She didn't want—or need—him to be involved with her strategy. She'd been doing this long enough without him. She drained her wineglass and continued. "A minute-long wrap-up with a call to action—more information, call the NET hotline. I'd like to get Tommy on film."

"You haven't even met him. You already said you didn't think he wrote the letter alone."

"That doesn't mean he won't have something to say. I'll take B-roll when Graham and his crew walk through the crime scene—"

"Detective Martin approved?"

"I didn't ask for anything more than to allow NCFI to analyze the crime scene and review the evidence and photographs," Max said. "Just the basics. Why would she *dis*approve? It's not like this is the number one priority for her. With Graham on board, I'll know exactly what evidence they have and don't have." She waited until the waiter refilled her wine. "Honestly, I should have thought of this before, but after my conversation with Grace it's clear. Three people were Snapchatting with Ivy prior to her leaving her house the night she was killed. She left shortly before ten thirty; it's less than a ten-minute drive to where she was killed. She didn't die until between one and two. Where was she the two to three hours prior to her death? The police never found out. No one came forward claiming to be with her. If Ivy was alone, what was she doing? Surely one of those Snapchatters knows *something*. Someone will break if I work the angle right. Someone always does."

Their food was delivered and Max began to relax, her headache finally disappearing altogether. After the bit of . . . *tension* . . . during their conversation, she and David settled into a comfortable silence. It wasn't until after they ate and Max ordered a brandy that she casually mentioned, "Austin Lake, Tommy's stepbrother, showed up outside the hotel today."

David said, "And you just tell me this now?"

She knew David would be irritated with Austin and with her, which was why she hadn't told him earlier. "He didn't talk to me, bolted when I spotted him. I didn't know it was Austin until I dug through my files and found a photo. I want to talk to him as soon as possible."

"You told Tommy where you were staying?"

"No—I hadn't even e-mailed him at that point."

"How did he know you were in Sausalito? At the Madrona?"

"Ben's looking into a possible leak from staff." She was just as curious, but planned to ask Austin outright. "I'll find out." Before David could get all security-conscious on her and start an argument—which she would inevitably respond to by reminding him she had been an investigative reporter for years before he was on staff— she said, "Tomorrow morning I'm meeting with Lance Lorenzo, the local crime reporter who covered the Ivy Lake homicide. Grace Martin doesn't like him, and I'd like to get his impression of the case. See what he'll share, where he thinks I should look."

"I'm not going to tell you how to do your job," David said.

Max laughed. "You're not?"

"Do I have to remind you of what happened the last time you reached out to the local press?"

"A totally different situation," she said.

"Hardly."

The last time was a confrontation with an old-time print reporter who had been taken by surprise by the Internet revolution. Not wanting to change his methods or format, he ended up a bitter drunk. Worse, he directed his animosity toward Max because she was young, attractive, and had embraced the new media. It hadn't been pleasant.

"I can handle Lorenzo," Max said confidently. "He's twenty-four. Graduated from Sonoma State with a degree in English and a minor in journalism. He's from Mill Valley, just like you. His parents still live there. He's looking to move up, I'm fairly certain, and he maintains a blog. Very active online. I'll bet he has both information and opinions. I wouldn't be doing my job if I didn't talk to him. And no—you can't come. You would scare him."

"And you won't?"

She arched her eyebrows. "I can be nice when I want."

David laughed, the sound brief but genuine. "Poor boy."

After his intense afternoon with Brittney, Max was pleased she'd gotten David to loosen up some. She paid the check and they walked back to the hotel.

Out of habit, David inspected her suite first. When he first started working for her, she'd been irritated by what she felt were far too intensive and intrusive security measures; now she was grateful to have someone looking out for her. Well, not *someone*. She doubted whether she would tolerate anyone else. It had taken her and David nearly a year before they stopped disliking each other, and even longer before they became friends. It had been two years since Ben hired him; now Max found him indispensable. That bugged the hell out of her.

David inspected the timeline she'd set up around Ivy's death. "You were busy this afternoon."

"I did most of the work back in New York. Once I sleep on it, I'll have more to add, but the timeline is accurate." She tapped the two hours prior to Ivy's murder, when no one knew where she'd been or who she was with. "This is key. I hope the segment on Thursday will give us the answer."

"You seem confident that Paula Wallace will agree to talk with you on camera."

"Her agreement is irrelevant. I would *like* to include her, but it's certainly not necessary for me." She kissed David on the cheek. "Sleep well. This will be a busy week."

She was about to close the door when David said, "Max—you're the one who needs to sleep."

"I'm fine."

He didn't respond.

"I've *always* had problems sleeping," she said. "This isn't because of what happened." She didn't want to talk about it. She would—if forced—but being kidnapped and tortured and nearly killed by an egotistical, jealous, brooding asshole was not her favorite topic of conversation. Not even with dear David.

"It's gotten worse," he said.

"Not true." She hated lying, and tried to avoid it. Worse, he knew she was lying.

He just stared at her.

"Okay, it's worse some nights," she admitted. "But I slept well in Lake Tahoe."

"If you can call five hours a night sleeping well."

"You were keeping track?" One look at his face and she knew it wasn't David keeping track. Her hand tightened around the door frame. "Nick! Do not discuss me with Nick! He had no right to talk to you about me."

David stepped forward, just as angry as she was. "If you were honest with me, and with Nick, he wouldn't be so worried."

"I'm not lying to you or anybody. And there hasn't been a night I've slept more than six hours for as long as I can remember. So when I say I'll be fine, I will be *fine*. And Nick can damn well talk to me about it if he's so damn concerned."

She shut the door. Terrific. Her night was officially ruined. She should never have vacationed together with both David and Nick. What a stupid, idiotic thing to do. Of *course* they had bonded, they were both former military. They were single dads, each with a kid they couldn't see as much as they wanted. They liked boating. Maybe they should start screwing each other, because Max was beginning to feel like the third wheel in this odd relationship.

She closed her eyes and shook her head. Her phone rang and she looked at the caller ID.

Nick.

Of course.

She declined the call and went to bed.

* * *

In his tree house, Tommy read the e-mail from Maxine Revere over and over again.

> *Dear Tommy,*
> *Last week I told you that I'd agreed to look into your stepsister's murder. I arrived in town earlier today and have already met with the police detective in charge of the investigation. I would also like to talk to you as soon as possible.*
> *Please contact me on my cell phone or e-mail me to let me know when would be a good time for us to meet. How about tomorrow after school? I can meet you anywhere you'd like. In your letter, you mentioned that you like ice cream. So do I. Online, I saw that there is a wonderful gelato shop not too far from your school. Maybe we could meet there?*
> *Sincerely,*
> *Maxine Revere*

She was here and she'd e-mailed him—just like she said she would! Wow. She really wanted to help him. He liked gelato, though he preferred real ice cream. But he would have gelato with Maxine Revere if that's what she wanted.

He was about to respond to the e-mail, then hesitated. Austin had wanted to know when Maxine Revere e-mailed or called. Tommy had come up to his tree house after dinner because he didn't want his mom to hear him talking to the reporter. His face grew warm. He didn't like to keep anything from his mom.

He forwarded the e-mail to Austin and added a message: *What should I tell her? Right after school? I don't have to be home until 5:30. I want you to come. I*

don't want to talk to her alone. I'm scared she'll think
I'm stupid and will leave and not help us.

He was waiting for Austin to e-mail him back when
the bell at the bottom of his tree rang. Tommy burst out
into a grin. *Austin?* Then he froze. Austin was going to
get in trouble for sneaking out of the house after dark and
visiting him. Tommy didn't want Austin to get in trouble.
Tommy opened the trapdoor in the floor of his tree house.
"Hello? What's the password?" He shined his flashlight
down the tree.

It wasn't Austin; it was his sister Amanda.

"I don't remember," she said.

"You can't come up without the password."

"Tommy, Mom sent me out to get you. It's after ten—
you should be in bed."

"I'm eighteen, I don't have a bedtime."

"You have school tomorrow." Amanda put her hand on
the ladder.

"Password."

"Ugh," she groaned. She didn't say anything for a minute, a frown on her face. Then suddenly she snapped her
fingers. "SpongePants SquareBob!"

He laughed. "See, you remembered!"

She climbed up the ladder and sat on the trapdoor
ledge. "What are you doing up here so late?"

"I sent Austin an e-mail. I'm waiting for him to send
one back to me." Amanda knew that Austin wasn't supposed to come over here, but she didn't tell on him to their
dad. As long as Austin was nice to Tommy, she wouldn't
say anything.

"Is Austin still grounded? I thought I saw him here this
afternoon."

"He's not grounded anymore." Tommy looked down
at his laptop. Austin still hadn't e-mailed him. It had been
fifteen minutes.

"Hey, Tommy, it's okay," Amanda said.

"It's my fault he was grounded."

"That's stupid."

He stared at his hands.

"Hey—I'm sorry." She took his hands. "I didn't mean that *you* were stupid, Tommy. I meant that it's not your fault that Austin was grounded. His mother told him he couldn't see you, and he broke the rules."

"Do you think that's fair? Maybe I should stay away from him so he doesn't get into any more trouble."

"No, it's not fair. And if you want to see Austin—if he is good to you—then you should see him. Paula is a bitch."

"Don't say that."

"She is, and I don't care if you don't want to hear it. She is a mean, nasty bitch. She hurt your feelings for no reason except that she's a stuck-up bitch. Austin knows he'll get in trouble, but he still comes over anyway. I think that means he really likes you."

"We're brothers. Brothers love each other, just like we do." Tommy smiled.

Amanda was sixteen and just got her driver's license last month. She took him to school every morning now. He put his bike in the back because she had stuff to do after school and he rode his bike home. She never once complained about driving him places. Amanda agreed with Austin that Tommy should be able to get his driver's license. She said she'd help him study for the test. She also said she'd talk to their mom about letting him get his license, but she hadn't done that yet. She said she had to find the right time. He didn't understand that, but maybe that just meant when their mom wasn't tired or upset. She was tired or upset a lot.

Amanda tilted her head. "You've been spending a lot of time in the tree house over the last couple of weeks."

"I like it here." That was true, but it felt like he was lying to her, and he didn't like the feeling. "You think tree houses are for little kids?"

"Who told you that?" Amanda demanded, suddenly mad. "Was it Austin?"

"No, Austin likes the tree house."

"Then who?"

"Why are you mad?"

"I think this tree house is fantastic. Even if Daddy built it for the wrong reasons."

Tommy had no idea what she meant. "He didn't want to?" He realized he was about to cry. The best thing his dad ever gave him was this tree house. "You're still mad at Daddy for leaving. He left a long time ago."

"Seven and a half years ago."

"Well, I guess—you think—I mean, Mom said once that the tree house was a guilt house. What does that mean?"

Amanda didn't want to tell him, he knew it. Sometimes Amanda treated him like a little kid, like his mom, but more and more she was treating him like Austin did, like a big kid. Now she said, "You always wanted a tree house, right? Ever since you saw it in *Little Rascals.*"

He nodded. He loved that movie.

"Dad built it right before he left. Mom says he did it because he felt guilty. She says he already knew he was leaving, and that he built it so you wouldn't hate him."

"But I don't hate Daddy. I don't hate anyone."

She hugged him tightly. "That's why I love you so much, Tommy. Now, let's go in the house. It's getting late, and we both have school tomorrow."

He glanced at his laptop and Austin still hadn't responded. He closed it and put it in the box that protected it from wind and wet. His tree house had one electrical socket that his dad had hired a man to put in, so Tommy sometimes left his laptop up here. He made sure it was plugged in so that it wouldn't die.

"Can we have a bowl of ice cream first?" he asked as they climbed out of the tree house.

"Sure," Amanda said. "You get the bowls, I'll dish up."

CHAPTER FIVE

TUESDAY

Max had been up since well before dawn, unable to sleep. Insomnia was a familiar part of her life. David thought her lack of sleep was a direct result of being drugged and tortured by a psycho nutcase last June, but sleep had never been easy for her, so she didn't know why he kept hounding her about it—like he had last night. She'd even seen a doctor about her insomnia—which was a waste of time.

"I can prescribe you sleeping pills," he'd said.

"No," she'd replied. Maybe three months ago she'd have gone the pill route if she was desperate for slumber, but after being drugged by the psychopathic whack-job, she refused even the mildest pain meds, so she wasn't going to take pills to sleep.

The doctor wouldn't let it go. Feeling quite sure that Max needed more sleep, he suggested another approach. "Doctor Olsen is the best psychiatrist I've worked with. She doesn't take many new patients, but I can convince her to add you."

Hell no, Max wanted to say. Instead, she'd politely declined.

A shrink. Absolutely not. Max understood her own problems, idiosyncrasies, and baggage. She didn't need anyone else telling her she was a judgmental bitch who let the past control her present. She was far more self-aware than most people. She didn't know who her dad was. She didn't have a birth certificate—she didn't even know where she'd been born. Hell, she didn't even know if her birthday was really December 31 or if her mother just made it up so Max's birthday was always a party. Her mother's disappearance when she was ten, and her college roommate's murder more than a decade later, had very clearly fueled her obsession with investigating cold cases. What happened in high school was simply more fodder for her neuroses. She didn't need to spend two hundred dollars an hour on a doctor to tell her she'd had an unusual and difficult childhood. She didn't need someone to explain why she didn't trust people or why she was unforgiving to liars. She knew why, and talking it out with some arrogant know-it-all head wasn't going to change her worldview. Max knew who she was and she was okay with it.

She just wanted an extra hour of sleep each night.

A benefit of insomnia, however, was early morning productivity. She drank coffee and updated her boards. The timeline was solid, as she'd told David the night before. She filled in additional details about the people involved in Ivy's life that she'd learned from Grace or through her staff notes. But it was that two-hour window that intrigued Max.

Max didn't have a copy of Ivy's phone records—she didn't have the authority to get them on her own, and Grace wouldn't give her a copy—but Grace had told her that Ivy's phone hadn't been used to make a call after she left her house just before ten thirty the night she was killed. She'd sent a dozen text messages to different people up until ten thirty, but Grace had spoken with each person and there was nothing incriminating. Nothing about meeting up, no arguments, nothing suspicious. Max wanted to see those messages nonetheless, and she hoped that when Graham and his team arrived tomorrow he could sweet-talk Grace into sharing.

Another fact: Ivy, who practically lived her life on social media, hadn't posted anything from ten the evening she died, until a single tweet at one ten in the morning. Her 10 P.M. update was a selfie taken in her bedroom, a close-up with her eyebrow arched in a mightier-than-thou pose. Below the pic were her last known words: *If you think I don't know what you did, think again, dipshit.*

According to Grace, no one claimed to know who the dipshit was or what Ivy was talking about in that post.

Max's producer and general pain-in-her-ass friend Ben Lawson called at eight in the morning. "I expected to hear from you earlier," she said.

"Three-hour time difference. Thought you'd need your beauty sleep. Or maybe your current bedmate was entertaining you."

"Don't be crude, Benji."

"Even you calling me that horrific name isn't going to ruin my spirits. I have good news. Paula Wallace has agreed to be interviewed. She's expecting your call this morning to set up a time. I'm sending Charlie Morelli out late tonight so he'll be ready for you first thing in the morning."

"Good—I need him at the crime scene when Graham and his people arrive. It'll make good B-roll. And I have a list of places he can film in the meantime."

"What about the cop?"

"I didn't ask her yet if she'd go on camera. I wanted to go slow. After she agreed to Graham—pending approval—she started to put the walls up. I didn't push. So what should I know about Paula Wallace?"

"You won't like her."

"That was quick."

"I call them like I see them, Maxie."

"Don't. Call. Me. That."

"Quid pro quo, babe," he said. "Remember Betsy Abbott?"

Her hand tightened around her cell phone. Betsy had been her friend Karen's roommate the year before Max arrived at Columbia. She came from the same wealthy, old-money family as Ben and Max, but class wasn't something that came with privilege. Betsy was selfish, demanding, and made everything about her.

When Karen disappeared on spring break and Max stayed in Miami to hound the police and FBI into doing their jobs, Betsy had contacted the media and made an embarrassing public plea. She set up candlelight vigils and created a scholarship in Karen's name, and each and every time she did *anything*, she sought out the press and made damn sure she got her face on camera. Nothing she'd done had helped, nothing she'd done had impacted the case in a positive way; she'd only served to humiliate her family and promote one person: Betsy Abbott.

"You're quiet," said Ben.

"You're saying Paula wants the attention. Then why didn't she do anything to get it last year?"

"She did—Jess is e-mailing you clips from a televised appeal she gave a few days after Ivy was killed. It was all over the news for a weekend, then gone."

"Sometimes that's the only way to get someone to step forward," Max said with sympathy. "Many parents go on-camera to spark interest in their child's murder. What makes Paula Wallace a self-promoter like dear old Betsy?"

"Her tone. Her questions. My instincts."

Max appreciated Ben's insight, but he hadn't had as much experience with grieving families as she had. After a year, Paula Wallace may have given up hope that anyone would be interested in her daughter's murder. Hearing from Ben could have excited her—at last, someone, finally, would listen. Maybe Ben was right . . . but Max decided to reserve judgment.

Paula Wallace already has an opinion—she thinks her stepson killed Ivy. Or is that just an easy way to cast blame?

"You're only going to have forty-eight hours to put this together, Max. I've restructured the show for this, and Charlie is going to bust his hump to edit and give us seven good minutes in time."

"Have I ever let you down, *sweetheart?*"

"You always cut it too close. Keep me in the loop, I don't want any surprises."

"I'll try my best," she said drolly and hung up.

Max took another look at the timeline. She needed to get ready to meet with Lance Lorenzo. She was taking him to breakfast—one thing she'd learned early on when dealing with local reporters was that they were far more forthcoming when well fed. Maybe that was true about everyone, she thought, feeling hungry right then.

She was about to step away when she saw an e-mail pop up from her staff with the clip from Paula Wallace's plea last year. Another glance at her watch—Max had a little time. She clicked on the link. It was only a forty-five-second clip.

Paula Wallace was impeccable—from her shoulder-length highlighted blond bob to her light application of makeup to her simple but expensive jewelry. She'd dressed for the camera. One week after the murder of her daughter, she was more than presentable. She could have walked into a boardroom and taken charge.

But Paula may have felt she would be taken more seriously if she was dressed well, or she could simply be vain and concerned about what she looked like on television. Or she could be fastidious, always leaving the house put together—no running shorts or tennis shoes or hair stuck up in a ratty tail.

The news conference had been held just before noon outside the police station. The chief of police finished speaking and handed the podium over to Paula. A man Max recognized as Bill Wallace stood in the background as Paula stepped forward.

"Thank you, Chief Reinecke." She took a breath, paused before looking directly into the camera lens. "I'm Paula Lake Wallace and Ivy was my daughter. As Chief Reinecke said, the police are doing everything they can to find out what happened to Ivy. But I want to ask the people of Corte Madera, as a mother who has just lost her daughter"—she paused, took a breath—"to think back to the night of July third. We are a small town. Ivy drove a white Volkswagen. Any tiny detail, even if you don't think it's important, may give the police the information they need to bring the person who killed my daughter to justice. You can remain anonymous. You can call the hotline at the number on the screen and the police will take every call seriously. Please." Paula paused, looking out at the group assembled. Max couldn't tell how many were in the audience, but Paula clearly had no fear of speaking to the press. "Bill and I need to know what happened. If Ivy was your daughter or your sister, you would want to know what happened. Just like we need to know. Thank you." She turned, chin up, and walked back to Bill Wallace. He put his arm around her and kissed the top of her head. The clip ended.

Max understood grief better than most people—not because she had suffered any more than anyone else, but because she often surrounded herself with people who grieved. She'd seen tears, anger, resolve. So she might not be inclined to trust Ben's impression that Paula was like Betsy Abbott . . . but Max sensed Paula Wallace was primarily concerned with appearances. And that was something she could work with during their interview.

Or maybe Ben's gut was right. He usually was.

Because he was late to school, Travis Whitman had to park his small pickup on the far edge of student parking. He didn't like being late, not that it mattered—he was a senior; he already had three top schools looking at him to play football in college; UCLA had offered him a scholarship; and his grades didn't suck. Still, he ran into the building and straight to the office to get a tardy slip.

"Mr. Whitman," the secretary said, her hand already filling out the green paper. She shook her head disapprovingly, but he saw her smile.

"Sorry, Ms. Brewster," he said, flashing his dimples. His dimples had gotten him out of more trouble than he could remember. He remembered Ivy telling him they were one of his prime assets, one of those compliments of hers that almost sounded like a dig. That was when they were still going out, way before they broke up, way before—he put it out of his mind and smiled Ms. Brewster's way. "I don't have a good excuse, I just hit the snooze button too many times."

"This is your second tardy in the first three weeks of school." She handed him the slip. "Let's try to do better."

"Scout's honor. Are you coming to the game Friday? We're playing West Valley."

"I wouldn't miss it."

"You never do. The team appreciates it, Ms. Brewster."

"Get along now, no more tardies this week."

He waved and strode down the hall to his locker. Most of the schools in San Francisco no longer had lockers, but there'd never been any problems with weapons in Corte

Madera, and they didn't even have metal detectors at the entrances like nearly every other big high school. Even drug use was low-key—though once a month the cops walked a drug dog through the school.

Travis steered clear of drugs because of football. His coach tested everyone at the beginning of the year and once randomly in the middle of the season. Their best kicker had been cut from the team last year because he'd become a dope fiend over the summer. Travis wasn't going to lose a scholarship just to get high. His parents couldn't afford to send him to college, he had to do it on his own. There was no way he was going to let them down.

He quickly spun his combination and pulled out his science notebook and a pencil. He was about to stuff his whole backpack in the locker when a phone rang.

He frowned, looked around, then shrugged and figured it was someone's phone in one of the lockers next to him.

It rang again and he realized it was coming from the top shelf of his locker. He reached up and found an unfamiliar phone. The screen showed an unknown caller. As soon as he opened it to answer the call, it stopped ringing. Then a text message popped up.

You disabled your ChatMe account. We have to talk ASAP.

His breakfast rose up his throat. He swallowed, his partly digested meal burning on its way back down. This could not be happening.

He looked around and saw no one. Of course not— Bailey had changed schools. Had the phone been ringing all morning? Why didn't she just call him direct? Why all this cloak-and-dagger bullshit? He wrote: *Who is this?*

It had to be Bailey. Who else could it be?

There's a reporter from New York asking questions about Ivy. Avoid her. She'll eventually go away.

He rested his head against his locker, the cold metal doing little to temper the rush of fever that hit him. This was not happening. Not now, not when the scouts were here, not when he was getting his life back together after that bitch nearly ruined it. It had been a friggin *year* since Ivy died. Why now? *Why the fuck now?*

He turned the phone off and almost tossed it in the trash, but at the last minute put it back on his locker shelf. It was about time that he and Bailey talked about this because there was no way in hell he was going to get in trouble for anything. He didn't *do* anything. Who did that bitch think she was, anyway? Always so perfect, so mightier-than-thou pretty girl, rich bitch snob. She had no right to come back now and fuck with him.

Travis slammed his locker shut.

Bailey Fairstein was no better than Ivy. People in glass houses and all that shit—and if she wanted to fuck with him, he'd destroy her.

He'd learned from the best.

CHAPTER SIX

Growing up in the digital era, Lance Lorenzo embraced social media as if it were a god. When Max woke up at three and couldn't get back to sleep, she read Lorenzo's online news archives. He maintained a blog where he "reported" news that could be taken as gossip; he covered not just crime in the small community, but politics and anything potentially controversial. He seemed to thrive on controversy, creating much of it in the bombastic way in which he reported the news. Based on his blog, Max wasn't a fan, but she needed his help. From his focus on San Francisco and the Silicon Valley, he definitely liked big-city news and politics. He seemed to be the type of guy who planned to move up and out of the small-town community quickly.

Max might be able to use that ambition to gain his favor and assistance. Because reporters often had their own agenda—personal or professional—Max didn't trust most of them. She understood that they wanted the story. *That* she got, but she didn't care as much about the by-line as she did about solving the crime. If Lance Lorenzo proved honest and useful, Max would help him any way she could. Which, considering her reputation and contacts, could be substantial. If he screwed her, she'd bury him.

She hoped she didn't have to explain all this to him.

It was nine when she walked into Peet's Coffee in Corte Madera where they'd agreed to meet. He was already there—she'd seen his photo online, but she would have quickly picked him out by the way he was sitting, eyeing everyone going in and out, a razor-thin laptop open in front of him.

She didn't pretend not to see him—she was five foot ten with dark red hair and tended to stand out in a crowd. She approached him and said, "Lance, I'm Maxine Revere." She extended her hand. "What can I get for you?"

"It's great to meet you," Lance said. "I was surprised when I heard you were in town." His hand was soft and damp. Either he was nervous or that was his natural state. He was of average height and build, and wore black-rimmed glasses that were popular a few years ago. He dressed like many Bay Area twentysomethings—khakis, button-down shirt with no tie, and loafers. Sharper than some beat reporters, more casual than others.

She kept her voice casual, but she was curious. "You heard I was in town before I called?"

He grinned. "I know people."

Crime reporter. He probably had a cop he talked to. She'd been at the police station with Grace for more than an hour yesterday, it was reasonable that news about her interest in the case would get out. But still, that was pretty fast.

"Coffee? Latte? Pastry?"

"Great, thanks. Large latte, triple, and maybe the wheat-free muffin?"

"Give me a minute," Max said and went to the counter. It was late enough in the morning that they had missed the rush. It didn't take long for her to bring back the food and coffee. She had her nonfat latte, plus a croissant. She slid Lance's order over to him. "Thank you for meeting me."

"I was curious. Ivy Lake, huh? Cold case. But that's your specialty." He tore off a section of muffin and ate it.

She couldn't tell if he had done research on her when he heard her name, like she did on him, or if he had already been familiar with her work. "When I looked into the news reports about the case," she said, "your name came up. You covered it from the beginning?"

He nodded. "We have a small circulation, but our online edition gets as many hits as a city five times our size. I cover southern Marin County. Murder is big news here—especially a teenager."

"You stated in one of your articles that Ivy's death may have been an accident, but the police ruled it a homicide. Why do you think it may have been an accident?"

"Because the police are jerks. They won't tell me anything. Maybe because you're from New York they'll be more forthcoming, but they treat me like crap. All they reported was that Ivy Lake fell off a cliff and cracked her skull on boulders in the ravine below. Why couldn't that be suicide? Or an accident? So I pushed, and they wouldn't give me a thing."

Not with that attitude, Max thought. She had an antagonistic relationship with several police departments, but she never initially went in belligerent. To get answers, she always tried the more flies with honey approach before calling upon her inner bitch.

If Grace Martin wasn't forthcoming with Lance Lorenzo, there was likely a good reason. Had he burned her before? He'd been a reporter for less than two years, but that was long enough to get a bad rep.

"Out of all the cold cases in the country, why'd you pick this one?" Lance asked.

Max decided not to tell him about Tommy's letter. She didn't want Lorenzo talking to the boy, especially before she had a chance to speak with him. "In cases like Ivy's, where there is little to no evidence, sometimes a national eye can bring forth a witness."

"So you're doing a whole show on Ivy Lake?"

"A 'Crime NET' segment," she said.

"Don't you need the family to cooperate?"

"I'd prefer it, but it's not necessary," she said. "Have the Lake or Wallace families been uncooperative?"

He shrugged. "They don't like me."

"Why is that?"

"I thought you read my articles."

"And your blog." She assessed him. "Nothing I read suggested why they might be annoyed with you. However, you did write extensively about the Brock lawsuit and what Ivy's death might mean to the Brock family."

"Bingo. I wanted Paula Lake Wallace to give me her side of the story—what their defense was to the civil suit. She never gave me the time of day. I had Ivy on record— I sent her an e-mail, to which she responded that she didn't do anything wrong. Pretty simple and straightforward. Her exact quote, 'It's not illegal to tell the truth.'"

Max had read that in one of Lorenzo's articles. She agreed with the sentiment, but not Ivy's actions. "And Mrs. Wallace didn't agree? Or maybe she didn't like that you reached out to her daughter?"

"No idea—she refused to talk to me. When Ivy was killed, I tried to speak to Wallace again, but she shut me down. I even said exactly what you did—sometimes media exposure can spark a memory. Then I wanted to do a one-year review of her death, and the Wallaces still didn't cooperate. I wrote something anyway, but it was short and didn't get a lot of interest."

"But it did get some interesting comments." She sipped

her coffee. "Several people wrote that she deserved what happened to her." She paused. "I also read a story under your byline that the Brocks had dropped their lawsuit."

"Yes, shortly after the one-year anniversary of Heather's suicide. I got them on record." He sounded pleased with himself. "In light of the tragic death of Ivy Lake, they decided not to pursue the civil suit, and all the money from Heather's college fund went to a nonprofit organization to prevent online bullying."

"You seem to have built a rapport with the Brock family."

He shrugged. "I guess." He stuffed the last quarter of his muffin in his mouth and didn't look her in the eye.

Something was off about Lance, something he wasn't saying. "There was an undercurrent of hostility toward the Wallace family in your reports," she said bluntly. "Not so much in the print articles, but certainly on your blog."

His spontaneous laugh didn't reach his eyes when he looked at her. "I don't think so."

She raised an eyebrow and didn't comment.

"I'm a good reporter," Lance said. "I've always wanted to be a writer, but with newspapers near death unless you're some financial expert or a sports guy, there are few openings. I started my own blog when I was thirteen. I used it to talk about things I liked. Video games. Movies. Books. I still get free books to review all the time. Science fiction, mostly, but I've started getting into crime novels. I guess I was a nerd in school. Ten years ago that bothered me, I was picked on by the jocks and preps and trust fund brats." He hesitated just a fraction of a second, and Max knew exactly what his story was and what he knew about her. And why he didn't like her. It all came clear, and she should have put it together immediately— maybe her increased insomnia was beginning to affect her instincts.

"The only reason my parents could afford to live in Mill Valley was because my grandparents bought the house fifty years ago," Lorenzo continued. "When my grandpa died, my grandma wanted us to live with her. My dad worked twelve hours a day, six days a week in construction until he died of a heart attack, and my mom owns a gift shop in Sausalito that is barely in the black. All so they could help me and my sister go to college. She's a sophomore at UCLA, got a partial scholarship. But we both needed loans and grants and scholarships. I'm still in debt and I went to a cheap state school.

"So when I see someone privileged like Ivy Lake tormenting someone privileged like Heather Brock, I just roll my eyes. It's just more of the same like when I was in high school. Except when Heather killed herself and I was assigned the article, I met the Brocks. And then I thought, none of it matters because their daughter is dead. Their money, their house, their cars, I knew just by talking to them that they would give up everything they had if it brought their daughter back.

"When I talked to Paula Wallace, I didn't get the same feeling. But when I reported on Ivy Lake's death, I didn't put any of that in there. Just the facts."

Far more information that Max could have hoped to get, but it said everything.

"You said Paula Wallace wouldn't give you the time of day."

"She didn't, but I cornered her a couple of times. She wasn't helpful either time."

Just the facts, he'd said. And a lot of opinion interspersed with those facts, but she didn't say that. "You reported on Ivy's murder, but your word choices—your adjectives—showed you had compassion for the Brocks when you wrote about Heather's suicide and the civil suit."

"I didn't write anything that wasn't true or attributable."

"I didn't say you did."

"Paula Wallace sure seemed to think so. She called my boss."

"What did she take issue with?"

He opened his mouth, then hesitated. "Why are you really here? Because the Wallaces are rich? One of your own? So they'll talk to you and not me, a lowly beat reporter?"

"When I first walked in, I'm surprised I didn't notice the chip on your shoulder, it's so big," Max said. While she didn't hide her heritage, or the fact that her family was wealthy, or that she was on the board of her family's half-billion-dollar trust that her great-grandparents had built from nothing, she didn't advertise it.

"I asked you here because you're the reporter who covered the Ivy Lake murder. I'd hoped we could share information," she said to Lance. "I was wrong about you."

He leaned forward. "I have been trying to get to the Wallaces for over a year. Just to talk. Interview. Do a fucking profile, *something* to get an in, and they shun me. You call and they welcome you with open arms?"

"I don't owe you an explanation—you have a preconceived notion about me and how I operate. But I'll explain something to you that I thought you were savvy enough to pick up on your own. I have a cable crime show. Not huge numbers, but every month we've grown. However, 'Crime NET' is big and the way we integrate the show with the Internet is innovative. That was all my producer's idea. When you call someone and say you'll give them airtime to help find the killer of their daughter, they usually want it. It doesn't matter if it was me or John Walsh or a random network. They think *television* will give them the exposure that the local media cannot." She stood. "Thank you for your time, but I'll do this on my own."

She walked out. She wasn't taking shit from anyone, especially a young reporter who hated her and the Wallaces just because they had money.

She was getting into her rental car when Lance ran up. "I'm sorry," he said quickly. "That all came out wrong. Yeah, you're right. I don't like the Wallaces. But not because they have money."

"Really?" Sarcasm edged her voice. "Because truthfully, I don't care if Ivy Lake is a millionaire or a pauper. I care that someone killed her and that person thinks they've gotten away with it."

"What do you want from me?"

"I had thought we could work together. You know the case, you know the people involved, you've been following it longer than I have. But I'm damn good at research and I'll stay here as long as necessary."

"The police don't like me."

"I'm not surprised. Most cops don't like me, either."

"Look, I want this."

"What specifically?"

"I want the article. I want the byline. You don't care about that, do you? I mean, you're a television reporter, you don't need a byline. I do. You think I want to stay here forever? I mean, I want to stay near my parents, but I want to work out of San Francisco. Or L.A. I don't want to be in Smalltown U.S.A. forever."

She'd certainly pegged Lance Lorenzo correctly.

"I don't want the byline. But I don't want you writing about what I'm doing until I tell you it's okay. It's not a secret that I'm here, but my movements aren't for public consumption. If you're discreet, I'll give you the scoop."

"You mean it?"

"Yes."

"Okay. What do you need?"

"You're close to the Brock family."

He paled. "Yeah," he said slowly, "but they don't want to talk to the media. They just want their privacy."

"And Justin Brock was a suspect. I want to talk to him, one-on-one."

"He won't."

"Lance, one thing you need to know about me is that I always get what I want. If not on the first attempt, then on the second. Or the third. I don't back down. I want to do this the easy way. Talk to him. Smooth the way. I'll drive down to Stanford to chat. But one way or the other, I will talk to him."

Lance was skeptical. "I'll call him."

"That's a start." Max handed him her business card. "That's my cell number on the back. Keep in touch."

She drove off and let him stew.

That went far better than she'd thought, but she wasn't going to hold her breath for results. She had the distinct impression that Lance Lorenzo planned to stab her in the back.

CHAPTER SEVEN

After Max left Lance, she went back to her hotel room and called Paula Wallace to schedule a time to meet prior to the taped interview. Paula sounded pleasant and professional enough, and suggested they get together tomorrow. She had to pick up her daughter from kindergarten at twelve thirty. Max said she could be at Paula's house at eleven thirty.

Next, Max called Graham Jones from NCFI.

"If it isn't my favorite reporter," Graham said as he picked up her call.

"Favorite? You don't like any other reporters." Max settled in a cozy chair on the mansion's balcony overlooking the bay.

"True." Graham Jones had retired young from the Sacramento County Sheriff's Department, putting in twenty years of service by the time he was forty-five. In the four years since, he and his wife Julia Mendoza had built Nor-Cal Forensics Institute, NCFI, into a successful private forensics lab and investigation unit. The idea had been Julia's—she'd quit her job as assistant director of the California State Lab when she found herself pregnant with twins at the age of thirty-eight. When the twins were five and in school, she wanted to go back to work full time, and was approached by a biotech company that wanted her to test their state-of-the-art equipment. Through Julia's foresight and the company's contacts, they created NCFI, and set the facilities on a college campus. The university was happy because their students had a chance to intern at a renowned crime lab.

Max had met Graham early in her career, long before the television show, when she had been investigating missing teenage girls in Sacramento County. At first Graham would have nothing to do with her—once he'd even arrested her for trespassing—but eventually Max won him over. She was pretty sure it had more to do with the information she'd been able to unearth than her winning personality, because to this day she and Graham butted heads. But Max and his wife Julia had really hit it off—odd, she sometimes thought, because Julia was a brilliant scientist and one of the smartest people Max had ever met, someone who focused on the evidence, while Max was a gut-driven reporter.

Graham said, "Are we on for tomorrow?"

"Yes. Detective Grace Martin says she's on board. But she still needs approval from her boss, basically for you to access the reports and lab results. I already sent you the information that's been made public."

"Got it—not much to go on."

"I know. This is going to be a legwork case. But I would love it if you can give me any additional insight into what you think might have happened on the cliff with Ivy. I know this isn't an exact science. Even though the police are investigating it as a homicide, they don't actually know if her death was an accident or if she was pushed or thrown off."

"You indicated that there were cuts on her arms consistent with a blade rather than a fall. Julia will need to see the report and photos."

"She's not coming down?"

"Work, Maxine. She's much busier than I am and can't drop everything for you like I can."

"I hear sarcasm in your voice."

"You always had good hearing. I won't be able to get there until the afternoon—I'll call you when I'm an hour away, give you an ETA. Likely between three and four."

"Thanks, Graham. Give my best to Julia."

As soon as lunch started, Travis Whitman left campus. He had no idea what time Bailey Fairstein had lunch at her uppity all-girls Catholic school, but he was determined to have a serious talk with her today. Enough of this bullshit phones, texts, and ChatMe account.

You'd think, after all these years, she'd just call him. They used to be friends. They used to talk all the time. It wasn't like with his buds, but it was still cool. In eighth grade Bailey had helped him pass math. She was a really good teacher, definitely better than the old fart he had that year.

Then Ivy happened.

Travis should have broken up with her after the whole Heather Brock thing, but, well, at the time he didn't think it was Ivy's fault. Ivy could be a bitch and everything, but who could have known Heather was so whacked? It totally came out of left field.

Bailey had completely lost it, though, and actually gave a deposition blaming Ivy for Heather killing herself. No way would Ivy ever forgive Bailey for that, not for something so serious and, like, legal. Travis joined Ivy's side because, well, to be totally honest, he was pretty obsessed with her and entirely happy when he could get in her pants. He hadn't exactly been thinking with his brains. Ivy was really fun when she wasn't snooping around and being so bitchy.

But she turned on him. For no effing reason. Just . . . snapped. Well, there was a reason. Travis had told Ivy to knock it off after she went after his buddy on her stupid blog. That was it: he'd called her blog stupid, and you'd think that he'd called her a stupid bitch. Then she came right at him, even *lied* about him on her blog. That's when Travis wondered if everything Ivy wrote was just made up or exaggerated crap.

He knew for a fact some of it was true, though—which was why he'd nearly lost his position in football when Ivy posted lies about him smoking weed. People were so stupid. They believed everything they read. And that sneaky fucking bitch, she used her reputation for only posting the truth to try and bring him down. If it wasn't for drug testing Travis would have been kicked off the team. And even now . . . Coach looked at him differently. If Travis wasn't the best quarterback the school had seen in a decade, he would have been benched or worse.

And he didn't fucking do *anything*. Being an idiot stoner was far down his list of appealing activities. He cared about two things: football and getting laid. Well, he cared about more stuff—like making sure he passed all his classes so he didn't lose the scholarship offer from UCLA, he liked helping his mom out because she was having trouble with her arthritis, shit like that. But really, getting stoned wasn't his cup of joe. Who needed that shit in their bodies? He saw what it'd done to his buddy, the kicker. Went from a decent runner to dead last in laps because he just couldn't keep up with the pack.

Lunchtime traffic through town sucked. By the time Travis got to Bailey's school, the girls were walking from the cafeteria and gym back to the main building.

Almost immediately, he spotted Bailey, even though all the girls were wearing the exact same uniform, plaid skirts and white blouses. Some wore blue sweaters, but most didn't because it was warm.

Bailey was drop-dead gorgeous, the type of pretty other high school girls would kill for, with beautiful long blond hair that she wore pulled back when at school. But looks alone were not what made her stand out from the other students. It was her poise. Bailey was tall and slender, and had a distinctive, confident stride.

But maybe she just stood out to Travis because he had known her since they were six.

The school yard wasn't fenced, but he didn't dare walk onto campus. He illegally parked in the school lot and ran over to an oak tree by the main entrance. He was probably breaking a hundred rules. Ignoring the many girls looking at him as he partially hid behind the oak, Travis kept his eyes on Bailey.

At first she didn't see him, then she did a double take and stared at him in shock. Finally she frowned and Travis felt the urge to run over and throttle her. They'd been friends for fucking *forever,* and now Bailey was playing games? What did she think he was going to do after finding that flip phone in his locker? Roll over and do whatever she said?

He motioned for her to come over. She said something to the other girls she was with, then glanced around before approaching him.

"What are you doing here?" she said. "You can't be here."

"Why'd you leave a phone in my locker? Why can't you just call me?"

She stared at him as if he'd grown a second head. "I have no idea what you're talking about, Travis. You need to go."

She was nervous, which told him everything he needed to know. "Fine, you don't want to talk about it here. Tell me what you know about the reporter."

"The reporter? What do you know about that?"

"Nothing! You must know more than me."

Bailey shook her head. "My mom and I were in Boston this weekend touring Boston College and Amherst. When we got home last night there was a message on our answering machine from someone named Maxine Revere. She said she's the host of a cable crime show and wants to talk to me about Ivy's death. My mom doesn't want me to call her back. She hopes she'll leave us alone if we don't respond. Did she call you?"

"No," Travis said. But she could have called his house today. His parents were working. There could be a message on his answering machine, too. His heart raced. What was he going to do? Ignore her. He'd ignore her, like Bailey.

"I have to go to class, I'm going to be late."

Travis still wasn't sure if she'd left the phone in his locker. But if it wasn't Bailey, who the hell would it be?

He said, "If you want to talk to me, just call me, Bailey. Stop with these stupid games."

She shook her head. "I'm sorry, Travis, but I'm not playing any games. We can never go back to the way things were, and I'll never call you."

She walked away. Travis didn't know if she was lying to him and playing with his head or what. But she knew about the reporter, she didn't deny it. Fine, if she didn't want to talk to him, he didn't have to respond to her stupid text messages ever again.

CHAPTER EIGHT

Parked across the street from Tommy Wallace's school, Max sat in the rental car with a clear view of the campus's special education wing: four large trailers on the school's southern edge. She'd learned the special ed kids were let out thirty minutes before the high school general population. When Max had spoken to Tommy last week, he'd told her that he rode his bike home from school every day. She kept her eye on the bike rack.

She'd sent him a message that she was in town, and was surprised when he hadn't responded. Odd, considering his stepbrother Austin had gone to her hotel.

Meeting Tommy spontaneously would benefit her. Give her an edge to determine his real motives in sending the letter, and whether he was as simple as he had sounded over the phone.

Max rarely, if ever, doubted herself. Yet sitting outside the high school, waiting for Tommy Wallace to leave, her confidence waned. She'd received one letter and had a brief conversation with a mentally challenged teenager, yet she'd devoted considerable "Maximum Exposure" time and resources to this investigation. Ivy Lake's murder was intriguing, but it wasn't her typical case.

Yet . . . she hadn't been able to get Tommy's letter out of her mind. From the moment she opened the envelope—odd in this day and age that he mailed her a letter—Max couldn't get his words out of her head. An unfamiliar emotional weight had filled her, propelling her to put aside a half dozen other missing persons cases she'd been considering for her next show, and instead latching on to a cold murder with little allure. Usually, Max was drawn to a case because of the victim profile—the need to see justice served, the need to punish the killer. This time . . . she had yet to develop any real affinity toward Ivy Lake. Instead, it was Tommy Wallace, and an overwhelming need to find out what happened to Ivy for *him*. Max was here because a teenage boy had written her an honest letter.

When she took a cold case, several things went into her decision, but she could never fully explain what drew her to choose one case over another. To Ben Lawson, her producer, Max would sell him on the ratings—that a particular case would be interesting to their audience. Sexy in some way, compelling, unusual. To David, she'd explain that it was the victim's family that drew her in—that she wanted to give them justice.

Both things were unequivocally true.

Still, Max would never have taken this case if it weren't for the letter from Tommy. In Max's estimation, Ivy wasn't an innocent victim. She'd used social media as a weapon, had bullied her peers, and her actions had a direct or indirect impact on a girl's suicide. There were no special circumstances to her murder—no sexual assault, no unusual violence, no repeat crimes, no serial killer, no threats, no suspect. The police had done a competent job investigating, so not even the allure of exposing an inept police department was an enticement for Max to investigate.

Now that she had a research staff and David, her traditional month-long prep and research was done in a matter of days. Still, Max profiled three major cold cases each month for the show, which meant she realistically could only spend one week on-site for each case. If she couldn't prove or disprove a suspect in a week, if she couldn't find the missing person dead or alive, Max had to move on.

It was the one thing she regretted about her agreement with Ben Lawson and NET. In the past, Max could stay on an investigation until she wanted to leave; now, business commitments pulled her in multiple directions.

Turning off the car radio, adjusting her seat, she checked her e-mail again, but there was nothing from Tommy or any of the others she wanted to interview. The only good news was a message from Grace Martin that her chief hadn't put up any barriers to Graham Jones and his people coming down to review the forensic evidence. Max e-mailed Grace, thanked her, then forwarded the note to Graham.

When she looked up, she saw kids pouring out of the special education classrooms. Some stayed in a line headed by a teacher; others were being picked up by parents in a designated roundabout; and a third group was being escorted to the school buses. The special education kids were mixed—some were handicapped, either with Down's or a serious physical problem. Some weren't obviously handicapped. Max didn't know how this particular school district ran their program, but the group appeared eclectic.

A few of the kids—including Tommy—walked over to a bike rack and unlocked their bikes. Others walked off campus and presumably toward home. The high school appeared to have between fifty and sixty kids in the special ed program.

Max watched as Tommy spoke to a couple of students,

then walked his bike out of the yard and across the street. Odd—he wasn't coming toward where Max was parked, which she'd picked because it was en route to his house. Instead, he was heading to the large, open block-long park that separated the high school from the middle school.

Max got out of her car and briskly walked toward the boy. It wasn't difficult to catch up because he moved along slowly, in no rush at all. Halfway through the park, Max caught up with him. "Tommy," she called when she was still several feet away, not wanting to startle him.

He stopped and turned, no worry on his face. He recognized her immediately and smiled. "You're Maxine Revere."

"Yes. And you're Tommy Wallace, right?"

He nodded. "How did you know?"

"I saw your picture in the newspaper when your dad got remarried."

"Oh. Is that what you meant when you said you had to do research before you came?"

"Partly. Did you get my e-mail last night?"

He bit his lip. "I should have hit reply. I'm sorry. I wanted to talk to Austin first because I always meet him after school. I want you to meet him."

"I would like to meet him."

"Great!" Tommy looked around, for a moment seeming confused. He looked at his watch. "Austin gets out of class in seven minutes. It takes him a couple more minutes to go to his locker and then to the bike rack."

"We can wait here." Max motioned to a nearby bench. "It's a nice day. I'd love to talk with you, Tommy. I just have a few questions," she added.

"Austin should be here."

"They're easy questions."

He glanced at the middle school. "I don't know."

"Did Austin tell you not to speak with me unless he was with you?"

Tommy looked torn. His pale face was expressive, his blue eyes inquisitive and concerned. He spoke clearly, maybe too clearly, like he was being extra careful to make sure each word was the correct one.

Max wanted this first meeting with Tommy to be without the influence of anyone else, especially an inquisitive young teenager who had made a point of going to her hotel yesterday.

"Let's sit, okay?" she said, trying to sound non-threatening. Ben had told her that she intimidated people with her tone just as David intimidated them with his physical presence. She didn't want to scare Tommy.

He hesitated. "Can we go over there?" He pointed to a bench on the park's far side, with a clear view of the middle school.

"Of course. Anywhere you want."

He led the way. "I always sit on this bench to wait for Austin. Do you still want to get gelato? Or maybe you prefer ice cream? A very good ice cream place is right next to the bookstore. You write books, don't you? Austin said you did."

"Austin is right." It seemed Max wasn't the only one doing research. "We can go anywhere you want," she said.

"Do you really like ice cream? Sometimes people say things they don't mean."

That was an interesting observation from Tommy. "Tommy, I would not have told you I liked it if I didn't. For me, it's really important to be honest all the time, don't you think so?"

"Oh, yes."

They walked to the bench Tommy had indicated. Tommy put his kickstand down, balanced the bike, and took off his backpack. He didn't let it drop to the ground, but carefully placed it on the bench between him and Max. He kept one hand on the pack. Security, maybe, a connection with his belongings. Keeping his distance from her, though friendly enough to talk.

"I saw Austin yesterday in Sausalito," Max said, after taking a seat. "He was at my hotel, then took off before we could talk."

"He wanted to make sure you really were here," Tommy explained, glancing at her then looking down. "Are you mad at Austin? Your forehead is squishy. That's how my mom looks when she's mad about something. Usually, it's about my dad."

This was the second time someone had made a comment about the wrinkles in her forehead. *Relax, Maxine. You don't need premature wrinkles.* "I'm not mad," she said calmly. Curious, maybe a bit suspicious of Austin, but not angry. "Before we start, I want to make sure that you understand what I'm doing."

"Austin already explained it," Tommy said with a nod. "Your job is to find out who killed Ivy. Austin said when the police get stuck, you get them unstuck."

Maybe this Austin kid was all right. She only wished it were true all the time. "That's what I hope for," she said. "On the phone, I told you that I'd do everything I could to find out what happened to Ivy, and I will try my best to do just that. But sometimes I can't find the answers. Or, sometimes, the answers I find don't make people happy."

Tommy wore a sad expression as he sent an unfocused gaze over to the school yard. "But . . . but if Paula finds out that it wasn't me who hurt Ivy, then I can go back home, right? She said I can't be there because I scare her. I don't want to scare anyone."

Max realized Tommy was a child in a man's body. Not a typical child. He had a solid grasp of the world around him and was capable of taking care of himself—going to school, riding his bike, any number of things—but he had a solid linear thought process. If A, then B. If B, then C. That did not mean he had the capacity to understand all the complexities of his situation. For example, Paula Wallace might have other reasons for banning Tommy from the house.

"You don't scare me, Tommy," Max said. "You seem like a nice guy. Anyway, as far as Ivy's case, we need to take this one step at a time. I've already done a lot of work. I spoke to the police, and—"

She'd lost him. At first Max thought he had just zoned out, but then she saw Tommy clutching the top of his backpack with tight fists.

"What's wrong?"

"I don't like all those people. I mean, I don't know them—I just don't like so many people around me. Cr-cr-crowds." He took a deep breath. "Austin said he would be late today because he has to meet with Mrs. Feliciano about his English essay." Tommy looked at his watch again. It was a nice digital sports watch with a large face. "It won't take long."

"Then maybe we have some time for questions without Austin," Max pressed.

"We should wait for Austin."

"Tommy, I promise you my questions aren't going to be hard. I only have one rule: tell the truth."

"I did."

"You mean you will tell the truth?"

"Yeah." He looked at his watch again.

"I like your watch."

He smiled and showed it to her. "I got it for my sixteenth birthday. Two years ago, but I take good care of it because it's my favorite. It has a timer and a stopwatch and an alarm. It's waterproof."

She showed him her watch, a slender Cartier band with small diamonds on its face.

"Pretty," he said, though sounding unimpressed. "Does it have an alarm?"

"I'm afraid it doesn't do anything but tell the time. It's not even waterproof."

"How do you wash your hands? Do you have to take it off?"

"No, I'm just really careful."

He looked from her wrist to his. "I like mine better."

"I like yours, too. Do you and Austin always ride home from school together?"

"We used to. But Paula said I couldn't anymore. I . . . I have to stop at the corner."

"You don't like that."

He shook his head. "I'm not lying. I mean, it's kind of like lying because I don't tell anyone I ride home with Austin. He's big enough that he can ride by himself, but it's one of the only times I can see him."

"Tommy, did you write the letter to me? The letter about how Ivy died?"

"Yes. Austin helped but he said it had to be in my words." Tommy paused, glancing over at her. "My first letter was too short, Austin said. I wrote it, I really did, but he helped me make it sound better. Was it okay?"

"Absolutely. I thought it was remarkable."

"Austin said it was really good but too short and I needed to give you more information. And it turned out he was right, because here you are."

"Why does your stepmother think you killed Ivy?"

The thought of that pursed his lips. "Austin says it's 'cause she's a bitch, but that's not a nice word." He put his hand to his mouth.

"I don't want to know what Austin thinks. I want to

know what *you* think, Tommy. Did you get along with your stepmom before Ivy died?"

He thought on that. "At first she liked me. I had my own room at my dad's house, and she always had my second favorite ice cream in the freezer. Napoleon, because I like vanilla and strawberry and chocolate."

"Why would Paula be scared of you?"

He shook his head and frowned. "After Ivy died. I was at the funeral. I went home with Dad and I heard Paula tell him she was scared of me. Later I asked him why, and Dad got really mad at me for *eavesdropping*." Tommy straightened his spine. "That means listening to a private conversation when you're not supposed to."

"Then what happened?"

"There was a lot of crying, Dad told her I was a gentle giant, but then later he said it was best if I didn't come to the house unless he was home. But he's hardly ever home! He was in Japan three weeks this summer and I couldn't see Bella at all." His voice cracked. "She's only five. She could forget me."

Max smiled. "Bella won't forget you, Tommy. You're unforgettable. What about your stepsister Ivy? Did you get along with her?"

"She didn't like me because I'm stupid."

Max tensed. "But you're not stupid."

"That's what Austin says. He also says my mom babies me and I need to grow up. I want to grow up. I want to go to college."

"Where do you want to go to college?"

"I wanted to go to University of California at Davis because that's where my dad went, but my mom said I wouldn't get in. She said I will set myself up for disappointment." He frowned. "I don't get it. I know it will be hard, but I want to learn more things so I can be smarter."

He sighed heavily. "But I can't go. I took the SATs last year and I didn't do good. I didn't finish. I don't do good when there's a timer." His lip trembled and his forehead creased with worry.

Max smiled. "My best friend Karen was very smart, but she got nervous whenever she had a test. She couldn't concentrate and kept looking at the clock. It took her three tries before she could pass her written driving test."

"My sister Amanda passed the first time," Tommy said proudly. "She's really smart, she has straight As. Did your best friend go to college?"

"Yes. That's where I met her, we were roommates."

"Austin says my mom doesn't think I can live on my own because people might make fun of me. But they make fun of me here, so I don't get what the difference is."

"Maybe she thinks you would be happier at home."

He shrugged. "It's a sad house. My mom works a lot. She works at work and she works at home. She misses Dad. She's still mad at him, but I know she misses him. My sister doesn't like being home. She's a junior and she'll go to college because she's really smart. She said she doesn't want to go to Davis because my dad went there. I think she wants to go far away, like where you live, in New York. I saw a big envelope from a college with Boston in the name. That's in Massachusetts. That's far away. So I'm alone in the house a lot, and I don't like that. Dad's house is never lonely because Austin is there. He's my best friend, but now I can't go there."

Tommy wasn't lying to Max but his perception of how things were at his dad's house or the situation with his stepmother could be clouded by feelings of banishment from that house and loneliness at his mom's home.

Tommy's face lit up. "There's Austin!"

Max looked across the street to see Austin standing next to a pretty blond girl.

A very familiar blond girl.

Emma.

Corte Madera was a small town and the neighboring smaller towns overlapped school districts. Max should have guessed that the thirteen-year-old Austin Lake might have known the almost thirteen-year-old Emma Stratton Kane, David's daughter.

Heads together, Emma and Austin stood at the corner. Emma must have told Austin about Max, and either Emma or Austin came up with the idea to write the letter. And Austin used Tommy to do it. Did it matter if it was Austin's idea or Tommy's? Max bristled at the idea of a thirteen-year-old kid manipulating her. And he'd done it well. Extremely well.

Tommy was completely ambivalent to her sudden anger. He said, "Sometimes Austin gets in trouble and has to go to detention after school. But he promised he wouldn't do anything wrong this week because you're here. That's Emma he's talking to. She's really nice."

Austin saw Max first. When the crossing guard motioned them forward and Emma and Austin began to walk, Max locked eyes with him. Austin stopped in his tracks. Emma glanced at him, then looked across the street to where Max sat with Tommy Wallace.

Emma's lips moved, and Max could read exactly what she said.

Oh, shit.

CHAPTER NINE

Tommy was oblivious to the tension as the four of them met by the bench. "Hi, Austin! Hi, Emma! We're going for ice cream. Do you want to come?"

Emma finally looked up from the ground and Max caught her eye. She didn't need to say anything, Emma knew Max wasn't going to keep this from her father. "I can't," Emma said quietly. "I have gymnastics."

"Oh. Okay. Next time?"

"Yes," she said.

Tommy smiled broadly. "Austin, this is Maxine Revere. You can call her Max. She likes ice cream. Emma likes double chocolate chip the best."

"Yes, I know," Max said. She gave Emma credit for standing straight and looking her in the eye. "Anything chocolate, right, Emma?"

Emma bit her lip.

Austin stepped forward. "What's this—a sneak attack? You can't just show up like this." Angry. Protective? Possibly. Austin had at first looked surprised, then sheepish, now he was confrontational.

Max didn't respond to him. "Tommy, where's the ice cream place?"

"It's not far. Two blocks down this street." He pointed. "Turn left, then walk six blocks, then turn right, and it's one block down."

"I need to talk to Emma," Max said. "Can I meet you there in about twenty minutes?"

"Sure!" Tommy said.

"No," Austin snapped. "Leave Emma out of this. This is between you and me and Tommy."

Max turned to Austin, sizing him up—he was of average height for his age, which meant much shorter than Max—the same height as Emma. Clean, brown hair that curled at the collar. He looked as if he was ready to hit someone, and he wasn't budging.

"Austin," she said, "this is actually between Tommy and me. He's eighteen, an adult. You're a minor, but because Tommy wants you involved in our conversation, I agreed to let you come."

Austin looked confused, but still angry—and suspicious. Good. That made two of them.

Emma said, "Austin, it's okay. Really. Go. Max will be there if she says she'll be there."

He obviously didn't want to leave Max and Emma but he said, "Okay." He looked at Max. "You shouldn't have just surprised us like this. Let's go, Tommy." Austin put his skateboard down on the ground while Tommy put on his backpack and grabbed his bike. Max watched after them for half a block.

"Can we talk later?" Emma asked. "I have to catch my bus to get to gymnastics."

"I'll drive you," said Max, setting a brisk pace toward her car, parked just a block away. "You have a lot of explaining to do."

"Please don't be mad." Emma said, following. "You're going to tell my dad, aren't you?"

"I don't keep secrets from David." Max paused.

"Though I think it would be best if I didn't mention that you were holding hands with Austin."

Emma blushed and Max would have laughed if she wasn't so irritated that these kids had manipulated her—and the entire "Maximum Exposure" news team—into investigating the Ivy Lake murder.

"I'm sorry about not being totally straightforward," said Emma.

"I'm thinking you had more to do with that letter than either Tommy or Austin. Is that why you were asking me so many questions at Lake Tahoe? Trying to figure out how I pick my cases?"

Emma nodded. "It's totally unfair that Tommy's being blamed for Ivy's death. If you knew him, you'd know he wouldn't hurt anyone. He just wouldn't."

Max unlocked the car and typed the address Emma gave her into her GPS system, then pulled away from the curb.

"And besides, Austin needs your help," Emma continued. "He's so angry all the time. And it's gotten worse, since the whole Bella birthday thing."

"Angry about what?"

"How his mother treats Tommy, et cetera. She's a total bitch."

Max cleared her throat. "Well, some people call me a bitch. It's not always a bad thing."

Emma gave her a half smile. "They don't know you like I do."

"Even people who know me well," Max mumbled.

"It's not the same. Mrs. Wallace is . . . I don't know exactly how to explain. She has a perfect house and perfect hair and perfect decorations and Bella—that's Austin's little sister—is spoiled, not in a good way."

"Is there a good way of being spoiled?"

"Yes—like when you took me shoe shopping in New York last year. Dad said you spoiled me."

"A girl can never have too many shoes," Max said. "And we only bought you four pairs." Max had been making light of the situation, but it was time to get serious. "You need to stay out of this, Emma. I appreciate your concern, and I admire that you want to help your friends, but you can't be involved."

"Does this mean you're not going to find out who killed Ivy?" Her voice cracked and she blinked back tears.

"I didn't say that," Max said.

"You have to. You just *have* to find the truth." Now the tears were coming steadily and Emma couldn't stop them. Max didn't know what to do. She drove the rest of the way to the gym in silence, trying to figure out why Emma was so emotional. Max always kept her feelings to herself. While some people might think that was a deficiency, it helped her do her job.

She pulled into the gym parking lot, parked several lanes away from the entrance, and shut off the ignition. Max looked in her purse for tissues. She found a small package and handed it to Emma. "I didn't mean to upset you, Emma."

Emma grabbed the tissues and blew her nose. "But if you don't find out who killed Ivy, no one will!"

"I will do my absolute best to find the truth. But I'm serious: stay out of this. Austin manipulated you into helping him, he's manipulating Tommy, and he knew where I was yesterday. I won't tolerate a lie coming out of his mouth, and I have a feeling he has a whole laundry list of lies he plans on telling me. You don't want to be in the middle of that. But the primary reason you need to walk away is because of your father. Not only will he not want you in potential danger—because *someone* killed

Ivy and that person is most likely someone she knew—but because if you're involved with one of my cases, your mother will have a fit. I will not be the cause of any more problems between your dad and mom."

Emma rubbed her eyes. "When are you going to tell my dad?"

"I'm not."

"You're not?" She sounded optimistic.

"You are. Before he figures it out on his own."

Emma shook her head rapidly. "No, please. I don't want to."

"It will come out sooner or later, and I'm not keeping it a secret. You have until eight tonight to call him."

"But you're staying, right? You're still going to find out who killed Ivy?"

"As I said, I will do my best."

Emma didn't make a move to get out. "Austin didn't manipulate me," she said. "He didn't even know about you or your show. I told him all about you. I said if anyone can find out who killed his sister, you could."

"I understand the situation between your mother and your father, but you could have called me."

"Dad says you're overcommitted."

"I am, but I'm used to it."

"He's worried about you," said Emma. "I noticed in Lake Tahoe. I asked him about it, if someone had threatened you or something like when he first started working for you, and he said no. But he didn't explain."

"You're wrong." Max had thought the same thing: the way she'd caught David watching her. The concern in his expression.

"No, I'm not."

Stubborn. Like her father.

Was David worried because of what happened over the summer? Or because she'd jumped back into work after the attack? That couldn't be it . . . she'd taken an entire week off to go to Lake Tahoe.

"Emma, you and Austin are friends and I'm not going to tell you not to talk to him. But I don't want you and Austin doing anything related to Ivy's murder. Don't start asking questions on your own. Do you understand?"

She nodded. "I promise. Max, it means everything to me that you're here."

Max said to Emma, "Don't forget to call your dad."

CHAPTER TEN

Looking around the ice-cream parlor, Max saw they sold far more than ice cream—turkey sandwiches, novelty gifts, newspapers, magazines, various beverages. The shop was half-filled with teenagers, and the other half mothers with young children.

Austin and Tommy weren't there.

She stepped outside on the sidewalk, irritated, and was about to call Tommy's cell phone when she spotted Austin leaning against a nearby light pole. He was watching her while eating the last of his cone.

She walked over to him. "Where's Tommy?"

"He wanted to leave." He wadded up a paper napkin and tossed it in a nearby trash can.

"No. *You* wanted him to leave." Max motioned toward a small table, as far as they could get from the ice-cream-shop traffic. She waited until Austin reluctantly sat down before taking a seat across from him. "We need some ground rules. Emma told me it was her idea to reach out to me with a letter from Tommy, and I believe her. But from this point forward she stays out of it."

Austin didn't respond.

That angered her. She didn't have kids—she didn't know how to handle them, and she didn't want to learn. "You've led Tommy to believe that I'm some sort of, of—" What word was she looking for? "Angel of justice," she said, "swooping in with answers so he can get his old life back. And I think you're smart enough to know that even if I find the truth about what happened to your sister, that's no guarantee your mother will welcome Tommy back into her house."

Austin stuck his chin out. She couldn't read his eyes, which seemed too old for a thirteen-year-old, but she recognized defiance. Maybe because she had spent most of her teenage years defiant. "I know my mom. She won't have any reason to keep him out. She needs a reason or she'll cave."

"Her reasoning sounds like an excuse to me. And if I prove someone else killed Ivy, she could find another excuse to keep Tommy out of her house."

Austin leaned forward. "Then everyone will know she's a selfish bigot."

Bigot. An odd word choice.

"I wanted to talk to Tommy," said Max. "You shouldn't have sent him away."

"And you shouldn't have surprised him in the park."

"We were having a nice conversation."

"Are you for real?"

"Excuse me?" That chip on Austin's shoulder was still there and growing.

"You want something and you're using Tommy. He told me what you were asking. You don't think he wrote the letter." Austin started to say something else but then stopped himself.

"What are you afraid of, Austin?" she asked.

"I'm not afraid of you."

"I didn't think you were. But why were you watching me yesterday? You could have approached me, told me who you were."

He shrugged. "I didn't really think you'd come. Emma said you were coming, but I had to see it for myself."

"I'm pretty certain you were listening in on my phone conversation with Tommy last week."

He glanced away, confirming her suspicion.

"I have a bad habit, Austin. And that's judging people when I first meet them. But honestly? I'm rarely wrong. Here's what I think of you, Austin: you're smart—really smart—but also manipulative. You lie, sometimes you're sneaky, and you're angry because things have happened that you think are unfair. And maybe they are. I don't have to tell you that we rarely have everything just the way we want it. You're not the only kid who has a screwed up family life. Yet you're going down a path that is eventually going to land you in serious trouble. You may be right about everything, but your methods are questionable. Tommy feels intense guilt because he thinks you get in trouble because of him, and he loves you. When he talks about you, his face lights up and I know he thinks of you as his *real* brother, not just a stepbrother.

"But, Austin," she continued, "you are the reason you get in trouble. That said, I have sympathy for you because it seems you have a redeeming quality: Tommy adores you. He listens to you. If I had never seen you talking to him, I don't think I would like you very much. The only time I haven't seen complete anger or total disdain on your grouchy face was when you were with Tommy. I believe you truly care about him, and it hurts you that he feels ostracized by your mother. I believe you would do anything to help him. So I'm going to be blunt with you, and you're going to have to find a way to explain this to Tommy, because the next time I talk to him, I will tell him."

Max searched Austin's face for something. He was watching her intently, on guard, but the anger was gone. He was curious, and Max understood curiosity better than anything. She leaned forward and spoke quietly.

"I believe with my entire being the truth is always better than a lie. Your mother deserves to know what happened to her daughter. You deserve to know what happened to your sister. The killer needs to face the consequence of his or her actions. And Tommy deserves to live his life without this cloud of doubt and suspicion hanging over him. But the truth doesn't always make things easier. The truth isn't always kind or tied up in a pretty bow. And why? Because of lies and secrets that give everyone a false sense of security. Sometimes the truth hurts."

Austin looked away. Max tried to read him, but couldn't. Maybe all thirteen-year-old boys were like this.

"There's a chance that I won't be able to prove who killed Ivy. You need to prepare yourself for that. *And* Tommy."

"I know," Austin said so quietly she almost missed it. Then he looked at her, and the anger was buried. It was there, deep down, but it was sorrow now that bled through. "Tommy is my brother, Ms. Revere. He needs me. No one else even really listens to him. You're our only chance."

"Austin, do you care who killed your sister?"

"Haven't you been listening to anything?" He glared at her, the anger back. "Of course I care. Because once you find out who it is, my mother will know it's not Tommy."

This kid—Max was in over her head. She didn't know what to say to fix things, to help Austin or Tommy.

She could only do what she could do.

And that was find out who killed Ivy.

"Tomorrow morning, can you meet with me before school?"

He nodded.

"I'll take you out for breakfast, my treat. What time does school start?"

"Eight fifteen."

"How about seven?" She glanced around. There was a diner at the end of the strip mall they were in. "Over there?"

"Okay."

"Bring Tommy. I need to talk to both of you."

"Fine."

Max got up, then turned back and said, "What do you tell your mom when you leave the house early and come home late?"

Austin shrugged. "Whatever I want. It's not like she cares."

CHAPTER ELEVEN

Max had three hours before dinner with David.

She knew he'd spent most of the day going through the thick binder of Ivy Lake's Internet activity—her social media pages as well as the blog she used to have. The explosion of social media had really just begun when Max was finishing college; now kids in elementary school had access to sharing anything they wanted with the world. In a decade, the world—and growing up—had changed, and was still changing exponentially.

David was good with research and had the patience to review the documents. Max had started it on the plane, but David was carefully combing through it again, making sure they hadn't missed someone whom Ivy had gossiped about online. He was analyzing every account of people connected to Ivy to see if there was someone they hadn't considered who might have motive. Time-consuming work, but it had to be done—and by someone intelligent enough to see connections that might not be obvious.

Max sent David a message about her meeting with Tommy and Austin—leaving out Emma's role. She'd give

Emma a chance to tell her dad the truth. Max added that she was going to Travis Whitman's house.

It had taken her well over a year of working with David before she adjusted to having a partner. Technically, David worked for NET and was assigned as her personal assistant, but that title didn't do him justice. He'd originally been hired as a bodyguard after there had been threats on her life while she covered a murder trial in Chicago; they had not liked each other. Neither she nor David expected him to stay after the trial. Yet in those few weeks, Max had grown to depend on him and when she asked if he would consider a permanent position—as more than a bodyguard—surprisingly, he agreed. He'd once told her that he didn't like her then but respected her, and she accepted that. A lot of people felt the same way. As they worked more together, she wanted his friendship as well as his respect.

She didn't have many close personal friends. Dr. Julia Mendoza, the forensic scientist—but Max rarely saw her, even though they'd worked together long distance on several of Max's cases. Detective Sally O'Hara in New York was a good friend—but even with Sally, there was an emotional distance. And though they both lived in New York, they rarely got together unless one of them needed a favor. That wasn't a good foundation for a friendship. There was, of course, her producer Ben who she'd met long ago in college. They, too, had disliked each other but became friends because they both loved Karen. They stayed friends, perhaps, to honor her memory.

David had become her closest friend, her confidant, the one person she could share anything with. She hated the cliché of the single New York career woman with the gay best friend, but that's exactly what they were. Only they weren't typical.

David had made it clear that if she didn't keep him in the loop he would walk. She believed him. Now sending him messages about where she was going and what she was doing had almost become second nature. Hence the text telling him she was going to Travis Whitman's house.

Travis Whitman's family lived in an older home on a narrow lot near the Corte Madera Creek that fed into the San Francisco Bay. The view was worth more than the house, which had been built in the late seventies and matched half of the neighborhood—slightly in disrepair, small yard, sagging porch. A few completely renovated homes made their neighbors' older homes look even shabbier and more tired.

Max had originally wanted to be confrontational with Travis, but had decided to change her approach. She knocked on the door. Almost immediately, a trim, petite older woman answered. She was pleasant-looking with dark graying hair pulled into a neat bun on the back of her neck. "May I help you?"

"I'm Maxine Revere with NET news. I'm in town to interview Paula Wallace about the murder of her daughter, Ivy Lake, in the hopes someone might recall seeing or hearing something the night she died. I'm speaking with many of Ivy's peers and would like to talk to your son Travis."

The woman blinked a couple of times. "You're a reporter?"

"Yes, ma'am. I'm talking with everyone who knew Ivy Lake. Is Travis here?"

Max knew he was; Travis owned a small pickup that currently sat in the driveway.

"I suppose it would be all right." Mrs. Whitman unlocked the screen door and let Max inside. Max handed her a business card. "I'll go up and get him," she said. "Please have a seat." She motioned toward the living room.

The house backed up to the wide creek. The drought had left the water ten feet lower than normal, according to the watermarks. Each house had a dock and the channel appeared deep in the center. Across the creek was another newer neighborhood. A biking path edged the creek and went farther than she could see, down toward the bay. It would make for a nice jog along the waterfront.

Max didn't sit. She turned slowly from the backyard view and assessed the Whitmans' home.

From photographs hanging on the walls, she saw Travis was the younger of two boys. His brother looked about ten years older, and was now married with two small children. A graduation picture showed he'd earned honors at UC Berkeley, but she couldn't tell with what degree. Travis's photos were primarily of him playing sports, baseball and football. What appeared to be a recent prom photo had him with a pretty redhead. With her cell phone, Max quickly took a snapshot of that picture. If it was taken during the most recent prom, that was roughly five months ago. Travis and the redhead may still be dating; she might have some insight into Ivy as well.

Travis was one of those all-around good-looking guys and by his smile and poses, he knew it. According to Grace Martin's notes, Travis wasn't a great student, getting mostly Cs with a few Bs, no honors or AP classes, but he was an all-star athlete, the star quarterback for the last three years.

Mrs. Whitman came down the stairs. "Travis will be right down. He just came back from football practice and was in the shower."

"I'm not in a rush." Max motioned to a family portrait that appeared to have been taken recently, since the two small children were in the photo. "You have a beautiful family, Mrs. Whitman."

She beamed. "Thank you. My son Greg is an engineer at JPL in Pasadena. He worked on the Mars Rover project, have you heard of it? They sent a robot to Mars."

"I've read about it. An exciting project."

"That's where he met Jill. She works with the software. I don't understand exactly what she does, but she's very smart, too. That's Johnny, he's three, and Sarah, she'll be two next month. I wish they lived closer. When my husband retires, we're thinking of moving south to be nearer to them. UCLA offered Travis a full-ride scholarship to play football. Two other schools may offer as well—Arizona and San Diego State."

"That's wonderful."

"That boy loves sports. Always has. If he put as much energy into his schoolwork as he did into football, he'd be a straight A student."

"What does your husband do?"

"George is a CPA, a partner with his firm. He loves his work, but I'm hoping he'll retire soon. At least work part time. I'm retiring from the school district in June—I'll only be fifty-five, but thirty years teaching elementary school is enough. I love the kids, but I'm ready to leave full-time teaching. Maybe substitute on occasion. With Travis going away to college, we're going to fix up the house and sell it, then travel—at least when it's not tax season."

Two smart parents who valued education and hard work. And a son who didn't do well in school. She felt a surprising empathy toward Travis—Max knew a thing or two about disappointing family.

"Did you know Ivy Lake?" Max asked.

"Not well," Mrs. Whitman said, her voice significantly cooler than when she was talking about her family.

Before Max could press her for more details, Travis came down the stairs. His hair was damp and shaggy and he wore gray sweatpants and a thin white T-shirt. He was tall and broad-shouldered. Max could see why teenage girls gravitated to him.

"Mom said you're a reporter?"

"Maxine Revere. You can call me Max." She handed him a card.

"May I get you anything?" Mrs. Whitman asked.

"No, thank you," she said.

"I'll let you two talk. I'm going to start dinner," she said to Travis. She patted his shoulder as he sat down on a worn leather couch.

"Thanks, Mom," he said. "I'll help in a minute."

"Take your time."

Max sat in a chair across from him. Though the furniture had seen better days, the chair was comfortable.

She said, "I'm in town to interview Paula Wallace for a segment of 'Crime NET,' a weekly cable show that highlights crime in America. I'm looking into the death of Ivy Lake, as you may have guessed, and I'd hoped you could help me by answering a few questions."

When he didn't respond, she continued. "You and Ivy had a yearlong relationship that ended two months prior to her death. According to police interviews, you said that you'd broken it off. Yet Ivy's mother said Ivy broke it off. Before Ivy died, she posted a photo of you and your girlfriend—not the redhead," she added with a nod toward the photo, "smoking pot under the bleachers at school."

"She nearly got me cut from the football team. And it wasn't me. I mean, it was me, but I wasn't smoking anything. I don't do drugs." He glanced toward the kitchen, then said in a quieter voice, "I've never smoked pot. Never. You probably don't believe me because half the kids I know have toked, but I don't. Ivy and I got in a major fight because she refused to tell me who sent her that stupid picture. Ivy didn't have the kind of skill to fake a photo like that. I mean, she was good with computers and posting photos and stuff like that, but she didn't know how to make something fake look so real. I had to jump through hoops to prove to my coach I wasn't smoking weed. I had to take two drug tests."

"You were angry at Ivy."

"Duh. Wouldn't you be? There're people who think I gamed the system, that I had someone else pee in the cup. I told the coach he could watch me pee if he didn't believe me. It sucks, having that hanging over my head."

Max said, "You told the police that you had no idea who might have killed Ivy."

"I don't. I mean, she pissed off a lot of people, but no one would *kill* her. That's just—ridiculous." He frowned. "I still think the whole thing was an accident."

"By accident do you mean that Ivy was up at the preserve at one in the morning and fell to her death? Or by accident do you mean that someone *accidentally* pushed her off the cliff?"

Travis opened his mouth, then closed it. He shifted positions and didn't look her in the eye. Was he hiding something or remembering something? Why had Grace Martin thought he was guilty? Max didn't get the killer vibe off Travis Whitman. He wasn't overly bright. If he'd accidentally pushed Ivy off the cliff, would he have been able to cover it up so well?

"I don't know," he mumbled. "I wasn't there. I don't know what happened. I'm sorry she died—I really am. But Ivy was bad news. She was bad for me. I totally fucked things up my sophomore year because of Ivy. She got me to do things I would never have done."

"Like what?"

"Like none of your business."

Max raised an eyebrow. "You broke up with Ivy. Why?"

"I don't want to talk about it."

Max held open her empty hands. "I'm trying to get a sense of who Ivy was, and what happened in the days leading up to her murder. Where she might have been during the hours before her death—time that is unaccounted for. Ivy's mother said she broke up with you, but she didn't know why."

"I don't know what Ivy told her mother, I don't really care." Travis glanced at the wall where all the family pictures were grouped. "I broke up with Ivy because I didn't like who I was becoming when I was with her."

"Something must have happened," Max said quietly.

She glanced over to where Travis was looking. His brother. He looked up to his brother, respected him. Smart, older . . . Max could see something his brother may have said sticking with Travis. Changing him. Getting him to think about who he was—and who his girlfriend turned him into.

"Have you ever said something to someone and wished to God you'd never said it?" Travis asked, but Max didn't think the question was directed at her.

Max was always conscious of what she said, understanding that there would be consequences to some of her opinions, questions, and comments. Yet, there were a few times when she wished she'd been more tactful.

"You hurt someone you cared about," she prompted.

"It doesn't matter. It was my fault, not Ivy's, not anyone but me. But I knew that I would be better off if I shed her. It took a while." He shook his head as if clearing his mind, then said, "Look, lady, I appreciate you want to help Mrs. Wallace find out who killed Ivy. But I think the police are wrong and it really was an accident." He got up. "I have to help my mom. She has real bad arthritis and I hear her cutting vegetables."

"I appreciate your time, Travis," Max said. "If you think of anything that may help in this investigation, call me."

"Yeah."

He wouldn't call. If Travis knew something, he wasn't going to share with Max or anyone. There was more to his story. She wanted to know what.

Mrs. Whitman came into the living room. "Travis, would you please take out the garbage for me?"

"Sure, Mom." He gave Max an awkward half smile then went to the kitchen. When she heard the garage door roll up, Mrs. Whitman turned to Max and said, "I heard most of your conversation. I wasn't intentionally eaves-dropping."

"That's fine. You could have stayed and listened."

"Travis went through a rough patch, and that included the time he was involved with Ivy. He was angry, sneaking out of the house, failing his classes, being mean for no reason. Drinking. He lost his best friend—and that changed everything."

"I'm sorry, I didn't know."

"Oh, Rick didn't die. But he and Travis had a falling-out, then Rick moved. They were best friends from the first day of kindergarten. Travis tried to fix things this summer. I don't think it worked—he doesn't like to talk about it. But I just want you to know that Travis is a good kid. Some good kids do awful things, but they're still good kids. And they learn from their mistakes. Do you understand?"

She did.

"And then—there are some kids who aren't very good. And they'll never learn."

"Like Ivy."

"I will not say a word about her, Ms. Revere. She's dead, poor girl. I'd like to think she would have grown out of her bad habits, and that's how I'm going to remember her. A lost little girl who didn't have a chance to grow up. And for that, I am sad for the Wallace family. I wish you luck—and I'm sure if Travis knew anything that might help bring peace to Ivy's mother, he would have told the police." But then her eyes skittered away just a fraction.

"What is it, Mrs. Whitman? What were you thinking?"

"I didn't like how the police treated my son. He grew a lifetime last year. That's what happens when the authorities put you under a microscope. They interviewed Travis three separate times. Searched his room. His computer. Cell phone. We allowed it because we knew he didn't do anything wrong. They found nothing because there was nothing to find, yet they still treated Travis as if he were a bad kid, a criminal. I didn't like it, but—looking at the silver lining—when it was done, Travis was a different person. A better person. He was forced to grow up, and he grew up the way he should."

Max could take that in two different ways. Maybe Travis really was innocent . . . or he was guilty, and relieved that he got away with it. Either way, Max wouldn't take him off her suspect list.

"Thank you for your time, Mrs. Whitman, I appreciate your insight."

CHAPTER TWELVE

Travis Whitman hadn't killed Ivy, so why was he nervous?

He finished his homework after dinner, but couldn't settle down. He had energy to burn, and a headache building. His dad was working late and his mom was watching TV. Sometimes he'd watch some of her shows with her. Over the last year Travis had realized that he hadn't been the best son to his parents. That was Greg's domain—the perfect son. And for a long time, Travis had resented his brother.

And then Ivy was dead and he was interviewed by the police and Travis looked into his mom's eyes and realized he'd hurt her.

He never wanted to see his mom like that again. He didn't want to be a selfish jock who didn't care about anyone but himself. He cared—he *wanted* to care—but Ivy had been intoxicating, worse than any drug.

Now she was gone and he could turn his life around. He *had* turned his life around. Colleges were courting him. His grades were up. He would prove to his parents that he was a good kid, that he deserved his scholarship and their love. He didn't want to make his mom sad or disappoint his dad. Travis desperately wanted to make everything right.

And now he didn't get why that reporter was here. He supposed he should call Bailey. Give her a heads-up. What if the reporter went to her house next?

Travis dialed the number he had for her. A recorded message said the cellular number was no longer in service. He tried again.

Invalid. She'd changed her number.

He should have brought the flip phone home from his locker. At least he could text her, convince her to call him.

Travis needed to clear his head. He changed into running shorts, a T-shirt, and Windbreaker. It was cool at night, but he liked running along the water, the fresh salt-tinged air clearing his lungs. He told his mom he'd be back in an hour and took off on a steady jog.

Four point five miles later, he was back in front of his house as the remnants of the sun disappeared. All thoughts of Ivy and her death and the reporter—gone. He'd just keep a low profile and it would all blow over like it did last summer.

Travis saw someone familiar sitting in a car across the street from his house. Watching him. When the guy got out of the car, Travis recognized him. The reporter. The *other* reporter.

Travis did not want to talk to him.

"Travis, Lance Lorenzo. We talked last year after the police interrogated you."

"I remember." Travis hadn't remembered his name, but now it came back to him.

"Do you have a minute?"

"No."

"Did Maxine Revere talk to you today?"

"How do you know that?"

"I had breakfast with her this morning," Lorenzo said.

POISONOUS   121

"I didn't buy Revere's story—that she's here to do a segment on her show about Ivy, hoping someone will come
forward. I did some research on her and this isn't the kind
of case she'd normally investigate. But she comes from
money, and Ivy's stepdad is big money. Those types stick
together."

"I don't want to talk about this."

"Revere is going to bring up every detail of Ivy's life,
all the shit she posted on the Internet, the people she went
after. That photo of you smoking pot."

"That was fake!" Was he never going to live it down?

"Help me, Travis. I want to shut her down and prove
once and for all that Ivy's death was an accident."

"Why do you care?"

"Because I want the police to admit that they fucked
up. You're not the only one who was raked through the
coals last year."

That was certainly true. "Look—she didn't say much.
She just wanted to know about Ivy as a person, and I told
her the truth. Ivy was a bitch. She messed up my life. I
broke up with her because I didn't like who I was becoming. End of story."

"That's all Maxine Revere asked you about?"

"I don't know, it's not like I wrote everything down
after she left." Travis was cold. He wanted to go inside,
take a hot shower, and crash.

"Did she ask about Ivy's whereabouts the night she
died?"

Travis hesitated. "Yeah—she said something about a
few hours unaccounted for. Ms. Revere said the police
think it was murder."

"The police are making it up as they go along. The results were inconclusive—the coroner refused to say it
was an accident, but he also didn't state it was homicide."

"I don't know what the fuck's going on, but I don't

want to be in the middle of this. Don't you dare quote me on anything, I'm not talking to you or anyone else."

"I don't need to quote you," Lorenzo said. "You already answered my question."

Travis watched the guy cross the street, get in his car, and drive off.

What question had he answered?

Travis went inside, told his mom he was going to bed, and ran upstairs. He turned on the shower and while he waited for the water to get hot, he pulled out his cell phone and downloaded the ChatMe app. He'd deleted his account and tossed the second phone no one knew he had after Ivy died, but now he really needed to talk to someone.

He sent a private message to ChatMe101.

QB17: Do you know what's going on with Ivy's family? That reporter from New York was here asking about Ivy. Then that other dick reporter Lorenzo came by asking about the first reporter.

Travis waited. No response. *Shit.* He stripped and took a quick shower. When he got back on his phone, she still hadn't texted him back.

QB17: Are you there? Dammit, I left the phone in my locker.

QB17: Fuck it, are you there?

ChatMe101: Chill, okay? What happened?

QB17: Maxine Revere is investigating Ivy's death. I looked her up. She's a legit TV reporter from New York. Lorenzo said it was an accident. This Revere lady says Ivy was murdered. I don't want to go through this again. It's not fair.

ChatMe101: I told you not to talk to her.

QB17: She showed up at my fucking house!

ChatMe101: What did you say?

QB17: Nothing! Because there's nothing to say. I didn't do anything. Why is this happening now?

ChatMe101: It's probably just something Ivy's mother wants. What she wants, she gets.

QB17: Revere wanted to know everything about Ivy. She asked why we broke up, shit like that.

ChatMe101: Chill. Out. Don't text me again. If you want to talk, leave a note in Locker 101. But there's nothing to worry about. I promise.

Travis didn't know what to believe. His life was finally in order, he had a great girlfriend, a scholarship, football . . . his life was almost perfect.

He turned out the light and fell back into his bed. Picked up his phone and reread the message from ChatMe. Sent a message back.

QB17: I hope you're right.

DamonServer5: The account you're trying to message has been deleted.

Locker 101. He'd never seen Bailey on campus after she changed schools. Had he been wrong all this time? How many people knew what he'd done? Who else could ruin his life?

Travis stared at the ceiling. Sleep would be a long time coming.

CHAPTER THIRTEEN

David was late to dinner.

Max went ahead and ordered an appetizer and glass of wine because she was famished. Emma must have waited until the last possible minute to call her father. Max almost felt sorry for the girl, but she had to own up to her actions and accept the consequences.

At long last, David strode in and sat down. He didn't say a word, but his face was set in a hard line and an almost imperceptible twitch pulsed along his square jaw. David always looked dangerous, and the crescent-shaped scar above his right cheekbone added to his dark demeanor. He rarely raised his voice, however, and tonight was no exception. Max could barely hear him when he said, "Explain."

Max said, "Emma should have told you everything."

"Should have."

She sipped her wine as the waiter approached. David ordered a scotch neat. Double.

"Scotch?" Max smiled.

When he didn't say anything, Max put down her glass and said, "It's simple. Austin and Emma are friends. Emma saw that Austin was angry about how his stepbrother was being treated. After they talked, Emma surmised that this might be a case I'd be interested in."

"So Tommy didn't write the letter."

"Tommy wrote *a* letter, but Austin and Emma rewrote it." Max hesitated, then said, "Emma's a smart girl. She asked me questions when we were in Tahoe that I didn't know at the time were helping formulate this letter. Things I look for. But it was still a crapshoot."

"Why didn't she call me?" David said.

"To protect you," Max said. "Emma doesn't want to give Brittney any reason to limit your visitation."

"She said that?"

"No, I inferred it." Max sipped her wine. David was still angry, or maybe he was more upset. "It's been better with Brittney, hasn't it?"

"We're not going to talk about Brittney," David said. The waiter brought his scotch, but David glared at him so he walked away.

"Great. He may never return and I'm starving," Max said.

"I told Emma not to run around and play Nancy Drew. There's a killer in Corte Madera and I will not have my daughter in the middle of it."

"Of course. I don't want her—or Austin—to turn over any rocks. But that makes this so much more important, David. I have to find out who killed Ivy. Not only for Tommy, but to make sure Austin and Emma are safe."

David leaned back in his chair. "For Tommy. Not for Ivy? Her parents?"

Max had no idea what he meant by asking that. "David, I was going to stay even before I found out Emma was involved. I have a plan—something I didn't have on the flight out."

Again with the look.

"What?" she asked again. "Spell it out for me, David, because I'm not understanding your silence."

"Let's set some ground rules for this case."

She rolled her eyes. "You cannot possibly expect—"

His glare had her closing her mouth.

"Once you start asking questions," David said, "the killer is going to hear about it. Just because Central Marin is one of the safest communities in the Bay Area doesn't mean that you won't set someone off."

"It's my charm," she snapped.

"You have it in spades," he said dryly. "And so your charm doesn't put you in the line of fire, make sure you keep me in the loop. You're getting better, but you still forget."

"You mean you don't want to tag along?" she said with intentional sarcasm.

"I reserve the right to 'tag along' anytime I see fit."

"Of course. That's why Ben pays you."

The waiter did return, and they ordered dinner. Then David said, "Tell me the plan."

"I want to see the tape of Travis's police interview. Travis didn't give me a bad vibe, but he gave it to Grace Martin. Why? After he and I talked, I was left wondering if he might know what Ivy was doing during those hours before she was killed. And maybe that he has some ideas about who was at the preserve with her, or at least who she might have been meeting. But I don't think he killed her."

She continued, "Graham Jones arrives tomorrow afternoon—he'll give me his assessment of the crime scene and the evidence, and hopefully Grace Martin continues to cooperate. She was impressed that NCFI was coming down."

"Most cops are."

"And I'm meeting with Paula Wallace tomorrow morning to prepare for the interview. Charlie will be here first thing in the morning. I also want to talk to the Brock family. I haven't heard back from Lorenzo, the reporter, who promised to contact Justin Brock on my behalf. Weasel. So I'm going to the parents."

"I should be there. As a parent."

She almost said no, but nodded. "And what about your day?" she asked. "Learn anything from the wealth of information our staff downloaded from cyberspace?"

"Quite a bit. Ivy was a busy girl."

"Tell me."

"The report is in your suite. Let's not discuss the photos in public."

The waiter came with their food and they ate in silence for several minutes.

"What happened with Tommy and Austin?" David asked eventually.

"Tommy is a rare person, completely open, unassuming. Austin and Emma helped him with the letter, but the sentiment was his." She sipped wine and considered what she'd been thinking that afternoon. "Austin is angry at everyone except Tommy. He's protective. The best thing I can do for both of them is find the truth."

"And what if the truth isn't what either of them want to hear? Tommy may still be ostracized. Sometimes, Max, the truth doesn't fix the problem."

"But it's better than not knowing," she said.

"Is it?"

She stared at David in disbelief. He knew—better than anyone—how important the truth was, especially to her. How could he even suggest that anyone live with the cloud of doubt—the agony of suspicion—hanging over them for the rest of their lives?

"Always." She drained her wine and stood up, her appetite gone. "I'm going back to my room. I have work to do."

In her room, Max changed into sweatpants and a tank top. She washed her face and put her hair up into a clip. She didn't want to think about her argument with David. Was it even an argument? He'd challenged her . . . but isn't that why she liked him so much? He always told her the truth.

And tonight, his truth was that maybe she shouldn't look for the answers. That was not acceptable. Why had David irritated her so much over dinner? It seemed like he did it on purpose.

She took a deep breath. Letting go wasn't easy for her, but she'd been working on it. Plus, she kept everyone at arm's length. She supposed she'd always known she did that, but it was the first time she wanted to change. It was difficult with her boyfriend Nick because he lived three thousand miles away, but with David, her closest friend, she worked to close the distance. He was street-smart. Efficient. Courageous. He observed people as well as she did, and sometimes he brought new insight. He had the calm, cool, rigid military aura that commanded fear and respect.

He had issues, and she didn't push. She didn't like being forced into talking about her private life, and she wasn't going to do it to him. David was an angry man. He'd gotten into fights in high school and been suspended twice. She wondered if he had been like Austin as a young teen, angry with everyone and everything. For David, it had been related in part to realizing he was gay. He'd once told her he'd hated himself and only the birth of his daughter had saved him.

"I pictured myself dead, a bullet to the brain because

I'd thought about killing myself so many times I knew exactly how I would do it. And then I saw my daughter growing up, believing that I was weak and full of self-loathing." He'd paused, not looking at Max. Not looking anywhere but in his soul. *"I still took risks I shouldn't have when I was in the army. I was willing to die a hero, but not a coward."*

Was Austin so angry that he would act out, too? On the one hand, Max admired the way Austin protected and cared about his stepbrother Tommy. But if someone hurt Tommy, what would Austin do?

She should go to bed because she would likely wake before dawn, but Max wasn't tired, and she wanted to get the case firmly in her head. She needed to understand—to know who Ivy was and what was going on in her life at the time she was murdered.

David had left a folder with his report on the desk in her hotel suite. She opened his report and started going through the sad summary of Ivy Lake's short life. Thirty minutes later, Max got up and opened a bottle of wine she had chilling in the suite's small refrigerator.

When Grace Martin had told Max that Ivy Lake used social media as a weapon, Max hadn't realized exactly what that meant. She was familiar with the Heather Brock suicide because she'd read the depositions from the civil suit that had been pulled after Ivy's death. Ivy had posted a video of Heather having sex with her boyfriend on a pornography Web site. Max still felt there were federal laws that could have punished Ivy, but she also understood that because these were two minors involved it wouldn't be treated the same way.

There was so much more.

Because he was meticulous, David had organized the information into three categories—innocuous, critical, and bully. Max didn't use the word "bully" lightly. She felt that too many people bandied around the word so it ended up losing its meaning.

However, Ivy was, in fact, a bully. In many ways, she was much worse than the thug on the playground who uses fists to resolve conflict.

Ivy started a blog when she was thirteen, but posted clips to several social media sites that linked back to her blog. Most of her posts were classified innocuous. Selfies, group shots, scenic photos, food, any number of things that had nothing to do with anything except sharing an everyday occurrence. Max would prefer an Internet filled with puppy and kitten photos to the crap most people posted.

A small stack of posts were critical—commentary on individuals, some named and some not. But even in the anonymous posts, clues could be picked up. Based on the information he found on her friends' social media sites from the same period, David had figured out nearly every person Ivy spoke about, even unnamed.

Nothing in the critical stack seemed to be reason enough to kill Ivy.

Though small, the bully stack was powerful.

David had included a memo written in his small, perfect block letters.

Ivy Lake seemed obsessed with four people in the year before she died.

First, Heather Brock. Prior to posting the sexually explicit video on a pornography site, Ivy posted humiliating details about Heather on her blog and unflattering photos and comments on her social media accounts, specifically: a photo of Heather tripping downstairs; a picture of her mimicking oral sex; and several comments about Christopher Holbrook only dating Heather because she "put out." Ivy also took Heather's personal photos and wrote her own captions that implied Heather slept around. It appears Ivy made Heather the negative center of attention and dozens of individuals at the school, mostly girls, joined in on the criticism and commentary. On one blog I counted ninety-four individuals who gave Ivy a cyberpat on the back or added a critical comment about Heather.

Second, and most recently: Travis Whitman. After Ivy and he ended their relationship, she also used his posted photos and wrote embarrassing captions. She humiliated a friend of Travis's named Rick Colangelo by outing him as bisexual. What I could put together from the public information is minimal, but my educated guess is that Travis told Ivy about Rick, and when Ivy and Travis split, Ivy used the information to out Rick in an attempt to hurt Travis. Rick had been on the football team and became the subject of ridicule and torment. He moved in with his grandparents in Scottsdale the summer Ivy was killed. A few days before Ivy died, she posted a photo of Travis smoking what appears to be marijuana under the bleachers with a girl. Comments from Travis accused her of doctoring the photo and he wanted to know where she got it, claimed it wasn't true. That issue is secondary. Betraying a friend like Rick would give Travis a far better motive to kill Ivy than a doctored photo. Especially since—based on my examination of both Rick's and Travis's social media profiles—they are no longer friends.

Third, Bailey Fairstein. According to older posts, Ivy and Bailey had been best friends until Heather committed suicide. Bailey then shut down all her social media accounts, and multiple times Ivy posted a photo of Bailey with the caption "Hypocrite." Others joined in and gave examples where they felt Bailey was a hypocrite. Shortly after this incident, Bailey transferred to a private school.

Finally, Tommy Wallace. Ivy repeatedly made fun of her stepbrother Tommy by posting unflattering videos of him stuttering or sounding unintelligent. She would ask him to say or do something, and he would do it and she would film him. Through the comments, I tracked Austin retaliating by posting embarrassing photos of Ivy. One month before she died, the posts about Tommy stopped.

Prior to the civil suit being filed after Heather Brock's suicide, Ivy used social media under her own name. When the civil suit was filed at the end of April, there was a six-week period of nothing. Then Ivy picked up where she left off on the day school was out for the summer—but she opened different accounts on all social media outlets and didn't use her real name. The only thing she didn't start up again was her blog, at least nothing that NET staff could find.

The last post that Ivy Lake made was on Twitter, not her Instagram account. It was posted at 1:10 A.M. July 4.

No show, no go. Payback's a bitch—are you sorry now? You will be. #sweetrevenge

That tweet wasn't directed at anyone. I called Jess at the office, thinking there might have been a mistake on her end, and she explained this is called a "subtweet" which means that it has a double meaning and is directed at one individual who knows it's directed at them. I don't fully understand the purpose, but it's apparently a passive-aggressive method of social media communication.

Max filled in the information David had uncovered on the timeline, drawing thick lines during the peak of Ivy's online attack on the individuals involved.

Grace Martin was right: they had many suspects and no solid evidence. Max pulled out the notes she had taken from her meeting with the police officer, along with the newspaper accounts, and what she'd learned from Austin.

According to Austin, Ivy had been gone most of the day and came home at eight the evening of July 3 in a really bad mood. When she found out that Tommy was still at the house, she told him to leave. Tommy was scared of the dark, so Austin walked Tommy home.

Austin returned home shortly after nine and argued with Ivy about how she'd treated Tommy. Ivy ignored him and went to her room. Austin was playing the Xbox in his room when he heard Ivy yelling at someone on the phone in her room. Ivy stormed out of the house just before ten thirty. Austin didn't ask where she was going or when she'd be back because he was mad that she hadn't let Tommy stay for the night.

Grace had looked into Austin's alibi—that he was home alone while his sister was killed—and he'd been on his Xbox playing online with several other people. The logs had been reviewed by the cybercrime unit and determined to be valid. Austin had been playing video games until just after three in the morning. While it was possible that he had someone come over to play his game for him—and therefore provide him an alibi—there was no clear motive, and he'd been twelve at the time. Not that a twelve-year-old couldn't plan and execute a murder, but it didn't fit with the other evidence.

The last conversation Ivy had on her phone was with her ex-boyfriend Travis—fifteen minutes before she sent the tweet. It lasted three minutes and Ivy had called him.

Travis claimed that Ivy had called to apologize for posting the fake picture. Mr. and Mrs. Whitman claimed Travis never left the house after they returned from a movie, but Grace wasn't holding much weight to that alibi. It would have been easy for Travis to drive to the preserve, kill Ivy, and return while his parents slept.

Max made a note: *What was that three-minute call to Travis really about?*

Justin Brock had the strongest motive for murder, in Max's mind, but David hadn't singled him out.

Justin was five years older than his sister Heather. They had an idyllic upbringing—their parents had been married for more than twenty-five years, they lived in a lovely home in Larkspur overlooking the bay, Dr. Brock was a surgeon and Mrs. Brock had been a stay-at-home mom until she opened an antiques store in town when Heather started middle school.

On New Year's Eve, six months before Ivy was killed, Heather committed suicide with pills and alcohol. A subsequent investigation revealed that Ivy had bullied Heather for the better part of a year. Heather had never sought help from her parents, her brother, or a teacher.

Cases like Heather Brock's should get more attention. Someone should have put a stop to that situation before it got so out of hand. Ivy had gone far beyond name-calling or mean-girl spats; it was cruel and humiliating, made worse because so many others remained silent and watched from the sidelines, some actively cheering on Ivy when she went after Heather.

The Brocks had filed a wrongful death suit in civil court, suing Ivy, her mother, and stepfather for ten million dollars. According to investigators, Ivy had posted no fewer than 180 comments or photos about Heather. Ivy had branded Heather as a slut, resulting in cruel teasing by her peers. Heather had lost weight, had become depressed, and her grades had suffered.

At one point, Ivy had written: *Poor Heather. She doesn't like her new reputation? If you don't want to be called a slut, don't act like a slut.*

The video of Heather that Ivy put on a porn site had been posted a day before her suicide. It had been shared with virtually everyone in the high school, but the Brocks didn't know about it until after Heather killed herself. Heather had kept the bullying private because she didn't want to tell her parents about things she'd done the summer before.

A summer of wild fun had ended in a suicide when it was revealed for everyone to laugh at, joke about, tease over. Heather was ridiculed and embarrassed, then dead.

It angered Max that so many people had jumped on Ivy's cruel bandwagon. They piled on those who didn't defend themselves, as if tearing down someone else made them better. And why hadn't anyone noticed Heather's weight loss and the depression? Had she made some excuse or was it sudden? Had she feigned being sick, or were the family and friends in her life simply blind to her pain and suffering?

A knock at her door made Max jump. She stretched and her back cracked. Two hours had passed with her hunched over her boards and reading David's findings; it was nearly midnight. She glanced through the security hole and saw David.

She opened the door. "I'm sorry I walked out," she said.

He held up a small bag. "I brought dessert."

"You were at the restaurant for the last two hours?"

"I went to high school with the bartender. Didn't realize

it until I was leaving and he flagged me down. We had a chat."

Chat? David wasn't someone who chatted.

He stepped inside and looked at her workspace. "You've been busy."

"You're right."

"Can I get that in writing?" He smiled.

Chatting. Smiling. Joking. "What did you do with my dark, brooding friend I had dinner with?"

David shook his head, still smiling. "Charlie is renting a car at the airport so I don't have to pick him up. He'll be here at eleven tomorrow morning."

"I'll be meeting with Paula Wallace then. Let's go to the Brock house at nine. And, if we have time, I want to talk to Bailey Fairstein's mother. Bailey will be in school, but her mother will have some of the information I want."

"Are you certain you want to do this?"

"Yes. I need to understand how all the pieces fit."

Max walked over to her timeline. "I need to confirm, but after the civil suit was filed, there was a six-week window of cyber silence." She pulled out David's notes. "You wrote that the alias she used was created with one of Ivy's e-mails. We need to triple-check that she didn't create additional accounts."

Max stepped back and looked at the board she'd created. Gestured toward the photo of Travis Whitman allegedly smoking dope.

"Ivy resumed her bad habits after her six-week silence. She didn't learn from Heather's tragedy."

"Six weeks hardly seems long enough for a punishment." David nodded to the bag. "Eat your dessert, go to bed. We'll leave at eight thirty."

"I'm meeting Austin and Tommy for breakfast at seven in Corte Madera, then I want to check in with Detective Martin."

"We'll leave at quarter to seven."

"Thanks, David. For understanding about tonight—I don't know why I got so emotional about this case."

"It's what you pay me for."

He walked out.

Pay him for? Is that all it was?

She tried to sleep, but it eluded her until well after two in the morning.

CHAPTER FOURTEEN

David dropped Max off at the diner where she was to meet Austin and Tommy for breakfast. He thought it would be less intimidating for the boys if Max met with them alone.

"You? Intimidating?" Max said with mock surprise.

"How many hours?"

She had no idea what he meant.

"Sleep, Maxine."

"Enough."

He didn't smile, but didn't comment again. She was irritated that David was watching her so closely, but instead of arguing with him, she got out of the car.

She walked into the restaurant and looked around. The boys weren't there. If Austin bailed on her, she'd track him down at school. She wasn't in the mood to be manipulated by a thirteen-year-old.

The waitress sat her in a corner booth where she had a view of the door. Max ordered coffee and a muffin. She was done with her second cup before the boys showed up—twenty minutes late.

Austin looked exactly the same as the day before—defiant, angry, a slight swagger in his step. Tommy was nervous. He kept looking around as if he shouldn't be here. She raised her hand. Tommy smiled and waved. Austin didn't. They slid into the booth across from her.

"Thank you for meeting with me," she said.

"I don't know why we have to do this," Austin said. "Emma said you know what you're doing."

"Yes, I do," she said.

The waitress came over and Max told the boys to order something. Tommy ordered bacon and eggs; Austin ordered nothing.

When she left, Max said, "I've already made progress on the investigation. I met with the detective, I spoke to Ivy's ex-boyfriend, and I'm bringing in a private forensics team to reexamine the evidence using state-of-the-art technology. But it's important to me to make sure you both understand this process."

They stared at her, waiting. Tommy openly curious; Austin openly suspicious.

"I will do everything I can to find out what happened to your sister. But sometimes, even if we know the truth, we can't prove it."

"That doesn't matter," Austin said. "All we need is to know what happened."

"Even if we do know what happened, that might not change your situation."

"Of course it will," Austin said. "All we need is to prove to my stupid mother that Tommy didn't do anything to Ivy."

"You shouldn't say stupid," Tommy said. "That's not nice."

Austin's mouth twisted, but then he relaxed. Interesting. Max had seen a bit of that yesterday when Austin was with his stepbrother. He controlled his irritation and anger much better with the older boy. It was a sign of maturity that Max hadn't expected.

"There's also the chance I may not be able to find out what happened," Max said.

The waitress came with Tommy's breakfast and a re-fill of Max's coffee. She put the bill facedown on the table and walked away.

"You have to," Tommy said, his lip trembling.

"I will work hard to find out exactly what happened to Ivy," Max said. "I promise you that. I will leave no stone unturned."

"I don't understand what that means," Tommy said.

Austin rolled his eyes. "It means she'll try her best but no promises."

The sarcasm was lost on Tommy. "You *will* try your best?" he asked Max.

"Yes, and my best is better than most people." She caught Austin's eye. "I told you from the beginning that cold cases aren't easy. There's a reason the police couldn't solve this murder fourteen months ago. There may not be enough evidence to arrest someone. There may not be enough evidence for the police to get a warrant. But I follow different rules. I can push and pull and talk to whomever I want. I don't have to get a warrant to ask questions."

"But you're really saying don't get our hopes up that you'll be able to do anything," Austin said.

"Don't get your hopes up that my investigation will lead to the arrest and prosecution of Ivy's killer."

"I don't care about that!" Austin exclaimed.

"I do," Tommy said. "Bad people have to go to jail. They might hurt someone else."

"That's right, Tommy."

Tommy seemed pleased that he'd said something she agreed with, and he began to eat.

Max watched the boys as she sipped her coffee. Austin pulled out an algebra book from his backpack and quickly did homework that should have been done the night before. He didn't seem to stumble over the problems. As she watched, he purposefully erased three answers and wrote down the incorrect solution. Twenty problems, three wrong, gave him a B.

Why would he do that? Math wasn't Max's best subject in school, but she'd gone through pre-calculus with a B-plus. Austin had all the questions right the first time.

He caught her staring at him. He stuck his homework back into his backpack. It had taken him all of ten minutes to do the work.

He was a smart kid. Too smart.

"You don't want to stand out," she said.

"We gotta go, Tommy," Austin said. He stood up and put his backpack over one shoulder.

Tommy looked at his watch. "Thank you for breakfast, Ms. Revere."

"You are welcome. I told you to call me Max."

He smiled as he slid out of the booth and carefully put his backpack over both shoulders. "If you can't find out what happened, I don't think anybody can. Thank you for trying."

She watched them leave the restaurant. They unlocked their bikes and rode off together.

Dammit, she had to prove who killed Ivy Lake. They deserved to know the truth.

Tommy deserved a chance to get his life back.

On the drive from the restaurant to the police station, Max again attempted to reach Bailey Fairstein's mother. It was eight in the morning and still the woman didn't answer.

"After we talk to Grace, let's pay Mrs. Fairstein a visit," she said to David. "I don't like when people avoid my calls."

They walked into the police station at eight fifteen. Detective Grace Martin had evidently just arrived in the building—Max caught her in the lobby with an oversized purse, gym bag, and file folders. Grace gave her a narrow glance, acting far less conciliatory than she had on Monday. Max introduced David, then asked, "Do you have a few minutes?"

At first she thought Grace was going to decline, then the cop motioned for them to follow her to her cubicle. "My boss is not keen on bringing in an outside forensics team." Grace dumped her stuff on her desk and motioned them to the same conference room that she and Max had used before. "You can do what you want, but I can't share anything that hasn't already been made public." She closed the door and stood, hands on her hips.

"Yesterday, you indicated that—"

"Obviously, things change," Grace snapped.

Max wasn't going to be deterred. "NCFI has an exemplary reputation."

"You, however, do not. The chief is not a fan of yours, to say the least."

Max bit back a comment that wouldn't have helped her or Grace resolve this. Graham was doing her a huge favor shifting things around so he could be here this afternoon. His insight would be invaluable, and being an outsider might bring another perspective. "Graham will expect to speak with you," she said coolly. "I hope that won't be a problem."

"So they are coming?"

"Graham and probably one of his techs," Max said. "He wants to look at the autopsy report, photographs, and the evidence log."

"The autopsy report is public information—I'll send you a copy. Photographs—that's not going to happen."

"How do we make it happen?"

"You're talking about our case files. It's an open investigation and therefore some of the information we don't release publicly. I shouldn't have to tell you that."

"This isn't public. I won't use anything without explicit permission."

David raised an eyebrow. Yes, Max was desperate. She would make any promise to get Graham the information he needed.

"I'll see what I can do, but don't hold your breath, especially now that you're working with Lorenzo. I was already raked over the coals for talking to you on Monday, especially in light of what that creep wrote."

Max froze. "What did Lorenzo write?"

"On his blog, posted first thing this morning." Now Max could just about see the steam coming out of Grace's ears. "I was unlucky enough to see it before my first cup of coffee."

David already had his phone out. He pulled up Lorenzo's blog and handed the phone to Max.

CONTROVERSIAL REPORTER MAXINE REVERE IN CORTE MADERA
*Television personality, author of four true crime books,
Revere seeks to find a "killer" in fourteen-month-old Ivy Lake
death investigation*

*Sixteen-year-old Ivy Lake died when she fell from a cliff at
the preserve off the main fire road in the hills of Corte Madera in
the early morning hours of July 4 last year. Though there were
no obvious signs of murder or a struggle at the scene, and the
coroner listed the death as "undetermined," the CMPA consider
Lake's death a homicide and have kept the case open.*

*Lake was the subject of a civil suit brought by the family of
Heather Brock, who committed suicide six months previous
after being bullied for months online and in person by Lake.
Lake posted humiliating and embarrassing photos and
information about Brock on her blog and in social media,*

where their high school peers joined in the harassment. For details on the civil suit, which was dropped by the Brock family shortly after Lake's death, go to the blog archives.

The police interviewed more than a dozen people as possible suspects in Lake's death, but never charged anyone with a crime. It has long been the opinion of this reporter that Lake accidentally fell to her death, but the police refused to back down after they used extensive resources to track down an alleged killer. Ivy Lake was a privileged girl from a wealthy family who have the contacts and resources to make the police jump when they say jump. If Lake was from Greenbrae, would CMPA have responded with the same resources? Little evidence, no obvious sign of foul play, and no official determination of homicide?

Maxine Revere, the host of a monthly crime show on the cable station NET, arrived in Corte Madera Monday. According to sources at CMPA, Revere spent more than an hour with Grace Martin, the lead detective in the Ivy Lake investigation. Revere said, "I'm confident of the CMPA's opinion that Ivy Lake was murdered, and I hope to give the family closure by finding out who killed Ivy."

Which makes me wonder, did CMPA share information with Ms. Revere that wasn't made public? If it wasn't made public, why not?

According to high school history teacher George Fong, Ms. Revere spoke to Ivy's intellectually disabled stepbrother, Tommy Wallace, yesterday afternoon. "Ms. Revere has a reputation for being a bully and I worried that she would push Tommy to say something that could then be taken out of context. Who's protecting his rights?"

When Fong went to approach them, he saw Tommy leaving with his brother and Revere leaving with an unidentified girl.

"I had Ivy in my freshman geography class," Fong said. "I'm heartbroken she died, but I question the integrity of any

reporter who would exploit a family's pain simply because events prior to her death seem scandalous."

Revere indicated that she would be talking to everyone the police spoke to, in the hopes of retracing Ivy's steps the night she died. "There are nearly three hours missing in the timeline," Revere said. "Where was she? What was she doing? These are questions that need to be answered because they could very well lead to her killer."

Three hours missing? That's news. Why didn't the police investigate where Lake was prior to her death? What haven't they told the public? Could they be covering up their own mistakes—like spending scarce resources on a wild-goose chase?

Only time—and money—will tell. And apparently, Maxine Revere has plenty of both.

Max's hand was shaking as she handed David back his phone.

She would destroy Lance Lorenzo.

"Now you see what I'm dealing with?" Grace said. "Why the hell did you talk to him? I told you he was an asshole."

"I didn't say any of that. Not in those words," Max added.

"A taste of your own medicine?" Grace said.

Max glared at the cop. "This is not how I work. If you read any of my books or articles you'd know that."

Grace didn't apologize, but said, "The chief called me at five this morning about Lorenzo. I've been dealing with it ever since."

With San Francisco in view of Corte Madera, Max had felt she was in a bigger place but clearly she wasn't. Small town, small-town politics. She had to remember that she was an outsider.

Lorenzo's bias was clear: the police protected the wealthy. And maybe Ivy Lake deserved to die. It wasn't what Lorenzo wrote, but the sentiment was between the lines.

Max didn't care if this case took weeks—or months—to solve. She would remain in Corte Madera as long as necessary. Lorenzo had called her out. And she was not going to back down from a bully who used the Internet as a weapon. . . .

"Maxine," David said, his voice low.

She glanced his way.

"I know what you're thinking."

"You do not."

Lorenzo was the same as Ivy Lake, only he was older and should know better. Worse, he used his position as a reporter—someone who was supposed to be fair and unbiased—as a crutch to say whatever he damn well pleased.

Grace said, "I can't help you anymore. I'm sorry. I wish I could, I like to think I was right about you, but I can't help—not when Lorenzo is looking for any reason to cause problems in our department."

"Why is he doing it?" Max asked. "Reporters don't generally stir the pot unless there's a reason."

"Because he's an asshole? Because he hates cops? He joined the paper two years ago and our department has been on edge ever since. This was shortly after the Police Authority was created, and while most people in the community believe combining three small police forces into one larger, better-funded police force was beneficial—both in saving resources and adding benefits—some people have agitated that we don't treat all areas of Central Marin the same. Which is BS, but people will believe what they want, regardless of the evidence in front of them. At least in my experience."

David asked, "Is it true that the coroner's report ruled Ivy's death as suspicious and not a homicide?"

"Yes, the evidence was inconclusive. Death from jumping or falling or being pushed is hard to determine. But we still believe she was murdered. Someone else was there in the preserve with Ivy—why would she be out there alone in the middle of the night? And why would that person not come forward? She had cuts on her arms not caused by the fall. *That's* the information I didn't give Lorenzo, and if you had spilled that to him I really would have been raked over the coals. Any less seniority and I could have already been relegated to desk duty. *That's* how pissed my chief is."

Still angry, Max tried to control her temper because ultimately, Lorenzo was to blame, not Grace. "Ivy's last tweet was about revenge. A subtweet—directed at someone specific, but without naming them. But she said someone didn't show when she expected them to. Do you know who that is?"

"How do you know about that? We pulled down all her social media accounts immediately after we learned about them." Grace put her hand up. "No, don't answer. I can't help you anymore. Have NCFI contact my chief directly."

"Grace," Max said, "I promised you I wouldn't write a word without talking to you first. But I am interviewing Paula Wallace this morning, and there will be a show tomorrow night aired nationwide about Ivy's murder. I would very much like your cooperation."

"Shit," Grace muttered and ran her hands through her short hair. "I can't—I really need to talk to the chief. He's going to fucking bite my head off."

She must be angry, because Max couldn't remember Grace swearing during their conversation Monday evening.

"We don't know who Ivy was talking about in that

tweet," Grace said after a moment. "My guess is that she thought she was meeting someone. That person never came forward, and we asked everyone we spoke to about that night. We have no way of knowing who she directed the tweet to, and no one responded to it. But the one thing I can point to is that we never told Lance Lorenzo about the three hours we can't account for in Ivy's last night. That came from you."

"No, it didn't." Max thought back to what she'd said to Lorenzo, and to everyone else involved. There's no reason Austin would talk to Lorenzo, but she would certainly ask the kid. Most likely . . . "It came from Travis Whitman."

"Lorenzo didn't mention Travis in the article."

"No, but I talked to Travis, and we discussed that time block, as well as what Ivy called Travis about shortly before she sent that tweet. Grace, I know you're angry, but we need to work together." Max decided to go for it, what the hell. "I'd like to watch the police interview with Travis."

"Shit, Max! I can't—"

"I'll watch it here, I won't take notes, I won't record anything. I need an impression of who he was last summer. When I spoke with Travis yesterday, he seemed to have a decent head on his shoulders. But you didn't like him, and cops who've been doing this a while like yourself tend to have good instincts about people." What Max said was true, and at the same time she hoped it would soothe Grace enough to give her access.

"I don't know," Grace said. "When is NCFI coming in?"

"This afternoon. I'd really like you there."

"I'll see. Text me the time and place, and I'll talk to my chief. No promises."

"Thank you, Grace."

They left the police station before Grace could change

her mind. David said, "I really didn't think it remotely possible that she would give in."

"She hasn't."

"She has. I guess sometimes you really do manage to charm people. She's going to bat for you with her chief."

"I don't know."

"I do. And if you were getting enough sleep at night, you would have seen it, too."

"Don't start." She pointed to a drive-through Starbucks. "Coffee. Please."

David pulled in. While waiting for the coffee, David brought up the directions to the Brock house and thankfully didn't mention her insomnia again.

She looked up the name and number of Lance Lorenzo's editor. She had a feeling that Lorenzo was freelance, but his blog was hosted by the newspaper servers, and they were responsible for ensuring that his information was accurate. He may claim his blog was simply his opinion, but he would be legally forced to remove the false quotes he'd created for her.

She called Ben on his cell.

"I'm sending you an article—"

"I've seen it."

"You didn't call me."

"I didn't feel like being yelled at this morning. I'm buried in work right now."

"I don't yell."

"I didn't want to be lectured this morning," Ben said. "What?"

"I want a retraction."

"Don't call the editor," said Ben.

"That's why I'm calling you, sweetheart."

"Dammit, Maxine, I don't have time for this."

"That jerk Lorenzo made up the quotes. I'm sending you a list of all inaccuracies. You're the diplomat—go be diplomatic with his editor. I want this resolved. This is my reputation, Ben, and my reputation directly impacts NET."

"Send me the bullet points. Laura will take care of it. If they don't correct it, I'll deal with it."

"Thank you."

"Anything else I should know about?"

"Not yet."

CHAPTER FIFTEEN

The Brocks lived in the hills of Corte Madera, not far from where Tommy Wallace lived with his mother.

"Lorenzo doesn't know what hornet's nest he's stepped in," Max said in the passenger seat. She'd read the blog again and had grown even angrier.

"He's not worth your attention," David said. He glanced in the rearview mirror and then switched lanes.

"He's causing problems in my investigation and that's going to stop today," said Max, glancing out the car window. "After Mrs. Brock, let's go see him."

"That's not a good idea."

"He put words in my mouth. He insulted me. He's screwing with my ability to do my job."

"And yet, you'll do the job and find out exactly what happened to Ivy Lake *in spite* of anything Lance Lorenzo does or doesn't do."

"I appreciate your confidence."

"It's well placed. Let it go."

"Jerks like Lorenzo don't stop. He'll get worse if I don't do something. I want you to follow him."

"You're really not going to let this go, are you?"

"It would be a mistake if I did. Lorenzo has an agenda.

What that is will determine how I deal with him, but I don't have time to work the Ivy Lake case *and* figure out what that twerp's up to."

David nodded once. He wasn't happy with the assignment, but he'd do it—and Max was confident that by the end of the day she'd know exactly what Lance Lorenzo was planning. Maybe he just wanted to stir the shit and see what happened. In short order, he'd find out, and he wasn't going to like the result.

"He has a relationship with the Brocks," Max said, partly to herself. "He's a couple of years older than Justin Brock, but they could have known each other. He has a younger sister in college . . ." She sent a message to one of the research staff at NET to dig around into Lance Lorenzo's background and find out everything about him, his sister, and his family—and specifically any overlaps with the Brock family. "I may ask the Brocks, if it somehow comes up," she said.

"But you sound like you think his attack on the blog is personal."

"It *is* personal. But is Lorenzo's animosity because of a personal relationship with the Brocks or because he doesn't like me? Or doesn't like the police? Or has a reason to dislike the Wallace family?"

"Maybe he hates everyone," said David as he parked in front of the Brocks' modest home in an exclusive neighborhood. Very typical of Marin County—the houses were older, well-built, and small . . . but it was all about location. High on a hill, the Brocks had a million-dollar view of the San Francisco Bay.

Max and David walked up the steep driveway, then up several stairs to the front door. She knocked. A moment later, a tall woman in her fifties wearing slacks and a lightweight sweater opened the door. "May I help you?"

"Mrs. Brock, my name is Maxine Revere and I'm an

investigative journalist. This is my assistant, David Kane. I'm airing a crime show about the Ivy Lake murder, and I'm asking for the public's help in finding out who killed her. I'd like to ask you a few questions."

Mrs. Brock stared at her, her mouth a tight, thin line. "Absolutely not."

"I can assure you that I will treat your daughter's suicide with the utmost respect. I'm planning a series of articles about cyberbullying and how it impacts young people and their families. Ivy Lake is just one small component of my series." Max hoped that worked, because she was stymied. She couldn't be too aggressive or too strong because the Brocks were only loosely involved in this case.

"I don't care to help you. Please leave." Mrs. Brock glanced at David as if she recognized him. "Kane? Your father—is he Doctor Warren Kane?"

"Yes, ma'am."

Mrs. Brock looked perplexed, and David continued, "I work with Ms. Revere, and I personally promise we're not out to make light of your tragedy. We hope to help others who may be in a similar situation find ways to get help."

The woman hesitated, then said, "I appreciate your sensitivity, Mr. Kane, but neither my husband nor I care to be involved in your interview in any way, nor can we discuss the civil suit, as per terms of the settlement."

Settlement? Max's ears perked up. Who had told her the case had been dropped? A settlement was different than dropping a case.

"I'm terribly sorry but you need to leave." Mrs. Brock closed the door. If it was anyone else, Max might have stuck her foot in, but this time she held back.

Max turned and walked back to the car. "You didn't expect another outcome, did you?" David asked.

"I'd *hoped* for more cooperation, but I'm not that surprised."

"Are you really writing those articles?" David turned the ignition and pulled away from the curb.

"Yes, for the wire. I've been researching cyberbullying, finding cases with horrific, sometimes violent outcomes. But that series will be after solving Ivy's case. I won't be bringing Heather's situation into the interview. I need to make sure that Ivy is seen as the victim, not the perpetrator."

"Good luck with that," David said.

"Ivy was a spoiled, immature teenager, but she didn't deserve to die. Whoever killed her got away with it. Doesn't matter if it was a premeditated crime or if it was spontaneous, this person—now emboldened—could snap again and kill someone else."

"I see your point."

"I didn't know your father was a doctor," she said, changing the subject. "I thought he was career military."

"He was an officer in the army," David said, "and went through medic training. When he got out of the service, he went to medical school and became a surgeon."

"You wanted to come with me today because Dr. Brock must know your father."

"My dad is fairly well-known in this area," David said. "I thought the connection might help ease the conversation."

"She was definitely friendlier after realizing who you were," Max said. "What else don't I know about your family?"

When David didn't respond, she said, "I'm looking forward to meeting your dad on Sunday." Max looked at her watch. "And right now we have just enough time before meeting Paula Wallace to talk to Bailey Fairstein's mother."

Pilar Fairstein and her daughter Bailey lived in the exclusive Richardson Bay neighborhood near the Mill

Valley–Corte Madera border. David's research hadn't yielded much: Pilar was a widow, came from old money, and was not employed. She volunteered extensively for nonprofit charities as well as serving on two boards, one for an art museum and the other for a theater company.

Max had been raised with people like Pilar Fairstein. They came in two varieties: snobs or true philanthropists. Max had both in her family. Her great-grandmother Genevieve "Genie" Sterling who'd founded the trust was a true philanthropist. She had believed in giving back to her community in every way possible. She established multiple full college scholarships at her alma mater for smart kids who couldn't afford higher education. She bought art, donated it to museums, and never said an unkind word about anyone.

Then there were snobs, like Max's Uncle Brooks, who used his wealth to control people and put himself above everyone else. And there were those who fell in between, like her grandmother Eleanor. Eleanor was judgmental— Max came by her attitudes honestly, she thought wryly— but she believed wholly in charity, both volunteering and donating. She was a true philanthropist as well as a snob.

Where did Pilar Fairstein fall in the spectrum?

It was nine A.M. Bailey would already be in school, so there should be no reason for Pilar Fairstein to avoid Max. There were no gates on the property. The house was smaller than the neighboring homes, but set farther back on the property with a sweeping lawn lined with manicured bushes, flower beds, and short, leafy trees. Some people might think the Fairsteins' home was less impressive than their neighbors', but their wealth and taste showed in subtle touches—double-paned windows, landscaping, and stone pathways. There was no opulence, but each detail was exquisite.

David parked on the street and followed Max to the

door. Max rang the bell and wasn't surprised when Pilar Fairstein answered.

"May I help you?"

"I'm Maxine Revere, an investigative reporter from NET. This is my associate, David Kane. I called and left several messages over the last two days, and was hoping you had a few minutes to talk."

If Fairstein hadn't recognized Max, she certainly recognized her name. Yet she remained perfectly poised. "Ms. Revere," she said. "I really don't know what I can tell you about Ivy Lake. My daughter was no longer friends with her when the poor girl died."

"I'm aware, and I would still like to speak with Bailey. However, I thought maybe we should talk first so you know why I'm in town and what I hope to learn from your daughter."

Fairstein hesitated, then opened the door fully. "Come in, please." She waited until they both entered, then closed the door behind them.

"Your home is beautiful, Mrs. Fairstein," Max said. The decor was a combination of old and new, antiques tastefully blended with modern furniture. Old money was quiet.

"Please call me Pilar. I'll admit, I recognized your name when you called. I know your aunt, Delia Sterling. We served together on the board of the De Jong Museum for many years; a lovely woman. She mentioned your work on several occasions, and always with great pride and admiration."

"Thank you," Max said, feeling pleased. Her great-aunt Delia was her favorite. She and Uncle Archer, Eleanor's only brother, had been married for fifty-eight years. Archer and Delia were more down-to-earth than Eleanor, and Max had enjoyed spending time with them. While they'd always gotten along well—unlike Max and her

other relatives—she was nonetheless surprised her aunt
had spoken of her to anyone. Max had left when she was
nineteen and rarely returned home. "Aunt Delia is amazing. She's in her eighties and hasn't slowed down. She has
a great appreciation of art."

"A genuine love," Pilar agreed. "Please, we'll sit in the
library."

The library was through double doors off the foyer.
Built-in bookshelves filled with books both new and old,
a stately wood desk, and two full couches facing each
other. A fireplace was a focal point. Three tall, rounded
windows looked out onto the bay, shielded by a wall of
fog.

"I appreciate you speaking with us," Max said.

"May I get you anything? Water? Coffee?"

Even though Bailey's mother was nervous—evident by
the way she kept tucking her short hair behind her ear
with long, elegant fingers—she never forgot her manners.

Max liked her.

"No, thank you," Max said, motioning Pilar to sit. They
sat in high-backed chairs around a small, low table.

"I'd really hoped we had put the last two years behind
us," Bailey's mother said, "but I suppose in the back of
my mind I knew it wasn't resolved."

Max glanced around the room. She could be comfortable here. It was formal, but not overly so; not too large
or too small. A wedding portrait hung on one wall, Pilar
with an attractive man in a formal air force uniform; on
the other side of the double doors was a portrait of the
same man in uniform.

David asked, "Your husband served in the air force?"

She smiled, but her eyes didn't. "Jonathan. Yes, he was
an officer. His plane was shot down in the Middle East
when Bailey was only six. We were living in Germany
then, near the American base, but moved back here to be

closer to family. Jonathan and I are both from the area and my parents live nearby."

"I'm sorry for your loss," David said.

"It'll be eleven years in February." She smiled sadly, then shook her head as if to clear the memories. "Please, tell me why you think Bailey can help you with your report."

"I primarily investigate cold cases—missing persons and murder victims where the police have exhausted all leads. I want to talk to Bailey because I think she knew Ivy better than anyone else. Even though the two had a falling-out, I think Bailey's insight would be extremely helpful."

Pilar took her time before speaking. "Bailey and Ivy used to be the closest of friends, but I put an end to it when I saw what Ivy was doing." She hesitated. "I should say, I attempted to put an end to their friendship, but Bailey snuck around behind my back. And with cell phones and computers and school—I couldn't monitor her every minute of the day."

"Why did you object to their friendship?"

"Ivy is dead, Ms. Revere. I don't see what saying anything about this will do to help you."

"Call me Max, please. I'm not looking to point fingers or blame Ivy for her fate. I want to know what happened to her for her family."

"Bailey has turned her life around. She was never a bad kid. But she had her moments . . . some lapses in judgment . . . that many young teens have. She's now a senior, and a good student. She plays volleyball, helps me around here. She's in the middle of applying for college. I don't want to upset Bailey in any way or overturn her life."

"I appreciate that," Max said, "but someone killed Ivy. And based on Ivy's life leading up to her murder, it's likely that someone who knew Ivy lured her to the preserve and killed her."

Pilar straightened her spine. "You're not accusing my daughter."

"No," Max said. "She was out of town that week."

"I see. And if Bailey had been here, you would have suspected her."

"So would the police."

"Bailey was at art school in San Diego for the entire month of July. I flew down there with her on June twenty-eighth, and she flew home by herself on July thirty-first," Pilar said. "She came for Ivy's funeral, just for one night. We were in shock, I suppose. Things like this don't happen in Corte Madera. Ivy had problems, but she was only sixteen. She had her entire life—" Pilar took a deep breath, shook her head. "I can't help but think about what Paula must be suffering. I spoke to her a few times after the funeral . . ." her voice trailed off, then she cleared her throat. "I can't even think about losing Bailey—she's my entire life. She's all I have left of Jonathan."

Everything about Pilar felt authentic, reserved, and honest. So Max responded in kind. "I want to talk to Bailey about the people in Ivy's life. Particularly about Heather Brock."

Pilar tensed.

Max said, "Based on the time frame of Ivy and Bailey's falling-out, I guessed that it had to do with Heather Brock."

"Partly."

Pilar was on the fence. Max let her sit in silence for a minute then said, "Nothing disappears from the Internet, Mrs. Fairstein. David and I have read Ivy's blog, her social media posts, seen the embarrassing photos. One of the last things Ivy did before she died was send out a message on Twitter, not directed to a specific person, but it was clear she was talking about someone. I'm hoping that Bailey can help figure this out."

Pilar glanced at David, then looked at Max. Her hands were clasped in her lap. "After Heather died, Bailey came to me. She was depressed and upset, and she told me everything. She held nothing back—some of what she said was deeply shocking.

"I'd tried to put an end to their friendship for several reasons, but the impetus had been a series of photos and e-mails I'd found on Bailey's phone. Here Ivy was outlining a detailed plan on how to 'get back' at Heather for stealing Bailey's boyfriend, Christopher. I was . . . in denial, I suppose you could say, until I saw the evidence. The plan was laid out meticulously, down to the time to post the photos and how Ivy would use a fake account to send revealing photos of Heather to her father. I couldn't even begin to imagine how Ivy obtained the pictures in the first place. They appeared to have come from a Webcam on a computer.

"When I confronted her, Bailey told me initially that it was just talk, but I had seen the evidence. It was a deliberate campaign to hurt that poor girl. I tried to reason with Bailey, to punish her, and ultimately I forbade her to see Ivy. When Heather killed herself, Bailey confessed everything. She said she'd helped plan with Ivy to hurt Heather, but then she told Ivy she didn't want to go through with it. I'd apparently said something that she thought a lot about, and she wanted to end the vicious campaign. That made Ivy very angry with Bailey, and I don't know specifically what was said, but that caused the final rift between them. Bailey thought Ivy wasn't going to post about Heather because they'd had this falling-out—Bailey assumed that Ivy wouldn't care about punishing the girl who allegedly stole Bailey's boyfriend. Bailey didn't warn anyone or say anything. My girl—

she's felt guilty every day since Heather killed herself. On her own, without me saying anything, Bailey gave the e-mails between her and Ivy to the Brock family so they could have evidence of Ivy's premeditation to hurt their daughter. Bailey agreed to testify for them. She gave a deposition for the lawsuit. It wasn't about the money for them," Pilar added quickly. "I know Miriam Brock through charity work. They don't need or want money from their daughter's death. It was the principle. They grieved. I understand grief. I was gutted when my husband died. I can only imagine it's as bad—worse—when it's your child. They grieved and wanted Ivy to admit to what she did and stop her from hurting anyone else."

"The lawsuit went away after Ivy's death," Max said.

Pilar nodded. "I don't know the details, of course, but I heard that Miriam didn't want to pursue it after that. Her husband wasn't as forgiving, but he deferred to his wife."

So Pilar didn't know there was a settlement. Was it a secret? An agreement between the two parties? Max wished she knew exactly what was settled.

"I have a copy of the civil suit and read the e-mails in question, though Bailey's name was redacted," Max said. "The police seriously looked at Justin Brock, Heather's brother, as a suspect in Ivy's murder, but there was no proof."

"Poor family. I hope he had nothing to do with it."

"I think your daughter knows more about what was going on in Ivy's life, or would be able to help dechiper some of the subtext of her blogs and posts."

"She hasn't lied to me since that time. It took us a while, but we have a good relationship. She's earned my trust. This has been a very hard, very brutal life lesson for her. Rehashing this with you—with anyone—would be devastating for her."

"I didn't say that she had lied, I believe Bailey might

know more without realizing it. I want to ask her questions—different than what the police asked. Questions about why Ivy did what she did. Why she wanted to hurt Heather, even though it was Bailey's boyfriend and Bailey wanted to back out."

Pilar nodded. "I see what you mean."

When she didn't say anything further, Max added, "Pilar, someone killed Ivy. A peer. Very likely it's someone that Bailey knows. That person may feel they did something right, something justified—and will they stop there? Others could be in danger."

Pilar was torn. Max saw it in her expression.

"I don't know," Pilar said, "but I'll talk to Bailey when she gets home from school. I don't want this situation haunting her for the rest of her life. If Bailey wants to talk to you, I will allow it. But it must be off the record. She can give you information, share what she knows, but you will not write about it. You will not quote her. You will not use her name. She's seventeen years old, and when she's eighteen, if she wants to go on record, that is her choice. But for the next seven months, it's mine."

Max admired Pilar's spine of steel. There was no hesitation, no fear in her statement. She would protect her daughter as much as she could because she was a mother.

Max wished all mothers were like Pilar Fairstein.

"Agreed," Max said. "I appreciate your support in this." She stood and handed Pilar her card. "But this is a timely issue. I'm interviewing Paula Wallace on my show tomorrow, and running with the details of Ivy's murder and the investigation thus far. Anything Bailey can help me with, steer me in the right direction, I need it sooner rather than later."

"As I said," Pilar said as she rose, "it's up to Bailey. But either way, I'll contact you by tomorrow morning."

CHAPTER SIXTEEN

Max and David were five minutes early to their meeting with Paula Wallace at the family's home in Corte Madera. The neighborhood was one of the oldest in the community, but the Wallaces' house had been completely renovated. They weren't near the bay, but they had more land. The house was set comfortably back from the street with a wide expanse of lawn.

Paula Wallace opened the door and before Max could say anything, she was shaking her head. "I've changed my mind."

"Why?" Max asked. She knew why, and she wanted to strangle Lance Lorenzo all over again. "When we spoke yesterday, you were feeling optimistic that reminding the community about Ivy's murder could generate new leads."

"I've had a half-dozen calls from people about that horrid reporter's article. I don't want to go through this again. I can't. He was absolutely *cruel* to me."

Cruel to *her?* From Max's reading of the articles, she'd thought he had been critical of Ivy more than anyone. Which, considering that Ivy had been murdered, showed him to be crass and insensitive.

"Mrs. Wallace, I understand your frustration and pain. Mr. Lorenzo has a theory of your daughter's murder that isn't supported by the evidence. He intentionally misquoted me in order to forward his own agenda. However, the NET platform is much larger than his platform. We can control the message and, I sincerely hope, find the truth."

Paula considered what Max said, then added, "There are many people who believe him."

"Mr. Lorenzo lied in his article," Max said, "and I've demanded a retraction. Today, I simply want to talk to you. There's no camera, just us. An hour to let you know how the show will unfold. You can ask me anything."

"This whole thing feels unreal. Why are you even here?" She glanced from Max to David.

"Because," Max said, "I believe I can find out what happened to Ivy the night she died."

"You? Really, when the police haven't done anything in over a year? Why do you even care?" The sarcasm rolled off her tongue smoothly. There was no anguish in her tone, just disbelief.

"I would be happy to answer all your questions if we can sit down and chat. If you're still uncomfortable when I leave, I'll run the segment tomorrow without an interview from you, but I'd prefer your cooperation," Max said coolly. "My job is to investigate cold cases. After fourteen months, the police have no new leads in your daughter's murder investigation. This is the best time to remind people about the crime, when it happened, what happened, how it happened. Maybe someone will come forward with information that will help the police find the truth. This approach has worked for me many times since 'Maximum Exposure' first aired. And 'Crime NET' has an even larger audience."

Max had hooked her. Whether because Paula Wallace

believed that Ivy's murder would gain exposure, or because Paula was curious, Max wasn't certain. Though still suspicious of Max, Paula was interested and opened the door wider.

"Thank you, Mrs. Wallace," David said. "I'm David Kane, Maxine's associate." He handed her both his business card and Max's.

The Wallace house was stately and impeccably decorated. And very white. Everything was white, from the rugs to the bleached floors to the kitchen that Max could see around a corner. Along the wide hallway were three pieces of framed contemporary art, each under their own light. Max saw nothing but thick strokes of bright white paint with a literal splash of primary colors in the middle. She almost asked Paula if one of her kids had painted the canvases, then she noted a faint gray signature the lower right-hand corner of each piece.

Max would bet a million bucks that some art dealer had talked Paula into overpaying for these marginal examples of contemporary art.

Paula led them to the formal living room. The couches didn't look like they'd been sat on, and nothing looked childproof. Max's grandmother had a room like this—to entertain people she had to talk to, but didn't like.

Max jumped into her normal explanation about "Maximum Exposure" and what she did for the television network, NET, then moved specifically to how she wanted to approach Ivy's death. "I'll ask you questions about Ivy, what she liked to do—for example, I'd read how she was a straight A student and wanted to go to USC or Stanford. That's a good human interest angle, and will really personalize Ivy for the viewers. I'll ask about the last time you saw her, her state of mind, how she was, general questions to lead into the details that we know about the investigation. We always close each segment with a call to action—and in this case, I'm going to ask viewers if they have any information about where Ivy was after ten thirty the night she died."

"I don't understand," Paula said. "I hardly think the person who killed her is going to come forward and admit it."

"True, but someone else might know something. Or someone may remember a detail because now they're thinking about this case in a different way. If people start asking questions again, the killer may feel guilty or panic and say something to someone. We don't require people to give their name or number. If someone knows something, they may feel more comfortable telling our anonymous hotline than the police."

"I see." Paula sounded interested for the first time. "And what do the police say about your involvement?"

"I've already met with Detective Martin. I'm bringing in a respected forensic auditor to review the evidence and crime scene and confirm CMPA conclusions, or extrapolate—they have far more resources than local police. So far, I've been working well with the detective, and I hope to continue. They have exhausted every lead they had, but if they have new information, they will pursue it. I truly hope I can find them that new information."

Paula harrumphed and frowned, but didn't say anything.

Max knew Paula wanted her to ask the question, and Max wanted to resist her curiosity because she had a feeling she knew what Paula wanted to say and Max wasn't going to like it. But she pushed anyway. "You don't think the police did a good job?"

"They did a competent job, but never pursued any suspect."

"You are aware they interviewed dozens of Ivy's peers,

and questioned both Travis Whitman and Justin Brock multiple times."

"Yes," she said, her voice clipped.

"Do you think they should have been pushed harder? Did Ivy say something that made you think her ex-boyfriend was dangerous?"

"Travis Whitman is harmless, a little boy in a man's body. Ivy broke up with him because he was immature and was more interested in sports and hanging out with his friends than her. They were both young—sixteen—hardly ready for any serious relationship. I told the police that Justin Brock had threatened Ivy—he came here, to our home, and screamed at her to come out and talk to him. Of course, I called the police, but my husband went out and told him to leave. He left before the police arrived. The police spoke to him, but refused to talk to us about what they were going to do. He apparently hadn't broken any laws." Again, a harrumph that told Max Paula didn't like the result.

"When was that?" Max asked.

"Before his parents filed that frivolous lawsuit."

"Wasn't the civil suit settled out of court?"

Paula's lips pursed in a thin line. "That settlement is confidential. Who told you about it?"

"I only know that there was a settlement, not the details," Max said.

"Well, no one is supposed to know about it *at all*. It had to be done, or Ivy's name would have been dragged through the mud when she's not here to defend herself against slander. Ivy wasn't perfect, but what teenager is? She was a good girl who made some mistakes."

"Honestly, Mrs. Wallace, no one—mistakes or not—deserves to be murdered. That's why I want to find the truth."

"Well, then you should look closer at Bill's son, Tommy. The police never seriously considered him a suspect." Paula said. She sighed and said, "Poor Bill. He's done everything for that boy. But he's brain damaged and dangerous."

"Detective Martin interviewed him and his mother, and determined that he wasn't involved."

"Honestly, Jenny would say anything to protect her son. He was suspended—twice—for fighting. He has a temper. He has always made me nervous."

"Why?" Max asked.

"You mean, over and above being suspended for physical violence? *Twice?* The way he looked at Ivy. It made her uncomfortable. I shouldn't have to spell it out for you. Ivy didn't like being alone with him, and he was at the house the night she died."

"According to witness statements, your son Austin escorted Tommy home shortly before nine that evening, and returned an hour later. Ivy then left on her own just before ten thirty."

"What does that matter? Tommy could have left his house at any point after Austin walked him home. The police said no witness saw anyone in the preserve or near the trails, not Tommy *or* Ivy or anyone else. What I know and what I can prove are different. But mark my words, Jenny had something to do with the police going easy on Tommy. She's lied for him before, I have no doubt she would lie for him again."

"When did Tommy's mother lie for him?" Max asked.

"Talk to her. You'll see what I mean."

"I'd like your opinion," Max said. "If the police didn't do their due diligence, I'd like to know."

"Meet with him, talk to Jenny, you'll agree with me. Because truly, who would hurt Ivy?"

Max could think of a half-dozen names that topped the

list of kids who would have hurt her if they thought they could get away with it.

And—obviously—one of them had.

"Do you believe that Tommy convinced Ivy to go up to the preserve? Why would she go with him if she was scared of him?"

"I suspect that he followed her."

"She had a car. Tommy doesn't have a driver's license."

"The preserve isn't far from his house. Tommy could have overheard Ivy making plans with someone, and then gone up there and waited for her. Why are you interrogating me? I thought you wanted to find out what happened to Ivy. Or are you just like everyone else, wanting to make her out to deserve being . . . being killed."

For the first time in the hour, Paula showed genuine signs of emotion. Though Max was irritated with Paula, her anger disappeared. As unlikeable as she was, Paula had lost her daughter. She was still a grieving mother.

"Mrs. Wallace," Max said quietly, "in no way do I think that Ivy deserved to die."

David said, "I think we have enough information to put together the segment. Tomorrow morning Ms. Revere and our cameraman, Mr. Morelli, will interview you here. We'd like to take some film of Ivy's room, the neighborhood, her school. We'd like to talk to your husband as well—"

"Bill is out of town until Friday night."

"What about Ivy's father?"

Paula shook her head. "Blaine has no interest in our children. He canceled the last two visits with Austin— over the summer and spring break. Like Bill, he travels for business, but Bill makes a point of being home every weekend."

David nodded, but didn't comment. Max wondered if Blaine's disinterest contributed to Austin's anger. Or, more likely, to Austin's attachment to Tommy—an older boy who would do anything Austin wanted to do. A big brother who was more of a playmate than a mentor.

Max said, "We'll handle the other interviews, you'll only need to be available for an hour."

"What other interviews?" Paula asked, her eyes darting from Max to David.

"The detective in charge of the investigation," Max said, even though Grace hadn't agreed. "The police chief, if he'll go on camera. Ivy's friends. Possibly her ex-boyfriend Travis."

"Travis did not kill Ivy," Paula said. "I told you, the police refused to consider Tommy. It breaks my heart to think that Bill's son could hurt my daughter, but I know what I know."

"The only way that this will work," Max said, controlling her temper and trying to remember where Paula was coming from, "is to leave as much open as possible, so anyone who watches the segment or reads it on the Web, won't be led into thinking one person or another was involved. We want them to consider what they might have seen or heard not only last summer when Ivy was killed, but among friends after the fact. Someone who was acting odd, or even a guilty confession. Teenagers don't keep secrets well."

The first "Crime NET" show that aired resulted in the killer confessing when he called in to the hotline. It was a hit-and-run of a mother of two young children. The killer had been a nineteen-year-old college student who was driving drunk. He didn't remember the accident, but had nightmares for a year. When he saw the segment on the Internet, he knew he'd been the driver. He made a plea deal and received five years in prison, a permanently suspended license, and would be paying restitution for years to come.

"Jenny Wallace has no remorse for protecting her son," Paula said. "She blames me for her failed marriage, and has been causing problems for Bill and me ever since we were married."

Max opened her mouth to point out that considering she'd had an affair with Bill while he was still married, Paula was more to blame than Jenny for the failed marriage, but David spoke first. "We have to be careful how to phrase certain information because of potential slander issues. I can assure you we'll treat this case with complete respect for Ivy. We know you want the truth; we want the same thing."

Paula nodded, satisfied with his response. David was certainly the diplomat in their partnership. Max's agitation was growing. At Paula, and at Bill. She certainly didn't give the husband a pass for cheating on his first wife. He had children. Max wasn't antidivorce—there were valid reasons to dissolve a marriage. But once you brought kids into the mix, you needed to think twice about your own selfish needs. Bill hadn't given a rat's ass about his two children when he screwed around with Paula Lake in Seattle for two years before he divorced Jenny. She'd been married as well with two kids. Was the sex that great that they had to screw up four children?

Max would never get married. It had nothing to do with trust, and everything to do with the fact that she was selfish. She liked her life the way it was, and if that meant she would be seventy and alone, so be it. She didn't want to change, and would resent anyone who tried to change her. But she also would never have an affair with a married man. That would make her no better than him.

"I have a few ground rules of my own," Paula said. "You're aware of the settlement; I will not discuss it."

"Understood. There is no need to bring up the lawsuit at all."

"In addition, I will not allow my daughter's memory to be tarnished, so you will not discuss anything that was brought up in the original civil suit."

"Mrs. Wallace, there is a line between childish teasing that hurts feelings and aggressive bullying that aims to destroy a person," Max stated. "I consider Ivy a victim, and her killer needs to be brought to justice. But I'm not giving anyone a pass on cruelty. It is highly likely that Ivy's online activities provided the killer's motive. Someone who was hurt so deeply, and blamed Ivy. That is no justification for killing Ivy," she repeated, "but without exploring all the possible reasons, we'll never find the truth."

"Then the interview is off."

"Fine."

Max wasn't going to beg. She wasn't going to capitulate. She would do this with or without Paula Wallace. But *damn* if she was going to jeopardize this investigation to feed into Paula's delusions about who her daughter really was.

Paula stood up and looked down her nose at Max. "I'm sorry that you won't help, but I'm not surprised."

Max stood and forced Paula to look up at her. "Your interview may be off, but I'm running the segment. I have more than enough information without your involvement."

Paula's eyes widened. She said, "I will sue you."

"Good luck with that."

Max walked out.

David followed, and when they reached the car he said, "You held back far longer than I thought you would."

"I've had it. Someone killed Ivy, someone who knew her, and it was directly or indirectly related to *something* she posted online. I will find the truth." Max slammed the passenger door shut. She'd faced grieving parents, shocked children, sorrowful spouses. Some victims were more saint than sinner, some more sinner than saint, but they all deserved justice.

Max didn't care what Ivy did or didn't do. She had acted like a bitch, but she'd been a sixteen-year-old mean girl. She could have changed. She should have had the *opportunity* to grow up. Someone stole that from her.

David slipped into the driver's seat and drove off. "Charlie just landed. He'll be at the hotel in an hour."

"He knows what to do. I'm not holding back any more punches. I haven't forgotten about Lance Lorenzo. You need to find out what he's up to."

"And where are you going?"

"It's time I met Tommy's mother, Jenny Wallace. I have enough information at this point. Let's drive back to the hotel. I'm sure the manager will let you borrow one of the company cars again. I'll take the rental."

"Better yet," said David. "I'll get you a driver for the rest of the day."

"I'm not in the mood, David." Max didn't have a good track record with rental cars. Sometimes the damage wasn't even her fault, but tell that to the insurance company. Still, she loathed being teased about it.

"Then don't argue with me," he answered.

CHAPTER SEVENTEEN

Before David, Max had always hired drivers, especially in New York City. But she'd become spoiled having David in the chauffeur's seat. She could bounce ideas off of him, talk through theories while generally enjoying his company. The driver he hired for her today was thin and wiry and didn't speak much. His name tag read: Richard.

Max sat in the back and reviewed her notes while Richard drove her to Jenny Wallace's workplace. Max's staff had pulled up most of the information last week, and the rest she'd filled in since she'd arrived in Marin County.

Jennifer Heston had met Bill Wallace in grad school. They'd dated three years while Bill was studying law at UC Berkeley after getting his degree at UC Davis. The year before they married, Jenny had received her master's degree in architectural history. She was originally from Los Angeles, Bill from Piedmont, a wealthy suburb of Oakland close to Berkeley. They both found jobs in San Francisco—Jenny restoring historic buildings and Bill as a lawyer for a prestigious civil law firm. When Jenny became pregnant with Tommy, they bought and renovated a house in Corte Madera. She'd won awards for her work on many projects, and shortly after the birth of her daughter, Amanda, who was two years younger than Tommy, Jenny became a partner in a San Rafael architecture company that specialized in historic renovations for both businesses and private homes.

Max had a copy of their divorce settlement—some people were stunned to find out that nearly every legal filing was available to the public unless sealed by the court. Jenny retained the house—which had more than quadrupled in value since they purchased it—and Bill retained his 401K. Jenny had custody of the two kids, Bill had liberal visitation rights.

Though the settlement seemed amicable on paper, it was the initial filing that was the most interesting. According to Jenny's statement, Bill had been having an affair with Paula Lake for nearly two years. He'd been traveling to Seattle often, ostensibly for work, but a chance encounter with one of his partners resulted in Jenny finding out the Seattle project had ended months before. After Jenny hired a private investigator, she learned about her husband's affair with Paula Lake. At first, there was extensive animosity—hence the initial rash and revealing filing—but on paper during the settlement, it seemed that they'd resolved their differences.

Once a cheat, always a cheat. Max couldn't imagine that Bill Wallace didn't have another mistress or two around the country. Why change his behavior? He'd already lost custody of his children—though there was no record of him fighting for them. In fact, there was no record of him doing much of anything other than agreeing to the terms of the divorce decree. He didn't counter Jenny's claims and didn't argue that he hadn't had an affair.

As far as Max was concerned, he was a cheating, lying prick who didn't deserve what Jenny had given him. Perhaps that was unfair.

But it wasn't unfair, Max decided after giving the situation a minute of thought. Bill allowed his new wife to banish his son from his house. Whether it was because he wasn't around enough to argue with her, or because he was complicit, Max didn't know and frankly, she didn't care. The end result was that Tommy felt ostracized and unwanted.

Nonetheless, she wanted to talk to Bill Wallace, even if she didn't expect it to go well. Maybe, if she was being honest with herself, she wanted a good, old-fashioned confrontation. She was in that sort of mood after speaking with Paula that morning.

She called Justin Brock at Stanford a third time; no answer. She left another message, ending with, "I would prefer to speak with you directly rather than stating that you and your family have no comment." It was hardball and she almost felt bad about it, considering what happened to Justin's sister. But there was a killer in Corte Madera.

And, she didn't like being ignored.

If Max needed to go to Stanford to see Justin Brock, she might be able to stop and see Nick. They wouldn't have a weekend, but one night might satisfy her.

Nick's voicemail picked up. She frowned, then left a brief message to call her.

She was making little progress. Two full days and she'd pissed off the detective, made an enemy of a local reporter, and lost the support of the victim's mother.

And she couldn't even talk to the man she called her boyfriend.

"Win-win all around," Max sarcastically muttered while pulling out the file David had created of Ivy's photos and posts.

Something Travis had said yesterday was bothering her, so she went back over the timeline. Ivy had Instagram accounts under two names—one for four years, and one for less than six months, the latter started shortly after Heather Brock committed suicide. There had been no claims that any of the photos Ivy had posted were fake, except the photo of Travis smoking pot.

One rather tame example was a photo of a jock with his arm around a cheerleader. The comment: *Interesting. Carl dumps ugly smart Gina Dole for the pretty dumb Ashley Adams.*

A distant photo of a blonde on her knees giving a blow job to a guy. Nothing explicit could be seen, but it was obvious what she was doing. The guy's face was clear; Max didn't know who he was, but anyone who knew him would. The girl wore a distinctive blue sweater with white stripes, but it didn't matter if she was recognizable in the photo: Ivy outed her. *Whoops! Tish caught with something in her mouth under the bleachers.*

A photo of a science test in someone's backpack. It meant nothing to Max until she read the caption: *Now we know why Vince gets As in science.*

On closer examination, the test was in fact an answer sheet.

The comments mostly piled on to whatever Ivy had written. Some people were angry—including Vince who wrote: *Bitch. You'll be sorry.*

Hmm. Who was this Vince and why hadn't David flagged him? She sent David a note and asked.

It only took him a minute to respond.

Vince Gustafson graduated the month before Ivy's murder and enlisted in the marines. He was in basic training in North Carolina when she died.

That explained that. She needed to remember that if there was something to see, David usually saw it.

"We're here, Ms. Revere," Richard said from the front seat. "Would you like me to wait for you or escort you inside?"

"You can wait here, thank you, Richard." Max said. As she got out of the car, Graham Jones from NCFI sent her a text message.

I'm on the road with Ruby and Hunt. Will meet you at the crime scene at three, provided traffic isn't hell.

She responded: *I'll be there. FYI: There may be a problem with the locals, but I'll fix it.*

When he didn't respond right away, she worried he was going to pull out. Graham didn't like working without the support and permission of the local police. A minute later he texted: *Don't know what you did, but I have everything I need. Detective Grace Martin e-mailed me the crime scene photos and measurements, and I received the autopsy report from you. Is there a new problem?*

Max immediately told him *no problem* and wondered how and why Grace had a change of heart.

She entered Jenny Wallace's office building in San Rafael, only fifteen minutes from Sausalito. Jenny was a partner in an architectural design firm located in a contemporary building featuring attractive sculptures and elegant furnishings. It was a pleasing blend of old and new, likely an example of the type of work done by Jenny's company.

The firm took up the top two floors of a six-story building. Max took the elevator to the fifth floor and checked in with the receptionist. Fortunately, she didn't have to jump through hoops. A few minutes later, Jenny came out to the reception area and said, "Ms. Revere? I'm Jenny Wallace. How may I help you?"

Max handed her a business card. "Is there someplace we can talk in private?"

Jenny looked at the card a moment before she said, "Sure, my office is right this way." She glanced at her watch. "I have about fifteen minutes before a meeting."

"I won't be long."

Her business was spacious, sparsely decorated, and each staff member had a large work area. Jenny's office was in one corner and included two desks, a drafting table, and a wall of blueprints to famous buildings. She was a minimalist, but her desk had three framed pictures: one of her with her two kids taken when Tommy was about thirteen, and one each of Tommy and Amanda, both recent shots. While Tommy looked more like his father, with blond hair and light blue eyes, Amanda's brown hair and dark blue eyes resembled her mother.

Jenny looked younger than her forty-seven years. She wore little makeup and had the long, skinny frame and movements of someone who rarely stopped moving. "When Crystal said there was a reporter here, I was surprised. Usually I would have you make an appointment through our media rep, but I had a few minutes."

"I'm not here about your business, though I've read up on some of your historic renovation projects—what an interesting career. Long ago, I wanted to work at a museum. I love art, and so many historic buildings are works of art."

"I can't imagine doing anything else. I only get to work about half my time on historic structures, but they're my favorite." She paused, smiled, curious but not suspicious of Max's motives. Max's gut first impression was that Jenny had a lot of nervous energy, but she was generally open, friendly, and trusting.

"I'm the host of an investigative crime show. We're running a segment on the murder of Ivy Lake, and I've been talking to everyone who knew her."

Jenny blinked. Her voice was flat. "She's my ex-husband's stepdaughter. I rarely saw her."

"But your children knew her well. They were over at

your ex-husband's house often. I'm trying to get a sense of how well you knew her, what you think might have happened, where the police should have been looking."

"I have no idea," The light had gone out of Jenny's eyes. She no longer was curious. She just wanted Max gone.

"Your son and Austin Lake are close," Max continued.

"How do you know that?"

"I spoke with them yesterday."

"You have no right to talk to my son without my permission."

Tommy was eighteen, and even if he were a minor, there was no prohibition with him talking to the media. There were ethical rules about publishing photos or interviews with minors, but Tommy was neither a suspect—nor a child.

Max wanted to tell Jenny about the letter Tommy had sent her, but decided to hold back for now. Instead, she said, "Though the police ruled out Tommy as a suspect, Paula Wallace has a different opinion. Do you know why?"

"Out."

Max didn't budge. "I'm trying to see the big picture."

"By accusing my son of a heinous crime? Just because he's a little slow?"

What a leap. "I didn't accuse Tommy of any crime. I'm asking why Paula Wallace banned him from her house. It seems harsh, considering the police had no reason to think Tommy had anything to do with Ivy's murder."

"Paula Wallace is a lying, manipulative bitch, just like her daughter."

Wow. Jenny had gone from friendly and sweet to full-on attack.

"You need to leave," she continued.

"With or without your cooperation, I'm running a

segment tomorrow night. Without any evidence, Paula seems to think that Tommy killed her daughter, and—"

Jenny cut her off. "Paula thinks Tommy isn't *perfect*. She doesn't want anything *imperfect* to touch her *perfect* life."

"Mrs. Wallace, please—I'm trying to help your son."

Her voice rose. "Tommy doesn't need your help!"

Max had been prepared for animosity, or denial, or co-operation . . . but blatant hostility was over the top. And Jenny wasn't listening.

"Tommy wrote me a letter," Max said clearly.

Jenny opened her mouth, then closed it. "You are either lying or mistaken."

Max reached into her briefcase and extracted a copy of the letter that Tommy had written. "Austin helped him, but Tommy told me the thoughts were his own."

Hand shaking, she took the paper from Max, then spent several minutes reading it over and over. She sat heavily on a leather chair next to her desk. Max took a seat on the couch across from her.

"I don't understand," Jenny said quietly. "How—he doesn't think like this."

"Jenny," Max said softly, "Tommy is hurting because he feels like half his family has been taken from him."

"He told me he couldn't see Bella, but I didn't know it was this bad."

"He told you what exactly?"

"That Paula didn't want him at the house anymore, that she didn't want him playing with Bella. He never said that she thought he killed Ivy. That—it's absurd. Bill would have told me."

"I came to California from New York because Tommy wrote me this letter. He doesn't deserve to be ostracized from his stepbrother and half sister. I know this situation is difficult for you, but I need your help. I planned to interview Paula, but she and I had a fundamental disagreement over how the interview would proceed."

Jenny shook her head. "Watch yourself with her. She's vicious."

"I can handle Paula Wallace," Max said. "But without Ivy's mother, it's going to be more challenging to engage my viewership. I have a seven-minute slot. Me talking and showing B-roll isn't going to cut it. I want to put Tommy on camera."

"No."

"I promise you I'll treat him with respect and will edit the program to make sure it puts the best possible light on him."

Still staring at Tommy's letter, Jenny seemed lost in thought. Max had to get through to her. "When I was in high school," Max said, "my best friend was murdered. Her ex-boyfriend—another friend of mine—was arrested. But without any evidence, the police couldn't make the case. Still, the accusation stuck with Kevin his entire life, until he killed himself after spiraling into a life of drug addiction. He was innocent, but everyone in town thought he was guilty."

Max paused and waited, but Jenny didn't respond. Max said, "I know you don't want that for Tommy."

"All he wants is to be a family," Jenny said, sorrow shaking her voice. "My divorce from Bill—it set Tommy back. The only thing that helped was, truly, Austin. He's no angel. He has a mouth on him, and I've had to make sure Tommy doesn't pick up Austin's bad habits. And Austin has been lying to Paula about how much time he spends at my house." She paused. "And I let him. It was a small way I could get back at Paula for destroying my family."

"She didn't destroy your family," Max said. "You have two children who love and need you."

"You've talked to Amanda, too?"

"No, but I'd like to."

"Amanda, though she was only nine, understood that her father left us for another family. It was that family that bothered her more than the divorce. Ivy was only a year older than her, and once Amanda told me that she thought Bill wanted a normal son. I lost it with her—I didn't mean to—but I won't have Tommy thinking he's anything but wonderful. He's not so severely mentally challenged that he can't learn or go to school. I let him ride his bike everywhere he wants—he's responsible and trustworthy. But he also understands when people tease him for stuttering or saying the wrong word or not understanding something. And that's why I'm nervous about letting him speak on television. People won't understand. They can be cruel."

"It won't be live. This will work because I have this very moving letter from Tommy."

"You're going to read this on the air?"

"I wasn't going to—until Paula Wallace cut me out."

"She won't like that—it might make the situation worse. She'll never let Tommy see Bella. He's already devastated."

"Maybe it's time you have a heart-to-heart with your ex-husband about what is going on with his son."

"Bill and I—we haven't been able to have a civil conversation since the divorce. I just stay away. We are cordial when the kids are around, but that's it."

Max was treading into unfamiliar territory. Just like Nick and his ex-wife Nancy, she didn't understand why Jenny didn't just tell Bill exactly what she thought and how he had affected their children. Why walk on eggshells? Tell Bill he's an asshole and fix it.

"If you prefer, I won't read the entire letter," Max said, capitulating in part. "I'll leave out the part where Tommy says Paula believes he killed his stepsister. Truthfully, Ivy wasn't a well-liked person and I don't see any viewer reaching out to help if I recite all of the sordid details. I need someone on camera that people will respond to, and I think—I *know*—that they'll respond to Tommy. He's a terrific young man."

"I don't like it." Jenny stared at the letter, her brows turned in. "If Tommy wants to do it, I won't stop him. But I'm not going to encourage him either."

It was the best Max would get. "Thank you. I'm going to ask Austin as well, which should help Tommy feel comfortable."

"Paula will never allow it."

"I wasn't planning on asking her permission." Max glanced at her watch. It was getting late, and she needed to meet Graham at the crime scene. "I was hoping I could meet your daughter later tonight or tomorrow morning—she was Ivy's peer, she might have some insight."

"Ivy and Amanda didn't get along. You're aware of the lawsuit, the civil suit filed on behalf of Heather Brock?"

"Yes."

"Amanda didn't know Heather well, but after the poor girl's death, Amanda told me that Ivy had posted all sorts of things about people on the Internet. True things, but embarrassing. Amanda said she didn't want to go to her dad's house because she didn't want Ivy to embarrass her online. That was one talk I did have with Bill and Paula, and it did not go well." She hesitated then asked, "Do you think Ivy was killed because of something she posted on the Internet?"

"I don't know," Max said truthfully, "but I think her behavior may have created the situation she found herself in, and someone snapped. The manner of Ivy's death suggests it was spontaneous. But I still believe that Ivy deserves justice. Tommy deserves to get his family back. And a killer needs to be punished."

Jenny nodded, but still looked troubled. "I hope you know what you're doing."

"I do," Max said. "I'm not leaving until I find the truth."

"What if you don't?"

"I will. I may not be able to prove it to the police, but I will know what happened."

Jenny glanced away for a moment, then said, "Come by the house tonight after seven. That will give me time to talk to Tommy and Amanda. But if they don't want to go through with it, that's that."

When Travis grabbed his shit from his locker at lunch, he'd found another text message on that stupid burn phone. He was sick and tired of all the game-playing. The bitch wanted to meet at *midnight* in the preserve!

Are you fucking kidding me? Where Ivy died? No way.

No response.

Bailey, I know it's you. I'll come to your house. Now. I'm out until practice.

He was 95 percent certain it was Bailey who'd been communicating with him through ChatMe for more than a year. Last summer he'd been 100 percent certain, but after talking to her yesterday, he had a small, niggling doubt.

Finally, an answer.

You can't come to my house.

Gotcha, bitch.

I'm not going anywhere near the preserve. We have to talk. Today.

It took her a few minutes but she replied.

I can't do anything until late tonight.

Well, he was done taking orders.

Tomorrow morning, the coffeehouse on Main, 7 A.M.

She didn't respond.

Well, screw her. This was out of control. Two reporters, that article, everyone at school looking at him, talking behind his back . . . he couldn't live like this. They had to do *something*. He wasn't going to lose his football scholarship over this.

Meet with me or I'm telling that reporter everything.

Nothing. Fine, if that's the way she wanted to do it, he'd do it.

He hesitated.

He wasn't about to lose everything he'd gained this last year. He hadn't even been up there when Ivy died. It was an accident, plain and simple, but how could Travis convince the reporter of that? He had no archives of the messages he and Bailey had exchanged because he'd used the phone she'd left for him last year. And she wasn't like a cop who could get a search warrant or anything. He didn't even think the ChatMe program kept an archive of old messages, it's why everyone used it.

Except he'd read about how some data could never be erased.

Would he be in trouble because he didn't tell the police he knew Ivy was going up to the preserve? Why should Travis get in trouble when he wasn't even there?

He rubbed his head. He felt sick. Really, like he was going to puke.

But he had this phone. He could use that, it would be something. Maybe he could tell someone anonymously to talk to Bailey Fairstein. Like the reporter.

Right. *Which* reporter? The one from New York or the guy? The guy of course . . . he really believes that Ivy's death was an accident. Because it was.

It had to be.

He was about to call the reporter when the bitch finally got back to him.

Fine. I'll be there.

He didn't know why he was so relieved. He didn't want to ruin anyone's life, not Bailey's or his, but he wasn't going to lose his scholarship or worse—go to prison—for something he didn't do. They could finally talk about what really happened when Ivy fell off the cliff.

If Bailey came clean, what's the worst they'd do to her? She wasn't even eighteen, it had been an accident, and her family had a fortune. It wasn't like she needed a scholarship like he did, or that she had meant for anything to happen to Ivy. Lawyers would get her off or maybe she'd do community service, something like that.

But with two reporters digging around, Travis could no longer risk keeping quiet. If Bailey didn't tell the truth, he'd leave an anonymous tip for the police and if they were halfway good at their jobs, they'd figure it out.

CHAPTER EIGHTEEN

After ten years in the Army Rangers, two years working as a bodyguard, and nearly two years working with Max—who seemed to have a knack for finding trouble—David Kane's instincts were sharp.

Lance Lorenzo was up to something.

David also knew that Max had good instincts. She could practically smell a lie, which sometimes surprised David. She had a knack for pushing the right buttons, usually making someone so angry that they spilled the truth. Her hunches paid off virtually every time, and David enjoyed seeing her proven right over and over again.

But her instincts about danger were pathetic.

Someone had wanted to get to Max last June, and they were willing to kill her driver to do it. It had taught David the uneasy lesson that even with the best-laid plans and procedures, if a bad person really wanted to hurt somebody else, they could—with enough time, money, patience, and cunning.

David didn't yet know if Lorenzo was dangerous, but he was certainly acting suspiciously. The newspaper he worked for managed several local weekly and daily newspapers with dwindling circulation. The Web site was clean and functional, and that evidently funded the business. Looking at the stats, David noted that Lorenzo was neither the most popular or least popular reporter or blogger, but he was the most prolific. Max had read everything he wrote regarding Ivy Lake and the Brock family, but David spent more time combing through his other blogs to figure out what made him tick.

Lorenzo was a rabble-rouser—creating controversy where there was none. Not that he wrote anything patently untrue, it was how he shaped his arguments, casting blame or aspersions on the motives of others. He was the consummate devil's advocate on various issues, taking first one side then the other, as if he got points for pointing out the flaws in every position. He had a deep disdain for anyone in a position of authority; as if simply by being in authority, they were either corrupt or corruptible. But he viewed authority as virtually anyone who had control over other people, from cops to teachers.

The comments on his blog fanned the flames but, surprisingly, Lorenzo stayed out of that end. Yet the anger and animosity in the uncivil debates in the comment section seemed to egg him on. Bitter and vindictive comments fueled more articles on that topic.

How was Lorenzo different than Ivy Lake? Under the guise of reporting news from all sides of an issue in the most confrontational way possible, he generated heated opinions from the community—similar to how Ivy's photos of her peers generated extensive comments from her smaller community.

David's disdain for the political process had only grown during his time in the army. Too often, elected officials made decisions that had affected his unit—and they had no idea nor did they appear to care about the negative repercussions. Most who made the decisions didn't listen to those in the field or even commanding officers, but instead often made choices that jeopardized the lives of soldiers and innocent civilians. It made David angry, but he had always been an angry man. He understood anger, and didn't know if he could live without it. Controlling it was the victory, and David controlled himself exceptionally well.

Lance Lorenzo's anger seemed manufactured. David couldn't put his finger on it, maybe because he didn't understand why someone would *try* to be angry. As David watched him that afternoon, it seemed clear Lorenzo was more excited than angry, as if controversy pushed him forward. This bastard would play both sides, then watch from the balcony with popcorn as opponents battled.

David tracked Lorenzo from a coffee shop. He followed the reporter as he drove to the Brocks' house. Mrs. Brock opened the door but didn't invite him in. They spoke for several minutes before Lorenzo left and drove to the police station. He parked on the edge of the parking lot. He didn't go inside but seemed to be waiting, on his phone most of the time. Ten minutes later, he pulled out and drove two blocks away, where he parked in a half-empty grocery store lot. Five minutes later, a patrol car pulled parallel to Lorenzo, so their driver's windows faced each other.

David photographed Lorenzo and the cop, a young, uniformed officer. David took a picture of the back of the squad car which included the unit number. Through the zoom lens, he noted Lorenzo typing rapidly into his phone but David couldn't make out any details. A few minutes later the cop pulled away and Lorenzo got back on his cell phone. Ten minutes passed before Lorenzo abruptly drove out of the grocery store lot. David followed.

Across from the high school, Lorenzo parallel parked next to the city park and turned off his car. David drove around the block, then found a space where he could observe Lorenzo's vehicle.

It was nearly two thirty. David suspected Lorenzo's plan and was ready to intervene. When the special ed students came out of the trailers, David almost opened his door, but Lorenzo didn't make a move. He simply watched.

Tommy walked his bike across the street and through the park. Lorenzo got out of his car and followed, but made no move to approach the young man.

David drove around the block again and saw Tommy sitting on a bench across from the middle school. He had a half smile on his face and looked around as if he had no worries. Several squirrels ran across the path in front of him, and he followed their progress with his whole body, tilting his head up to watch as they disappeared in the leaves. He grinned when the squirrels ran back down and then up a different tree.

Lorenzo was sitting on a bench three over from Tommy. Tommy had no idea he was being followed. David took a couple of photos, then drove around the block again and parked not far from Lorenzo's car. He had a clear line of sight to Tommy, and a partial line of sight to Lorenzo.

The middle school let out a few minutes later, and Tommy's attention shifted to the kids who came out of the school. Max had said that Tommy waited for his stepbrother every day.

A few minutes later, Tommy jumped up and waved. It looked odd, a grown man over six feet tall with shaggy blond hair and a bright green backpack on his shoulders waving like a little kid. Now David understood why Max was so protective of Tommy. He needed protection. She had often told David she never wanted children, but when it came to those who couldn't take care of themselves her protective instincts were well developed.

David looked at Lorenzo. He hadn't moved, but his attention was diverted to where Tommy was waving.

Austin Lake crossed the street, holding hands with a familiar blond girl.

His daughter, Emma.

David got out of his car as soon as Lorenzo stood up. But Lorenzo was closer and met up with Austin and Emma before David could get there.

"Hey, Austin, do you and your brother have a minute?" Lorenzo said. "I'm working with Max Revere and have some follow-up questions."

To Austin's credit, he narrowed his gaze and said, "Really? She didn't tell me she was working with another reporter."

David walked up to the group, putting his body between Emma and Lorenzo. "Go. *Now,*" he said to Lorenzo.

Tommy glanced at David, eyes wide, and took a step back.

Emma's mouth dropped open.

"Excuse me, sir," Lorenzo said, not intimidated. He should be. He had no idea what David could do to him. "I'm a reporter following up on a story."

"I'm not asking again," David said, not taking his eyes off him. David stepped a fraction closer to Emma, in front of her, and was surprised when Austin did the same. The kid had good instincts.

"I don't know who you are, but you're scaring these kids," Lorenzo said. "Leave, and I won't call the cops."

"Dad," Emma said and put her hand on his arm, "let's go."

Austin stared at him. "Oh, shit."

Lorenzo looked confused. "Sir, I'm not here to talk to

your daughter. Feel free to take her. I'm working on a story, and—"

It was Austin who spoke up. "Bullshit," he said to Lorenzo. "You said you worked for Max Revere? That's a fucking lie. Get out of here, and don't talk to my brother again."

"I'm just trying to—"

"You heard the kid," David said.

"But—" Lorenzo took a step back, looking even more confused. "Look, I don't want any trouble, I'm just—"

David stepped forward. He didn't need to do anything else. As he shifted, his gun was visible under his jacket. None of the kids saw it, but Lorenzo did, and the reporter stared, eyes wide, before walking quickly away.

David made sure that Lorenzo got into his car before he turned to face the teenagers. He was about to speak when Tommy said, his voice shaking, "He-he said he worked for Max Revere. W-why did you do that?" He stepped away from David. David felt like crap that he'd scared the kid, but he had to protect him. At times he forgot how intimidating he was. David didn't know how to be anything else.

Before he could explain, Emma took both of Tommy's hands and said in a quiet voice, "Tommy, that man doesn't work for Max. I know Max very well, remember? This is my dad, David Kane. Remember, I told you about him? My dad works for Max."

"B-b-but why would h-he lie?" Tommy refused to look David in the eye.

"No good reason," Austin said. "Don't talk to him. Ever. Promise me."

Tommy looked at his feet, a deep frown on his face. "Okay, Austin, I promise."

Austin turned to David. Both worried and defiant, the kid was not at all cowed by David. The brief moment of panic that had crossed his face when he realized David had seen him holding hands with Emma was gone. "Who is he, Mr. Kane?"

"Lance Lorenzo, a local reporter."

"So he *is* a reporter."

"But he's not working with us," David said. "Max doesn't trust him."

"Lorenzo—I think I've heard about him."

Emma said, "He's that blogger who wrote all that stuff about Ivy last summer." She turned to David. "Why are you here, Dad?" Emma glanced around. She was nervous, and for a split second David thought she was embarrassed of him, and his heart twisted painfully. Then he remembered what Max had said—that Emma was worried that Brittney would screw with their custody agreement if David saw Emma without prior permission. He hated that his daughter was trying to protect him. He hated his arrangement with Brittney, but there was not one damn thing he could do about it.

"I was following Lorenzo," David said. "He's gone—I'll catch up with him later." He turned to Tommy. "I didn't mean to scare you, Tommy."

Tommy nodded rapidly, but still wouldn't look at him.

David was getting a headache. "Austin, may I have a word with you alone?"

He phrased it as a question, but there was no question in his tone.

"Dad—" Emma began.

David discreetly winked at her, then steered Austin twenty feet away. Emma still didn't look happy.

"Sir, I promise I'm not involving Emma in this situation. We're just friends."

"I know you're *just* friends," David said in a low voice. "Emma will be thirteen on Sunday. There can only be *just friends.*"

"Yes, sir."

"Max says you're a smart kid."

He shrugged, but looked up at David. He had to give the kid points for not averting his eyes. Austin Lake was one tough teen. But David also recognized the anger in his stance and his eyes. It was all too familiar, and this was a potentially volatile situation.

"I'm going to give it to you straight. I don't know what Lorenzo is up to, but he's working around Max and causing problems in our investigation. You told your brother to stay away; you do the same."

"Yes, sir."

"If you see him again, call me or Max, anytime." David handed Austin his business card. "That's my cell phone, I always answer it because I don't give the number out to many people."

"Um, thanks." Austin put it in his pocket.

"I'll give you a heads-up—Max and your mother had an argument this morning about the interview tomorrow. I don't know how it's all going to play out, but if Lorenzo thinks he can mess things up for Max, he'll do it—and approaching your mother might be his next move."

"Why?" Austin asked. "Max is trying to find out who killed my sister, why does another reporter care?"

"Good question, and I will find out. Not you."

"Is that it?"

"If my daughter is hurt in any way, you will answer to me. Understood?"

Austin nodded and shifted on his feet, the first outward sign that he was nervous.

David smiled. Not a big smile, but he liked this kid. So he gave him a bone. "By the way, Austin, I appreciate how you stepped up a few minutes ago and were looking out for my daughter."

"I don't understand."

"You have good instincts. Listen to them, and you won't go wrong."

"Okay," Austin said, though it was clear he didn't know what David meant.

"Take your brother home."

"Thank you." He turned to leave, then stopped and looked back at David. "You're the only one who's ever called Tommy my brother, not my stepbrother. Thanks for that."

David watched the three teenagers talk, then Emma ran over to him and gave him a spontaneous hug. "I love you, Dad." She smiled and waved goodbye as the three of them walked off, Tommy walking his bike alongside.

David's eyes burned. He wished things were different. He wished he could see his daughter every day. But one reason he didn't return to Marin County after the army was because living so close to Emma and knowing he couldn't see her would have tormented him. Unless Brittney was completely on board, David wasn't confident that the court would change the custody arrangement. He'd never married Brittney, and diligently paying child support apparently didn't give him any rights. Brittney didn't even want the money from him, she had wanted nothing to do with him after he called off the engagement, but support was nonnegotiable. He would provide for his daughter. Brittney's mother helped convince Brittney to accept the money, and they agreed that the money would go directly into a college fund for Emma.

Neither David nor Brittney had gone to college, and sending Emma to a good university was one thing they agreed upon. Perhaps the only thing.

David went back to his car and drove around the block, hoping Lorenzo was still around. He wasn't. David drove by Austin's house, then Tommy's house, but didn't see Lorenzo's car. David went back to the newspaper office. He was bound to show up here sooner or later. David sent Max a quick message that he wouldn't make it to the preserve to meet with her and Graham, but to call him if she needed anything. Then he waited.

CHAPTER NINETEEN

Jogging and biking trails, open spaces for picnics, seasonal creeks, and a five-mile hike marked with posts every half mile, made the thousand-acre preserve a nice place for a day trip. Max pocketed her phone and stood in an uneven wooded area that was too big to be called a hill and too small to be called a mountain.

Vehicles were forbidden in the area, but a fire road bordered the west edge of the preserve, locked on both ends and used only for emergency crews. Each access point opened into a neighborhood.

Her research revealed that the preserve was used sparingly during the week except for morning joggers, most of whom lived along its perimeter. Though the preserve was technically closed an hour after sundown, it was easy enough to access on foot and Max suspected teenagers often came up here to drink or make out. But this afternoon, it was quiet. Too quiet. No sounds of traffic, people, construction . . . only nature and Max.

She wondered why she didn't get the warm fuzzies when she was in the middle of such peace. She craved her privacy, loved her penthouse apartment off Greenwich in New York, and she adored her cabin in Lake Tahoe where she could sit on the deck, watch the sun dance upon the water, drink wine, and relax.

But it was *too* quiet here. No water, only trees and trails. The only sounds were those of birds, and even they weren't all that noisy.

She'd had Richard park at the end of a sparsely populated road where the southern end of the fire road was accessed. She asked him to stay with the car—David had hired him as a driver, not a bodyguard, and she didn't want him tagging along and distracting her while she was thinking. She'd told Richard to direct Graham and David up the trail when they arrived.

Richard had parked their vehicle on the same stretch of road as Ivy had the night she died. According to the police report, they'd canvassed the neighborhood, but no one had seen Ivy driving into the neighborhood or leaving her car. Her car had been off to the side at the end of the road, ten feet from a sign that said no parking after 10:00 P.M. The police patrolled the area two or three times a night. Ivy's car hadn't been there at 10:15 P.M.; it had been ticketed at 3:30 A.M. But that made sense because according to Austin, Ivy left the house just before 10:30 P.M.

A public trail led Max to an open area on the hilltop. Aside from the trails and the one large open space at the top, most of the preserve below was covered with trees and dense foliage. The main fire road branched off into several fire access roads, which doubled as dirt bike paths. Houses had been built into the hills on both sides of the access road. To the west was a golf course and then beyond that, Mill Valley. Max walked to the far western edge of the open space and she could see the green fields at the base of the hill, but couldn't make out any details.

Ivy had fallen to her death from the northwestern edge of the clearing. The steepest part of the area was a three-story drop before the incline leveled off to a more gradual downslope. A seasonal creek bed was lined with rocks, branches, and debris.

The clearing was approximately four acres, with evidence of a recent party—some effort had been made to clean up, but Max found several empty beer bottles and a pair of women's underwear near the eastern edge of the space, where it was partly shielded by trees. Max was hardly a prude, and she'd enjoyed sex in a variety of places, but in the middle of a clearing where any hiker, biker, or jogger could chance upon them? She'd pass. She liked sex, not voyeurism.

She looked around and tried to picture Ivy here. She couldn't. Why had she come? To meet with a boyfriend? But that didn't explain the tweet, as if Ivy was waiting for someone who hadn't shown up. The tweet sounded angry, not upset.

Turning around in a circle, Max surveyed the space.

Ivy had parked on the south side of the preserve and had died on the north side of the clearing. If she were running from an attacker, wouldn't she have run *toward* her vehicle? It was nearly a mile down the trail, but still closer to residences than the northern trail.

But Max was presuming that Ivy was running *away* from someone. Maybe she had *met* someone here and it got out of hand. Maybe it really *was* an accident.

But why the cuts on her arms? There had been no signs of rape, but maybe an attempted rape?

Max heard a faint noise. She turned, surprised to see Grace Martin emerging from the trail. Max met her halfway across the clearing.

"I'm glad you're here," Max said.

"Unofficially," Grace said.

"What happened today? First you tell me you can't help, then you're sending NCFI everything they need."

Grace looked around and for a minute didn't say anything. "Off the record," she cautioned.

Max nodded. "Of course."

"My chief is a cop's cop. He spent twenty years as a deputy sheriff in Los Angeles County before taking this post two years ago when we consolidated. He supports the staff, is good with the public, and keeps the department within its budget. There is really only one thing he hates: threats."

Max couldn't imagine that anything she'd done or said would constitute a threat. Not that she *wouldn't* use a threat if warranted, but this time she'd been playing nice. Or she'd thought. "I'm not following."

"Paula Wallace called the chief and said if he allowed you to run with the segment on your show with his cooperation, she and her husband would sue the city and the department."

Max was rarely at a loss for words. She knew she'd angered Paula Wallace, but had no idea how much.

"The chief told her that no one with CMPA was going on camera related to your story, but that you had every right to use public information as you see fit. I don't know what Paula said after that—he wouldn't say—but when he got off the phone, he told me to send NCFI anything they wanted. I'm still banned from speaking on camera, but the chief is going to let you put our media rep on if you wish. She'll only give you the standard spiel, but it's better than nothing."

"I owe your chief a bottle of scotch."

"He doesn't drink. But if you had football tickets, he's a die-hard Forty-niner fan and the tickets at the new stadium are hard to come by."

Football—Max wasn't a fan, but she'd bet her trust fund that one of her relatives had season tickets.

"For what it's worth," said Max, "Paula Wallace

wouldn't agree to the interview if I mentioned anything about Ivy's social media bullying, the Brocks' lawsuit, or the settlement."

"Why didn't you agree?"

"Because Ivy's death wasn't sexually motivated, it wasn't a crime of passion. It was either an accident or a premeditated push off that cliff." Max gestured to the north, where Ivy had fallen to her death. "That suggests that it was related to something personal, and the only thing Ivy had going in her life was her blog and Instagram feed. She wasn't involved in athletics, she had good grades but wasn't involved in any extracurricular clubs, no hobbies that she talked about online. Her entire life seemed to focus on spreading gossip, proving it with photos if possible."

When they heard a small group making their way up the trail, the two women turned. Max immediately recognized Graham Jones, the retired deputy sheriff from Sacramento County who now ran NCFI. With him were Ruby Jones, his sister-in-law and one of the best crime scene analysts Max had ever met, and Donovan Hunt, the former Public Information Officer for the sheriff's department. He only answered to the name Hunt.

Max made the introductions and stood to the side while Graham, Ruby, and Hunt did their thing. She didn't like staying on the sidelines, but she'd worked with Graham often enough to know he'd walk if she irritated him.

Her phone vibrated with a message from David.

I'm tracking Lorenzo. Won't make it to the crime scene.

Good. That meant David suspected the lowlife was up to something.

Just when Max was getting irritated that Charlie was late, her cameraman/editor/assistant producer emerged from the trail. Charlie was the best on the road, and could fill multiple roles as needed. Her driver Richard walked behind him, helping carry his equipment.

Charlie was tall and skinny, with a smooth baby face and a thick head of hair that had gone completely gray by the time he was twenty. No one ever got his age right, but Max knew he was thirty-six.

"Before you yell at the poor guy," Charlie said, "I needed his help. You didn't tell me this place was in the middle of bumfuck nowhere."

"You're late," Max said. "Your plane landed at eleven oh nine this morning."

"Ain't you the stalker boss," Charlie snapped. "I've been doing my job. What have you been doing, pissing off the locals?"

Grace watched the exchange, bemused. Max couldn't expect her or anyone to understand her relationship with Charlie Morelli.

"You know me all too well," Max said. "But you're still late, and you didn't text me. So get off your high horse and catch up with Graham and his people. Hunt will make the official statement for NCFI."

As Charlie spoke, he was unpacking his equipment, checking film and batteries. "I've already been doing my job, Maxine. Took B-roll of the school, the Wallaces' house—or is it the Lakes' house?—the town, the bay, and the bridge."

"Bridge?"

"Setting, baby, it's all how we splice it."

Charlie was right—set the stage for the segment with a shot of the Golden Gate Bridge, the bay, Sausalito, the town of Corte Madera. Bigger to smaller, bringing the dead to the viewer. That this was a crime that could happen anywhere to anyone, that they should care because murder didn't just happen in big cities. It affected everyone. The cyberbullying spin was—in Max's mind—the big selling point of the story, but she would minimize it for the show. Her audience skewed older, with women forty-five to sixty-four being the largest viewer group, so the Internet wasn't going to be sexy enough for them. Murder in a small town? Might as well write a cozy mystery and rake in the bucks with that demographic.

Charlie knew this. He understood stats and demographics better than anyone, even Ben. Even though he could be annoying, Max liked working with him.

Max and Grace remained silent as Graham and his team methodically surveyed the crime scene. It didn't matter that more than a year had passed—they weren't expecting to find any evidence the original investigators missed. But Graham would match up his measurements and photos with the official forensic photos; he sent Ruby down the gulley to take measurements and photos of the rock Ivy had hit. He had a copy of the police report. Hunt was inputting the details into a specialized forensics computer program that another person from NCFI had developed to help analyze data and work through scenarios. They worked for more than an hour, then the three huddled together.

Max had waited long enough. She walked over to them.

Ruby stopped speaking as she approached. Max arched her eyebrow and said to Graham, "Is this a private conversation, or can the person who's paying you listen?"

He smiled with half his mouth. "I expected you over here fifteen minutes ago. You really are learning patience."

She wasn't amused. "I missed lunch, Graham."

Grace had followed her over and Graham turned to include the detective in their conversation.

"Detective, we input the data collected into a computer model, then added additional information that wasn't available—the exact distance, for example, of the cliff to the base, of the cliff to the rock, the angles in question, and statistical probabilities of all falls that are known to be accidents and those that are known to be homicides. Meaning, using only solved cases over the last twenty years that we have in our database, we can extrapolate that there is an eighty-five percent chance that your victim was pushed off the cliff—that she didn't slip, run off, or jump. Of course there's still a possibility it was suicide, but truthfully, based on known suicides, it's highly unlikely she would have fallen on her back that far from the edge."

"So you're simply confirming what we already know," Grace said, sounding both irritated and disappointed.

"There is one inconsistency, however. We downloaded all weather data from this area before leaving NCFI. Based on the actual temperature at this elevation, the coroner's report, the forensics report, and the fact that Ivy Lake's body was found less than twenty-four hours after her death which makes TOD easier to determine, I am comfortable stating that she was killed between ten and twelve midnight the night of July third."

Grace didn't say anything, but Max wasn't keeping quiet. "Ivy posted to social media at one ten in the morning on July fourth. That was in the notes I sent to you."

"To be accurate," Graham said, "Ivy's *phone* was used to post to social media at one ten on July fourth. There is no evidence that Ivy herself uploaded that message, at least no evidence that was submitted to NCFI."

"Your time frame isn't much different than the coroner's," Grace said.

"Correct. The coroner gave you a range of eleven at night to two in the morning, which is a good hypothesis, but I'm telling you based on a computer analysis that factors in all the nuances of the weather including moisture and the actual state of rigor mortis, liver temp, and visual examination, that my estimate is more accurate. I've narrowed the window down."

"A witness stated that Ivy's car was not parked outside the fire gate at ten fifteen when he was walking his dog," Grace said. "According to her brother, she left the house just before ten thirty the night of July third."

"And according to her phone records," Graham said, "the last message she sent via Instant Chat was at ten twenty, which is the approximate time she left the house according to your witness." He looked at Ruby, then Hunt, and they exchanged a silent message. He then said, "I'll leave Ruby here for the next day or two. She is a certified forensic pathologist with a master's in both entomology and biology. She can work with your coroner or the state lab to confirm our findings. Hunt and I have to return to Sacramento."

Max considered the time window. Austin had last seen Ivy just before 10:30 P.M. The preserve was a ten-minute drive from Ivy's house. Which meant she was killed after 10:30 P.M. . . . but before midnight. It was a brisk ten-minute walk from her car to the clearing. "Can you narrow the window anymore?"

"It may surprise you, but time of death is not an exact science."

Max just stared at him, then turned to Ruby.

Ruby didn't speak at first. She looked at Graham for permission. He nodded once.

She said, "The computer states based on the information we input that the victim died at 11:03 P.M. However, there is always a window. We don't know what her exact body temperature was when she died, if it was elevated because of exertion or a fever. We don't know—"

Max put up her hand. "I understand. We know she was alive at ten twenty and you're stating she was absolutely dead by midnight."

Ruby nodded.

"She didn't go anywhere else," Max said. "She came directly here from her house. We assumed she went elsewhere because of that one-ten tweet."

They all thought on that for a minute. Grace turned to Max and asked, "How does this work? Are you going to reveal this new information tomorrow on your show?" She looked disturbed—and worried.

"We'll talk about that," Max said. "I'm not going to jeopardize your investigation, but this is key information. I've been working off the assumption that Ivy went someplace for the nearly three hours between leaving her house and sending the tweet, ending up here to meet someone or, perhaps, spy on someone—knowing that she liked to take photos of her peers behaving badly. But if she was already dead, someone else had her phone. Someone, perhaps, who has no alibi between ten thirty and midnight and sent that tweet in an attempt to cover his own ass."

David's phone vibrated in his pocket. It was nearly seven, and Lorenzo had shown up at his office at four thirty, then left again thirty minutes later. He ended up in a sketchy bar shortly thereafter where he met a man David didn't know. He took a couple of pictures, then went back to the hotel to wait for Max who was still at the preserve with Graham and his team.

He saw it was Jess calling, one of the researchers for "Maximum Exposure."

"It's late in New York," David said.

"I'm working from home," Jess said. "I got something on Lance Lorenzo. Max said he had a sister, right?"

"Yes."

"Her name is Laura. She's three years younger than Lance, a junior at UCLA majoring in psychology and biology. That's a standard double major for someone who wants to go into medicine, probably psychiatry. She's a year younger than Justin Brock—and they went to his senior prom together. Justin came up for the weekend to take Laura to her senior prom the following year."

"High school sweethearts?"

"It's more than that—neither Justin nor Laura have much of a social media presence, which isn't surprising considering Justin's little sister was cyberbullied. So I dug around a bit and I think they're engaged."

"Think?"

"There hasn't been an announcement in the newspaper or anything, but I spent hours going through every psych major at UCLA on Facebook and found Laura's name and photo pop up a few times here and there—not tagged because she doesn't have a profile. Stanford gets out for the summer three weeks before UCLA. Memorial Day weekend, there's a photo of Laura and Justin on who I'm thinking is Laura's best friend's page. No names, but the caption is, 'Prince Charming just made my BFF the happiest girl on earth.' Laura was sporting a rock the size of Gibraltar."

"Good work, Jess. Get some sleep."

David hung up and let himself into Max's suite. He wrote down the dates—if Laura Lorenzo was a college junior, four years ago she was a high school junior. Justin was four years older than his sister, which meant Laura was a senior when Ivy and Heather were freshmen. They'd all gone to the same school.

Lance was older than all of them, but he must have been privy to the connections. Corte Madera was a small town, and half the kids from Mill Valley went to the high school in Corte Madera. It definitely fit that Lorenzo knew the Brock family well—his sister was marrying into the clan—which could explain why he had shaped his articles on the Brock civil suit to make the Wallace family look particularly bad.

But why was Lorenzo pushing so hard that Ivy's death was accidental? David looked in Max's master case file and saw that Justin Brock had been in town the weekend that Ivy was killed. He'd been with his girlfriend until midnight, then gone home—alone. The girlfriend's name wasn't in the file, which meant that the CMPA hadn't released the name to Max. His parents had been in Europe for the month. His girlfriend was likely Laura Lorenzo. If they were dating in high school and engaged a few months ago, chances were that they were involved last summer as well.

It wouldn't be the first time that a friend covered up for another friend. With the power of the press—and the lack of physical evidence—it would be relatively easy for Lance Lorenzo to sell the public on the fact that Ivy Lake's death was purely an accident. She'd been up at the preserve at night alone and fell. Write it off as a tragic accident.

Except for the not-too-small detail of why she was at the preserve in the middle of the night in the first place.

Max walked in. She looked a bit surprised to see David in her room, then said, "Did you learn something?"

"Lance Lorenzo's sister is engaged to Justin Brock."

She stared, then smiled. "That's my in."

"In?"

"I want to talk to Justin. I couldn't get through to his mother, but I can get through to him."

David frowned. "He could be the killer, Max. And Lorenzo is protecting him by running with the story that Ivy's death was an accident."

"Graham proved it wasn't an accident. Well, his computer model gave him an eighty-five percent chance that she was thrown off the cliff."

"Thrown? Not pushed?"

"Thrown or pushed hard. And he has some more questions about the body. The chief had a change of heart and is giving NCFI full access. I just checked Ruby into the hotel, she's meeting with the ME tomorrow morning, then the state lab that processed biological evidence. Graham and Hunt went back to Sacramento."

"What questions does Graham have?"

"Specifically, time of death. TOD was sketchy. According to Graham, when there are extreme fluctuations in temperature and moisture, time of death can be off by hours, sometimes days, unless you bring in an entomologist."

"And is that what Ruby is?" David had only met Graham Jones and his wife Julia once. He didn't know anyone on their team.

"Ruby is an expert on damn near everything. The girl is brilliant. And younger than me."

"Jealousy or pride?"

"Pride. If I were gay, I'd be in love. But she's married to Graham's younger brother, so I'm shit out of luck."

David laughed. Max didn't joke much, especially over the last few months. Hearing her lighten up eased his mind. He'd been worried about her, which was no surprise considering she was attacked and nearly killed three months ago. He'd once broached the subject of PTSD causing her insomnia, and she'd dismissed him. He knew she'd seen a doctor, but refused both sleeping pills and a shrink.

Max dumped all her stuff on the desk and said, "We're going to Jenny Wallace's house. I sent her a message that we'd be there by eight, I just want to change."

David called into the bedroom. "So what's off about the time of Ivy's death?"

"I think she went up to the preserve to meet someone,

and they killed her. I think they sent the tweet from her phone hours later."

"To give themselves an alibi."

"Exactly. If Ivy was killed closer to eleven, perhaps different questions would have been asked to different people. We don't know. But Grace is going to go through her notes and the witness statements and see if there is anything to pursue. Ruby is going to work her magic with bugs and fly larvae and see if she can confirm that Ivy was killed earlier than first thought. The computer says she was—but Ruby's one of those people who has to confirm it with physical science."

"Do they still have that kind of evidence?"

"If they collected it, they have it since it's an open case."

Max came out of her room dressed in gray slacks and a royal blue sweater. She'd put her hair back in a ponytail and had taken off some of her makeup. She looked years younger.

"What's with the getup?" he asked.

"I want Tommy to feel comfortable, prepare him for going on camera tomorrow. Dressing down helps the comfort level with kids. On your other question, Ruby said she may be able to make a finding if the photographs are detailed enough. Graham said we can have her as long as we need her—provided she's back in his lab on Monday."

"That's generous of him."

Max laughed. "Generous? He and Julia are taking the girls up to my cabin over Christmas. Ten days. And I had to call in a favor to my uncle Sterling to get me tickets to a Forty-niners game for Grace's boss. This investigation is costing me."

"Have you eaten?"

"We'll eat after we see Tommy."

David opened the cabinet, took out a banana, and handed it to her. "We didn't have time for lunch."

"I grabbed a smoothie on my way to the preserve."

"Just eat it."

She peeled the banana and took a bite.

"I may have scared Tommy today." David explained what happened while following Lorenzo.

"That bastard said he was working with me?"

"Cool down. Right now, I'm the bad cop in this situation. I don't like that he knows who my daughter is, but fortunately, Austin is quick on his feet and didn't give anything away."

"You mean that you work for me?"

"Exactly. Lorenzo will be able to find out, but it'll take time. I'm not the public face of 'Maximum Exposure.'"

"You like Austin."

"He was holding Emma's hand. I wanted to pound him into the ground. But the kid has good instincts. He was immediately suspicious of Lorenzo."

"Why did Lorenzo want to talk to Emma?"

"He didn't—he followed Tommy from school. He wanted to talk to Austin. He knows you're working with Tommy. He knows Tommy is slow, and that Austin is the one to talk to. He wants to know what they told you, and what you're doing. That's my educated guess."

"Because you think he's protecting Justin Brock."

"Or he could be working on another story for his blog. I have photos of him with different people, one of whom I couldn't identify. Your staff is working on it. And he met with a uniformed cop. Young cop, looks like he's a rookie. I have his unit number, should be easy to find out who he is."

That certainly explained how Lorenzo got some of his inside information. Max said, "Grace is not aware of that—or if she is, she didn't say anything to me."

"You're going to tell her?"

"Of course I am. They need to know—but I'm going to mull over this a bit first. Lorenzo made an enemy of the wrong person. I said I would destroy him, and now I have a way to do it."

CHAPTER TWENTY

A teenaged girl with sun-streaked brown hair answered the door. She eyed Max and David with both curiosity and suspicion. "You must be the reporters," she said.

"I'm Maxine Revere, this is David Kane. Your mother is expecting us. Amanda, right?"

She nodded and opened the door to let them in.

Like her workplace, Jenny's house was an eclectic mix of old and new. The design and furnishings worked together, from the rustic stained wood floors to the large colorful throw rugs with geometric shapes; from the plush oversized denim furniture paired with small, antique tables. Every surface had some sort of decoration on it—like the dried flower arrangements in the middle of the bookshelves to a collection of antique brass frames with ancestral photos on a corner table to an alcove off the kitchen with small shelves supporting a collection of antique salt and pepper shakers from around the world.

A little too much clutter for Max, but it was cozy.

Jenny stepped out of the kitchen, looking nervous, but she smiled politely when Max introduced David.

"Do you have homework, Amanda?" she asked.

"Finished," Amanda said. "I want to stay, Mom. This affects me, too."

"I just hate dragging you into this."

"Where's Tommy?" Max asked.

"He and Austin are playing video games in the den. Tommy was agitated and upset, I don't know that this is a good idea. I told him I read the letter he wrote you, and then he was worried he hurt my feelings. I assured him that he didn't, that he didn't do anything wrong, but he's so very sensitive."

"I didn't bring a cameraman because we're just here to talk to Tommy about what to expect tomorrow," Max said.

"I'm livid," Jenny said. "That . . . that *woman* would make my son feel as if he were banished."

"Unfortunately, as I told Tommy, even if we solve Ivy's murder, things may not change at his father's house."

"Well, my ex-husband will hear a thing or two from me about that," Jenny said.

Max understood Jenny's anger, but it wasn't going to do them any good now. "I didn't show you Tommy's letter to create friction between you and your ex—"

"Don't worry about it. There's been plenty of friction ever since that adulterous bastard left us for them."

Odd, Max thought. *Left us for them.* Did Jenny think that Bill had traded one family for another? Maybe she did . . . but it had been more than seven years since the divorce. Max wanted to tell the lady to get over it . . . but who was she to talk? Max's mother had walked out on her more than twenty years ago and she still had a lot of anger about it.

Anger, yes, but a deeper need to know *why.*

David cleared his throat. "It might be best if you avoided that particular conversation for the next few days.

Our goal is to run the news segment, detail the facts, speculate on motive based on those facts, and encourage people to call the hotline."

"We have some new information that may spark someone's memory," Max said.

"What is it?" Jenny asked.

"I haven't decided how to present the information, so I'm going to hold off sharing right now—and I'm hoping Detective Martin will go on camera with it. That will have more impact." Grace said she didn't want to make public the revelation, but had also seemed swayed by Max's argument that new evidence could bring out new witnesses. They'd agreed to discuss it again in the morning after Grace reviewed all the statements and alibis and talked to her chief.

"Can you direct me to Tommy?" said Max. "I only want to make him comfortable with this process." She always tried to work with the victim's families before an interview, but she'd never felt so compelled to make it as easy for someone as she was for Tommy Wallace.

"I'll get them," Amanda said and went down the hall.

"Can I get you anything?" Jenny asked. "I just made a pot of coffee—half-caf."

"That would be nice, thank you," Max said.

"Yes, thank you, Mrs. Wallace," David said. "Let me help."

"I'm fine, I'll bring a tray to the living room." She went back to the kitchen.

"Nervous," Max said.

"Worried about her son," David countered. "Angry." He was about to say something else, but closed his mouth.

Amanda returned with Austin and Tommy. She sat next to Tommy on the couch while Austin took a seat across from David. Tommy was positioned to be as far from David as possible and still be in the living room.

"Hi, Tommy," Max said. "David told me what happened this afternoon."

"The reporter said he worked with you. He lied. That's wrong." Tommy was tense, his hands clasped tight in his lap, his posture rigid.

"Tommy, it's more than wrong. Lying is the coward's way out."

He frowned. "I don't understand what that means."

"When people lie, a lot of times it's because they don't want to get in trouble for something they did. Or they lie to trick people into telling them something. Like what Mr. Lorenzo tried to do today. I trust David, though. I know he looks a little scary, but do you know how he got that scar on his face?"

"How?" Tommy said, eyes wide with curiosity.

"When he was in the army. He was helping his unit evacuate a hospital that was in an area being bombed. Shrapnel—that's metal and debris that is flying around when bombs go off—hit him in the face."

"Max," David said quietly.

David didn't like to talk about what he did in the army, but Max had researched him shortly after Ben hired him. He'd done far more heroic things and had many more scars, but few that could be seen when he was fully dressed.

"Really?" Tommy asked, interested.

Austin said, "Emma said you saved a kid who was trapped in a bombed building and got shot in the back. She also said you rescued girls from an illegal school that was under attack. And—"

"I'm not going to talk about this now," David said sharply.

"My point is," Max said, "sometimes people aren't what they look like. They might look nice and friendly, but they aren't. Others might look gruff"—she glanced

at David and resisted the smile that wanted to come out—
"but they're kind."

Tommy's eyes lit up like he'd made a huge discovery.
"I know! I know! 'Don't judge a book by its cover.' My
teacher, Mrs. Haserot, says that all the time. She's my favorite teacher."

"She's smart, and it's good that you understand what
that means. It's important. That's how the police solve
crimes. They look at the facts, at the evidence, and all
the people involved, but they can't or they shouldn't
make judgments just because they don't like how someone looks. When I talk to you tomorrow, I don't want you
to think about me, or how you might look or sound, I want
you to be honest. To tell me what you think, what you feel.
Don't worry about how it's going to sound. I promised
your mother, and I promise you, I'm going to make the
show exactly what it needs to be to find the truth."

Jenny came in with a tray of coffee and hot chocolate.
She put it down and took a few moments to hand everyone their drink.

Jenny sat down next to her daughter and squeezed her
hand. "I'll admit to being concerned about what's going
to happen after this segment airs. You said Paula isn't going to support the show."

"That's her right," Max said. "But I think we'll find the
answers we need."

"My mom's a bitch," Austin said.

"She's your mother," David said firmly. "Show her some
respect."

"Why? She's hasn't earned it."

"She lost a child," David said.

"What was her excuse before Ivy was killed?" Austin
looked David in the eye and didn't waver even when David stared back.

This conversation was going to deteriorate if Max

didn't steer it back on track. "Austin," she said, "in light of the fact that your mother doesn't want to go on camera, would you feel comfortable talking about Ivy?"

"What do you want me to say?"

"What do you want to say?"

Austin shrugged. "That Ivy was a bitch but she shouldn't be dead because of it."

"Yeah, let's avoid that," said Max. "Tell me something positive. A good memory with Ivy."

He shrugged again, didn't answer.

"Bella," Tommy said. "Ivy loved playing dress up with Bella. Remember, she would put lip gloss on her and that pretty pink tutu and have her twirl and take a bow? Bella's curls would bounce up and down. My little sister is so cute," he said to Max. "And she has the best laugh."

"Bella was a doll to Ivy," Austin said. "A toy."

"Was not," Tommy said.

"If you don't want to go on camera," Max said, "that's okay. You don't have to."

"I want to. I want the truth. I don't like what's happened to our family," Austin said. "There's this dark cloud over us and it's never going away until we know what happened to Ivy. It's like—it's like we're all just in a daze, stuck in the same place because of all these unanswered questions."

Max nodded. "That's what you say."

Jenny said, "And what happens if Paula comes out with her ridiculous accusations? What if she turns people against us? I don't care about my reputation, but Tommy is innocent. He shouldn't have to go through any more trauma."

"He is going through it," Max said quietly. "When this is over, then you and your ex can have that heart-to-heart."

"If *she* allows it," Jenny said with an eye-roll worthy of a teenager.

"I can't solve your family problems," Max said, growing irritated with Jenny's attitude. "but I can find out what happened to Ivy. The rest is up to you."

"No, it's up to Paula, because she's obviously the one who controls what everyone else thinks and does," Jenny said. She glanced at Austin. "I'm sorry, Austin. I shouldn't have said that."

His mouth twisted into a half smile. "Truth."

"Can we all agree to take it easy for the next two days?" Max asked. She didn't want the family drama and infighting to get out of hand or go public before the segment. If there was a sense that the family didn't deserve answers because they were sniping at one another, Max was going to get nothing from this. And even if everything went right, she still might get nothing from it. All she could do was keep looking.

Talk to Bailey Fairstein. Push Travis Whitman again.

And dammit, talk to Justin Brock. He still hadn't returned her call. If she didn't have to film tomorrow, she would drive down first thing in the morning to hunt him down and get a statement.

Jenny turned to her son. "Are you really okay with this, Tommy?"

He nodded. "Max said that even if we know who hurt Ivy that maybe I still can't go to Dad's house. But the truth is always better than not knowing, right? And I think if Paula knows the truth, she won't look at me funny anymore."

Max hoped so.

David was silent most of the drive back to the hotel.

"Good news," Max said after checking her phone messages. "Pilar Fairstein said I can talk to Bailey tomorrow morning before school. Seven at their house."

David grunted a response.

"Should I call Richard to drive me or are you taking me?"

"I'll drive," he said.

"You're angry," Max said.

"You don't want to hear about it."

"Of course I do."

He grunted again. Well, this was fun.

She mentally replayed the conversation at Jenny's house. At first, Max thought David might have been angry that she'd told Tommy and Austin about the bombing that scarred his face, but he'd seemed more embarrassed by the story, typical of his humble attitude about his years in the military. He had never talked to her about it, over answering a few questions. She'd learned everything through an extensive background check. She hadn't kept that from him, but he still refused to discuss it.

"You don't see it," David said after a few minutes. "For someone as smart as you are, Maxine, you're entirely dense."

"Excuse me," she snapped, "it's been a long day. I guess I missed something obvious. Enlighten me."

"This is why I don't say anything about Brittney to Emma."

She was lost. "I didn't say anything to Emma about Brittney."

"Dense," he said. He parked the car and got out.

Max grabbed her briefcase from the backseat and got out as well. David was in his bodyguard protective mode, looking around, and that was fine with her, she didn't want to talk to him. She went through everything she had said to Emma, and she couldn't remember anything that could have been construed as being critical of her mother.

She unlocked the door to her suite and David followed her inside, putting his arm in front of her as he checked out the space.

"You can stop," she said. "You're not a bodyguard on this assignment."

He didn't respond, but closed the door and stared at her. "Amanda is sixteen. She was nine when her parents went through what was a nasty divorce. Jenny cares about her kids, but she made a number of biting comments about her ex-husband and his wife."

Max hadn't noticed. Or, if she had, she hadn't thought about it. Well, she had noticed that Jenny was still angry about what happened with her ex-husband. And she had considered how public bickering might damage her ability to do her job and air a productive show. But Max had never been married, and that sort of betrayal would be difficult, especially if you thought everything was just fine.

But she didn't say anything, because David obviously had more to say.

"Tommy didn't pick up on the comments like Amanda did," David continued. "She's quiet, a smart kid, and she'll probably grow up just fine. There are millions of children of divorced parents who grow up to lead relatively normal lives. But to live with that kind of anger and animosity for half your childhood . . . no child should have to deal with that. It's our responsibility, as parents, as adults, to protect them. The world is a dangerous place and there is enough hatred and anger out there that they shouldn't be subjected to it in their own homes."

"You're talking about Nick."

"No, I'm talking about Amanda and her relationship with her mother and her father. And me, and why I've made certain choices related to Emma and Brittney—choices that I know you disagree with."

"I don't."

"Don't lie. First, you're shitty at it. Second, I know you think I've made more than one mistake."

She bit her lip. "They're your decisions to make. As you've often said."

"Your unconscious mind is very loud, Maxine."

"Well dammit, David, kids should be protected, but they shouldn't be lied to."

"Refraining from calling your husband an adulterous bastard is not lying to your children. It's showing respect and restraint in a difficult situation." David paused. "I haven't always been so restrained, Max. But with Emma, I wasn't going to use her as a pawn between Brittney and me."

"And you don't think Emma knows exactly who her mother is?"

"Emma loves Brittney. I got Brittney pregnant in high school. She was barely nineteen when she had a baby. She didn't go to college. She made sacrifices to raise Emma—personal sacrifices. I respect that. I don't like that I can't see my daughter whenever I want. I don't like that I'm not in the house, raising her, teaching her, going to her school plays or gymnastics meets."

"You've made sacrifices, too, not just Brittney."

"Yes. And I don't have to like the law that gives mothers all the rights, but I respect the law and I've made this work and I will have a relationship with my daughter in spite of everything. But I will not have Emma hear me utter one word about Brittney. Emma is smart enough to figure out how the world works, and she will. She knows I love her and that's going to have to be enough for now. It's all I can control."

Max shook her head. "It's not fair."

David stared at her, then laughed humorlessly. "Since when have you *ever* thought that life was fair?"

"You don't understand."

"I do. It's you, Max."

"Fine."

"You really don't understand, and I don't know how to explain it to you. Don't let Austin go on camera tomorrow."

"That subject is closed."

"You're making a mistake."

"It's perfectly legal. All he will be doing is what I would have had Paula do, share about his sister and his desire to find out who killed her."

"You'll be damaging his relationship with Paula. Coming between a child and their mother is a recipe for disaster."

"She damaged her relationship with him," Max said. "I do listen. And if you couldn't hear how angry and hopeless Austin feels over what his mother did to Tommy, then you have selective hearing."

"I heard everything, Maxine. *Everything.* It's you who has selective hearing."

"The subject is closed, David. Austin has something to say, and he deserves the right to say it."

Maybe because she was wound up after her fight with David, or maybe because her mind was working overtime on the case, she pulled Laura Lorenzo's contact information out of her staff's notes and called her. It was ten in the evening, and Max usually didn't like to call people so late, but Laura was a college student and likely still awake.

She answered on the first ring. "Hello?"

"Laura Lorenzo?"

Pause. "Who's this?"

"Maxine Revere. I'm an investigative reporter working on a television segment for 'Crime NET' about the murder of Ivy Lake. I'd like to talk to you about—"

"I have nothing to say to you," she said.

"Justin Brock said he was with his girlfriend the night that Ivy died. Was that you?"

"I can't believe you're dragging Justin into this. Haven't he and his family suffered enough?"

"I'm just looking for the truth."

Laura began to cry. "The truth is that . . . that *girl* bullied Heather to death. Literally. And no one cared about that, but you care about an accident? My brother is an investigative reporter too, and he said the police have their heads up their ass. Why don't you investigate what Ivy did to Heather?"

"Ivy was murdered, that's not in dispute. I'm afraid your brother has been spreading disinformation and inaccurate stories." Max took a deep breath. This wasn't how she wanted the conversation to go. "Laura, I just want the truth. I know you do, too. Nothing justifies what happened to Heather; nothing justifies what happened to Ivy."

But Laura had already hung up.

Max had just stepped out of the shower when her cell phone rang. It was nearly midnight but when she was working, late calls were par for the course.

It was Nick.

She almost hit decline—it had taken him this long to get back to her?—but the hot shower had calmed her down.

"It's been a long time," she answered.

"I'm sorry, Max. Really."

She wrapped her damp body in a terry robe and walked through the bedroom into the living room. With her free hand, she poured herself a glass of red wine and took a sip.

"You're not talking," Nick said.

"Ah, now you know how it feels."

"I'm trying to juggle things around so I can come up there this weekend."

"I don't know if I'll be done."

"You can take one night off."

When she didn't respond, he said, "Or I could come up and wait for you in your hotel room."

She almost laughed. "Let me know if you do juggle things around, and then we'll talk."

"I suppose I deserve that."

"I did want to see you, Nick."

"You don't anymore?"

"I do."

"I'm glad to hear that."

Max's phone vibrated with another call. She glanced at the caller ID and didn't recognize the number. She almost ignored it, but she'd given her card out to many people lately and this could be related to her investigation. "Hold a second, I have to take this. If I lose you, I'll call you back."

"I'll wait."

She clicked to the other call. "Maxine Revere."

"How dare you threaten my fiancée!" said an angry male voice.

Justin Brock. "I thought that might propel you to return my calls," said Max.

"Stay away from me and stay away from my family."

"Meet with me. Tell it to my face."

"You've got a lot of nerve."

If she had a quarter for every time she'd heard that, she'd have already doubled her ample trust fund.

"I'm doing a story about Ivy Lake with or without your blessing. I will find out who killed her. I have questions only you can answer. Or I can sit outside your parents' house until they talk to me."

"Do you know what my mother has been through? Do you even care?"

"I do care, Justin. I care about the truth. I'm sorry about Heather, deeply sorry about what happened. And I also believe that Ivy's online activities led to her death. I'm not leaving until I find answers."

"I don't care who killed that little bitch."

"But you care about your sister and your family."

"Are you threatening me? You're no better than Ivy, dragging people through the mud."

Her stomach flipped. Why did that bother her? She was used to people hating her, she was used to people accusing her of atrocious things. Didn't make it true.

"I can meet you in Palo Alto at a place of your choosing first thing Friday morning."

He didn't answer.

"I want your side of the story," she said.

"I didn't kill her. That's all you need to know."

"Please, Justin," Max said, her voice calmer than she felt. "I promise to treat your sister's memory with respect. I have no intention of mentioning anything that she may or may not have done. Heather was a victim. But in the end so was Ivy. Others might be in danger, and you have a unique insight that I can't get from anyone else."

"I'll think about it." He hung up.

She took a deep breath. Then another. Max didn't know why that had been so difficult. She switched her call back to Nick. "Still there?"

"Yes."

"Are you working tomorrow night?" she asked.

"No."

"Then I'll be at your house for a late dinner. I'll text you when I have a better time."

"You don't need to come down here. I said—"

"I have an early meeting Friday morning in Palo Alto.

Instead of fighting traffic for hours, I'd prefer to be in bed with you. Unless you have other plans."

"I'd rather be in bed with you, too. Tomorrow night. And I'll still come up this weekend."

"If you can juggle things."

"Max—"

She held her breath. Was he finally going to tell her what was going on with his wife and son? She sat on the couch, not far from her wineglass.

"Be careful," he said after a moment. "You're good at your job, but you stir things up and I worry about you getting hurt."

"I'll be fine." She hung up when she realized she was about to make a snide comment about his ex-wife. She leaned back on the couch and closed her eyes.

Don't take this relationship so seriously.

That was becoming harder.

Austin couldn't sleep.

He turned on his Xbox and put on his headphones, but even his favorite game *Destiny* couldn't distract him.

He'd made a huge mistake and he didn't know how to fix it.

No one could. No one could help him.

He would just have to see this through. All the way through.

CHAPTER TWENTY-ONE

THURSDAY

At five in the morning, Travis's phone vibrated. He groaned. Thinking about everything that could go wrong today, he'd slept like shit last night. His head pounded and he grabbed his phone.

It was a text message from an unlisted number: *Hey, it's Brian.*

Ever since Rick moved, Travis had no one he considered a good friend, but Brian was cool. They'd been on the football team together since they were freshmen, the only two sophomores on varsity.

Run before school?

Over the summer they'd gotten into the habit of running in the mornings a couple times a week because Brian lived nearby, but they hadn't done it since school started. Brian had a new girlfriend, though he was being low-key about it.

Sure. On the track?

Brian replied: *How 'bout the marsh?*

Travis stretched and got up. If they ran the entire perimeter, it was just over three miles. He'd be back in time to shower and meet Bailey.

Usual spot?

Brian agreed, and Travis pulled on his sweatpants, Windbreaker, grabbed his car keys and cell phone, then ran down the stairs.

His mom was making coffee, dressed in her robe and slippers.

"You're up early," she said.

"I'm going running with Brian."

She smiled. "That's nice."

He kissed her on the cheek. "If I don't see you when I get back, I'll see you tonight."

"You'll have to get yourself dinner, sweetheart—I have Open House at the school, so your dad is picking me up after and we're going out."

"I'll see if Brian wants to come over and we'll get a pizza."

He left, hopped into his truck, and drove the mile to Industrial Way. At the end of the dead-end street, you could access the marsh trails. It was still dark, though the sun was creeping up.

He was glad Brian had reached out to him. Even after the whole thing with Ivy was over, he'd felt that he'd lost more than just his buddy Rick. This summer he and Brian had hung out again, and that was good.

Brian lived in the mobile home park between the freeway and the marsh, and he didn't like people coming over. His mom wasn't around and his dad was a prick. So Travis and he always met at the dead end. The businesses here were mostly auto body repair and construction shops and no one gave them trouble. The area was kind of trashy, but when Travis was younger, he and Rick used to ride dirt bikes on the trails. The best was when it had been raining, and the marsh was really a marsh and not just a dried-out low-lying plot of land. Then in eighth grade, they'd come out with a wildlife biologist who talked about the animals and birds that lived in the marsh. Travis didn't remember any of that, but he, Rick, and Brian had a blast the following weekend when they came out to the marsh and got drunk for the first time.

It was already after five thirty and Travis didn't see Brian. The light was getting better, but it was still friggin' cold, so Travis stretched and jogged toward Brian's place, expecting to meet him on the path.

He rounded a slight curve that dipped down. Salt grass and pickleweed overran the area, especially now with the drought, and it came almost to Travis's waist. Some bushes were even taller, so he almost missed the movement as another runner came toward him in the twilight. For a second he assumed it was Brian, but then he realized the guy in the dark hoodie was too short. Travis nodded a greeting as they were about to pass, then hesitated. There was something familiar . . .

A sharp, burning pain spread through his chest. He was having a heart attack.

Except he heard a loud noise. A gunshot. And saw the gun. And then he recognized the shooter.

Suddenly Travis had answers to all his questions about what happened to Ivy, except for one.

Why?

Max was glad David was quiet driving to the Fairstein house. She hadn't had enough sleep or enough coffee and was, frankly, in a crabby mood. And she shouldn't be. They'd made progress on the Ivy Lake case in less than three days, had the support of local law enforcement (to a degree) and already had more information than the police had started with. Narrowing down Ivy's time of death was huge. Max knew that even though Grace didn't make a big deal about it yesterday, she had been very interested in the information.

David pulled up to the Fairsteins' house and cut off the engine. "I'll wait here," he said.

"Fine," she snapped, then hesitated before getting out of the car. "Look, I'm sorry about last night. Not about disagreeing with you, but about arguing. I might not understand, but I care about you. I know the situation with Brittney and Emma is tough."

"You want to fix something that you can't fix," David said.

"I just want everyone to listen to me and do what I say because I'm usually right."

He almost smiled. "I'm okay, Max."

"Good. I'm going to take the car tonight and visit Nick, then tomorrow morning I have a meeting with Justin Brock."

"He agreed?"

"He's thinking about it, but I'm not giving him the chance to say no. I pushed last night, and I won."

"You usually do."

"I wish that were true."

She walked up to the house and knocked. A full minute later, Pilar Fairstein answered the door. Already dressed and ready for the day, she didn't look happy that Max was there but still let her in.

"I made some coffee," she said, "but Bailey doesn't have much time. She leaves for school at seven thirty. She was up early to get ready. In fact, I heard her before dawn. Bringing up this whole affair is troubling for her, I don't think she slept at all."

Pilar led Max down the hall into the kitchen. Max admired the vast, open space—two ovens, a six-burner stove, a large chopping block adjoining the center island. The view outside was of the swimming pool and a lawn that appeared to roll all the way to the bay.

"I love kitchens," Max said. "I took cooking classes

when I got out of college and had my apartment kitchen remodeled. This is amazing."

"My grandmother was a wonderful cook; I learned everything from her. It's one of the few things that relaxes me."

Bailey Fairstein walked in wearing a Catholic school uniform, no makeup, her long blond hair braided down her back. She was almost as tall as Max, with a fine bone structure and porcelain skin. Her eyes were sad and wary.

"My mother told me you wanted to talk about Ivy— about before she died, what she was like," Bailey said, preempting Max. "I'm not sure what you want to know."

Pilar poured Max a cup of coffee and asked how she liked it. After she put it on the counter, she poured another cup, added a liberal amount of milk, and handed it to her daughter. "Bailey, I'm going to let you talk with Ms. Revere alone. But you don't have to answer any questions that make you uncomfortable, you know that, right?"

"Yes, Mom." She smiled thinly. "You can stay if you want."

"If you'd like, but I suspect you won't couch the truth if I'm not here."

"I don't want to upset you, Mom."

Pilar squeezed her daughter's hands and left.

Bailey sat down at the counter opposite Max. "My mom cried last night. She doesn't want me to know, and she doesn't cry like other people. She's very quiet about it. But her eyes were red when she woke up. I hate upsetting her. She worries about me, and she misses my dad."

"I appreciate you talking to me. I know you have to go to school, so I'll get right to the point. I work on cold cases. My cases are different than traditional investigations because much of what I do the police can't—because of time or rules or money. I'm trying hard to understand who Ivy was and who might have wanted to hurt her. I read the Brock lawsuit, though I didn't know at the time that you were the unnamed witness. Your mother told me yesterday."

Bailey nodded. "She told me about your conversation. She didn't want me talking to you—she thinks that it'll make me sad or depressed, because I was really torn up after Heather killed herself. But I have nothing to hide. I regret everything I did, and I wish I'd stopped Ivy. I wish I'd known how to stop her."

"It took courage to admit your part in Ivy's plans," Max said.

"I didn't see it at the time . . . but Ivy was mean. Like, deep-down mean."

"I want to understand her. Maybe then I can figure out what was going on in her life the week she died."

"*I* don't even understand her." Bailey paused, then added, "We'd been best friends for a long time, ever since she moved to Corte Madera. Ivy wasn't always that way . . . she could also be nice and fun. She had a rough time when she first moved here—her parents getting a divorce, her mother remarrying, leaving her friends in Seattle, all that stuff. We were in the same class and played soccer together and became friends. She used to *actually* listen to me. It really wasn't until eighth grade that she changed."

"What happened then?"

Bailey looked down at her entwined hands, her long delicate fingers twisting around each other until the knuckles were white. "It's going to sound really stupid."

"It doesn't matter how it sounds. If you think that it was important to Ivy, I want to know."

"Ivy moved here in the middle of fourth grade. She was real quiet. She didn't like her new family or stepdad and was mad at her mom for making them leave Seattle. But she was mostly scared."

"About?"

"I don't know—looking back, I think it was coming to a new school in the middle of the year. Not having friends. This is a small town, really. We all know one another. But I started school in the middle of the year, back in first grade, so I kind of remembered how it felt. So I was nice to her, and she was nice back. We became inseparable."

She looked back down at her hands before talking. "There was another girl we hung out with, Rachel Beyers. The three of us—we did everything together. But when there's three, it doesn't always work out. Like there'd be a fight, and one of us would take sides, and then we'd say and do mean things, then a day later make up. It seems so silly now, and I don't remember most of what we argued about. Stupid things, probably. Then everything would be good . . . until the next disagreement.

"In eighth grade, Ivy and Rachel had a huge fight. Rachel accused Ivy of cheating in a game—some dumb online game—and Ivy said she didn't. Rachel didn't believe her. They didn't talk, and then Rachel started hanging out with a group who didn't like Ivy for whatever reason. You know how girls are—cliquey. Rachel is the type of girl who is always popular no matter what. I think more things happened between her and Ivy because Rachel completely shunned her, and then everyone else shunned her, too. Near the end of eighth grade, Rachel spread a rumor that Ivy liked this guy, Rick Colangelo."

"That name is familiar." Max had seen it somewhere.

"He was Travis Whitman's best friend until Rick moved—and that was Ivy's fault. But I'm getting ahead of myself. Anyway, Ivy had a crush on him, it was true, but when you're thirteen you don't want anyone to know. Rachel let it out, then told Ivy that Rick wanted to go to the graduation dance with her. So Ivy asked him—and he said he was already going with Heather."

"Heather Brock."

"Rachel had already known, but she'd wanted to humiliate Ivy for whatever it was that Ivy had done to her. And it worked. After that, Ivy changed. Her image meant everything to her."

Just like her mother.

"What happened to Rachel?" Max asked.

"She went to Branson, a private college prep school. She plays volleyball and softball and has probably never thought twice about Ivy—or me—since she left. So that left Heather. Ivy hated her so much, even though none of it was Heather's fault. By the time Ivy posted that awful video, I don't think she even remembered why she hated Heather."

"It seems that a lot of people were angry and upset with Ivy and what she posted on the Internet—their secrets, photos. Embarrassing them like Rachel did to her."

"Not really."

Max leaned forward. "I don't understand."

"I guess some people were upset, but everyone knew that Ivy would post *anything* on her blog. The picture with Heather and Christopher in, um, you know . . . well, more people 'liked' that picture than any other picture Ivy posted. I think . . . well, I guess, Ivy thought the more people who liked her photos, the more popular she was. I mean *hundreds* of people clicked 'like.' It kind of egged her on, you know?"

Max hadn't thought of the situation from that perspective, but it made sense as soon as Bailey said it.

She was about to ask another question when Bailey continued. "The more scandalous the photos, the better,

and Ivy kept looking for things to post. She said if people didn't want the attention, all they had to do was screw
around in private. And it wasn't just, you know, sex . . . it
was anything. Like when Missy and Kyle were smoking
pot on the beach . . . *someone* told Ivy about it, and she
practically ran down there and took a photo. Sometimes
she didn't even need a photo. She saw Missy and Doug
lip-locked under the bleachers when Missy was supposed
to be all hot and heavy with Kyle, but Ivy's phone was
dead so she just posted an update about it later that night.
She was actually pretty strict about that—she had to see
it herself or someone had to send her a photo. And people
did—Ivy didn't take the first picture of Christopher and
Heather." Bailey took a deep breath. "That was me. I
gave it to her." Her voice cracked. "I wish I could have a
do-over. I was just so angry when Christopher dumped
me . . . I really liked him. And he wasn't nice about it.
I . . . I wouldn't do something he wanted and he just said
if I didn't, he knew girls who did."

"What about the video?"

Bailey shook her head. "I didn't know about the video
then—I was so mad at Ivy about posting the photo after
I told her I changed my mind, I didn't talk to her for
weeks. And then she posted the video and Heather killed
herself and I felt so awful, so guilty. That's why I went to
the Brocks in the first place. I know I can't bring Heather
back, but they needed to know the truth."

"One thing I noticed reading the police statements and
reviewing social media is that Ivy never really talked
about herself."

Bailey thought about that a minute. "I guess that's
strange, huh. Ivy was very private."

"She had a boyfriend who broke up with her a few
weeks before she was killed. But Ivy never talked about
the breakup on her blog."

"She did—subtweets."

From how David had explained it earlier, Max was vaguely aware of the practice but she didn't quite understand it. She must have looked confused, because Bailey explained, "It's when you're talking about something or someone without mentioning their name, but everyone knows who you're talking about. Ivy was so mad at Travis. I stopped going on social media after Heather, and transferred schools . . . but people talk all the time. Right before I left for San Diego, I heard about the photo of him smoking pot. I was stunned, because Travis is a jerk, but he's one of these 'my body is my temple' athletes. It's *all* he cares about. If you told me he took steroids, I'd believe it. But pot? Not his style. But . . . I didn't doubt the photo. I don't know who gave it to her or if she took it herself. Then I heard Travis claimed it was fake."

"And Ivy didn't post anything else fake?"

"Not to my knowledge."

"So you could say that Ivy saw her social media presence as a popularity measure."

"Yeah—yeah, I guess that's what it was."

Max pulled her iPad out of her purse and flipped to a page where she'd typed the names of everyone Ivy had humiliated in the three months leading up to her murder—at least the names David and her staff had identified from the archived pages. Rick Colangelo was on the list. Now she remembered—Ivy had posted something about him being bisexual.

"You said that Rick Colangelo was Travis's best friend?"

"Yes. What did Ivy say about him? I'm serious that I didn't follow anything she wrote. I don't use social media anymore."

"She outed him."

"Rick—he's gay?"

"She claimed he was bisexual."

Bailey looked stricken. "I didn't know. I guess . . . I don't think anyone knew that. I'd always seen him with girls. He dated a girl from my school."

"Maybe he didn't want people to know. Maybe he was unsure himself."

"Travis—oh, God, I'll bet Travis said something to her, and Travis totally egged her on when he didn't like someone. But that wouldn't be right because he and Rick were tight."

"Where's Rick now?"

"I don't know."

Max made a note to find out everything about Rick Colangelo. And to talk again to Travis Whitman. If Ivy outed Travis's best friend, it would give both Rick and Travis a motive.

She showed the list to Bailey. "Did any of these people have lasting or serious repercussions from Ivy's postings?"

Bailey frowned. "I don't feel comfortable doing this. I know what you're asking: would any of these people have killed Ivy?"

"The police have a theory," Max said. "They think that whoever killed Ivy didn't plan on killing her. That they met up with her to scare or threaten her, and in the heat of the moment killed her. A crime of passion, I suppose some would call it. Anger. Spontaneous. The police don't have solid evidence tying any of their key suspects to the crime scene."

Bailey reluctantly looked at the list of names. There were dozens, a rather intimidating list. Max watched Bailey's reaction as she scanned the names. She went from pale to white. "I . . . I never realized how many people she hurt. We hurt."

Pilar walked into the kitchen and cleared her throat. "Honey, you're going to be late if you don't leave now."

Bailey handed the iPad back to Max. "I'm a senior and can't wait for high school to be over. I have no friends anymore, at least no one I trust. Some people avoid me because I was friends with Ivy. Some people come up to me with the latest gossip, to see what I'll do or say. Most everyone is superficial, secretly thrilled that another person has been exposed for being a slut or a pothead or a cheater or whatever. As if the fall of one person makes them somehow better, higher up on some invisible ladder. After Heather, I hated myself. It'd be a lie to say it was easy, because there were days I didn't want to go to school, I didn't even want to get out of bed. Then I thought about my dad." She closed her eyes and didn't say anything for a minute. When she opened them, they were moist. "I don't remember much about him. A few things— but I was six when he died and even before then he was deployed for months at a time. But when he was home, he would take me fishing. We would sit at this lake near base for hours and I would just be so happy that he was safe. And he would talk to me about his childhood, how his grandpa took him fishing because his dad was always too busy with work. And he said, and I'll never forget, that even though he's gone a lot, he's always thinking about me and my mom. And the first weekend after he gets back, we'd always go fishing. Because he said it was while fishing that he learned how to be a good friend, a son, a grandson, a husband. He said the solitude of fishing made him a better human being.

"I hated myself because I had disappointed my mother, but mostly, because I didn't live up to my dad's expectations. He told me many times that courage was the most important thing. Courage, because it wasn't always easy to do the right thing. It took courage to say goodbye every time he left. Courage to go to school and make friends. And my dad . . . he was the most courageous person I knew. Mom tells me stories . . ." Bailey's voice drifted away as her eyes locked on Pilar. "Anyway, I thought of him looking down at me and being disappointed, and I couldn't live with that. So I got out of bed and went to school, and I still do it even when I want to hide. Because I'm not going to let my dad down, and my mom needs me.

"There's only one person on this list who you didn't mention who *might* have had a reason to go after Ivy. Sarah Thomsen. She's a year older than us. Someone told Ivy that Sarah had cheated on her SAT test. Ivy ran with it, and Sarah—who'd been accepted into early admission at Stanford—was then denied admittance. They rescinded their acceptance. She was the valedictorian, but the school decided to take that away. Sarah lost it. She went after Ivy big time . . . she also claimed that she hadn't cheated. She appealed the decision. She ended up being valedictorian because the school couldn't prove she cheated, but Stanford still refused to admit her. I don't know where she ended up going—but I know she blamed Ivy."

"Who gave Ivy the information?"

"I don't know."

"Do you think it was true?"

Bailey hesitated, then shook her head. "I really don't know, but if I had to guess, I would say no. Sarah was always the smartest girl in school. Honors society. AP classes. If you told me Christopher or Travis cheated? Yeah, I'd believe it. But why would Sarah cheat?"

"Sometimes, smart people panic, and fear a poor test score would hurt them. Or they don't do well on standardized tests."

"I get that, and maybe that's what happened—Ivy was certain it was true. She didn't outright say it, but implied that she witnessed the cheating. I didn't know Sarah well—she was a year older than me."

"And you don't know where she went to college?"

"No. It's a good college, but on the East Coast. Pennsylvania, I think. Maybe Carnegie-Mellon? I could find out if you think it's important."

"I don't know that it is, but having the information only helps." Max paused, then asked, "Do you know Laura Lorenzo? She would have been a senior when you were a freshman."

Bailey considered, then shook her head. "The name kinda sounds familiar, but CM is a big school. I can't picture her."

Pilar said, "Ms. Revere, I really have to end the conversation now. Bailey's going to be late."

"Thank you for your time. Would it be all right to call tonight or tomorrow if I think of something?"

Pilar looked at Bailey, and the girl nodded. Max slipped her a card and said, "Please, if you think of anything else, no matter how unimportant, call me. And please watch the 'Crime NET' segment tonight. It'll air at nine on NET in this time zone, or through our Web site at seven, as soon as the East Coast airs the broadcast. It's archived, so you can watch it at your convenience. Something you see or hear might spark a memory."

Bailey nodded and walked Max to the front door. She said, "Is it really important to find out who killed Ivy? If it was an accident, as you say—not premeditated—is it really that important to know?"

"The truth is always important," Max said. "Ivy's family is torn apart. Her mother thinks Tommy Wallace is responsible, and that's affected everyone in the house."

"Tommy?" Bailey was surprised. "Tommy is a sweet kid. He wouldn't hurt anyone."

"He's been in a couple of fights."

"But he never started them. He was always defending Ivy's little brother, Austin. If anyone has a temper, it's him. I don't think I've met an angrier kid."

She closed the door and Max was already walking down the path when Bailey opened the door again and called, "Ms. Revere?"

Max turned.

"I did remember something about Travis," Bailey said as she walked down the path toward Max. "He came to see me at school on Tuesday. It was really weird. He was talking about you, asked me what I knew. But he said one other odd thing—he accused me of putting a phone in his locker."

"A phone?"

She nodded. "I have no idea what he was talking about. I completely forgot about the phone comment because he'd heard that you were in town and wanted to know what I knew—which was nothing. My mom and I were out of town, looking at colleges, and all I knew was what you'd said on our answering machine."

CHAPTER TWENTY-TWO

Max got on the phone after directing David to drive to Travis Whitman's house. She called Jess directly, not wanting to go through a middleman. "Jess, it's Max. I need you to background a couple of people. Are you ready?"

"Give them to me."

"Rick Colangelo. He would be a high school senior this year, David's research indicated he moved to Scottsdale shortly before Ivy's murder. The other is Sarah Thomsen. She graduated valedictorian from CM two years ago and goes to college in Pennsylvania—or in that general area."

"Got them. What do you want to know other than the basics?"

"If you can find out if they were in northern California the night that Ivy was killed, that would be great."

"That might be a bit harder, but I'll see what I can turn up."

"Thanks." She hung up. To David she said, "Travis knew I was here on Tuesday at lunch—before I spoke to him. He confronted Bailey at school and asked what she knew about me and what I wanted. Said she'd left a phone in his locker."

"Did she?"

"She says no."

"He must have had a reason for thinking she left it," David said. He avoided the freeway, slow with commute traffic, using side roads to cross into the adjoining town of Larkspur. "Travis has probably already left for school."

"Let's check anyway, it's only a couple of minutes."

His truck wasn't in his driveway, and neither of his parents were home. David and Max drove by the school and didn't see his pickup in the student parking lot.

"How did he know you were in town Tuesday?" David asked. "Who knew?"

"The police knew. Lorenzo, since I met with him Tuesday morning. Austin and Tommy."

"Paula Wallace, because Ben called her," David added, "Bailey and her mother, because you left messages. Who else did you leave messages for before lunch Tuesday?"

"The Brocks. But I met Lorenzo in a public place Tuesday morning—someone could have seen me with him."

"But would they have known why you were here?"

"Lorenzo could have told anyone," Max said. "Maybe not even on purpose; he was calling around, trying to dig up dirt."

Their cameraman, Charlie Morelli, was already at the police station by the time Max and David arrived. "I can't fucking believe you, Revere," Charlie said.

"Cool it," David muttered.

"Did you see the schedule? We're going to be shooting at *four in the afternoon?* I'd expected to be in the city slicing and dicing the tape by two."

"Tommy and Austin have school until three. I can't get them out of school for this. Austin is a minor."

"And where's Paula Wallace on this schedule? You sent me to her house, but we're not interviewing her?"

"She backed out," Max said.

"You're killing me."

"I've prepped the boys. We'll have everything else done. I only need thirty to sixty good seconds of the kids."

"Do you even understand what goes into editing twenty hours of tape into seven minutes?"

"Ben sent you because you're the best," Max snapped, "so act like it."

"You're fucking impossible."

Charlie knew damn well they were on a tight schedule, and there was no doubt that he'd already pulled the B-roll he wanted to use. He had the interview with Donovan Hunt, the NCFI spokesman, and a Skype interview Max had done with an expert on cyberbullying in the UK late last night. They would have the police spokesman, the boys, and of course Max. She'd already shot part of her segment yesterday at the preserve, they'd do the voice-over as soon as they were done with the Central Marin Police Authority, and Max hoped one of Ivy's teachers agreed to speak on camera. Then there was Ruby Jones, who would hopefully have confirmation on time of death after analyzing the organic evidence preserved at the lab in San Francisco. They wouldn't have time for an on-site interview, but a Skype interview would work.

Max let Charlie walk off his frustration and went into the station. Grace Martin met her almost immediately. "The chief wants to talk to you."

"Am I in trouble?" Max asked.

"He's letting me go on the record."

Max lit up. "Really? Why the change of heart?"

"Time of death—he wants to release the information in a controlled manner, and I suspect he thought if I went on record with you, you'd let us shape the revelation."

Max would have deferred to them on this point anyway, but she didn't say that. "You found something."

"Travis Whitman's alibi is gone. He was home alone

until eleven fifteen when his parents returned from a movie. But I checked the movie times again. His parents had said they'd arrived home 'around' eleven fifteen, take or leave. The movie got out at eleven ten, and walking to the car and driving—going as fast as I could imagine them going—they wouldn't have been home until eleven thirty. At the earliest."

"And no one can confirm that he was in fact home while his parents were at the movies."

"Correct. The problem is any defense lawyer would skewer the prosecution if we arrested Whitman solely on this lack of an alibi and time of death."

"You want him to confess."

"We're going to ask him to come in this afternoon."

"What about Justin Brock? Is his alibi more or less solid?"

"When we interviewed his girlfriend, she said he left her house just after midnight. She could be lying, so we'll talk to her again, but his alibi is more solid if Ivy was killed between ten thirty and eleven thirty. I have a list of other potential witnesses who could have seen Brock with the girlfriend, but after a year I can't trust them as being reliable memories."

"Was his girlfriend at the time Laura Lorenzo?"

"Yes, how did you—wait. Is there a relation between her and that damn reporter?"

"Yes. Younger sister."

"Well, that explains a lot, doesn't it?"

Chief Reinecke came out of his office and into the lobby. He introduced himself and said, "I just spoke with Graham Jones of NCFI. Impressive operation he runs."

"Yes, it is," Max concurred.

"He'll have his report to me by noon today, including the entomology report from his colleague who's working with the state lab. I rarely allow detectives to speak to the press, but I'm making an exception in this case. However, I told Martin only the facts. We will not discuss individual suspects, and I would appreciate if you don't ask the question."

"Understood."

Reinecke still seemed nervous. Max said, "I told Detective Martin that my objective is to find the truth, not to vilify the police department. I appreciate your cooperation."

He nodded but didn't respond. "Our spokesperson will go on record with a formal statement, and then you can talk to Grace. But I'm going to sit in."

"Absolutely," Max said. "Let's do it—I'm sure Charlie's ready."

They went to the chief's office, and first the official spokesperson gave a perfunctory statement that Max doubted she'd use at all, and then Grace sat in the chief's chair. While Charlie rolled the camera, Max had Grace verbally document the investigation, starting at the point the CMPA was called to the preserve. Grace went on a bit too long, but it could be edited down. Max then asked the key question. "Northern California Forensics Institute sent a team down to review evidence. Have you received their report and what did they find?"

"We have a preliminary report. Based on a state-of-the-art computer program that takes in all environmental factors, plus an analysis of the organic material, they have narrowed the time of death to between ten forty-five and eleven fifteen at night."

"Isn't that earlier than you'd initially thought?"

"The coroner originally gave a wider time of death, but based on other evidence—such as the fact that Ivy's phone was used at one ten—we determined she was likely killed closer to one thirty or two in the morning."

"And have you changed that theory?"

Grace nodded. "We believe that whoever killed Ivy Lake used her phone at one ten and pretended to be her. This was likely done to establish an alibi for her killer."

Max liked working on a rush segment; the time flew by. After Grace came an interview with one of Ivy's teachers, then the Skype session with Ruby, a Skype session with Graham, and a follow-up with the psychologist, and finally Max's voice-over. Charlie edited between filming, and they already had a good chunk of the show complete.

When they were finished it was time to meet Tommy and Austin at Jenny Wallace's house. The final clip, the part that was going to twist the hearts of Max's viewers.

Max told Charlie to shoot film of the tree house while she settled Tommy down. He was antsy and nervous, and he began to stutter.

Jenny didn't want him going on camera at all, but Tommy insisted he wanted to.

As soon as the camera started to roll, even if they told Tommy it wasn't on, he froze or stuttered or mumbled. Austin gave his interview like a well-trained actor, but in the end, Max realized it wasn't working out the way she wanted. They left at four thirty and Max knew they were cutting it close. Charlie was stressed, and she was headed in that same direction.

David saved the day.

David said, "Richard will drive you to the city so you and Charlie can work on the segment on the road. Hopefully, by the time you get there, it's just a matter of fine-tuning."

"And you?"

"I'll follow and you can take the car when you're done. I'll head back with Richard. I know you want to see Nick, though I still think I should come with you. Justin Brock could be our killer."

"If he is, he's not going to admit it to me. He only agreed to meet because I got through to his fiancée. I have questions, and since neither his parents nor the Wallaces are going to answer them, I need to convince Justin to talk. Specifically, I want to know the steps the Brocks took prior to Heather's suicide."

"What do you mean?"

"They had to have known Heather was being bullied. They pulled her from school, sent her to the all-girls school, they must have talked to Ivy or the school or her parents. Austin said he recalled Paula and Bill talking about a visit Paula had from Mrs. Brock—but I don't know the details. Paula isn't going to tell me. Mrs. Brock isn't going to tell me."

"Why is it important?"

"Because it might reveal other people whom Ivy had humiliated online."

David didn't say anything, and Max glanced over at him. "What aren't you saying?"

"Some crimes shouldn't be solved."

Max shook her head. "I don't believe that. You're thinking, someone—likely a teenager—reacted to Ivy's machinations by pushing her off a cliff. Possibly spontaneously. Possibly by accident. And that I can believe. But the problem is, Ivy might have been a bitch, but she deserved a chance to grow up, to redeem herself. Further, the person who killed her—if they had come forward—would likely have been given a minimal charge if there were extenuating circumstances like cyberbullying. If the person was a minor, they could have had their records sealed. They could have felt remorse."

"Teenagers don't think that way. They panic. They lie. They conceal, because they think, 'Oh shit, no one can ever know about this.'"

"Yes, but do they then set up evidence like the tweet

from Ivy's phone two hours after she died? In order to give themselves an alibi? If Graham's team is right, Ivy died within an hour of leaving her house. The killer met her in a remote location, pushed her off the cliff, and either left and returned two hours later to send the tweet and throw the phone over the edge with Ivy's body; or sat up there for hours, thinking how to cover up the crime. And all the while, two teenage boys are stuck in the middle of a hate-filled divorce and remarriage.

"If Paula and Bill had stopped Ivy when it was first brought to their attention that she was tormenting Heather Brock—and possibly others—Heather would likely still be alive and so would Ivy," said Max. "So talking to Justin Brock is paramount. If I get any sense that he killed her or knows who did, I won't tip my hand. Plus, I'm meeting him in a public place only two blocks from the police station."

"Just be careful."

"I was doing far more dangerous things and talking to far more dangerous people before Ben hired you," Max reminded him.

"Those days are over," David responded.

CHAPTER TWENTY-THREE

She'd left San Francisco at seven thirty that evening, after the segment aired in New York, but not yet in California. It took her an unreasonable ninety minutes to drive thirty miles. By the time Max arrived at Nick's house, she was irritable and stressed.

Nick answered the door and opened his mouth—she didn't know what he was going to say, but she stepped inside and said dramatically, "I despise traffic. I'm starving. And I really wanted to see you." She shut the door before wrapping her arms around his neck and pulling him in for a kiss.

Nick's hands fisted in the small of her back as he embraced her. Her tension headache all but disappeared.

"How hungry are you?" Nick asked, his voice low and rough.

"Very," she whispered.

He reached up to the back of her neck and slowly pulled down the zipper of her dress. She shivered as he reached her waist and he slid his hands down and gently, purposefully, pushed her pelvis toward his.

"Me, too." He looked at her and smiled, his eyes dark and mischievous. Nick walked backward through the living room, down the hall, pulling Max with him. He didn't have to pull too hard. By the time they reached his bedroom, her dress was on the floor and Nick's T-shirt was no longer covering his chest.

This was exactly what Max needed.

It was nearly eleven by the time Nick and Max crawled out of bed, and Max was truly famished. "I'm going to pass out if you don't feed me," she said, breathing deeply. "I smell oregano. And tomatoes!" She slipped on one of his shirts, he put on sweats, and they dashed to the kitchen.

He grinned. "I made lasagna when I got home, all it needs is to be warmed up."

"Good in bed and you cook, too," she said, taking a seat.

"Only good?"

She smiled and accepted the wine that he offered. "I wouldn't want you to rest on your laurels."

"I don't think either of us will be resting tonight."

Nick slipped the lasagna into the warming oven, then sliced a loaf of fresh sourdough bread. He poured olive oil onto a shallow dish and added fresh minced garlic. He put both on the kitchen table in front of her. She immediately dipped a chunk of bread into the garlic oil.

"Your stomach is loud," Nick said.

"I told you I was hungry. I could eat the lasagna cold at this point, but the bread will tide me over."

"Fifteen minutes." He poured himself a glass of wine and sat down across from her. "I know you're angry with me."

"Yes, I always have two orgasms when I'm mad."

"For canceling our weekend."

"I'm fine."

"Are you?"

"Of course I'm fine. I'm not the one with a manipulative ex."

He bristled, and Max regretted being so snippy. "Okay, I'm a *little* upset," she admitted. "But I'll get over it. Sex and food works for me."

When Nick didn't say anything, Max didn't know if he was angry with her or upset with the situation. She shouldn't have responded with sarcasm, but she wasn't someone who held back what she thought. David told her to stay out of it, and she was *trying* but she cared about Nick and she hated that his ex-wife was using his son to hurt him. She wasn't someone who could sit back and let things just *happen*. She wanted—needed—to solve problems. Isn't that why she'd picked the Ivy Lake homicide to investigate? Because she wanted to fix all of Tommy's and Austin's problems? To fix two families who were destroying each other from the inside out?

"Max, I'm really glad you're here," Nick said. "But I need to handle the situation with Nancy on my own, in my own way. I need you to respect that. I can't talk to you about it."

Max had a laundry list of things she wanted to say about the situation between Nick and Nancy. Max was stunned, however, at the twist of pain in her chest when he said *I can't talk to you*. It didn't matter that it was about his ex. It was that Nick didn't want or value her insight. He was keeping her at arm's length.

It hurt. More than she would ever admit to Nick, but Max had long ago promised that she would always be honest with herself. She was falling for him. Part of the reason their relationship was working—and had been for five months—was because they lived three thousand miles apart. Seeing Nick was fun, exciting, a vacation from her busy life. But she found herself wanting to spend more time with him, and not wanting to leave.

"I understand," she said.

"Do you?"

"Yes," she lied. It was better this way. Keep Nick at a distance. He had a major problem with his ex-wife, and he didn't want Max involved. Intellectually, she knew she should accept it. That Nick enjoyed her company, she liked being with him, and that the other stuff didn't matter.

But it *did* matter. And it bothered her that he was letting it happen. Worse, it pained her that he wouldn't share with her. But all these feelings and emotions told her she was getting too close to him.

She had to step back and reassess. They were good in bed. That wasn't a surprise. Nick was a thirty-six-year-old healthy male and she was a nearly thirty-two-year-old healthy female who enjoyed sex. Attraction was a good thing. It worked. She didn't need anything more than that. When did Maxine Revere really have the time for a relationship anyway? And really, how much time had they spent together? A few stolen weekends over the last five months. One week in Lake Tahoe—with David, Emma, and Nick's son Logan. She hadn't seen Nick in six weeks, and Skypeing twice a week didn't count.

Max was too independent and confident for most men. With Nick, Max thought she'd found someone who truly accepted her life choices, who respected her career even when he sometimes disagreed with her methods. Nick was grounded, there was no rush to make a commitment. They had a nice balance. But Max wondered if she wanted more from her lover. Because the idea that he was intentionally separating part of his life from her deeply bothered her.

Or was all that just an excuse for Max to keep *him* at arm's length?

"Max—" Nick began.

She put her hand up. "It's fine. You know what you're doing." As she said it, she realized she didn't believe it. She'd just lied to Nick. *Again.* She told him she understood, then she told him it was fine. She wanted to backtrack and tell him that she *hoped* he knew what he was doing, but she bit her tongue. She didn't want to fight tonight. She wanted to eat, she wanted more sex, she wanted to sleep.

The timer beeped and Nick retrieved the lasagna. The silence was uncomfortable.

"I saw your segment on 'Crime NET' tonight," Nick said. "Watched it on the computer as soon as it was posted."

"What did you think?"

"You were fantastic, as usual."

"Of course I was," she said, lightening the mood. Maybe this was really for the best. Keep her distance, don't get too involved. Enjoy the company and the sex, but remember that she had a completely separate life, one that Nick didn't want to participate in, just like she wasn't part of his life.

The only difference, she figured, was that she wouldn't mind Nick letting her in a bit. She'd shared as much about her life as he wanted to know, but maybe this was the boundary of that.

"It was well edited," Max said between bites.

"What happened? You said earlier this week that you planned to interview the mother."

"She set up rules I couldn't follow," Max said. "I had to go around her. Ben told me I wouldn't like her, and he was right. I've worked with people I didn't like before. But this time—no way was I agreeing to her terms." She sipped her wine. "I hope we had enough and can generate a lead from the program. Our Nor-Cal affiliate is running the show again later tonight, and of course it's on the

Web page. I caught a break that the police cooperated—
they weren't inclined to at first."

"You can be persuasive."

"It wasn't me. It was Paula Wallace, the victim's
mother, ordering and threatening them not to talk to me."

"Why would she not want this publicity? It would seem
to be the only real chance of finding out what happened to
her daughter."

"I'd like to say I don't know why, but I do. I suspect
that Paula Wallace convinced herself that her cyber-
bully daughter didn't do anything wrong, or that Ivy
was just being an average teen when she drove another
girl to kill herself. She called the Brock family's civil
lawsuit frivolous. She's in denial—or even more likely,
she lies to herself and believes only the good about her
daughter."

"That's a common reaction when a parent loses a child.
Blinders. Losing a child . . . it isn't easy nor does everyone respond the same."

She nodded. "I don't blame her for the rose-colored
glasses. I blame her for her attitude before Ivy's murder.
But as far as the investigation, I did what I came to do. I
helped gather additional evidence because I have the resources and desire to do so. Because I pushed, the police
have more than they had last week."

"Without new evidence or a witness, they had no direction," Nick said.

"Exactly."

"And what do you think?"

"I don't have an opinion yet."

"You always have an opinion, Maxine."

She leaned back and sipped her wine. She'd cleaned
her plate. The lasagna was delicious.

"More?" Nick offered.

She shook her head. "Maybe for a midnight snack."

"It is midnight." He stared at her. "You don't want to tell me what you think?"

"I haven't finished my interviews," she said. "On paper, Justin Brock has the strongest motive. He blamed Ivy for his sister's suicide; his alibi is his girlfriend—who's now his fiancée; and he confronted Ivy the day before she died." Max paused, then finished her wine. Nick poured her another glass. "The local reporter is Justin's future brother-in-law. He's been pushing—very hard—the theory that Ivy's death was an accident. She went up to the preserve alone and fell to her death."

"But there's solid evidence of a homicide."

"Depends on how one looks at it, I suppose. *Someone* else was up there with her. Graham is confident that based on where her body was found and other injuries, she was pushed off the cliff." Max rose and stretched. After the tense drive to Nick's then vigorous sex, she was sore and stiff.

Nick got up and rubbed her shoulders. "What's bothering you?"

She couldn't tell him, because what was bothering her was why he wouldn't talk to her about Nancy, and he'd already asked that she stay out of it. Ordered her to stay out of it.

"I hate traffic."

He kissed her neck, then steered her into the living room. He tossed a couple of throw pillows onto the floor. "Take off your shirt and lay on your stomach."

She raised an eyebrow. "Bossy, aren't we?" She pulled off her shirt.

"Well, that's my shirt. Maybe I want it back."

She tossed it at him.

She did as he asked because Nick's hands were truly magic. He straddled her, supporting himself on his knees, and worked through her muscles. "You're tense."

"I'm going to melt."

"Tell me about your theories."

She waited a few moments and let Nick's fingers relax her. "Ivy had cuts on her arms. Forensics said they were caused by a thin blade, not the fall. They appeared to be defensive wounds, but none were deep enough to kill her. Based on where her body was found, forensics believes she was pushed. I brought in a private forensics team to look at the evidence and give me possible scenarios."

"And the police detective was okay with that?"

"I didn't ask her permission, but I told her what I was doing and she ended up observing. Graham—the director of NCFI—gave her a copy of their findings. They're experts, it's not unheard of to bring in a private consultant. I've used them on other cases."

"I wasn't being critical."

Max had to get over this mood. She had only this one night with Nick, and her wounded ego was making it difficult to enjoy their time alone.

"One theory is that Ivy's death was an accident. She went to the preserve to meet someone; they argued and fought. The killer had a knife, maybe brought it out to scare Ivy or maybe in the heat of the moment wanted to kill her. Ivy put up her arms and was nicked several times as she backed away."

"And she couldn't have backed off the cliff?"

"Unlikely. The cliff was nearly vertical, but if she walked off it, she would have fallen closer to the base.

"A more likely scenario is that after the knife attack, the killer pushed Ivy. It had to be a good, solid push and right at the edge. The photos taken the morning after show that there may have been a scuffle at the top, but revealed no clear shoe prints. The ground was too hard and dry."

"Any more theories?"

"She ran off the cliff to get away from her attacker, not realizing how steep it was."

"You don't sound like you buy that."

"I don't. And my forensics people think it's less likely, based on how her body was found—she landed on her back and the back of her skull, not her side or front, which would be more likely if she was running away. However, there was some brush and saplings she hit on the way down that could have altered her fall, especially if she reached out and caught onto something. Torn clothing halfway down on a jutting tree branch matches her clothes."

"So you think she was pushed. And the detective thinks she ran away from an attack. Either scenario doesn't make the killer less guilty."

Max looked at him over her bare shoulder. "How do you know Grace thinks she ran away?"

"Because, based on what you've told me, that's what I think. If someone is being attacked with a knife, if they have a chance, they run away. Why do you believe she was pushed?"

"I don't know," Max admitted. "Ivy's personality was to push back, not run. She lived in Corte Madera half her life. She would be aware of the area, the cliffs, the risk. I don't see her running off a cliff."

"But you don't know her."

"I feel like I do." Max didn't know if she could explain it. It was more intuition than anything else. "She reminds me of Lindy."

"Your high school friend."

Max hadn't articulated these feelings, and they were still confusing.

Because it really wasn't Lindy who seemed the most like Ivy.

"I graduated from high school nearly fifteen years ago. There was no Facebook, no Twitter, no Instagram. I keep thinking—if Lindy had a blog, would she have kept her secrets in her diary? She had a mean streak, especially if someone had hurt her, perceived or real. She hated hypocrites."

"That sounds familiar," Nick mused, still rubbing her shoulders.

"It might be one of the reasons Lindy and I got along so well. But Lindy was two-faced. She kept her sexual relationship with my cousin a secret. She spied on people. Blackmailed them. Knowing secrets made her feel superior, but it also depressed her. It was as if she expected the worst, dug around until she found it, then used the information when it suited her."

"And Ivy?"

"Did the same thing—except she revealed everything immediately. She had no filter." Max paused. "I'm just like her." Her voice cracked, and that she didn't expect.

"You're not."

Max didn't say anything. The thought had been circling around all week. Was that, more than the insomnia, why she was in such a foul mood? Why she was arguing with David?

"Is it because you speak your mind?" he asked.

"No—well, yes, I speak my mind, but that doesn't bother me."

Max hadn't slept well the night before. Everything had been jumbled around, from the Brocks' civil suit to Paula's claim that it was frivolous; from Jenny Wallace's hatred of her ex and his wife to her argument with David, only Emma and Brittney had been replaced by Nick's family, Logan and Nancy. Lance Lorenzo's ridiculous but annoying article angered her, but there were some hidden truths. Not to mention that Tommy and Austin had put everything on her to resolve, as if their future depended on whether she solved Ivy's murder.

But something Bailey had said this morning had stuck with Max. That Ivy only posted the truth. Travis said something similar: because Ivy's gossip was usually true he had a hard time proving her photo of him smoking pot was fake.

Max believed the truth deserved to be heard. That lies destroyed, they tore apart families. Yet did that mean that Heather's mistakes should be spread far and wide for no reason except to hurt her? When Max thought about the truth, she thought first about lies—the lies her mother told to her over the first ten years of her life, the lies her uncle Brooks had told when he was cheating on his wife, the lies her cousin had told to his friends and family when he was secretly sleeping with Lindy in high school. Lies that nearly cost her cousin his freedom, and did cost him his marriage.

"Max, what's wrong?"

She rolled over to face Nick. She didn't care that she wore no shirt; she'd never been falsely modest and she and Nick and been sleeping together for some time. "Ivy posted photos of Heather in compromising positions with two different boys. She posted a short video of Heather having sex with her boyfriend. Photos of Heather drinking at a party, dancing provocatively at another. Heather was a bit wild, I suppose, but the pictures of her and the boys were taken when she thought she had privacy. When they were exposed on the Internet, she lost that privacy. The kids at school branded her a slut, largely because those boys had other girlfriends. Boys expected her to put out. Girls shunned her because she tried to steal someone's boyfriend. All high school drama . . . except with a dark edge. A meanness. Even though she changed schools,

Heather couldn't get away from it. Ivy continued to push, enjoying her reaction. That's all I can think it was, Ivy took pleasure in hurting Heather. All because Heather had embarrassed her back in junior high. Ivy took that pain and humiliation and escalated it until someone died. In this case, Heather.

"When I was in high school, I learned my uncle Brooks was having an affair. I exposed him. At a family dinner where he couldn't get away from it, couldn't lie, couldn't threaten me to keep quiet. And I wonder . . . if I was sixteen now, would I have exposed him on Facebook? Would I have stalked him until I got a photo of him and Lindy's mother doing the deed? Because I certainly didn't keep the truth a secret then. Yet I hurt the one person I never wanted to hurt—my aunt Joanne. Brooks has never forgiven me—I don't care about that—but Aunt Joanne hasn't forgiven me, either. She was embarrassed—humiliated—and I caused that."

"There are so many differences between what you did then and what Ivy did," said Nick.

"Are there? Because I was glad that I exposed him." Max paused. "If I wasn't sixteen, I might have done it quietly. Without the theatrics."

"I can't believe you don't see it."

"I do—really. Ivy humiliated Heather with the sole purpose of hurting Heather. It was mean and vindictive. And yet I exposed Brooks because he was a hypocrite who had hurt me, and I wanted to get back at him."

"What did he do to you?"

Max realized what she'd said. She hadn't thought about this in a long time, and she certainly didn't mean to bring up the past with Nick tonight.

"It's ancient history. He hated my mother, took it out on me. It's not worth going into. The point is, I never saw myself as being mean and vindictive, but I was. And yet . . . I would do the same thing today. Even knowing all this, I would still expose him. It bothers me that it *doesn't* bother me that I would do it."

"I think you're reading too much into this. You're identifying with the victim."

"I don't see Ivy as a victim. I see her as a mean little bitch who took extreme joy in exposing everyone's secrets and flaws for the world to see, all because it gave her a false sense of popularity."

"And that's the biggest difference between you two. When you exposed your uncle, you did it within the family. You didn't take out a newspaper ad and announce it to the world."

"I announced it at a family dinner between the first and second courses."

Nick laughed and pressed his body against hers, leaning in for a kiss.

She wasn't laughing.

Nick leaned up and frowned. He eyed her, as if just realizing something. "You still have that bastard messing around in your head, don't you?"

Nick was right.

She pretended she didn't know what he meant. "No," she said. "I'm fine. That was nearly three months ago."

Max hadn't articulated it but Nick had nailed it. She'd been doing a lot of soul-searching ever since a psychopathic shrink had kidnapped her, drugged her, tortured her . . . the physical scars were nearly gone, but the emotional scars from him digging around inside her psyche had brought back memories and unwanted feelings that Max hadn't been able to shed, even in the time since her brief captivity. She'd always prided herself on knowing who she was and what she did; now she felt raw from the experience and had begun to question her own motives.

"Max," Nick said, lowering his body on top of hers,

"you are hardly perfect, but you care about the truth. About justice. You can't possibly know what you would do if you were a teenager today. They face a different world. For all your flaws, you're not a mean person. You have far more compassion than you give yourself credit for."

"That sure sounds like a backwards compliment," she whispered.

"It is a compliment." He kissed her. "You're one of a kind, Maxine Revere. Never forget it."

CHAPTER TWENTY-FOUR

FRIDAY

Max woke in Nick's bed to her vibrating cell phone and the smell of coffee. When she moaned, Nick rolled over and put his arm around her, pulling her against his hard, naked body. "It's six o'clock. You don't have to get that."

"It's nine in New York," she muttered, reaching for her phone on the nightstand.

He kissed her shoulder and traced the small memorial tattoo on her shoulder. The one she'd had designed after her friend Karen was killed.

She put the phone to her ear, but didn't have to say a word. "Where are you?" her producer demanded.

"Good morning, Ben."

"David said you left town."

"I'm in bed with Nick."

"Shit, Maxine."

"It's six in the morning."

"I just spent the last fifteen minutes trying to soothe Paula Wallace. She saw the show last night, you ignored her calls, David ignored her calls, the police said there's nothing they can do about the show, and she's been fuming ever since. Her husband is a fucking *lawyer*, Max. A *corporate* lawyer."

"I know."

"You should have told me!"

"It's in my report."

"Like I have time to read all your notes?"

"I didn't do anything illegal."

"She said she didn't give permission for Austin to be on the show."

"I didn't ask her. I didn't put him on camera, except in B-roll and from behind. Can't even tell it's him."

"I suppose I can thank David for that."

She fumed. "And even if I had put him on, we're clear. *Ethically* I should get parental permission, but it's not mandatory."

"You quoted him."

"I have an unaired segment where I interviewed Austin. If it will help calm her down, I'll show it to her."

"We may be beyond that. Her husband is coming home from his business trip early and our lawyers are having a cow."

"Relax, Ben." Max sat up and swung her legs over the side of the bed, but she didn't get up. She was exhausted. They didn't get to sleep until two, but she'd had four solid hours of sleep. More than she had any other night this week. "This case has turned, I feel it."

"Why did you leave town? We have calls coming in, clips you need to listen to, follow-up—"

"Because I have David and he's worth three assistants. I'm interviewing someone important to the case this morning, and since I worked all weekend and didn't get to have sex with Nick, I deserve a night off."

"You're impossible."

"You're high-strung. I'll be back in Sausalito by noon. I'll deal with Paula Wallace."

"Let the lawyer handle her."

"Normally I'd agree with you, but I know what I'm doing."

"Don't get arrested."

She laughed. "Getting arrested is half the fun."

"Dammit, Maxine!"

"Don't worry, this time I have the police on my side."

"A first for everything."

Her good humor dried up. "Goodbye, Benji." She pressed End and put her phone back on the nightstand. She turned to her naked lover. Nick was watching her with a combination of apprehension and lust.

Max said, "I don't have a lot of time, but I need a shower."

"We have a drought here in California. They ask that we limit showers to seven minutes."

"Seven minutes for me, seven minutes for you . . . that's fourteen minutes together." She walked her fingers up his chest. Nick grabbed her wrist and pulled her in for a kiss.

Max had an early morning breakfast with her grandmother, Eleanor Revere. She hadn't told her she would be in town until yesterday, and part of her wished that her grandmother had had plans. Yet, Max hadn't seen her since April and while they had an understanding and mutual respect, Max still didn't approve of what Eleanor had done. Specifically, getting a judge to send Lindy's killer to a sanitarium instead of prison.

Max appreciated her wealth and the opportunities it afforded her—such as paying for NCFI to re-create the Ivy Lake crime scene, or being able to fly first-class cross-country to spend a weekend with Nick. But she didn't approve of using money and connections to circumvent the justice system, and that's exactly what had happened when Eleanor got involved.

But family was family. And while on the surface El-

eanor's motives might have seemed pure, the simple fact
was her grandmother did not want to be associated with
a felon. She wanted the problem to disappear. Image was
everything. That Eleanor preferred to have a mentally ill
relative locked up in a hospital for the criminally insane
rather than a felon locked up in maximum security bog-
gled the mind.

Especially since Lindy's killer wasn't crazy. Narcissis-
tic, twisted, a borderline sociopath—but not insane.

Maybe Eleanor was the reason Max understood Paula
Wallace. Her grandmother was the same . . . with one
crucial difference. Eleanor would never have allowed
Max or any of her children or grandchildren to go as far
as Ivy had with her blog and social media.

The morning was too cold to eat outside, so she and
her grandmother sat in the glass-enclosed breakfast nook
off her opulent, Tuscan-style kitchen.

Eleanor always drank tea, and Max joined her. Max
didn't particularly like tea, but she loved the ritual, and
no one did it better than Eleanor. There had been days
when Max was younger when she missed her mother for
reasons she didn't understand—it wasn't like her mother
had ever acted maternal—when Eleanor would brew a pot
of tea and they would sit in the rose garden or here in the
breakfast nook. Rarely talking, just being together. There
was a peace Max longed for that she'd only attained in
those quiet moments with her grandmother.

"You're staying with Detective Santini, I assume." Eleanor wasn't a prude, but she thought Max should be dating
CEOs and senators, not cops and FBI agents.

"Just last night," Max said. "I'm at the Madrona in Sausalito."

"You've been here all week?"

"In Sausalito. I've been working, otherwise I would
have come down sooner."

"Hmm." That was Eleanor's way of showing disapproval. "You haven't been sleeping," Eleanor said.

"When I get involved in a case, my mind doesn't stop working." Max had never told Eleanor or anyone in the family about what happened in New York three months ago. They knew she'd been attacked—that had been on the news—but she hadn't given them more details than had been revealed publicly. She didn't know exactly why she wanted to keep it from them—maybe she just didn't want to talk about it anymore.

"No, it's more than that," Eleanor said, studying her.

Max didn't like how her grandmother analyzed her. It wasn't like Eleanor was psychic, even though at times she had an uncanny ability to see through people.

"How's William? The boys?" Max asked, changing the subject.

"I invited him over for tea. He declined."

It had been nearly six months since Max had turned his life upside down with her investigation into Lindy's murder. Max hadn't apologized; she'd found the truth. It had to come out. There was nothing she'd done that she wouldn't do again.

But she missed seeing her young cousins.

"Tell me about your work," Eleanor said. She took a dainty bite out of her scone.

Instead of rehashing the investigation, Max said, "What do you think of social media?"

"That's a broad question."

"You don't have a Facebook page, for example. But Uncle Arthur does." Arthur Sterling was Eleanor's brother—they were close in age, and Max knew enough retired people on Facebook that she didn't think Eleanor's age had as much to do with her disdain for the medium as her personality.

"I've heard of it, of course. I'm old, not ignorant."

"That's not what I meant. My investigation involves a teenager who revealed other people's private business on social media. Embarrassing things."

Eleanor raised her eyebrow and look pointedly at Max. "Familiar."

Well, that took the knife and twisted it. Maybe this was a bad idea, coming here—and asking Eleanor for her opinion. Max knew what she would say—yet she came anyway. Eleanor loved her, Max didn't doubt it, but the two women sometimes had very different perspectives.

"Ivy did it to be mean, to hurt people. Things that between two people aren't embarrassing, but when exposed for the world are humiliating."

"Sex," Eleanor said bluntly.

Max almost blushed. Eleanor was not a person who had discussed sex with her when she was growing up.

"Basically."

"I would imagine this girl did such things for attention."

"Attention and popularity."

"There are better ways to hurt people."

"But the Internet is faster."

"Hmm." Eleanor sipped her tea. "And perhaps that's why I don't care for social media. I've found that in the heat of a conversation, people sometimes say things they may mean but would never utter if given another moment to think. Social media takes away that . . . hesitation, I suppose you might call it. That moment of contemplation. When I write a letter—any letter, for business or personal, I think about what I want to say. Then I reread the letter to make sure that my meaning is clear. If I'm upset about something, I'll sit on the letter for a day to make sure I want my feeling on the matter known, and how I want it to come across. Civil society requires civility. It requires individuals to consider the repercussions of their words as well as their actions. Today I fear people—not just teenagers, who did not exhibit self-control even in my day—rarely consider the repercussions of anything they do or say."

Max leaned back. Her grandmother had always been regal, judgmental, and wise. But she said something that put Ivy's behavior in a completely different light.

Ivy didn't post anything spontaneously. She did it with purpose and full knowledge of how it would be perceived by her peers. She planned and orchestrated the cyberattack on Heather over months. She had the photos of Heather and her boyfriend for weeks before she posted them—as if waiting for the most devastating time to reveal them to the public.

"Do you disagree?" Eleanor asked Max.

"No," she said. "I was thinking about this girl Ivy's image. How she wanted to be seen, but more than that, how she wanted *others* to be seen."

"So she attempted to make herself look better by making others look worse."

"Yes, that's exactly what I was thinking."

"Crass," Eleanor said.

"Her mother is concerned about image as well."

"She must not have known what her daughter was doing."

"She did."

Eleanor looked surprised. "Oh? And she allowed it?"

Max almost smiled. "What would you have done to me, Eleanor? Some parents have no control over their teenagers."

"You would never have been so pedestrian."

"I did things to expose people's lies. Ivy would likely say she was doing the same, calling people out for their hypocrisy."

"Posting sexually explicit material is hardly calling

someone a hypocrite, unless that person has put them-selves out as some sort of saintly individual, like a min-ister or a married woman. It's the public spectacle that this girl created, as well as the private information she shared. It's one thing to have a secret; it's quite another to reveal that secret."

"You're right about one thing, Grandmother. I would never have used the Internet to expose anyone. Not be-cause I'm noble or good, but because I wouldn't want your disapproval."

Eleanor laughed, and Max was surprised. "Dear, if you feared my disapproval, you wouldn't have done half the things you've done in your life. But you wouldn't have done what that girl did because it was wrong. You're a much better person. Maxine, never have I doubted you knew right from wrong and acted accordingly."

Max cleared the table and hugged her grandmother goodbye. As she drove to meet Justin Brock, she realized that she was glad she'd taken the time to visit. Eleanor *was* eighty-two and if something happened to her and Max had not told her that she loved her and that she appreciated how Eleanor had taken her in when her mother walked out—well, Max didn't want to take her for granted.

Warts and all, a dysfunctional family was still a family.

Justin Brock was staring into an extralarge cup of coffee when Max walked into the coffee shop in downtown Palo Alto. She recognized him from his pictures, but he'd also sent her a message that he'd be wearing a white Oxford shirt with jeans. He was a handsome young man of twenty-two, a senior in college, prelaw, of average height and build, but with the tan of someone who spent a lot of time outdoors. The research she'd done into the Brock family supported an adventurous lifestyle—skiing, waterskiing, swimming, running. Justin had played baseball in high school, but hadn't continued in college.

Max slipped into the chair across from him. "Hello, Justin. I'm Maxine Revere. Thank you for meeting with me." She slid over a business card.

He glared at it, didn't pick it up. "I only agreed to see you because I don't want you talking to my parents or to my fiancée."

Max hadn't actually promised not to talk to his parents, but she said, "I appreciate your concern for them. I'm sure you're having a difficult time as well."

"It's not the same." Justin stared at her, anger etched on his face, perhaps permanently. He looked both young and old at the same time. Max recognized the expression. "Heather was my little sister. I miss her. But she was my mom's baby. It's just not the same."

"You're in prelaw."

"Prelaw and psychology. I had planned on going into family law, but I'm leaning toward criminal justice. But I don't know anymore. I'm rethinking whether I can even be a lawyer." He cleared his throat and it was evident from the way he shifted his position that he hadn't intended to share any of that with Max.

Max understood what Justin was going through. When tragedy hit close to home, everything changed. Fifteen years ago, Max had planned on majoring in literature and art history, or possibly archeology, with the idea of working at a museum.

But when your college roommate disappears and there's enough of her blood found to declare her dead—but no body and no conviction—priorities changed.

Max would never let anyone else decide her fate. And maybe that, more than anything, was why the events in New York had affected her so deeply. That bastard had taken away her control, her ability to make her own choices. She'd been drugged and restrained and that niggling fear in the back of her mind, the fear from her childhood that her life wasn't her own, that she had no choice about where she would go or how she would live because her mother moved on a whim.

Max refocused on Justin. He was contemplative, sad, protective. She said, "I read the civil suit your parents filed against Ivy Lake and the Wallaces but the settlement is sealed."

Justin's jaw tightened. "And you're trying to defend Ivy, I don't believe it."

"I'm not defending her. I'm trying to find out who killed her."

"The question you should be asking is who *wouldn't* have wanted her dead? She destroyed my family. It's been nearly two years and my mother still cries nearly every day."

"Someone killed Ivy," said Max. "Evidence is thin, suspects are plenty. But no one fits perfectly. Solving Ivy's murder is important—not just to her parents, but her siblings."

"Her parents? Maybe they now understand a little of what we suffered because of their daughter."

She raised an eyebrow. "Is that what you want? For Paula Wallace to cry every day like your mother?"

"Don't twist my words."

"I get that you're angry. I would be, too. What Ivy did was cruel. Her parents should have stopped it. But sometimes parents can't prevent their children from doing bad things." Though Max suspected Paula Wallace had been in denial up until the civil suit was filed. And possibly even after. Then when Ivy died, Paula decided to ignore all the bad things that Ivy had done. Not just ignore, but declare untrue.

Max waited until Justin looked at her, then said, "The

end result is Ivy intentionally, deliberately, methodically set out to tear your sister apart."

He stared at her, expression open in disbelief. "If you believe that, why are you helping them?"

"Her parents? I'm not investigating this case because the Wallaces asked me to."

"Then why are you?"

"Because Tommy Wallace asked me to."

At first, Justin's face was blank. Then he leaned back, confused. "Tommy? He's, um, retarded, isn't he?"

"He is more than capable of understanding what's going on in his life—and Ivy's murder has greatly affected him, as well as Ivy's brother, Austin. They deserve to know what happened to their sister or it will hang over them forever.

"But beyond that," Max said, "*someone* killed Ivy."

He scowled. "I honestly don't care. Ivy Lake might as well have killed Heather herself. I'm sorry about her brothers, but there's nothing I can do. I don't even know why you wanted to talk to me, except to find out about Ivy and my sister. Well, here it is: Ivy hurt a lot of people. She destroyed my sister's life to the point where Heather didn't think she had anything to live for. Ivy should have paid for that, but now she's dead and my parents won't go after her parents. They agreed to settle, to keep silent about what happened. Why didn't her mother stop her? My mother talked to Mrs. Wallace several times. She *knew* what Ivy was up to and did nothing to stop it. My father confronted Mr. Wallace and he claimed to not know anything about it. Said girls could be mean and would grow out of it. *Grow out of it?* They were sixteen! It had been going on for nearly two years. I don't care what Heather *may* have done to Ivy, *nothing* justified what that little bitch did to my sister. Nothing."

"Your future brother-in-law has made it his life's mission to prove that Ivy's death was accidental."

It took Justin a half a minute to calm down and switch gears. He shrugged and leaned back in the chair. "Lance is Lance," he said. "He thinks the police were pressured to rule that Ivy's cause of death was inconclusive, because the Wallaces want someone to blame. I honestly don't care. I don't have any problem with what the police did—they interrogated me, I told the truth, end of story. I get that they had to talk to me—I'd had a confrontation with Ivy in public. But I didn't kill her, accidentally or on purpose."

"Forensically, Ivy's death is a homicide. There's proof that she was pushed off that cliff."

"Lance sent me several scientific reports that state it's virtually impossible to determine whether a person jumped, fell, or was pushed."

"*Sometimes* it's hard to determine, sometimes it's conclusive, and sometimes forensics can prove what happened."

"Like I said before, who wouldn't want her dead?"

Max looked him in the eye. "Maybe Lance is pushing the accident theory because he's trying to protect you."

Justin stared at her blankly. As the realization of what she meant came clear, he swore under his breath. "Lance warned me about you, that you're a shark reporter from New York City who will do or say anything to get a story."

Max tensed. "Lance is a liar. He lied to me, he lied to the police, and he printed erroneous information in the newspaper that I could sue him for if I were so inclined. As it is, I'll be satisfied when he's fired."

Justin frowned, but didn't say anything.

"You said you had an argument with your girlfriend and went home alone the night of July third."

"I don't have to talk to you about this. I gave my statement to the police."

"I believe you didn't kill Ivy."

He looked confused. "Then why are you even talking to me?"

"Because right now you're the only one I'm reasonably confident did not kill her. Your statement to the police was that you were with your girlfriend all evening until just before midnight when you had an argument. You didn't elaborate on what the argument was about, but it was serious enough that you left her place and went home. It couldn't have been too serious, because you're now engaged to Laura, but at the time it gave you a weak alibi because the police believed that Ivy was killed between one and two in the morning of July fourth. However, they now know she was killed closer to eleven on July third. Someone posted as her on social media at one ten. Which means that they were either covering their tracks, or they were trying to cast blame elsewhere."

Justin let everything she said sink in. Then his curiosity got the better of him, and he asked, "Then what the hell do you want from me? You tried to talk to my parents, you scared my fiancée, why me? Why us?"

"You told Detective Martin that in the bookstore you saw Ivy and saw red, that you went up to her and told her she would pay for what she'd done. A threat. You had no alibi for the original TOD before the new forensics report. Who else was in that bookstore? Who else could have heard your threat?"

He opened his mouth, and then closed it. "You think that someone intentionally set me up?"

She nodded, watching him closely. Justin Brock was angry, he was grieving, but he had an inner restraint and solid sense of right and wrong. She could see him confronting Ivy in the bookstore like he had, but not luring her to the preserve and pushing her off a cliff.

"We were standing outside the bookstore," he said, after thinking for a moment. "There are several shops in the area, it's a small mall. And Ivy wasn't alone. She had some people with her, but no one I recognized."

"Some people? Boys? Girls? Peers?"

"A couple of girls, I didn't know them. Why would anyone want to frame me?"

"Convenience? I really don't know for certain. Maybe the killer heard your threat and determined that if Ivy showed up dead, you would be the primary suspect. There was no evidence against you, other than your threat to Ivy—and your motive, of course, to avenge your sister's own death. There was no evidence against Travis, except that he and Ivy had a confrontation the week before because she posted a doctored photo of him."

"According to Ivy, she only posted *the truth*," Justin snapped.

She only posted the truth.

Ivy didn't know that photo was doctored. She really believed Travis was smoking pot and she exposed him because she was angry with him. Either because he dumped her or because he was with another girl.

Who altered that photo? Who'd sent it to Ivy?

"In the civil lawsuit, your parents identified a witness who would testify that Ivy intentionally sought to hurt Heather. I now know that the witness was Bailey Fairstein."

"I can't discuss that."

"The initial civil suit is public information. I spoke with Pilar Fairstein and Bailey and they confirmed that Bailey went to your parents after Heather killed herself. Bailey indicated that she had been privy to Ivy's plan because she felt that Heather moved in on her boyfriend. Here's where I'm stuck. What Ivy did to Heather went far beyond the slight that Bailey spoke of. Meaning, what Heather did in eighth grade seems to pale in comparison to the intensity of Ivy's response over the next two years. Are you aware of anything else that transpired between these two girls—both of whom are now dead?"

"I can't even imagine how anyone could do what Ivy did. It went beyond being catty and gossipy."

He was right about that.

He continued. "I thought after Heather changed schools it would get better, but it didn't. In some ways it was worse because Heather *thought* it would get better. She lost weight, she grew depressed, and then the video that Ivy posted—we didn't know about it until after Heather killed herself, but it was the reason, I'm certain of it."

"Which brings me to another question: who recorded the video?"

"I wish I knew. If it wasn't Ivy, that person is just as guilty as she was."

"Did your family try to track down any other victims of Ivy's abuse? In the civil suit, you'd indicated that you would bring additional witnesses and victims of Ivy's cyberbullying to support your case. But because of the settlement, none of those names were listed."

"I honestly don't know who."

"Would your parents?"

"Please don't." He rubbed his eyes. "They hired a private investigator, but I don't know how far he got before the settlement."

"Did you watch the 'Crime NET' segment last night?"

"No."

"You should."

"I told you, I don't care about Ivy, I don't care who killed her, I just want . . . hell, I don't know."

"Maybe if you watch, you'll understand what I'm trying to do." When Justin didn't respond, Max said, "I'd like to see the investigator's report."

"I don't know that we can share it—the terms of the settlement were very strict. The Wallaces paid a lot of money to keep that information private."

"Legally, if his report was never part of the civil suit to begin with, it wouldn't be covered under the settlement." Max had no idea if it was true—but it sounded good.

He hesitated. "I'll call my dad. It's the best I can do at this point. It's up to him. And all I ask is that you respect his decision."

She agreed. It was the best she was going to get.

CHAPTER TWENTY-FIVE

Driving back to Sausalito, Max used the rental car's Bluetooth system to talk to her staff and follow up with David on the calls the 'Crime NET' hotline received the night before. He had one in particular that he wanted her to listen to. She had just merged onto the Golden Gate Bridge when Detective Grace Martin called.

"Are you back?"

"Almost. What happened?"

"Travis Whitman is missing. The last time anyone saw him was yesterday morning. He left the house early to go running with a friend."

"And?"

"We talked to the kid, who said he had no plans to go running with Travis. Travis's phone is missing and it's off—we haven't been able to track the GPS. We put an APB out on his car. He didn't show up at school, but no one was suspicious until last night when he didn't come home. His father called this morning—they had a late night, and he had a message from the coach that Travis wasn't at practice or at school, wanted to make sure he wasn't sick."

"Did he bolt? I looked for him yesterday morning—but didn't find him. I wanted to get him on camera."

"If he reaches out to you, contact me immediately."

Max hung up and only a few minutes later arrived at the Madrona. David had brunch waiting for her in her suite where he was working. "How'd you know I was starving?" she asked.

"When you're hungry, you're even crabbier than usual."

She picked up a croissant and took a bite, then poured coffee. She told him about Travis Whitman.

"Maybe he got scared something would come out on the show," David said.

"Why leave before it was even cut? It makes no sense." She shook her head. "There's nothing I can do about him now. Let me listen to the call you flagged. And did you follow up with the neighbor of the Wallaces?"

An elderly neighbor of the Wallaces had called the hotline and insisted on talking only to Max.

"I set up a time this afternoon to talk," David said. "I don't know what she knows—she was emphatic that she wanted to talk to the 'no-nonsense redhead in charge.'"

"I like that—no-nonsense. It's way better than *bitch*."

David cracked a smile as he cued up the flagged call on his laptop. "Nothing else panned out, but New York is still weeding through calls. We had over a hundred—most were worthless—and a few more are coming in today."

"Hang ups?"

"Yes, they're running a report for you."

Max's ex, Marco Lopez, had told her about a case years ago where the killer had made contact through an anonymous tip line the FBI had running on one of Marco's cases. He called and hung up three times, each time staying on the phone a little longer, listening to what the operator was saying. By the time the fourth call came in, the operator had alerted Marco and he picked up the call and talked to the guy. At first, the guy said nothing, but Marco kept speaking. Eventually, the caller gloated about the murder, revealing details that hadn't been released to the public, thinking that the police couldn't track him. He didn't realize that an anonymous tip line wasn't truly anonymous—that the 800 number logged each caller's number. The killer had called from his cubicle at work. Because of Marco's case, Max always wanted a hang-up list.

"This call came in twenty minutes after the West Coast show aired," David said. "From San Rafael."

"Crime NET hotline, this is John Rutgers," the operator answered on the recording. On Thursday nights—the first airing of "Crime NET"—most of the operators who answered the hotline were retired law enforcement or trained counselors. The hotline received 90 percent of their calls within four hours of the first broadcast.

Max knew John well. He was sixty-two, a retired beat cop from the Bronx. He and Max didn't get along—he despised any and all reporters. Why he came in every Thursday to man the phones, Max didn't know—it couldn't be for the modest stipend the show paid—but he was one of the best they had. Every time she asked him anything about his career or his personal life, he'd only glare at her and stomp away. Ben told her to leave it alone, but being naturally curious, she couldn't. Max would get him to talk to her. Eventually, everyone did.

A female voice on the other end said something indistinct.

"Ma'am?" John said. "I didn't hear that."

"Is Maxine Revere there?" The voice was youthful—not a child, but a teenager or maybe a college student.

"I'm helping Ms. Revere answer the phones tonight. How can I help you?"

Silence.

John asked, "Are you calling about the 'Crime NET' show that just aired?"

"Yes," the girl's voice whispered.

"Would you like to tell me your name?"

In person, John was huge—six feet four, two hundred twenty pounds. But on the phone he didn't sound scary. He sounded like a kind but firm grandfather.

"Do I have to?"

"No, you don't. What would you like to tell Ms. Revere?"

"I really wanted to talk to her."

"I understand. I might be able to make that happen. I work with Ms. Revere and I can get her a message, and she may call you back. But she'll want to know what you want to talk about."

He was good. That's exactly what Max wanted the operators to say. No promises that she would call, but the assurance that it was a possibility. The more information the operator could elicit from the caller, the more efficiently they could separate the wheat from the chaff.

"I—I knew Ivy."

"How did you know her?"

"School."

"You were in her class?"

"No, she was a year older than me. And it was a long time ago."

"How long ago?"

"I changed schools. I had to."

"Why did you have to change schools?"

After a pause, the girl said, "Can you just tell Ms. Revere that I think whoever killed Ivy sent me a letter?"

John's voice took on a cop edge. "Do you know who killed Ivy?"

"No!" Too quickly? Or fast because she was surprised at the question? Or because she expected the question? "But—never mind. I'm reading too much into this. I just—"

"Honey," John said, his voice soft, "you called for a reason. Even if you don't think it's important, you must have a reason to think that Ivy's killer reached out to you. Do you believe that you're in danger?"

"Oh, no, nothing like that. I think—it was just—nothing. I'm reading too much into it. My dad says I overthink everything. I don't want to get anyone in trouble."

"You won't get anyone in trouble." Smartly, John changed the subject. It was easier to get someone to talk if you made them comfortable. "You said you knew Ivy in school. When was that?"

"When she moved to Marin. It was the middle of the year. She was a grade older than us."

"Were you friends?"

"No, no—she didn't like me. I stayed away from her. But—" She stopped.

"But what?"

"Look, I'm sorry I called. I shouldn't have. I don't know what I was thinking. It's stupid. I'm stupid. I gotta go."

Click.

Max jumped up. "Do we have her number?"

"Yes. It belongs to Stephen Cross in San Rafael."

"A parent?"

"Good guess. He has two daughters, Madison and Kristin. Single dad, wife died ten years ago."

"Is that when they moved?"

"I went through property records and Stephen and Anne Cross were married in San Francisco twenty-two years ago. They bought a house in Larkspur nineteen years ago. According to Anne's obituary, ten years ago her daughters were six and five."

"How did she die?"

"Car accident. Weather related—fog. Her daughters were in the car at the time, both in car seats in the back, and survived. Mom didn't."

What a tragedy. Were the girls too young to remember? Max remembered quite a bit from when she was five and six. Not everything, but sometimes she wished she could forget what she did remember.

"Madison or Kristen . . . one or both of them knew Ivy. When did they move to San Rafael?"

"The summer before Ivy was killed," David said. "At least, that's when Stephen Cross purchased the house in San Rafael and sold his house in Larkspur."

Max strode over to her timeline. Ivy moved to Corte Madera nine years ago . . . that put her in fourth grade, as Bailey had said. Under that year, Max made a note: *Cross*. Then two years back from today—the summer before Ivy's murder—she wrote *Cross moved*.

The girl had said they had to move. Why? Family? Or Ivy?

Heather Brock changed schools at the beginning of her sophomore year in an effort to stop the cyberbullying.

Bailey Fairstein changed schools after Heather's suicide to get away from Ivy and her shenanigans.

Rick Colangelo moved out of state after he was outed by Ivy.

Max turned to David. "Did you ever talk to Colangelo?"

David nodded. "Spoke to him last night. Straightforward. Rick and Travis had been friends since early childhood, and Travis was one of the few people who knew that Rick was bisexual. Rick was blunt—he said he'd experimented as a freshman, started liking guys. Travis picked up on it, said he'd keep it secret."

"This is twenty-first-century California. You'd think being gay or straight wouldn't be a big deal to most people."

David shook his head. "It's a double standard, Max. Gay athletes usually keep quiet. Same with the military. Don't ask, don't tell. Sometimes it's better that way. It's not perfect but, dammit, we just want to do the job and not have our personal shit get in the way." He pinched the bridge of his nose. "I understood where Rick was coming from. He was furious with Travis because he'd betrayed that trust by outing him to the school's biggest gossip—his words. When Ivy posted the information, he said most people were cool, but a few big mouths created problems for him. He wanted a clean start so went to live with his grandparents. Seems to have his life in order. A hell of a lot better order than I did as a high school senior. He visited his parents this summer and Travis reached out. Rick said he forgave him, but had no desire to be friends again. He hasn't spoken to Travis since."

"You believe him." It was clear to Max that David took what the kid said at face value.

"I didn't ask if he killed Ivy, but unless he lied about being in town that weekend, he couldn't have."

Maxine mentally checked Rick Colangelo off her suspect list, pending confirmation of his alibi. Grace Martin might have already done so.

"I can see why Rick's parents let him move away," Max said. "Changing schools like Bailey and Heather did to get away from Ivy would be relatively easy. But the Crosses moved lock, stock, and barrel out of town. The family—both families, the Crosses and the Wallaces—must have known *something* about why. A kid can't just go to their parents and say, 'Hey, quit your job let's move out of town.'" She turned to David. "I need to talk to the Cross girls."

"They're minors. We'll contact the dad first."

David was right, especially in light of the fallout from her quoting Austin—which she still believed was right.

"Okay, but if he says no, I'm going to track them down anyway."

"Of course you are. But we're going to try it this way first."

Max looked at her timeline. "Madison is a year younger than Ivy, Kristin two years younger. Either of them could have been the caller—they're now fifteen and sixteen. Knew Ivy, didn't like her—sounded scared of her almost." She frowned. "No, that's not right. She said Ivy didn't like her and she didn't know why. Do you think the killer really contacted her?" As she said it, Max shook her head. "This girl thinks that Ivy's killer contacted her, but she didn't sound threatened. There's a reason for that. We need that letter. She didn't pull the idea out of thin air. Maybe she hadn't thought about it at all—until she saw the show."

David nodded. "Something she heard or saw sparked her memory. Or reminded her of the letter."

Max glanced at her watch. It was already well after the lunch hour. "I want to talk to her today."

"Stephen Cross teaches math at a private high school in San Rafael. I'll call the school first. If he doesn't call me back, I'll call his cell phone."

"You tracked down all that information today?"

David just cracked a smile. "As soon as John flagged the call."

"This girl knows something." Max stared again at her board. "Austin might know about her. Or Tommy. Or Bailey Fairstein."

"How did the conversation with Brock go?"

"Better than I thought. With the change in time of death, if Laura Lorenzo is telling the truth, then he's not the killer. And after meeting him, I don't think he did it. He's a grieving brother who is worried about his mother and how Heather's suicide affected her. Justin also told me that his parents hired a private investigator who was let go when they settled. He was gathering information about other people Ivy bullied in order to bolster the civil case."

"And you have those names."

"Not yet. He's going to talk to his father."

"And where does Lorenzo fit in all this?"

"To convince the public that Ivy's murder was an accident to protect Justin."

"Because he thinks Justin killed her?"

"Maybe Lorenzo knows something, maybe he doesn't. Or what he thinks he knows isn't accurate. The guy is an ass, and he high-jumps to conclusions. He thinks Justin snapped and to Lorenzo it's justifiable, but Justin would lose his scholarship, lose a future as a lawyer, lose his girlfriend and his freedom. So Lorenzo, in his own way, was trying to protect him."

David raised an eyebrow.

"He's playing with fire, and he's wrong, and he lied about me and to me. He's not getting away with it. But I have my own way of dealing with him now."

"We can't assume that Lorenzo's sole motivation was to protect Justin because he thinks Justin killed Ivy."

"I'm certain that's not the only reason. I suspect he has an ax to grind with the police, though whether it's simply because of his own authority issues or if it's specific to this department, I don't know. Send me the photo you have with him at the bar and with the cop. I'm going to give them to Grace."

"They're already on your phone."

"You're so good." She smiled and forwarded both photos to Grace. No caption required on the first of Lorenzo chatting with the cop; on the second she added, *Do you know this man?*

It may have nothing to do with the Ivy Lake investigation, but Max wasn't going to take any chances.

Austin had PE right after his lunch break. He changed into his gym uniform and was there for roll call, then said he needed a bathroom pass. His PE teacher barely remembered his name, wrote out the pass, and Austin headed for the gym. He went through the gym and out the back doors, then ran across the soccer field toward the high school. The high school was about to start their lunch break. Austin crossed over to the trailers where Tommy's classes met.

Tommy could have gone to the regular school, but Jenny coddled him. She thought it would be too hard for Tommy to compete with the other kids. She didn't get that Tommy would do better if more was expected from him. Sure, he had problems with reading—he got the letters confused—but he was great at math and his special ed classes bored him. He wouldn't say anything about it, because that was Tommy. He was just happy to be at school at all.

Austin walked into the special ed office. He flashed the bathroom pass to the secretary who was on the phone, then quickly pocketed it. "My brother accidentally put my essay in his binder when we were doing homework last night. Can I get it from him?"

She nodded, still listening to whoever was talking.

Austin didn't wait, and went down the row of trailers to where he knew Tommy was about to get out for his lunch break.

Tommy's teacher opened the door for her students to

exit the classroom and head for lunch. She was surprised to see Austin standing there. "Austin? Do you need something?"

"Tommy has my homework in his backpack."

"Oh—go ahead, then send Tommy to the lunch tables, okay?"

Austin nodded and pulled Tommy back into the trailer classroom.

Tommy's eyes were wide. "You can't be here. I'll get in trouble."

Austin made sure no one heard him. "That restraining order is bullshit, Tommy."

Tommy frowned. "You lied to my teacher. I don't have your homework. We didn't do homework together yesterday."

"I had to talk to you. I'm going to find a way to fix this. Please, Tommy—I know it's hard, but we need to stick together. You're my big brother."

Tommy looked so sad that Austin wanted to scream. "I don't want to go to jail."

"Who said that?" Austin asked, angry.

"My mom said if I go near you or Bella, I will go to jail. I want to see you, Austin, but I don't want to go to jail."

"First, the restraining order hasn't been filed yet. That means that no one has signed anything, okay? I won't let her. I swear to God, Tommy, I will not let her do anything. I'm sure your dad won't let her, either. She's just mad that she didn't get her way."

"Like when Bella threw her new Barbie across the room because it was the wrong Barbie?"

"Yeah." Austin adored his little sister, but she could be a brat. He took a deep breath. "It's my fault, Tommy. Everything is my fault. Ivy left the house that night because of me."

"I don't get what you mean."

"We got in a fight. Like always. She said she'd make me pay. I shouldn't have—"

The teacher stepped inside. "Tommy? Austin? Can this wait until you boys get home this afternoon?".

No, Austin wanted to say. He wanted Tommy to cut school so he could tell him everything about the night Ivy died. But Tommy would never break the rules.

"Yeah," Austin said. He wanted to hug Tommy because he looked so miserable, but that would make both of them look like dweebs, and the other kids would make fun of Tommy.

Austin almost cut class, but didn't. Cutting class would put him on the radar, and right now he wanted to avoid his mother at all costs. He hated her. He went back to his class but didn't hear anything his teachers said the rest of the day. As soon as the final bell rang, he grabbed his backpack and, without even waiting for Emma, ran to the park, hoping Tommy would be there. Wanting to explain that he would fix it, he'd make sure his mom never filed the restraining order, that they could be brothers again.

But Tommy wasn't there.

CHAPTER TWENTY-SIX

Max waited in the park across from the high school for Tommy Wallace. Though his memory wasn't as sharp as Austin's, he might remember who Madison and Kristen Cross were. If not, she wouldn't have to wait long for Austin.

She sent him a text message that she hoped he'd see when his class was over. She wished she'd had the chance to talk to him after the broadcast aired last night, to answer any questions he might have. There were too many things on her plate as it was, why had she thought she could escape for a few hours and have a romp with Nick? Especially when the only thing positive had been the sex. He hadn't talked to her about anything personal, and while he was a good sounding board for her investigation, she had gone there to connect with Nick, not work the case.

Her life was becoming overcomplicated. And it had never been uncomplicated.

While she waited for Tommy to get out of school, instead of working on her phone, she sat on the bench and enjoyed the warm, breezy day. Ten minutes to relax. Ten minutes to not think about Ivy, or Nick, or Paula's threats, or Justin Brock's pain. Not think about dirtbag Lance Lorenzo and what he might be up to, or where Travis Whitman had gone, or her guilt that she might not be able to solve this case and Tommy would remain ostracized.

And that got her thinking about Bill Wallace. So much for relaxation.

Ben said Wallace was coming back from his business trip early. How early? She sent David a text.

I need everything we have on Bill Wallace.

Max knew she shouldn't get in the middle of this triangle, but when had she ever done the easy thing? Why hadn't *someone* stepped up and told Bill Wallace that his indifference was hurting his own children?

She thought back to what David had said about Jenny Wallace, and how she was critical of her ex-husband around her kids. What would Max have done in the same situation? But of course she'd never be in that situation. Married, two kids, career, Jenny's husband cheating on her—lying to her—then moving his new family to within miles of his old family. And then still keeping his distance from his kids by traveling constantly on business. Did he have yet another girlfriend in the wings? Max wouldn't be surprised.

Because of his build and shaggy blond hair, Tommy was easy to pick out. He walked his bicycle across the street. At first Max didn't notice anything wrong, but as he approached she realized he was upset. His face was flushed, his eyes bright and wet.

She rose from the bench and strode over to him. "Tommy, what happened?"

"I don't want to talk about it." He carefully put the kickstand down on his bike and made sure it wouldn't fall before he sat down on the bench. He didn't take off his backpack, but perched on the edge and stared straight ahead.

She sat next to him. "Someone upset you."

He shrugged and wiped his nose with the sleeve of his blue hoodie. "I have to be home by four."

"Tommy, was it about the show last night?"

"Was what about the show?"

"What got you upset. I never meant for anything I said on the show to hurt you."

"You didn't do anything. You're nice. You want to find out who killed Ivy."

"Yes, I do."

"Why's it taking so long?"

If it were anyone else, Max would have snapped that she'd been here less than a week and she already had leads the police never had. Instead she said, "Some crimes take longer to solve than others."

That didn't make Tommy happy.

Max said, "My best friend was killed when we were in high school. It took thirteen years before her killer was brought to justice." Justice? Was living life in a mental hospital for the criminally insane justice? Perhaps, considering who was locked up, it was a twisted, ironic punishment.

"In thirteen years, Bella will be in college."

"You're good at math."

"It's my best subject. I always get an A in math."

"What other subjects do you like?"

He shrugged. "I like science class. Not history. I can't keep all those dates in my head or remember what happened first."

"What do you like about science?"

"My teacher said that for everything that happens there is an equal and opposite reaction. I didn't understand that at first, but then we went on a field trip to the aquarium and watched fish swim and my teacher explained that the fish is pushing the water and the water is pushing the fish with the exact same force! We watched and watched—I could have stayed at the aquarium all night. I have a gold-fish and I like him okay, but it's not the same thing as the aquarium."

"I have a couple of questions, do you mind if I ask you?"

He shrugged. "I have to be home at four."

"I won't keep you that long. Do you know Madison or Kristin Cross? They moved away two years ago."

He nodded and smiled. "Maddie is Amanda's best friend. They have matching Mickey Mouse necklaces. Amanda's says Madison, and Madison's says Amanda. They got them when they were twelve and Madison's dad took Amanda with them to Disneyland. I wanted to go, but it was girls only. I went to Disneyland once when my dad was still married to my mom. I was eight and Amanda was six. I didn't like Mr. Toad's Wild Ride. I cried and Amanda cried because she thought we'd have to go home because I was crying, but then Dad took me on the train and that was my favorite. We went on the train six times, all around the park."

"I was eight when I went to Disneyland, too," Max said. It was Disney World in Florida, and her mother had left her there for the day. Her mother hadn't wanted to go—she had plans with friends to go sailing—and Max had begged her to take her to Disney World. Instead, Martha bought tickets for both of them, walked her into the park, and gave her two hundred dollars. She told her to have fun; she'd pick her up at midnight when the park closed.

Max tried to have fun. At first, she did because it was so new and exciting. The food smelled great, Disney characters were everywhere and she shook their hands. She went on every ride, some of them twice. But everywhere there were families. Parents with kids. Kids with friends.

Grandparents and grandchildren. Young couples. Parents taking pictures of their kids with Mickey Mouse or Goofy or Daisy Duck. Max paid a park photographer to take a picture of her with Chip and Dale, the two chipmunks. She'd given it to her mother and never saw it again.

Max had never felt so alone. To be surrounded by thousands of people and feel like the loneliest person in the world. . . .

She hadn't thought about the first ten years of her life until the psycho shrink got into her head three months ago. Now she thought about the past too much.

She had to get over this. It was tearing her up. It's why she couldn't sleep. It's why she was drinking too much. If she didn't find a way to forget, she'd implode. David was right. She was losing her edge. He hadn't said that, but he'd thought it.

"Ms. Revere?" Tommy said. "Are you okay?"

"I liked the train," she said, "but my favorite ride was the Pirates of the Caribbean."

"My mom thought it would scare me so my dad took Amanda on it and my mom took me on the train again."

"It's a dark ride."

"I'm not scared of the dark. I have a night-light, but that's just so I don't trip if I have to get up in the middle of the night to use the bathroom. I didn't like how we went through Hell in Mr. Toad's Wild Ride and it got all hot and the mean bully was hurting Mr. Toad."

"That sounds scary."

Tommy nodded and looked at his hands.

She asked, "Are Amanda and Madison still friends?"

"I guess so," Tommy said. "But Maddie moved away. Why?"

"Sometimes when people move away, they don't really talk anymore."

Tommy thought on that. "Amanda talks to her a lot.

I've heard her sometimes in her room, talking on the phone. Does that count?"

"Yes, of course it does. That helps a lot."

"Why do you want to know about Maddie?"

Max didn't want to lie to Tommy, but she doubted he would be able to keep the information to himself. "Part of being a reporter is research. Not only do I need to look at Ivy's life—her friends, her classmates, her teachers, her family—but I look at the same things for everyone close to her. Someone said that Maddie's family might have moved because of something Ivy said or did to her. I'm trying to find out if that is true."

Tommy nodded solemnly. "It's true."

"What do you remember?"

"I—I don't really know. It was a long time ago, and Amanda doesn't talk to me like that. But Amanda cried a lot when Maddie moved, and she blamed Ivy, I don't know why. When Amanda cries, it makes me sad."

Suddenly, Tommy jumped up. He looked at his watch. "I have to go."

"Aren't you waiting for Austin?"

He suddenly started crying and shook his head. "M-m-my mom s-said I can't. Austin's mom got so mad at him last night. H-he's grounded a-a-and Paula said I can go to jail if I talk to him."

Max's heart sank. "Tommy, you will not go to jail."

"Y-yes! It's a *straining* order. M-mom explained it to me. Paula is getting one so I can't see Austin or Bella ever again. It's legal. My dad is a lawyer. I gotta go, I gotta get out of here before Austin gets out of school so I don't go to jail."

He pedaled away.

Max wanted to throttle Paula Wallace.

David called her.

"What?" Max snapped.

He cleared his throat. She rubbed her eyes and mumbled, "Sorry."

"I just got off the phone with Stephen Cross. He agreed to meet with us tomorrow morning, but I should warn you, he has a lot of anger built up over what happened between Ivy and his daughter."

"What exactly did happen?"

"He didn't want to say over the phone—however, he commented that he'd spoken to the Wallaces twice about Ivy's behavior and that he'd been contacted by the Brock family regarding their lawsuit."

"Where are you?"

"The hotel."

"I want to talk to Amanda Wallace tonight—I don't want to go into the conversation with Stephen Cross blind and she's friends with one of his kids. Is Madison going to be there?"

"Cross wants to talk to us first, then he'll decide if he'll let his daughter talk to us."

"I really need your help on this one—you're a dad. You have a daughter. I just see Madison as a fount of information. I don't see the big picture."

"Where is this coming from?"

"I've screwed up, David. I should never have come to Corte Madera."

"That's not true."

"I've made a bad situation worse. Now I have no choice other than to find the truth. And even then . . . I don't know that the truth is going to help anyone." She couldn't believe she'd just said that. The truth was *always* better than lies.

Except this time, would Paula Wallace even care about the truth? Would she change her opinion about Tommy or would she still keep her children away from him?

"Meet me at the bookstore and we'll go together to the

Wallaces' neighbor's house," Max said. "And then we're going to talk to Mr. and Mrs. Bill Wallace."

"Sounds to me like this won't be a friendly conversation," David said.

She ignored his comment. There was a pattern—parents complained to Ivy's parents about her behavior, yet the behavior didn't change. Ivy was old enough to be responsible for her own misbehavior, but the parents had known. Had they even tried to stop her? Try to get her counseling? Take away her phone? Her computer? Ground her? Toss her in a dungeon? Maybe that's what it would have taken to knock sense into that kid. Max actually understood Ivy and her motives. She craved attention, any kind of attention. Her popular blog convinced her that *she* was popular. Her thousands of followers on Twitter and Instagram fed into that belief.

It must have been difficult, as a teenager, to see the numbers and believe you were popular, yet have no real friends. Ivy was smart, she must have sensed that disparity. And then what did she do? Pile on more shit for the gossip mill? Was she confused? Frustrated? Lonely? To have all those cyberfriends and to feel like the most isolated person in town. She hadn't made the connection. Would she have, had she lived?

They would never know.

What else did Ivy's parents know that they hadn't told the police? Because they hadn't told Grace Martin about Stephen Cross or any of the other people who spoke to them about Ivy. While the fact that Stephen moved his family out of the area might take them out of the suspect pool, the Wallaces should have informed the police about everyone and everything in Ivy's life. But then, as far as Paula Wallace was concerned, Ivy was an average teenager who didn't do anything that any other teenager wouldn't have done.

And now the situation between Tommy and Austin had gone from bad to worse. Before Max came to town, at least they could see each other—even if Austin had to defy his mother to do it. Now Paula was making it a legal matter.

It wasn't right.

"Thirty minutes, David. Thanks." Max hung up and got out of the neighborhood before the junior high students left the building.

CHAPTER TWENTY-SEVEN

Based on the recording of Mrs. Dorothy Baker, both David and Max had first assumed that when she said she was a neighbor of the Wallaces that meant she was a neighbor to Paula and Bill Wallace, who lived closer to town. But Dorothy Baker lived down the street from Jenny Wallace, Bill's ex-wife.

She was in her eighties and petite. Two dogs greeted Max and David as Mrs. Baker opened the door—Pomeranians, which matched Mrs. Baker in both size and temperament. They barked nonstop; one growled.

Mrs. Baker glared at David through narrowed eyes. "Becky and Cassie don't like men."

As if being a man was David's fault.

"Come in, come in, I can't be chasing these girls down the block at my age."

They walked into the foyer and Mrs. Baker closed the door behind them.

"Mrs. Baker, you have a lovely view—maybe if we sit out on the deck?" Max suggested.

She turned to Max and looked up at her. "You're taller than you look on television." Her tone suggested that Max had been deceptive.

"I'm five foot ten."

Mrs. Baker looked at her feet. "Then why do you wear heels? Landsakes, you must be over six feet tall in those shoes!"

Max liked being tall, except when she wanted to go undercover. Height, especially on a woman, stood out. She squatted and put her hand out for the dogs to sniff. One ran down the hall, turned around and continued barking. The other sniffed, turned around in three circles, and licked Max's hand.

Mrs. Baker nodded sharply, as if Max had passed some sort of test, but with a suspicious expression that maybe she'd cheated. "This way," she motioned toward the sliding-glass doors.

The house was decorated in old lady clutter—antique furniture, plastic on couches, doilies on every surface. Glass-enclosed cabinets filled every available wall space, their insides crammed full with every possible knick-knack.

Mrs. Baker told them to sit, then she left them and went back into the house.

"I should have come here alone," Max said.

"We shouldn't have come here at all," said David. "You're a total softie, Max."

"Me?"

"Little old lady wants to meet you, you rush out and meet her. Not that you don't have a dozen other things you need to be doing."

"I want to talk to Amanda anyway, about her friend Madison. We're not that far. In ten minutes, get me out of here."

"If I can survive ten minutes with that barking."

"They're annoying, but they're cute."

"A golden retriever is cute. Those things are fluffy rats. Rats aren't cute."

Max almost laughed, then Mrs. Baker emerged from the kitchen with a tray of cookies and tea.

Max didn't want anything, but she didn't want to be rude. Too often, families neglected their elderly relatives, and all they wanted was a little company. When she'd been undercover at a senior care facility in Miami—the year before she started "Maximum Exposure," when she could still go undercover—she'd learned that many children and grandchildren left their elderly parents in a home and rarely, if ever, came to visit them.

David stood to help, but Mrs. Baker told him to sit back down. She took her sweet time pouring hot tea and, with shaking hands, passed cups and saucers to David and Max.

Finally, she sat. Max sipped, then put the tea down.

"Mrs. Baker, thank you for your hospitality. We have another meeting this afternoon, so I was hoping you could share with us why you called the hotline last night."

"Right to it, aren't you? But that's the way you are on your show. I thought that was an act. Guess not." She sipped her tea. "I watch the NET shows on Thursday and Monday—your show and Ace's shows. I like Ace Burley, he has a good voice."

"Yes, he does," Max said, restraining from saying anything negative about her coworker. She didn't hate Ace, but he could be extremely difficult.

So can you, Maxine.

"And watching your show, I remembered that night the retarded fellow tromped through my yard again."

"The night of July third?"

"Yes."

"You can remember the exact day fourteen months later?" Max asked.

"I may be eighty-three, but my memory is intact."

"Yes, ma'am."

"This wasn't the first time. His mother had to put alarms on their house because of his sleepwalking."

Sleepwalking?

"Tommy Wallace sleepwalks?"

"Has since he was a little boy. Nearly got himself killed once or twice. Before they got the alarms, his mother found him sitting at the bus stop at the corner three times in the middle of the night. All ready for school, but in a daze. He's not right in the head, that boy."

"The bus stop? Doesn't he ride his bike to school?"

"This was a while ago, when he went to a special school for those kids, before high school. The high school has a special education program, I've heard. My granddaughter is the girl's PE teacher, she told me about it."

Max bristled. She didn't like that she hadn't known about the sleepwalking, but she also didn't like the way Dorothy spoke about Tommy.

"When was the last time you heard him in your yard?" Max asked.

"I saw him. Last month. It was midnight. I couldn't sleep. I was sitting at the kitchen table playing solitaire. Saw him clear as day walk across the front yard, like Frankenstein."

Max resisted the urge to correct Dorothy that Frankenstein was the doctor, not the monster he created.

"I called Jenny right away. Told her her alarm didn't work, her boy was out wandering again. He did it as a little boy, then it stopped. Jenny explained it all to me one day in the garden, so I paid it no mind. Then it started up again when his father left poor Jenny for that Seattle floozy." She harrumphed clearly, looking thoroughly disgusted. "Jenny said the sleepwalking was stress-related and the doctor said it would stop on its own like it did when he was six, but it hasn't. That alarm is so loud it wakes me up! Anyway, I think most nights she forgets to set it. She's one of those people who forgets everything. She'd forget her head it if weren't attached to her body. I may be turning eighty-four next month, but I don't forget anything. Prunes. My papa ate prunes every morning, lived to one hundred and two, his mind all there. I plan on doing the same."

"In your call last night, you said you had information related to Ivy Lake's murder."

"Well, I just told you! That boy is out at all times of the day or night. When I was a girl, people like Tommy Wallace were put in institutions so they wouldn't be a danger to themselves or others."

Max had just about had it with the woman. "Mrs. Baker, I think you're—"

David cleared his throat. "Ma'am, you said you saw Tommy out the night of July third last year?"

"Yes." She glanced at Max, her mouth in a tight line. "I heard him."

"You recognized his voice?" Max said through clenched teeth.

"The dogs were barking. In the middle of the night! It was after one o'clock in the morning. Woke me up and I couldn't get back to sleep. I went to the kitchen to warm some tea and heard his bike. His old bike—he got a new one for Christmas, I believe. His old bike made this go-dawful sound when he shifted gears. A *clunk-clunk* sound."

"Are you suggesting that Tommy, a sleepwalker, was riding his bike in his sleep?"

"Stranger things have happened. But he was out and about that night, the night his stepsister died, and everyone knows that boy isn't right in the head." She leaned forward conspiratorially. "My bridge partner Meredith Moore told me Paula Wallace thinks he killed her daughter, but the police won't do anything about it. Political correctness and all that. And I know for a fact that she won't let him in the house unless her husband is there, and he's traveling on business half the year. No wonder those kids are all over town doing God knows what. They need a firm hand, and they don't have one in Bill Wallace. Tommy and his stepbrother. That kid is even worse that Tommy. At least Tommy has an excuse, being retarded and all. But that kid—Adam. Andrew? No, no . . . whatever his name is. The one with the skateboard, sneaking around all the time. He doesn't even go to Jenny's front door. Hides his bike in the bushes and jumps her back fence all the time. I can see from my sewing room upstairs, clear as day. Why don't his parents do something about him? I know he trampled my flower beds last spring."

Max was glad that David had prevented her from verbally assaulting Dorothy Baker. She had always liked the elderly—they had lived history. They deserved respect and appreciation, even this old biddy who reminded her of Miss Gulch in *The Wizard of Oz*.

Old or not, Max did not like this woman.

It was all she could do to say goodbye and thank you.

"Last year, you would have given her a tongue-lashing," David said when they were in the car.

"It wouldn't have done us any good."

"She knows some truths."

"About Paula Wallace? She hasn't kept quiet about her opinion on her stepson Tommy."

"Ask his mother about the sleepwalking," said David.

"Do you actually believe it's possible Tommy killed Ivy in his sleep?"

"I don't know."

David didn't have to say anything else. If Tommy was prone to leaving the house, sleepwalking or not, his mother may not have always known when he did it. Or she may be covering for him. Jenny Wallace was over-protective of her son, and it wouldn't be the first time that Max had encountered a mother who lied to protect her child.

"Tommy is not a killer," Max said.

"It could have been an accident."

"Tommy wouldn't have been able to lie about it," Max said. "I haven't met many people incapable of lying, but Tommy cannot lie. If he killed Ivy, he'd have confessed."

"We don't know a lot about his condition," David said. "Maybe he doesn't remember."

"Oh, please."

"I never thought I'd say this, Max, but you've grown too attached to a suspect. You're not objective."

"My feelings about Tommy are irrelevant," she said. "I know he's innocent. The evidence at this point doesn't support it, and nothing he has said or done has made me think he's lied about anything. Mrs. Baker said one in the morning. We know Ivy was killed two hours before that."

"She said he was returning after one in the morning. On a bike. He might not know what he did."

"Then there would have been evidence. He's not a criminal mastermind. Kill Ivy at eleven, hang around her dead body for two hours, send a tweet using words and phrases Ivy used, then return home?" She shook her head. "No."

"He has a protective mother who may have destroyed evidence. A knife. Dirty clothes."

"I can't believe you are saying this."

"And I'm just as surprised you aren't considering it."

Why was she so upset? Max had no stake in this case. All she wanted was to identify whoever killed Ivy Lake.

Except . . . she wanted the truth because of Tommy. She wanted Tommy to have a normal life, as normal as possible considering his challenges and his dysfunctional family.

"I would be more apt to believe that Austin killed his sister than Tommy," she said. "He's a smart kid. Cunning. But he has no real motive, and he was twelve at the time. While a twelve-year-old can kill . . . I don't see him bringing me in to investigate if he's the killer. It was his idea."

"It was Emma's idea," David corrected. "And Austin may not have expected Tommy to be accused. Maybe he didn't see the potential ramifications. Ivy hurt Tommy, Austin hurt Ivy. Austin was the last person to see her alive. And based on the new timeline, she died less than an hour after he said she left the house."

"Just because I'm more inclined to believe Austin could do it doesn't mean I think he did."

"What are you going to do now?"

"Talk to Amanda about Madison Cross, just like we'd planned." Max paused. "And we'll have a conversation with Jenny Wallace about Tommy's sleepwalking. Ask to look at their security system." But she didn't think Jenny would let them.

"Max, you can walk away," David said.

"I've never walked away from an investigation. I'm not going to start now. The truth may be inconvenient, but it's better than anything else. And that's all I can do."

Max and David drove the block up the hill to Jenny Wallace's house. It was five in the evening, and Max was surprised to find Jenny home. She had hoped she wouldn't be.

Jenny smiled at them, but her eyes were rimmed in red. "Come in," she said. "Can I get you anything?"

"No, thank you," Max said. "Do you have a few minutes?"

She nodded and closed the door behind them. They sat in the living room.

"Are you okay?" David asked. "You look upset."

"I am. I'm sorry." She squeezed her eyes shut and took a deep breath. "It's Paula. She's furious about the show last night. When I saw it, I thought it turned out so well—you showed Tommy as I see him, as a sweet, loving young man. You've been so kind to him, Ms. Revere. You listen to him. So many people don't listen to kids like Tommy. Explaining all this to him has been . . . challenging."

"I saw Tommy after school today," Max said. "He told me about the restraining order."

Fresh tears slid down her cheeks. "Paula called me last night and we argued. She said she was getting a restraining order. I didn't believe her, but then she called me this morning at work and said Bill had agreed. I-I— It took me hours to reach him. We're going to sit down with our lawyers on Monday and work it out. We have to work it out, for Tommy's sake. Bill just can't allow this to happen. He told me he didn't agree to the restraining order, Paula told him about it on the phone just before he boarded a plane in New York. She lied to me because she didn't think I'd be able to reach him."

"I'm glad you're going to talk," Max said.

"I don't know what to do—I thought the show went well. I didn't know Ivy, but I was heartbroken when she died. Any mother would be. I went to Paula, but . . ." Her voice trailed off. "That was last year. And now, with someone like you taking an interest, I really thought it would mend fences. And for her to be so angry with me, with Tommy, with Austin. I don't understand how she could possibly think Tommy would ever hurt anyone, especially a girl he considered his sister. No matter what she did, Tommy loved Ivy because she was his family."

"I'm culpable," Max said. "The situation with your ex-husband's wife is partly my fault for continuing this investigation."

"I don't know why Paula is so upset," Jenny said. "You showed Ivy in a much better light than most. Anyway, the really rotten thing is that Austin is good for Tommy. And honestly? Austin is a nicer kid when he's around my son."

David said, "She may be more upset that Austin broke the rules than about what he was actually doing."

Max disagreed, but didn't say it. "I hoped I could speak to Amanda."

"Why?"

"Some of the leads we received on the hotline related to other people who were bullied by Ivy. One of them was Madison Cross, a friend of Amanda's."

"Maddie—she moved away two years ago, before high school. Her father got a job teaching in San Rafael." Jenny looked from Max to David, then back to Max. "What does that have to do with Ivy?"

"Were you aware that Madison had been bullied by Ivy? That the family moved away because of her?"

Jenny shook her head, her eyes wide. "Amanda has never particularly liked Ivy, but I didn't know why. Other than the obvious."

"Obvious?"

"Amanda has expressed concern that her father spends more time with his stepdaughter than his own daughter. I tried to explain it to Bill, but he doesn't look at things the same way. That he's living in the house with his new family doesn't apparently *count* in the time he spends with his new family—only the things he does outside of the house. And he keeps a log of the hours he spends doing things with Tommy and Amanda."

"Without realizing," David said, "that it's the home life that Amanda is missing."

"Exactly." Jenny was pleased David understood. "Amanda is sixteen now, she's adapted like most children of divorce do. It was harder when she was younger."

"May we speak to her about Madison? I'd like to find out specifics on the incident that had the Cross family moving."

"How will that help find who killed Ivy?"

"I don't know, but it's one more piece to the puzzle." Max didn't want to tell her about the call or the letter Madison claimed came from Ivy's killer. "The more we know about how Ivy operated helps us retrace her steps the day she died." That sounded lame, but Jenny nodded as if she understood.

"She's in her room studying," Jenny said. "I'll get her."

She left, and David turned to Max. "I'll talk to Amanda alone."

"Okay," Max said.

"No argument?"

"You built a rapport with her the other day. She responded to you. I'll check on Tommy, see how he's doing." Max paused. "In his letter, Tommy wrote that his sister thought Ivy's best friend killed her. Maybe you can find out if she meant Bailey or someone else."

Max waited until Jenny came out with Amanda.

The girl looked both curious and a little scared. "You want to know about Maddie? Why?"

Max said, "We're putting together a timeline of everyone Ivy may have embarrassed or hurt with her social media postings. Madison's name came up."

"That was so long ago."

"It seems that way," Max said, "but she moved only a few months before Heather Brock committed suicide. It might be connected. And it might not—but until we can piece together Ivy's life before she died, we won't be able to solve the case." Max glanced at her watch. "Jenny, would you mind if David talks to Amanda? I want to see Tommy before we have to leave."

"Of course," Jenny said. "He's in the den watching his favorite movie. He was so confused about the restraining order today, I needed to distract him."

Max left with Jenny, and David turned to Amanda. "How are you holding up?"

She shrugged. "Fine. Why wouldn't I be?"

"You were on television last night. Sometimes at school things can get weird."

Again, the shrug. David didn't like when Emma shrugged her answers, it seemed elusive to him, like she was holding back. But Amanda had a lot she was holding back. He'd only caught a glimpse of it before.

"Sit down," he said.

She sat. He hadn't meant for it to come out as an order, but his voice was naturally commanding.

"Your mom told you we want to talk about Madison— it's important, Amanda."

"Why?"

"I'll tell you something that isn't public information. But you need to keep this between us."

She nodded and leaned forward.

"Madison called the 'Crime NET' hotline last night. She didn't say much, except that Ivy was the reason she left Corte Madera."

Amanda's eyes widened. "She called? She saw the show?"

David nodded. "She wouldn't say why she left. But I think you know."

"That was forever ago."

David waited. He could see that Amanda was thinking—maybe she didn't want to share Madison's secret.

"Is it true that the police took down everything that Ivy wrote on the Internet?" she asked.

"They removed her social media profiles and archived the information. That's important in case there's a trial down the road. It's not easy to find, but everything that's been posted online is still out there somewhere. And the police have the original archive. Our tech people at NET are working on rebuilding her profile for Maxine's story."

"Story? I thought that's what you did last night."

"She's looking at a bigger story, instances where social media was used to facilitate a crime. Meaning, it was one of the reasons behind a crime. Cyberbullying is only one part—people hurting other people online, usually because it's anonymous."

"Ivy was never anonymous," Amanda said. "She seemed proud of what she was doing."

"I've seen that in what I've put together. And Madison?"

Amanda frowned. She didn't want to talk about it. David was about to push when she said, "Maddie moved two years ago, right before we were going to start high school. I've barely talked to her since. Her dad doesn't let her go on social media, so I can't keep in touch. She has an e-mail, but rarely checks it. Last summer we got together for a weekend, but . . ." her voice trailed off.

"Things weren't the same."

"Yeah."

"What did Ivy say or do that was so awful that Madison had to leave town?"

It took Amanda a good two minutes of David remaining silent—and her fidgeting—before she said, "Maddie used to cut herself. Ivy found out when she caught her in the bathroom at school. Ivy was in eighth grade, we were in seventh. Ivy told everyone. At first, I didn't think it was all that bad, because I knew what Maddie was doing, and

I didn't know how to make her stop, and I didn't want to go to her dad, you know? Unless it got really bad. That would be like betraying your best friend. Maddie worked so hard to stop, and she did for a while, but then when Ivy went to high school and we thought she was done tormenting us, we went to a football game—and someone said something to Maddie. And she was horrified. That's when she discovered that Ivy was still talking about her online."

"Ivy was talking about what?"

"That Maddie was seeing a psychiatrist. She didn't actually say Maddie, but she put in enough information that people who knew her even a little bit knew the post was about Maddie. Like, how many people have a mother who died in a car crash when they were little whose dad is also a teacher at the high school?" She rolled her eyes in frustration—there was pain and anger there. "People are mean, Mr. Kane. They teased Maddie about it. Her dad was worried about her because she started cutting again, so they moved, he said, to get her out of the 'toxic environment.'" Amanda frowned.

"And?"

"And that's it."

"That's not it, Amanda. You said that Ivy was tormenting 'us,' meaning both you and Maddie."

"I didn't."

"You did."

She fidgeted. "I guess—I don't know. I feel like it's my fault that Maddie moved. Ivy was my stepsister, and she hurt my best friend. I think Maddie blamed me for it. I mean, we talk sometimes, but it's not the same. I never told Ivy anything about Maddie, I wouldn't do that. I never talked to Ivy anyway. She wanted nothing to do with me, and that was fine. Her mom is a phony, and I didn't like going over there anyway."

"I'm sorry you had to go through all this."

"Last time I talked to Maddie she sounded happy, so that's good, right?"

"Yes, it is."

"I have homework," Amanda said, fidgeting.

"One more thing. When Tommy wrote to Max, he said you thought Ivy's best friend killed her."

Amanda frowned, clearly confused. "I never said that. And I don't even know Ivy's friends."

"Perhaps Tommy thought that because of something you said?"

Amanda shrugged. "The only thing I can think of is that I was surprised to see Bailey Fairstein at the funeral because while they used to be friends, Bailey hated Ivy. Maybe Tommy thought that meant she had a reason to kill her. I don't know."

Tommy looked both happy and nervous when Max walked into the den. It had been turned into a media room, with a large screen TV, a computer on a desk, books, and at least a thousand movies and video games. He paused his movie and stood up politely. "Hey, Ms. Revere."

"I said you can call me Max."

He nodded and glanced at his mom.

Jenny went over and rubbed her son on his back and smiled. "Max came by to see how you're doing, isn't that nice?"

He nodded. "I'm watching *Shrek*. Have you seen *Shrek*?"

"No, but I heard it was good."

"It's the best. Or at least it's in my top ten favorite movies. I keep a list. I moved it to number eight when I got *Guardians of the Galaxy* for Christmas. That's number seven now. I had to take off *Star Wars*. I still like *Star Wars* a lot, but it's not in the top ten anymore."

"You like making lists?"

He nodded. "So I don't forget anything."

"I do the same thing."

He beamed. "I can go back to the beginning if you want to watch *Shrek* with me."

"I wish I had the time." When was the last time Max had seen a movie? Some indie movie in New York with Ben. One of his friends had produced it. It was crap and she'd told Ben it was a waste of two hours and fifteen minutes of her life. That was a year ago. When she was in college, she, Karen, and Ben had gone to the Film Forum nearly every week to watch old movies, anything from spaghetti westerns to Hitchcock to classics like *Casablanca*.

She hadn't been to the Forum since Karen died.

"I don't want to interrupt your movie," Max told Tommy. "I just wanted to see how you're doing, and make sure you didn't have any questions. Like I told you this afternoon, just call me. You have my cell phone number."

"I memorized it," he said, then recited the number.

Jenny said, "Tommy has always been very good with numbers. We had to make sure when he was a little boy that he knew his address and phone number. Just in case." She kissed his cheek and said, "Go back to your movie, sweetheart. I'll call you when dinner's ready."

"Okay, Mom." He sat back down and pressed the play button.

Max and Jenny stepped out and went back to the living room. There they found David and Amanda were laughing about something.

"Amanda is a smart kid," David said.

"Straight As," Jenny said. "She's always done well in school. We're taking a week next spring to tour colleges on the East Coast."

"Can I go to Tanya's house?" the teenager asked.

"Dinner will be ready in an hour."

"I'll be back by then."

"Go ahead," Jenny said.

After Amanda left, Jenny said, "This situation has been hard on both my kids. Amanda has always been a rock, though. It breaks my heart that her father is such a selfish ass. She's going to go off to college in less than two years and he's going to realize he's done nothing to keep the relationship going. He can't turn back the clock and make up for all the damage he's done."

"Kids are resilient," Max said. "We were talking to your neighbor, Mrs. Baker."

Immediately, Jenny's demeanor changed. She went from friendly to suspicious in a blink.

Max said, "She claims that Tommy has a history of sleepwalking. Not just in the house, but that he gets outside."

"Yes, but he's stopped. The doctor said once he went through puberty it would likely stop on its own, and it did."

"According to Mrs. Baker, she saw him just last month walking across her front yard at midnight."

"She can't see anything with her old eyes. I set an alarm every night just in case, and Tommy is *fine*. He hasn't walked in his sleep in *years*. The last time he was fifteen and the alarm went off and I found him in the backyard before he even left our property. Got him back to bed and he didn't remember anything."

"You're certain," Max pushed. Jenny was lying. Max saw it in her stance and her tone. She was overly defensive, but why would she lie?

Because she knows Tommy was out the night Ivy was murdered.

"How dare you. Get out of my house. You've already turned a bad situation worse, stirring up everything about Ivy and my husband's bitch wife."

"Jenny, I only want to find the truth."

"The truth? Paula's truth? That my son killed her daughter? Is that why you befriended Tommy? Has this all been a trick? Because you think we're all stupid? You used him!"

"You must know that's not true," Max said. "Please listen—"

"Out. Get out. Do not come here again. I forbid you from talking to my son. Stay out of our lives!"

Tommy stood in the doorway, frozen. He heard his mom shout, and muted the movie. Listened. His mom was talking about his sleepwalking. Then she started yelling at Max. He couldn't hear what Max said, but his mom was really mad. Had he done something wrong again?

He closed the door and sat back on the couch, staring at the silent television. Fiona the princess was singing and about to make a bird blow up. Tommy didn't like that part and always closed his eyes.

He turned the TV off.

His head hurt.

He sometimes woke up in places he didn't go to sleep in. It's why his mom wouldn't let him sleep in the tree house, even if Austin was there to sleep over the door.

Last month he'd woken up, and his feet had been cold and wet. He thought he peed in his bed like he sometimes did when he was little but only his feet were wet. And the bottom of his pajamas. Like if he'd walked through wet grass.

The door slammed and his mom started banging pots and pans in the kitchen. She was really mad about something, and Tommy worried that it was Max. He ran to the window and looked out. Max was getting into a car with Mr. Kane, Emma's dad. Mr. Kane was really scary-looking, but Emma was really nice and said that her dad was nice, too. Tommy didn't want to judge a book by its cover. Like when people thought he was stupid or scary because he didn't think as fast as everyone else.

His mother got quiet, so Tommy went out to talk to her. Sometimes she didn't tell him everything, and he didn't really want to know what happened. He just wanted to know that everything was going to be okay. He didn't want his mother to cry anymore.

He stopped before he entered the kitchen.

His mother was making dinner and talking on her cell phone.

"Ginger, I don't know what to do!"

Aunt Ginger. His mom's older sister. She lived in Colorado Springs, Colorado. They had to take a plane to visit her, which was scary and fun. They went every summer for two weeks. He liked Aunt Ginger, but didn't like all her rules. They didn't make sense to Tommy. Like, she wouldn't let him touch the DVD player because it was only for grown-ups. But she let Amanda touch it and Amanda was two whole years younger than him.

"I just need to leave. To start over. What was I thinking, that Bill would actually be a real father? That he would regret his choices? I should have moved seven years ago when he moved that bitch *two miles* from us."

Move? His mom wanted to move? He didn't want to move. He didn't want to go anywhere. He liked his school and his teachers and Austin and . . .

His mom said to his aunt, "You're right. It's best to do it now. Amanda and Tommy will adjust, they're such good kids."

Tommy went to his room and climbed under the covers even though he had all his clothes on. He didn't want to move. He didn't want to leave his friends and family and tree house.

Nothing would ever be normal again.

CHAPTER TWENTY-EIGHT

The best thing about parents who didn't give a shit what you did was that they never questioned the obvious.

After dinner, Austin had told his mom that he was going to spend the night over at Jason's house. He picked Jason, first because the asshole would cover for him, and second because his mother admired Jason's mother, a rich bitch just like her—with even more money and even snootier friends than his mom. She'd been pushing for Austin to hang out with the "right people," and Jason Dunlap was "the right people."

If she only knew that Jason was the biggest drug dealer under the age of sixteen, she'd flip. Or maybe not. Because she wouldn't want to offend potentially fancy friends or anything.

Lucky for him, his mom had forgotten all about how Austin was already supposedly grounded for letting "that unscrupulous reporter" put words in his mouth.

Truth was, Max had toned down everything Austin had said. He'd wanted to go on camera, and she said it would be best just to show him and Tommy in the background. Austin watched the show, thought it was pretty good, though he thought it would have been better if Max put his interview up. He didn't realize until later that his mom had gone off the deep end.

The anger in Austin had been growing all day, and especially after he'd talked to Tommy during PE. Tommy was so sad, and it hurt. It wasn't fair. His mom had said if Tommy came within one hundred feet of Austin, Tommy was going to jail. Austin told her she was a stuck-up bitch and he hated her. She sent him to his room. He kicked his door closed and cracked the wood frame.

When his stepdad came home late that afternoon, it was like his mom was a whole different person. Over dinner, Bill was trying to calm her down about Tommy, so she turned on the waterworks. Claimed she was scared, didn't feel safe. Then Bella saw her crying and she started crying. That's when Austin took his little sister from the dinner table and they played with her Barbie house until she calmed down. Bella was like Tommy that way—easy to distract.

But his anger had not gone anywhere. Austin would not let his mom tell him what to do and who he could talk to and hang out with. He hoped Bill would grow a pair and tell his mom that she was wrong, but instead he just did this weird, there-there, pat-pat thing and didn't say anything more. And when Austin's mom was going to say no about the sleepover, Bill told her it would be good for him to be with friends.

"And it'll give us a chance to talk this through, Paula, sweetheart. I'll take Bella to my mom's house, and it'll just be you and me tonight."

She got all sappy and agreed.

Austin packed a change of clothes in his backpack and sent Jason a text message. Jason responded almost immediately.

I'll cover for you, but you owe me one, Lake.

That was fucked, but Austin would deal with Jason when he had to.

Tonight, he had to make sure Tommy was okay.

He rode his bike up to Tommy's house, but parked it on the opposite side of the house behind the bushes so no one could see it. He went around through the back and up into Tommy's tree house, then sent Tommy a message.

I'm in your tree house. We need to talk. It's okay. Your dad is talking to my mom and trying to stop her from being a bitch.

Tommy didn't respond, and Austin thought he might not have his phone with him. Tommy would sometimes leave it charging in his bedroom after school. Jenny had made him paranoid about always having a charged phone, so much so that he plugged it in whenever he was home and carried an extra charger to use at school.

Austin waited. Fifteen minutes later, Tommy climbed into the tree house.

"My mom didn't want me coming out here."

"Did you tell her I was here?"

Tommy shook his head. "No, but it's like lying."

"You just didn't say anything."

"You can't stay."

"Why not? My mom thinks I'm at Jason's house."

"Jason Dunlap? I don't like him. He's mean to me. He's mean to you, too."

"He's a prick, but he'll cover for me. We have an understanding."

"Max Revere came over this afternoon and said something that made Mom cry."

"What?"

"I don't know why she was crying, but Max said Mrs. Baker told her that I walked in my sleep. And now Mom is talking to my aunt Ginger about moving to Colorado Springs. I don't wanna move to Colorado Springs."

Austin fumed. That old bat. Why didn't she mind her own business? "You don't sleepwalk anymore." Not exactly true.

"That's what Mom said, but maybe Mrs. Baker is right."

"And?"

"And Mom got really mad. She told Max to leave and never come back. She told her never to talk to me again." Tommy frowned. "I like Max. She's nice and real smart and doesn't talk to me like I don't understand. And when I don't understand, she explains things to me and doesn't sigh like I'm stupid. I don't like Emma's dad. He's scary."

"He's not scary."

"I've had some weird dreams, Austin. Maybe I'm sleepwalking and don't know it."

Austin was more than a little familiar with Tommy's sleepwalking. When Tommy used to stay over at his house, Austin put a bell over his door so he'd hear if Tommy got up. Before that, the first time it happened, his mom had freaked out because she'd found Tommy asleep in Bella's rocking chair when Bella was still in a crib. Tommy told her that he heard Bella crying and thought she wouldn't be scared if her big brother was sleeping in the same room. No one else had heard Bella cry, but Austin believed Tommy. He also knew Tommy had vivid dreams.

After that, Paula wouldn't let Tommy sleep over for months but once she calmed down about it Austin made sure that he woke up if Tommy got up. Austin read everything he could on sleepwalking. Most of the time, he just followed Tommy and usually Tommy went back to bed after doing something—once he made everyone's school lunches. Another night he walked out of the house, stood at the corner for ten minutes, then went back to the house.

Once he left the house and it was raining—Tommy woke up in a panic and if Austin hadn't been there, he didn't know what would have happened. Tommy might have been locked up, even though he was just scared because he didn't know where he was.

But Jenny had told Austin that Tommy had grown out of the habit. Jenny was weird, really smart in some ways and stupid in others. She let Tommy go to and from school by himself, but wouldn't let him get his driver's license, even though Austin had been studying with him and knew he'd be able to pass the test. Tommy sometimes got confused about events—especially in the past. The more time that passed, the more confused he got. But he remembered what he read. Not like a photographic memory, but when he wanted to remember, he studied. Sometimes it was annoying—like when he refused to go biking unless Austin wore a helmet because that was the law. Or when the signal was broken but the sign said DON'T WALK so Tommy walked six blocks out of his way just to cross the street at a crosswalk.

"Have you been sleepwalking lately?" Austin asked.

"I don't know. A few months ago—it was right before my birthday, I remember that because we were planning our trip to the Exploratorium, remember that?"

"Yeah." They went, and Austin was grounded for two weeks because he wasn't supposed to be with Tommy unsupervised. Austin didn't care because it was one of the best days ever.

"That was the most fun I had all summer," Tommy said, grinning. "I love going on the ferry. Maybe we can do it again. Oh, and also Dad said he'd take us to a baseball game again. That was my second best day ever, remember? And the Giants won and Dad bought us hats and I ate three hot dogs. Do you still have your hat? I have mine."

Austin wanted to hit something. Bill Wallace had no intention of taking them to a baseball game. Bill used to be pretty cool, but Austin's mom had rubbed off on him. Shouldn't Bill know better than to make promises to Tommy that he had no intention of keeping?

The day he and Tommy had gone to the Exploratorium, Tommy's birthday, Paula had made a huge scene when they got back on the ferry. She'd actually called the police and was waiting for them at the dock in Larkspur. Tommy cried when Paula yelled at him. That was the day Austin knew he had to prove Tommy hadn't killed Ivy. Apparently just because the police said Tommy didn't do it didn't mean anything to his mom.

But Paula didn't know about the sleepwalking. Jenny had told Bill that Tommy wasn't doing it anymore. Austin didn't know why she lied, but that was fine by Austin, he wasn't going to say anything.

"Tommy, are you saying the last time you walked in your sleep was in June?"

"I opened the back door and the alarm went off. It scared me." He bit his lip. "And Mom was talking about it to Max and then to Aunt Ginger. I didn't want to listen."

"Are you sure you didn't eavesdrop?"

Tommy always eavesdropped. He didn't really mean to most of the time, but he heard everything. It's why he knew Paula thought he'd killed Ivy—not that she was trying to keep it a secret.

"Mom was really mad. And crying. A crying mad. It was different. She looked scared. Why would she be scared? I haven't seen her so mad in a long time. I came here, to my tree house, because I don't like seeing my mom like that. She looked like that when Dad left to marry your mom. And when she told Max to leave and never come back. And I thought maybe I have been sleepwalking and no one told me. My feet were wet last month."

Austin didn't hear the last part. He could barely breathe.

"Is Max leaving? She's not leaving, is she? She promised she'd help. What did she say?"

Tommy's bottom lip trembled. "I-I don't know. Mom told her never to come back and she and Mr. Kane left. Maybe we'll never find out who killed Ivy."

"She's not leaving," said Austin. "She *can't* leave. I'm going to talk to her."

"It's dark. It's almost nine o'clock."

"The bike trail has lights. This is important."

"I don't think you should."

It was all Austin could do not to snap back at Tommy. Didn't he know he was doing this all for him? Didn't he know that everything he'd done, he'd done for them?

"I have to talk to her," he said through clenched teeth.

"Text me when you get back so I know you're okay."

"I'm sleeping in your tree house tonight."

Tommy shook his head. "I don't want to go to jail."

"You won't. I'll be okay, I promise. It's only a thirty-minute bike ride," Austin said.

Before Tommy could argue with him—not that Austin would listen—Austin climbed out of the tree house and left.

CHAPTER TWENTY-NINE

Austin sped down the bike trail and it only took him twenty-nine minutes to get to Sausalito, and another five to arrive at Max Revere's hotel.

He locked up his bike. His heart pounded in his chest from the ride, and he breathed heavily from his mouth. He was hot from the exertion, but his hands and face were like ice. The hotel was spread out into multiple buildings, more like oversized houses, and he headed for the building where he knew she was staying. Austin didn't want to call her first—what if she didn't want to talk to him? Or if she was mad at him for not telling her about the sleepwalking? As if that mattered! Austin had learned, especially in the last year, that adults looked for any excuse to tell you that you were shit out of luck.

After Paula banned Tommy from the house, Austin had gone to see Bill at his office in the city. He'd waited two hours for Bill to finish a meeting and talk to him. Bill listened—Austin gave him credit for that—but then his stepdad said, "Austin, I'm glad Tommy has a friend like you. I've talked to Paula about this, and I think deep down she knows that Tommy would never hurt anyone, but she's still grieving for Ivy. We need to give her some space to let her sort through this on her own. I'll find time to take you and Tommy to a ball game or maybe a fishing trip like we talked about last summer before . . . before Ivy died."

Nothing happened. Austin's mother hadn't budged, Bill was never home. His mom devoted herself to Bella. That kid had more activities and playdates than anyone Austin knew. She had even modeled for some kids' clothing magazine.

Austin didn't care about all that. His own dad was a jerk, too. Even more of a workaholic than Bill. More often than not, he canceled their scheduled visitations. Austin hadn't seen him since last Christmas. Before that, he'd come for Ivy's funeral. Flew in that morning, out that night.

Austin tried the door into Max's building. Damn! He needed a keycard to get in. He waited fifteen minutes before someone walked out, then he slipped inside. The couple noticed, but didn't say anything. He didn't care, let them call security. He'd be gone before they got here.

He ran up the stairs to her room and knocked on her door. Louder. Why wasn't she coming? He pounded again. "Max! Ms. Revere! It's Austin Lake. Please! I have to talk to you!"

Had she already left? Why? Did she think Tommy killed Ivy, too? It wasn't fair!

"Damn you, Maxine Revere!" he screamed.

David Kane jumped up from the couch in his hotel suite. He'd been reading an e-mail from Dr. Arthur Ullman, one of Max's contacts, answering his questions about sleepwalking. David grabbed his gun and opened the door.

Austin. He was standing in front of Max's door, raising his fist to pound again.

"Austin!" David said sharply.

The kid jumped around, surprised and scared. And angry. Anger and fear was etched in Austin's face so clearly, it was as though David was looking into a mirror of his own past.

"I need to talk to her *right now!*" The kid stepped toward him, anger dominating his fear. "She's leaving, isn't she? She doesn't care. Joke's on me, huh? Who cares what I think? Who cares about Ivy? I don't. I don't care she's dead. I don't care!" Through the rage, he was crying, a thirteen-year-old kid trying to deal with a situation that was completely out of his control.

"Come in my room," David said.

"She's gone. She left. She's not going to help, is she?"

A hotel security officer came down the hall, his hand on his radio. "I've called the police, Mr. Kane," he said. "I'll take him to the office."

"It's fine, Jay. I've got this."

Jay looked uncertain. "He slipped in behind two guests. They came immediately to the front desk. I know—"

"I said all's good. He won't make any more trouble."

"If you're sure."

"Thanks for coming so quickly," David said. He opened the door wider and pulled Austin inside and closed the door behind him.

"You need to calm down, Austin. Pull yourself together and then tell me exactly what happened."

Austin rubbed his face with the sleeve of his jacket and stood in the middle of David's suite but didn't budge.

David grabbed a water bottle from the minifridge and handed it to Austin. The kid just held the bottle, as if not knowing what to do with it.

"Sit," David said.

The kid glared at him. He was debating his options,

and obeying seemed to win out. He sat on the edge of the chair, ready to bolt.

David sat across from him. "Max is out working the case, but she'll be back."

"Why should I believe you?"

"Why shouldn't you?"

Austin jumped up. "Because you and Max are just like everyone else!"

"Sit!" David ordered.

Austin waited several seconds before he sat down. A power play. A way to show David that he would sit when he wanted to.

"What happened?" David asked.

"You talked to that old hag, Mrs. Baker. Why'd you have to do that? Mrs. Baker hates kids. She hates Tommy. She called him an idiot." Austin took a deep breath, and David appreciated his effort to control himself. "Tommy doesn't sleepwalk anymore, not much anyway. And it doesn't matter if he does, that doesn't have anything to do with Ivy. Now everything is all fucked."

"Max told you and Tommy that the truth is sometimes difficult to hear. She doesn't investigate cases unless someone in the family wants her to because inevitably, some people aren't happy with the truth."

"So she's quitting?" Defiant and scared, and mad as hell.

"No." David sat down across from Austin. "You're an angry kid. I saw it at the school when the reporter Lorenzo came up to you." David didn't say anything for a minute. He suspected the anger had been simmering for years. Besides the divorce and all the family turmoil, there was also the fact that Austin didn't understand his mother and didn't like his sister. When you didn't like someone who then ends up dead, that's when guilt seeps in, and there was no stopping it.

David had more than his fair share of guilt. Even now, when he knew he had no control over events in his past, guilt ate at him. He could have done more. *Should* have done more. Even when he knew in his gut that nothing he did would have made a difference, guilt that he was a lesser man always stayed with him.

"If Tommy wants her to leave, will she?" Austin asked.

"Did he say that?"

"Not exactly."

"What do you think is going on here, Austin? Why do you think Jenny had such a negative reaction?"

"I don't know," he said quickly, but he wasn't looking at David.

He knew. He might not be able to articulate his thoughts, but Austin was a smart kid and he had an idea of what Jenny Wallace was thinking.

David let Austin sit for a minute. The kid squirmed, his brow furrowed, his hands clenched in his lap.

"What if we never find out what happened to Ivy?" Austin said, his voice quiet.

It wasn't a question David could answer.

"Have you eaten dinner?"

"My mom cooked."

"Did you eat?"

The kid shrugged.

"I'll call for room service. Cheeseburgers? Fries?"

Austin shrugged and nodded at the same time.

David made the call, then sat back down. Austin was calm, contemplative.

Still angry.

"Max doesn't stop an investigation just because it becomes difficult," David said. "She might not be able to solve Ivy's murder, but it won't be for lack of trying. And the more someone tells her not to do something or to stay away, the more determined she becomes. She doesn't like anyone telling her what to do. Does that remind you of anybody? Regardless, before she leaves, Max will exhaust every lead."

"My mom wants a restraining order," Austin said. "Why is she doing this? Tommy never hurt anyone. He's the only person who has never said a mean word to anyone in his life."

It was late, long past sunset, two hours after Max grabbed a quick sandwich in her hotel. But Grace had called Max and asked her to meet, so Max put aside preparing her interview questions for Stephen Cross and drove to the edge of the bay, down a dead-end road lined with industrial shops. A broken-down block bordering an affluent community.

There were a half-dozen police cars, a fire truck, and an ambulance, but there was no urgency. Lights had been put up in the area, along a running path that cut through a flat open space. Bushes and grasses and some low growing trees lined the marsh.

She found Grace talking to Chief Reinecke near the headlights of two cop cars. She approached, surprised when no one stopped her.

"Revere," Grace said.

"You were cryptic on the phone."

"We found Travis Whitman."

Max glanced around the area. The cops. The dogs. The lack of urgency.

"He's dead."

Grace nodded. "Been dead for a while, probably since yesterday morning when he left to go running. He's in sweatpants and a Windbreaker. Running shoes. His body isn't in good condition."

"Why wasn't he found earlier? This is a pretty open area."

"Look, we've only been out here for an hour. I don't have much information yet. It was dusk when a runner heard some yelping. Thought it was an injured or lost dog and went to inspect. Found two juvenile foxes fighting over the body. Called it in. We sealed it off. The coroner's here now. All I can tell you is that it looks like Travis was shot at least twice. His body was dragged off the path and into the vegetation. We can't do much tonight, but I'll have a crew here to protect the crime scene, and a full team come in at dawn to canvass the area."

Chief Reinecke looked pained. "I'm going to notify his parents."

"I can do it, Jim," said Grace. "It's my case."

"I'll do it. Whatever happened—" He glanced at Max. "Well, you're a smart lady, you suspect it's connected to Ivy."

Max did. But how? Travis was killed before her "Crime NET" segment even aired. "Do you have a theory?"

Grace shook her head. "Here's the kicker—we can't find Travis's phone. It's not on his body, and so far it's nowhere near his body. It's not in his truck, which was parked at the dead end. Joggers use this area often. Hikers. Marine biologists. The marsh is used by schools. Because of the drought, it's drier than usual. This section of the marsh is always useable, but as you get closer to the bay the tides come in. I don't know if the killer thought the tide would come in this far or not—but it doesn't. Still, his body was in a damp area, and there was animal and bird activity."

"You don't think it was robbery."

"His wallet was in his jacket pocket."

"He knew something," said Max

"We can't speculate," Reinecke said, "and I would appreciate if you didn't, either. I didn't want to call, but Grace said you have an insight into this case and have interviewed people we haven't spoken to in over a year. She assured me you wouldn't give away anything."

"I'm not that kind of reporter," Max said. "I don't have a nightly news deadline I need to meet. I'm here to find out who killed Ivy Lake." She paused. "And I suspect whoever killed Ivy also killed Travis."

"And we're back to square one," Grace said.

"No, we are not," Max said.

Grace arched her eyebrow. "We?"

"Like the chief said, I have insight into this case." Max paused, considered how to give Grace the information she had. "Bailey Fairstein, Ivy's former best friend, told me Travis had cornered her at her school on Tuesday. He knew I was in town and accused Bailey of putting a phone in his locker. She didn't know what he was talking about, and because I was talking to her about Ivy's psychology, it didn't really stick with me. I'd planned to follow up with Travis."

Grace glanced at the Chief. "We have access to school lockers?" she asked.

He nodded. "Call the school deputy and tell him to seal the locker. He'll contact the principal, but there's no warrant necessary. When you're done here, you can search it."

Max said, "Bailey told me she'd had no contact with Travis until he came to her school, and that he'd seemed . . . agitated. Upset."

"Because of your questions?" Reinecke asked.

"This was before I spoke to him. Before most people knew I was here. It seems that Travis knew something about Ivy's death. Whether he was involved in her murder remains unclear, but he knew something that he didn't share with you or me. And that knowledge got him killed."

"He told his mother he was running with his friend Brian," said Grace. "Brian claimed not to have spoken to him that morning. After I search Travis's locker, I'll go over and formally interview him. He lives in the mobile home park not a quarter mile from here. I don't think that's a coincidence."

Reinecke said, "I'm going to check in with the coroner, then go see Mr. and Mrs. Whitman. Keep me informed of every step of the investigation."

"Yes, sir," Grace said.

After he left, Max said, "I had a few calls on the hotline. Nothing specific, but I'm going to interview a family who moved from town, possibly after something happened with Ivy. They live in San Rafael."

"Who?"

She hesitated, then said, "Their name is Cross."

Grace shook her head. "Not familiar. If you learn anything that can help—"

"Of course." That wasn't completely true. Max didn't tell Grace about Tommy's sleepwalking. But would that help or hinder the investigation? Tommy didn't shoot Travis Whitman. There was no doubt in Max's mind that Tommy couldn't kill a person in cold blood. Besides, she had no proof that Tommy was actually still sleepwalking except for the word of an eighty-three-year-old bitch who didn't like the kid. And his mother's overreaction when Max brought it up. None of that would hold up in court. Max wasn't going to say anything right now without additional proof that it was relevant.

Max wasn't going to further ruin Tommy's life.

Reinecke came back from down the path looking grim, and walked to his squad car without saying anything else.

"Thanks for the info about the phone." Grace hesitated, then said, "You want the exclusive?"

Max didn't know whether to be angry or irritated or offended.

Or none of the above.

She changed the subject. "Did you get my texts earlier? The photos?"

Grace bristled. "Yes."

"Do you know who that guy is?"

"The cop? He's a rookie. Been here for less than a year.
I told Reinecke—it's his call on what to do about it."

"I mean the other guy, in the bar."

"Yeah, Robert Carr. Not a favorite. He quit the police
force under the consolidation because the council voted
to hire an outside police chief instead of promoting
him—he was the chief of the Greenbrae division. The
only one who adamantly opposed the consolidation of
CPMA."

"Local politics." So not directly connected to Ivy's
murder investigation.

"I'm not surprised Lorenzo is chummy with him—and
it explains a lot about what that guy prints in the paper.
Carr has been making noise about running for police
chief—under the consolidation, the joint council ap-
pointed the first police chief, Reinecke, but the position
is elected. Under the charter, the first election is next year.
He basically got three years to prove himself before facing
the voters. I suspect Carr is going to challenge him."

Grace glanced at Max. "Two murders doesn't help
Reinecke, but solving them will. I'm very motivated to
solve them."

CHAPTER THIRTY

Max took a deep breath before entering David's suite. He'd texted her a heads-up that Austin was there.

Though David had opened the doors to the balcony, the smell of hamburgers and french fries filled the room. It was chilly, but not uncomfortably so. Max kicked off her heels and sank into the corner of the sofa.

"It's been a long day," she said to no one in particular. This time last night she'd been in bed with Nick.

Austin looked tired and more like a little boy than the aggressive young teenager she'd met only days ago. He looked at David. Max watched the silent exchange, and David gave Austin a brief nod.

"I didn't tell the entire truth about the night Ivy died," Austin said, eyes fixed on David and not Max.

Silence.

"Tell her." David's voice was low but commanding.

"Ivy—" Austin began, then stopped. He started over. "I hacked into Ivy's Instagram account the day she died. Not hard because I'd figured out her password. I'd meant to just delete the account, but instead I changed her profile. I put up a picture of her that she hated for her profile picture, and then wrote for her bio, 'I'm Ivy Lake—bitch, bully, phony, fake.'"

Max raised an eyebrow but said nothing.

"She found out immediately and changed it back, but she was freaking furious. When she was younger, there were these girls she hated, who always called her a phony, and had even spray-painted it on her locker in eighth grade 'Lake is fake.' It always bugged her, and I knew it."

When Austin didn't say anything else, Max was going to tell him guilt was normal and what he did really isn't at issue, but David put up his hand before she opened her mouth.

"Tell her the rest," David said.

"Everything I told the police was true—that Ivy was gone most of the day, she came home really pissed off about something, same old same old, and she demanded I send Tommy home. With him right there, Ivy said, 'Get that fucking retard out of my house, loser.' I told Tommy to get his bike and meet me out front—that's when I hacked her account. When I came back from walking Tommy home, she told me she knew what I'd done. That she'd fixed it, no one saw it, but that I could have ruined her life. I finally stood up to her. I never had before— she'd picked on me my entire life, especially after we moved here. I don't know why, she just didn't like me. And so now I stood up to her. Told her she was a stupid bitch, that Tommy was a better person than she would ever be, that no one liked her, they just liked hearing whatever gossip she had. Ivy really thought she was the most popular girl in school because she had more Instagram followers than anyone else. She *obsessed* over it, as if each person who liked one of her photos liked *her,* personally. Which was why I wanted to delete her account."

He bit his lip. "I should have known better. She went to the kitchen and came back with a knife. She cut her left arm with the knife, then her right arm. They weren't deep, but she was bleeding. At first I thought she was going to kill herself because of what I said. I just stared. I didn't know what to do. I didn't even think about calling 911 or running out of the house. Then she pointed the knife at me, and I thought she was going to kill me. I backed away and fell over the ottoman in the family room. She laughed. Then she told me that she was going to tell Mom that Tommy tried to rape her, and when she pushed him away he grabbed a knife."

Tears ran down Austin's cheeks. There was no doubt in Max's mind that everything Austin said was true. But it still seemed unbelievable.

"I told her I'd tell Mom and Bill what she did, and she just laughed at me and said no one would believe me. That Tommy had always creeped Mom out, especially when he got big. Then she got a phone call, and went up to her room. She was arguing with someone on the phone, and fifteen minutes later she left the house. Just before ten thirty, like I told the police."

"Why didn't you tell anyone the truth?"

"Because they might think I killed her! Or worse, that Tommy killed her. I never told anyone what she did. Especially Tommy. He wouldn't understand. He told me once that he loved Ivy because she was family. Even though she was mean to him, she teased him, she was embarrassed by him—he never hated her. I hated her. I hated her!"

Max rubbed her temples.

"Don't go," Austin said to her. "I made this mess. I should never have written that damn letter. I told Tommy everything was going to be fine, and now it's even worse. I need to fix it. I don't know what to do."

"I'm not leaving," Max said. "But the police believe whoever pushed Ivy off the cliff cut her first—that he attacked her with a knife and pushed her off the cliff. But now you are saying that she had those cuts before she went to the preserve. What happened to the knife, Austin?"

"Ivy took it with her," he said. "I don't know why the police never found it."

"Wouldn't the coroner have noticed the cuts were made earlier?" David asked.

"I don't know," Max admitted. "Her body wasn't found for twelve hours, give or take. The fall caused scrapes and cuts, but the cuts on her arms were made with a knife and it was surmised they were made by her attacker. Is Ruby still here?"

"Yes. Graham told her to stay through the weekend, in case you needed something else."

"I want Ruby to look at the photos again," Max said. "I don't know if she'll be able to tell if the cuts were an hour old, but since Ivy's body was cremated we can't get an exhumation order—if that would even help after a year."

"I'll send her a message," David said.

Max assessed Austin. He'd pulled himself together, but his face was still splotchy from the tears. The anger that had been simmering beneath the surface since she met him seemed to have dissipated some. In its place was resignation, sorrow, and hope.

Hope that she would be able to fix everything.

How had she gotten herself into this position of being the savior to a teenage boy and his mentally challenged brother?

And Austin had just put himself on the line as a suspect. He'd lied to the police, he'd withheld evidence, and he had a motive. A motive not to protect himself, but to protect Tommy.

"You need to tell Detective Martin everything you told me," said Max.

David cleared his throat.

"You have something to say?" Max said.

"He needs to tell his parents. Get a lawyer. Protect his rights."

Max didn't see it working out that way. But she said, against her better judgment, "David's right. You're a minor, but you have just as many rights as an adult in the criminal justice system."

"I didn't kill Ivy."

"But you lied to the police. And my forensics team believes that Ivy was killed closer to eleven than one thirty. Which means that your alibi isn't as solid. You didn't go online with your computer game until after eleven."

"I didn't kill her," he repeated, his voice cracking.

"I don't think you killed her. But you can see why others might be more suspicious? You could have followed her to the preserve."

"She was driving her car."

"You could have overheard her tell someone that's where she was going. Taken bike paths up there. Been there even before she was."

"I didn't! Why don't you believe me?"

"I do, but you have to see how this might look to others. To the police. The police had to look at everyone's alibi again, because they assumed based on a tweet Ivy supposedly sent that she died after one in the morning. Now they need to know that her wounds were self-inflicted."

"My mom won't believe me."

"I'm sure she knows you didn't hurt Ivy."

"Not about that! She won't believe Ivy cut herself. She'll think Tommy did it, that Tommy killed her and I covered it up, or something dumb like that."

Max feared Austin was right. Because in Paula's mind, Ivy was perfect, Tommy imperfect. She said, "You have my number memorized, right?" Austin nodded. "If anything goes wrong, if your parents don't get you a lawyer—or if they tell you not to tell the police—call me."

"Why do they even need to know? It's not important."

"It is important! Those cuts on Ivy's arms tell another story, and it changes the way the police will investigate her murder."

"You mean it's my fault they couldn't find the killer?"

"No," she said. "It means that they would have assumed it was an accident if she hadn't had any cuts on her arms at all. They would have investigated and determined that she fell. There would have been no need to bring in experts who had a theory that isn't an exact science. Time of death can be difficult to pin down. It means that they take other evidence, coupled with the physical evidence, and make an educated guess. And sometimes they're wrong. Even if they're wrong by only an hour, it can make the difference in someone's alibi, which is why they look at a block of time."

Max glanced at David, then looked at Austin. "How well do you know Travis Whitman?"

He shrugged. "He dated Ivy. He was okay, kind of a jerk."

David looked at her quizzically, but didn't say anything.

She wanted to tell Austin about Travis's murder, but Grace hadn't yet publicly released the information. It wasn't Max's information to tell. Chief Reinecke could still be with Travis's parents. They had to hear it first.

"I'll take you home," David said to Austin.

"I don't want to go home."

"Where do your parents think you are?"

"At a friend's house."

"You need to talk to them," David said.

"You don't get it, do you?" Austin shook his head. "They'll never understand. Never!"

"I'll go inside with you."

Austin stared at David, stunned at the offer. "You'd do that?"

David said, "Austin, you're not alone in this."

He thought a minute. "I have my bike."

"And the car has a trunk." David stood. He said to Max, "I had room service put a sandwich and salad in your minifridge because I didn't know if you'd eaten."

"Thanks, David. Do you want me to come with you?"

"It's best if you don't. You're a lightning rod as far as Paula Wallace is concerned. I'll bring him home, explain the situation, and make sure he's okay before I leave. You get some sleep."

She leaned over and whispered to David, "Travis was shot and killed yesterday morning. They just found his body. That's why Grace called me."

David frowned. "We'll talk when I get back. And Max? Don't leave the hotel."

Austin walked down the stairs with David Kane. He was shaking inside. David didn't know his mother. She'd never let him tell the police anything because that would bring bad attention to her. Even Ivy getting killed had brought unwanted attention.

Paula Wallace wanted to be known for her charity work. For her perfect family, as the wife of Bill Wallace, successful and wealthy corporate attorney. She wanted to be known for her giant house, her expensive clothes, her pretty daughter, Bella. A mentally retarded stepson didn't fit in with her idea of perfect, a daughter who drew a civil lawsuit didn't fit in with her idea of perfect. Austin's mom twisted the truth around so that up was down and right was wrong and good was bad. He hadn't figured it out when he was younger, but this last year he felt like he was no longer a kid. He was thirteen, but he felt a lot older. Everyone had their problems, he guessed, but other kids seemed to complain a lot about stupid shit. Homework, being grounded, having their phone taken away, or not being bought the latest video game.

David was cool. He listened, really listened, and Austin thought he understood, mostly. But not totally because if David really got it, he wouldn't take Austin home. He didn't see that Austin's mother would just go about her business as if nothing happened.

"I'm not going to tell you that everything is going to be fine," David said as they walked out to the front of the hotel, where Austin had locked up his bike. "You're smart enough to know that things might get tough for a while. But they will improve. It won't be bad forever. I didn't believe that when I was a kid, so I suspect you don't believe it, either. I had my own problems, stuff that happened to me and my family that felt like the end of my world."

Austin turned to face him. "Like what?"

"My mom died of cancer when I was fourteen. My father's a doctor—I blamed him for not saving her. I blamed her for not going through chemo a third time. I thought she'd given up. That she didn't want to live anymore. I didn't know then how painful chemo and radiation therapy could be. How draining. How much she'd already sacrificed to give my brother and me and my dad a few more years. It was the end of my world and I was so angry, so grief-stricken. I couldn't see anything else in my life. I got into fights, I wanted the pain, because I was numb. Physical pain was the only thing I felt.

"I still miss my mom, but now without the grief or the pain or the anger."

"I'm sorry about your mom," Austin said. He unlocked his bike lock and wrapped it around his frame, then locked it again. "My mom isn't your mom."

"I know that, Austin, but what I'm saying is that bad things happen and we have to find a way to get through it. And it's worse when you're a kid because you don't think anyone understands the anger and pain. You think you're alone. Max understands more than you think."

"No, she doesn't. She has everything."

"Her mother abandoned her when she was ten. Her mother wasn't much better than yours. She did some unforgivable things. But you'll get through it, just like Max did."

"Do you believe in God?"

"Yes."

"I don't. Because your good mother is dead, and my bad mother is alive. If there was a God, he wouldn't take good people away from kids who need them, and he wouldn't let bad people have kids in the first place."

"It's not that simple."

"It's never simple. That's what grown-ups always say."

David popped the trunk of his car and leaned over to move some boxes.

Austin didn't think twice. He jumped on his bike and pedaled as fast as he could.

He didn't know where he was going, but he was never going home.

Tommy woke up when he heard voices outside his door. He looked at the dull red letters on his clock: 11:35. He sat up, a bit disoriented, and listened. His mom. Talking to his sister. He picked up his phone and checked his messages. Austin hadn't texted him that he was back.

He wished Austin hadn't gone off like he had. He wished Austin hadn't come to the tree house. Tommy felt really scared, but he didn't know why. And Austin was so mad all the time, sometimes Tommy thought he was mad at *him*. Tommy's stomach hurt when he thought Austin was mad at him.

"It'll be okay, Mom," Amanda was saying.

Tommy frowned. Was his mom still upset?

He got up so he could give his mom a hug. She always told him that his hugs were the greatest and made her feel better.

"You can't tell Tommy," his mom said.

She was right outside his door but they were walking down the hall, toward the kitchen.

He couldn't hear them anymore, so he stepped out of his room and slowly walked toward the kitchen. Still out of sight, he stopped as they kept talking about him.

"Tommy wouldn't understand," his mom said. She was getting milk out of the refrigerator. Water in the teapot. She was making tea because she couldn't sleep. She did that a lot when his dad first left. "If it gets out he was sleepwalking the night Ivy was killed, the police will think he did it, and they'll twist everything around when they interview him. And he'll end up agreeing with whatever they tell him."

"No one could think Tommy did anything wrong," Amanda said. "He's a sweet kid."

"The sweetest. Did you set the alarm when you came in?"

"Yes."

"Did you double-check it?"

"Yes, Mom. I swear. Are you sure Tommy was out that night?"

"No . . . but the alarm wasn't set and Mrs. Baker heard him." She paused, then sighed. "As much as I hate to say it, I think we should move."

"Move?"

"I know it'll be hard on you—changing schools your junior year. If you really want, you can live with your father."

"No!" Amanda said. "Never. I don't want to live with him. I hate him."

"Don't say that, Amanda. Your father loves you, he just doesn't know how to show his emotions."

"He doesn't love us. I don't think he ever loved us."

"He does—he loves you and Tommy."

"If he loved us so much, he wouldn't let that bitch be mean to Tommy."

"Don't say that—I know I've called her worse, but I'm trying to be better."

"You are better, Mom. I love you. This isn't your fault."

The teapot whistled and there was a rattling of cups and saucers. A shuffling of chairs. Tommy wanted to go sit with his mom and his sister and have tea. He loved nights when the three of them had tea together. It made him feel grown up and special.

But he was frozen.

If it gets out he was sleepwalking the night Ivy was killed . . .

"Where will we go?" Amanda asked.

"Ginger wants us to move to Colorado Springs, but I don't know. . . . My firm is bidding on a job in Boston to renovate an entire block of historic buildings. The history of the area is rich and wonderful, and it would be a terrific experience for you and Tommy. The project will take at least two years—normally, we'd hire a local architect to work with us, but I can relocate there and manage it myself. By the time it's finished, you'll be out of high school and going off to college. Would it make you terribly sad to leave California?"

"No. There's nothing for me here. And Tommy needs to get away from Austin."

Tommy almost shouted *No!*

"As much as I hate to say it, I think you're right," his mom said. "Austin has always been sweet with Tommy, but this whole thing with the reporter and Paula threatening a restraining order . . . the move would be good for him, too."

Tommy didn't want to move or leave Austin. Bella would never remember him.

He frowned, felt tears in his eyes. Paula would never let him see Austin or Bella again.

His own mother had lied to him.

If it gets out he was sleepwalking the night Ivy was killed . . .

Tommy turned slowly around and walked back to his bedroom.

He picked up his phone. Austin had sent him a message.

I'm fine, but I don't want you to get into trouble so I'm going to Jason's. Love you, Tommy.

CHAPTER THIRTY-ONE

David dropped Max off at a coffeehouse around the corner from the police station on his way to San Rafael. Though Max wanted to talk to Stephen Cross, she trusted David—and she needed to see Grace Martin.

She'd called the police station and learned Grace was in the field, so Max left her a voice mail on her cell phone, then sent her a text and an e-mail.

We need to talk. Where can we meet?

Along with a ham and cheese croissant, Max ordered a nonfat latte with an extra shot of espresso—she was tired. David had searched half the night for Austin, but Max told him not to alert his parents. They assumed the thought of David escorting Austin home had triggered him bolting. Max didn't know if she was doing the right thing in not contacting Paula Wallace—she knew David didn't agree with her.

Max was halfway done with her croissant and thinking about alternative ways to track down Grace Martin when Lance Lorenzo walked into the coffee shop. As he approached, he took one look at her and scowled.

"You are such a bitch," he said.

"Good morning," she answered and tilted her chin up.

He sat across from her.

"I didn't invite you to sit."

"You actually went and talked to Justin in Palo Alto."

She didn't respond.

"Hasn't that family been through enough?"

She was not going to be baited by this asshole.

He narrowed his eyes. "I see you don't read the news. Maybe you should."

He walked out without getting coffee or food.

Now Max was curious. And concerned.

She pulled out her iPad and went to Lorenzo's blog. He'd posted the article only two hours ago.

MEDIA BLITZ FALLOUT

According to Maxine Revere, hostess of NET's "Maximum Exposure" a cold-case true crime show, she came to Corte Madera to investigate the death of high school junior Ivy Lake who died in the early morning hours of July 4 last year. A family member contacted her, and she claimed to be interviewing Ivy's mother on her show, but when the show aired, Paula Lake Wallace was nowhere to be seen. Why? Because she opposed any effort of Ms. Revere to exploit the death of her daughter.

"The Corte Madera police are thoroughly capable of investigating Ivy's murder," said Mrs. Wallace. "We don't need a New York reporter creating problems. She used my thirteen-year-old son—a minor—on her show without my permission, claiming that he contacted her. My attorney is already looking into possible violations of privacy law and child exploitation."

While some people like Mrs. Wallace believe that her daughter was murdered, others believe that Ivy's death was an accident. The Marin County Medical Examiner's final report indicated that the evidence was "inconclusive" as to whether Ivy accidentally fell off the cliff at the Kings Preserve. Forensic expert Dr. Josh Davies said, "It is virtually impossible to tell whether a person was pushed or fell from a high point based solely on how the body landed on the surface. Additional evidence would be needed—such as witness statements, a sign of struggle at the top of the cliff, or physical evidence on the body that is inconsistent with a fall."

Yet Ms. Revere called in a private forensic science company—paid for by the multimillionaire Ms. Revere herself—to refute expert testimony with a bells-and-whistles computer analysis stating, "With 85 percent certainty, Ivy Lake was pushed from the cliff." When Nor-Cal Forensics Institute was contacted and asked about the methodology, their spokesperson Donovan Hunt said, "The computer program is proprietary. We have provided law enforcement with the documentation, and are available to testify in the event of a trial."

Isn't it interesting that the grant that NCFI has been endowed is partly funded by Maxine Revere herself? That she paid for their scientist to stay in a ritzy Sausalito resort? That she also paid their consulting fee for this case? Isn't that a conflict of interest? She came to town believing that Ivy Lake was murdered and she'll do anything and everything to prove it—even if it's "proving" an unsubstantiated theory.

Ms. Revere even went so far as to use her relationship with her "assistant," David Kane, to get close to the Lake family. Kane, the son of renowned local surgeon Dr. Warren Kane, is a graduate of CM High and a former Army Ranger. He is introduced by Ms. Revere as her assistant, but his official title is Chief of Security. Because our small town is so dangerous Ms. Revere needs a personal "bodyguard"?

Kane's daughter attends CMJH with the Lake boy. Kane has been seen staking out the school and intimidating Ivy's younger brother and Ivy's mentally challenged stepbrother,

Tommy Wallace, an eighteen-year-old high school senior who attends the CMHS special education program.

Lorenzo had inserted a photo of David talking to Austin, with Tommy and Emma in the background. Austin and Emma weren't clearly identifiable, though anyone who knew them would be able to recognize them. David's scar was visible and made him look dangerous. Max realized that Lorenzo had doctored the photo to make the scar more prominent.

But what is the real cost of so-called investigative journalism? Perhaps the human toll.

The seven-minute segment on Crime NET resulted in 213 potential tips to the NET hotline, according to a spokesman for Ms. Revere. "A handful" are being followed up on by staff and Ms. Revere herself. In the segment, Ms. Revere went through the already public information, then put an emotional spin on Ivy's death by exploiting Ivy's intellectually disabled stepbrother.

But the true tragedy is that in the segment Ms. Revere rehashed the arguments that alleged suspects had with Ivy in the days before her death. These people have since been cleared by police from any wrongdoing—including Ivy's former boyfriend, high school senior and star quarterback Travis Whitman. Because of the unproven report by NCFI, Whitman appears to have disappeared. Does he think he's being railroaded?

UPDATE: 7:45 A.M.: A Central Marin Police Authority spokesman said that Travis Whitman was shot and killed as early as Thursday morning, his body dumped in the Corte Madera Marsh. The detective in charge of the investigation, Grace Martin, who has been assisting Ms. Revere with her so-called investigative report, has refused to answer any questions.

> *Travis Whitman was cleared of any and all crimes until Ms.*
> *Revere came to town and concluded that his alibi wasn't solid.*
> *Could the star athlete's tragic murder be vigilante justice?*
> *Should Ms. Revere be held responsible?*

Tommy rode his bike to the police station Saturday morning at nine. Since most businesses opened at nine, he thought that would be safe. And it was foggy. Tommy didn't want to wait outside. Fog made his clothes damp and uncomfortable.

He walked in and said to the policeman behind the glass wall, "I need to talk to Detective Grace Martin please."

"Detective Martin is in the field right now. Can I find another detective to speak with you? Can you tell me what this is about?"

Tommy frowned. "I-I have to talk to Detective Martin. It's about my sister."

"Who is your sister?"

"Ivy Lake. Detective Martin is the policewoman in charge of finding out who killed her. I know who killed her."

"Who?"

"I can only tell Detective Martin."

Tommy was trembling. He thought for a moment that he shouldn't have come. But now that he was here, he was going to do the right thing.

"What's your name, son?"

"Tommy Wallace."

"Have a seat. I'll call Detective Martin."

"Thank you, sir."

He sat down on a hard plastic chair and waited.

Thirty minutes later, Detective Grace Martin entered the station through the front door. Tommy recognized her right off, and relief flooded through him.

"Tommy? What's wrong?"

He stood and waited until the detective was standing right in front of him. "I killed my stepsister," he said. "You need to put me in jail." Saying it felt good and bad. It felt good because he always needed to tell the truth, and it felt bad because he didn't remember killing Ivy. Also, Tommy didn't want to go to jail.

The policemen in the room looked at him like he was a bad guy and that made Tommy feel worse. He looked down at his feet.

"Come with me, Tommy," she said.

"Don't you need to put handcuffs on me?"

"No."

She walked him through the big room to a row of rooms with windows. She opened one door. There was a table and two chairs. It was a small room and he didn't like it.

"Sit down, Tommy."

He took a seat and folded his hands on the table in front of him. He looked around. There wasn't a lot to see. There was a camera in the corner. He raised his hand to wave at whoever was watching.

"Tommy, I'm going to record our conversation for your protection as well as mine," she said.

"Okay."

"I'll be right back. Stay here."

"Okay," he said again.

There was a high window on one wall that looked outside, and Tommy stared at the blue sky. Were there windows in jail? He didn't like scary shows, but he'd seen one that had a prison and it scared him. He didn't want to be locked up in a cage, but if you hurt someone you have to be punished.

He wanted his mom really bad, but he couldn't call her. She'd already lied to the police and he didn't want her to get into any trouble.

Tommy didn't get mad at other people. He only got mad at himself when he couldn't say what he thought. He could think better than he could talk. He knew he should be mad at Austin, but instead he was just sad. Austin was his best friend. Tommy had friends in his special class, but none like Austin. Because he thought Tommy could go to a community college and take classes, Austin was helping him with his reading. Tommy still struggled when reading. Numbers were so much easier. But even in math, you had to know how to read. He was the best reader in his class, but he wasn't as good as other people like Austin, and no one else helped him get better. And sometimes Amanda when she wasn't too busy.

Tommy didn't want Austin to get into trouble. He wished he'd never let Austin help him write the letter to Max. Tommy didn't want to know what happened to Ivy anymore.

Maybe because he was the one who'd hurt her.

The lady detective came into the room and handed him a can of orange soda. His favorite.

"Last year when you came in to talk to me about Ivy, you asked for orange soda. You still like it?"

He nodded.

"It's cold. Drink it."

His mom didn't like when he drank orange soda because his lips always turned orange for the rest of the day. He hesitated, then reached out and opened the can. It was cold and yummy.

"You're not under arrest, Tommy. I'm telling you that right now. But because of what you told me outside, I need to inform you of your Miranda rights. I need you to listen to me carefully."

"Okay."

Then she said a lot of stuff about his rights, and ended by asking if he understood.

"Yeah," he said, a bit uncertainly.

"Do you need me to explain anything to you?"

"Austin told me never to talk to the police because they twist things around," Tommy said. "But you're recording this, right? So anything I say is on that camera, right?"

"Yes, Tommy. I can call your mother to bring in an attorney for you. Would you like me to do that?"

"No. No, I'm going to tell you the truth. I promise." He crossed his heart. "Cross my heart, hope to die, stick a needle in my eye." He frowned. He'd said that when he was little. He straightened and hoped this police lady took him seriously. She wasn't laughing. She looked at him with kind blue eyes.

He remembered that Max told him she was helping the police. Suddenly he was relieved. Max had told him from the very beginning that she would help. Maybe she left, but she tried real hard, and it's not her fault that his mom yelled at her.

He said, "Max told me that the truth is really important. She also said that sometimes people don't want to know the truth. I didn't get what she meant. My mom told me never to lie, and I never lie. Well, I guess I sort of lied. Is it a lie when you don't say something because you don't want to get in trouble?" He backtracked. "I mean, not if you're asked a question, and then lie, because that's wrong, but if you know something but don't say anything because if you say something then everyone will be mad at you?"

"I think it depends," she said.

"I'm sorry I sent the letter to Ms. Revere. I . . . I didn't write all of it."

"Austin did," she said.

His mouth opened and his eyes widened. "H-h-how did you know?"

"Ms. Revere said that Austin helped you write the letter," Detective Martin said. "What did you want to tell me, Tommy?" She spoke very softly and he almost couldn't hear her. He spoke softly, too. Paula, his stepmom, told him he was too loud.

"I will tell you the truth because it's the right thing to do," he whispered. "But, please, I don't want my mom to get into any trouble for not telling the truth. She didn't mean to do anything wrong. My mom is a really good person."

The police lady didn't say anything, so Tommy continued, hoping he was doing this right. "Ever since I was little, I walked in my sleep. Sometimes I leave the house and I don't know. A couple times I've woken up in my tree house and didn't know how I got there. I like my tree house, especially when Mom is sad and crying.

"I didn't know I was walking in my sleep that night. I never remember anything. When I was twelve I climbed into my tree house and fell out and broke my arm." Tommy showed her his right arm. There was a faint scar from the cut he'd gotten when he fell. "She told Dad that I don't sleepwalk anymore, that I outgrew it, but that was a lie. Because she thought that I wouldn't be able to spend the night at his house because his wife is sort of mean."

"Can you go back to the night Ivy was killed? Do you remember anything?"

He shook his head. "I went to bed and woke up at six thirty in the morning. I always wake up at six thirty, even in summer when I don't have to set my alarm. But last night my mom told my sister that she found me outside the night Ivy was killed. Mom didn't tell me because she didn't want anyone to know, but she told Amanda. I think because Mrs. Baker told Max that I was sleepwalking last month. I don't remember that, either. She said I walked through her yard and squished her flowers. I don't remember. But sometimes I wake up and my feet are dirty." He paused. "I didn't want to kill Ivy."

"Tommy, do you recall anything about the night Ivy died? Like, did you have a dream maybe? And in the dream you did something?"

He shook his head. "I don't really remember dreams. Only if they're happy or scary."

"So you might not have done anything wrong, just walked outside."

"Then why would my mom not tell the truth?"

"I'm going to have to talk to her, Tommy. You know that, right?"

He felt the tears come back and he didn't want to cry. "I know." His voice sounded funny. "And you need to talk to Austin, too."

"Why?"

"Because I think he lied, too." Now the tears did come. Tommy thought he was doing the right thing, but he was so darn sad. "Why do people lie to me, Detective Martin? Is it because I'm not smart?"

"I think you're smart."

"Now you're lying to me. I'm not smart. That's why I have to go to special ed. Austin says I can go to college if I try really, really hard, but I still read slow, and I have to think hard about which way is left and which way is right." He showed her the small mole on the top of his right hand. "This is my right hand because of that mole. Smart people just know, they don't need a mole."

"I'm going to let you in on a secret," Detective Martin said. "I've gotten lost many times because I turned right when I should have turned left. It confuses me, too."

"You're just saying that to make me feel better."

"No. I'm not." She took off her glasses and rubbed her eyes. His mom did that when she was really tired or really frustrated. She looked at him, really looked at him. He squirmed, then froze when she asked the question, "Tommy, did you ever think about killing Ivy? Before or after she died?"

Tears burned. "N-n-no," he said. "I swear. I didn't know what I did. I don't remember. Do they have a special jail for people who don't remember they did something bad?"

Someone knocked on the door. Tommy jumped.

Detective Martin said, "Stay put, Tommy. Drink your soda. I'll be right back."

Grace stepped out of the interview room and closed the door. She could not see that boy killing anyone, but she couldn't discount that his mother had lied to her about where her son had been the night Ivy died.

"What?" she asked the cop who interrupted them.

"That reporter is here, Revere. She said it's urgent."

"Tell her to cool her heels, I'll be done in a minute. And call Jenny Wallace and ask her to come here to pick up her son. But don't let her leave—I have some questions for her."

"What about the boy?" he nodded toward the interview room.

"He's fine where he is."

Grace took a minute to compose herself. There was no evidence that Tommy had killed Ivy, but no evidence that exonerated him, either. If Paula Wallace found out that he wasn't at home sleeping the night her daughter was killed, she would push it, and the DA might lock Tommy up for evaluation. That could do more harm than good. And Grace was very skeptical about psychiatrists and children. She'd seen too many instances of children being led into believing something that wasn't true or only partly true. While Tommy was a legal adult, he had the mental capacity of a child. He easily believed what his mother told him, what Austin told him, or what anyone told him.

She went back into the room. "Tommy? I'm going to call your mom and let you go home."

He frowned. "You can't. Shouldn't I go to jail?"

"I need to verify your statement."

He stared at her blankly.

"I need to talk to your mom."

"She's going to be mad at me. She's going to cry."

"I'll try not to make her cry, Tommy. I need her to tell me the truth. Just like you did. Do you understand?"

He nodded, still looking upset and confused. Grace didn't want to leave him alone.

She pulled out her phone and sent one of the civilian staff members a text message. A few minutes later, John Ogilvie popped into the room. John was tall and skinny and looked much younger than his thirty years. He brought with him snacks, paper, and crayons. She nodded her appreciation. "Tommy? This is John. He's one of our computer technicians. He's going to sit with you for a bit while I do some work."

John pulled a deck of cards from his breast pocket. "Do you play cards, Tommy?"

Tommy smiled. "I love Crazy Eights."

"Me, too." John sat down and dealt the cards.

CHAPTER THIRTY-TWO

While Max sat at the police station waiting for Grace, she sent the article Lorenzo wrote to her producer Ben. Max told him to move heaven and earth to get that garbage off the Internet or, at a minimum, correct the inaccuracies.

Ben e-mailed back that he was skeptical that he could do much since it was Lorenzo's blog and not an official newspaper. But he'd still try and do his best.

As a journalist, Max was a huge proponent of free speech. There was no right more important than the First Amendment. Lance Lorenzo had a right to his opinion. But lies? That photo of David was taken out of context.

Maybe Max was more upset because she feared how Brittney was going to react to that picture. If she used it against David because it was an unofficial visitation . . . if she tried to keep him away from Emma . . . Max couldn't think about things she couldn't control.

She had to focus on the present. She might not be able to do anything about that idiot who called himself a reporter, but she would absolutely find out who killed Ivy Lake and fix all the damage she'd done.

She rubbed her temples. It wasn't even ten in the morning and she had a splitting headache. Not enough sleep, coupled with that article and the pressure of this investigation. She considered all the things she could have done differently, thought more about her choices.

There were a few people Max had worked with whom she genuinely liked, people she admired and respected. Sally O'Hara had been in law school when Max met her, frantic to find her younger sister who had been abducted. Now Sally was a detective in Queens and Max's closest friend outside of David.

Lois Kershaw, the octogenarian who had brought her into the elder abuse case in Miami. Max went down every year to visit her on her birthday, which was the day after Max's. She'd be ninety on January first.

Dr. Arthur Ullman, the retired FBI agent and criminal psychiatrist who was instrumental in expanding the Behavioral Science Unit, and now taught a seminar at NYU. Max had met him while he was still an active agent and assigned to Karen's disappearance.

And now there was Tommy. Max had an odd protective feeling for him, and she didn't exactly understand why. It couldn't simply be because he was handicapped, because she didn't think of him like that. She wasn't a patient person when dealing with most people but with Tommy—Max never had that sense of rushing, that she had to get through the conversation, get to the next point, get to the next part of the job. It pained her that he'd been treated so poorly by the people who should love and care for him the most.

If Max was going to be entirely honest, she hadn't been as aggressive as she might have been with people because she didn't want Tommy to be damaged by it. She hadn't pushed him because she didn't want to intimidate him. And now, he'd been out sleepwalking the night Ivy had been killed, and not once did Max think that he could have killed her. Even as she struggled against the thought, she wondered if her subjectivity had blinded her to the truth.

David's research said deep sleepwalkers did things they wouldn't do during waking hours. That they were almost different people. Arthur Ullman had concurred, though he'd qualified that he couldn't give an opinion without meeting Tommy.

No wonder her head hurt.

"Max."

She looked up as Grace approached. "I called you earlier," Max said.

"I've been busy—didn't get much sleep last night. Follow me."

Grace led her down through the heart of the police station. Instead of upstairs, she walked down a long row of smaller offices and interview rooms. She opened one door and stepped into a narrow room.

Through the one-way glass Max saw Tommy playing cards with a tall, lanky man. "Why's Tommy here?"

"He told me he killed his sister."

Max didn't know what to say.

"He sleepwalks. He overheard his mother telling his sister that he was sleepwalking the night Ivy was killed."

"I talked to her about it yesterday," Max said.

"You knew?"

"A neighbor told me she heard Tommy's bike that night. Elderly woman who keeps a log of every time someone makes her dogs bark. Which is often."

"So Tommy was riding a bike while sleepwalking?"

"David researched it—it's possible. There are some proven oddities with people walking in their sleep. One woman went out and had sex with men other than her husband and had no recollection of it."

Grace stared at her blankly. "Do you actually believe that?"

"It was written up in a respected medical journal. It seems far-fetched, but I don't know. That's out of my area of expertise."

"Mine, too. I had to call Tommy's mother. I'm not going to hold him, but now I need to investigate his claim."

"Austin is going to come in to talk to you."

"About?"

"Something he didn't tell anyone about the night Ivy died."

Grace pulled at her short hair. "His parents are throwing a shit-fit over your show. And that article this morning has caused us nothing but problems."

"That wasn't an article."

"I didn't know your partner Kane was from Marin. That his family lives here."

"Lorenzo is an ass." Max had already made the calls. Lorenzo was done. "Any new developments on Travis's death?"

"He was shot three times, twice in his chest, then once in his head, likely after he was already dead. We found the gun at the scene—in the water. It's at the lab now. They've already run ballistics and it's not a match to anything in the system. We're sending the report to all local police, FBI, other states. I don't expect anything from it. We're running the serial number."

"Ivy thought she was meeting someone the night she died. Travis thought he was meeting his friend Brian to go running."

"We went through Brian's phone and there were no messages, but he's letting us dig deeper, see if something was erased. We have a warrant for both Brian's and Travis's phone records."

"And the phone in Travis's locker?"

"Not there. However, we have a witness, a teacher, who said she saw Travis texting on a small flip phone, which he then put back in his locker. His personal phone was a smartphone."

"Are there cameras at the school?"

Grace raised an eyebrow. "Look, Max, I know how to do my job. Yes, there are cameras at the entrances. There are no cameras in the hallways. His parents let us take his computer and gave us full access. We're going as fast as we can, but there's a process. What we do have is a camera near where his truck was found. There's footage of him getting out of his truck after sitting there for five minutes. Then he starts to jog down the path toward the mobile home park where Brian lives. That was at five fifty-four Thursday morning. Travis didn't return. The coroner is performing the autopsy shortly, but I had a cop go through all the tape, and I think he was killed shortly after he left his truck. No one was seen coming out of the marsh for more than an hour, until three joggers started down the path at seven oh-two. There are no other cameras that show that part of the marsh."

Grace paused. "There's no evidence that the two murders were connected. One a push off a cliff, the other a gun."

"But you know they are."

"I'm treating them as connected, but of course I have to look at all possibilities." Grace's phone vibrated and she looked down. "Well, your young friend Austin is here. So many people seem to be dropping by today."

Max was relieved. She followed Grace out to the lobby.

Austin got to his feet as soon as Grace and Max approached. He was in the same clothes he'd worn last night, Max noted. She wondered where he had slept.

"I want to talk to you in private," he said to Grace, followed by a glance at Max. "I mean, Max can come, too, but I don't want my parents here. You can't make them come, can you?"

"What's this about?"

"Ivy. Something I didn't tell you about that night."

Grace looked pained. Another gray area. "Austin, I should call your parents."

"No." He swallowed nervously and then blurted out the whole story. "I didn't tell you before because I didn't think anyone would believe me. I mean, I didn't think my mom would believe me, but I swear to you, this is the truth." Austin told her about changing Ivy's Instagram profile and embarrassing her, how she cut her arms with a kitchen knife right in front of him. "Max says that those cuts change everything. I swear, I didn't think it would matter."

Grace stared. They'd drawn a bit of a crowd as well, but Austin seemed oblivious.

"What time did this happen?" she asked.

"Everything else I said is true. Ivy came home at eight, mad. She left after ten and didn't come back."

"Austin, do you remember that you told me you went online around eleven that night?"

He nodded. "I know—this means I have no alibi. But I didn't kill Ivy. I don't know who did, but it wasn't me. Max said you might look at the case differently if you knew Ivy cut herself."

Grace glanced at Max. "You're right."

Jenny Wallace ran into the station. "Tommy, is he okay? An officer called me and said he was here. What happened? Is he hurt?"

"Calm down, Mrs. Wallace. Tommy is fine. But we need to talk."

David drove to San Rafael and located the Crosses' home. As he was about to knock on the front door, Emma called him. He sent her a quick text message that he was going into a meeting and would phone her back in an hour.

Fortunately, Brittney hadn't been able to cut off his cellular communication with his daughter. He was looking forward to the birthday dinner he had planned at his dad's house tomorrow. He just hoped Brittney didn't change her mind.

When Stephen Cross opened the door, David introduced himself. He saw one of his daughters sitting in the living room beyond. "Maddie told me she called your hotline, and why. I decided to let her talk to you."

Cross closed the door behind David. Max should be here, she knew how to talk to people and get them to tell her things they didn't want to. But David was on his own.

Cross brought out coffee for the two of them, black, and they sat down. "I didn't see the show about Ivy Lake until after Maddie talked to me last night, then I watched it on the Internet. I didn't realize her murder was still unsolved. Maddie told me she called the hotline but got cold feet. She then showed me this."

He pulled a folded piece of paper from his pocket and handed it to David. "She doesn't have the envelope anymore, but said it had been postmarked from Corte Madera the second week of July last year."

David read the typed letter. It was short but creepy.

I thought you might like to see this clipping from the local paper. Karma.

Attached was a printout of the news story about Ivy's death. David had read it before. It revealed that Ivy had been killed early in the morning of July 4 and the cause of death was a fall from the cliffs at the preserve, autopsy pending.

"Maddie didn't tell me about the letter until last night," Cross said.

"I didn't think—it kind of creeped me out, but I just

thought it was sent by a friend who knew how much Ivy hurt me."

"What exactly happened with Ivy before you moved?"

"That girl just wouldn't leave Maddie alone," Cross said. "I even spoke to her mother, but Mrs. Wallace didn't consider it important. She said she'd talk to Ivy, but I could tell she wasn't going to do anything."

Maddie said, "Ivy told everyone that I was cutting, but that wasn't the main reason I needed to get out of there. She . . . she told people about my therapy. I was going through a bad time and everything was worse because of that. And my therapist was prescribing me antidepressants that didn't work, and my moods were all wacky."

"We changed psychiatrists when we moved, and found that Maddie was being overmedicated," Cross said.

"One day in class I started crying, and then Ivy posted on her blog that I had gone off my meds."

"That was it," Cross said, his jaw set. He wasn't a large man, a bit soft around the edges, but it was clear his daughters meant everything to him. That, David understood. "My girls have been through enough in their young lives. They lost their mother in a car accident, and Maddie still has nightmares about that night. I took the job here in San Rafael and we moved. It was the best decision I ever made."

Maddie nodded. "I wish I could have been stronger then."

Cross squeezed her forearm. "You are strong."

"Do you still talk to Amanda Wallace?" David asked, although he knew the answer.

"Poor Mandy," Maddie said. "She and Ivy didn't get along, and I don't blame her. Between the divorce, and then they moved so close. Ivy was a year older than us. Ivy was just flat-out nasty to Amanda's brother."

"So you're still friends."

Mandy glanced at her father. "No, not really."

"What happened?"

"We go to different schools. I mean, we're not that far away, but we don't have the same friends."

Cross interjected. "Maddie had a hard time after the move, and Amanda had as well. They'd been friends for a long time, but Amanda started calling Maddie every day. At first, it wasn't that big of a deal, but she didn't stop."

"I didn't want to hurt her feelings," Maddie said. "We'd been best friends since forever, our entire lives. But I couldn't go visit her all the time, and I couldn't talk every night. It got to be too much."

Cross concurred. "I called Jenny Wallace and told her that Amanda had sent Maddie two thousand text messages one month."

"Two *thousand*?"

"Mostly short. Like, what are you doing, did you see this movie, read that book. Amanda told Maddie everything that was happening in her life. We ended up changing her phone number."

"I didn't want to," Maddie said. "Amanda was so lonely. I was really her only friend. When we were younger, it was cool. We liked the same things, the same books, the same clothes. We used to say we were twins."

"Amanda was a nice kid," Cross said, "but her mother was a basketcase during her divorce, and Amanda started spending more and more time at our house. At first, that was fine, but then I had to put an end to it when Amanda started staying over every night. Moving her clothes into Maddie's drawers. I assumed she was trying to move in because she was so miserable at home."

"And how was Amanda when Ivy posted about your cutting and your therapy?"

"Horrified," Maddie said. "But . . ." She glanced at her dad.

He said, "This is your story, Maddie. You choose who you share it with."

"Amanda knew about the cutting. My psychiatrist thinks Amanda didn't want to tell anyone because it was *our* secret, even though she knew it was bad for me. I couldn't stop—like people who can't stop drinking alcohol. And Amanda would be there for me to talk to, but I think she was one of the reasons I kept cutting myself. She was . . . needy. Oh, God, that sounds so bad."

"It's accurate," Cross said. "Maddie started getting sick, trying to keep Amanda happy by responding to all her messages, doing her schoolwork, juggling chores and her therapy, and making friends. It was too much."

David suspected he knew the answer but asked anyway. "When was that?"

"I had a talk with Jenny Wallace in her office," said Cross, "shortly before the Fourth of July holiday. Two or three days before."

"This past summer?"

"No, a year ago. About eight months after we moved."

"And what did you say?"

"I told her about all the texts, the phone calls, the e-mails. And that Amanda had shown up at our house that weekend with an overnight bag. Jenny was shocked—she thought the sleepover was planned. She'd brought Amanda to the house on a Friday right after school got out, and picked her up Monday. I didn't say anything when she picked her up, but that weekend was hell for Maddie."

He looked at his daughter.

She said, "I realized that Amanda wanted to be just like me. I mean, we always liked the same things, but when I came here, I started doing other things, you know? Like I always liked soccer, but Amanda didn't so I never played. Here I made my high school team. And then she said she was going to play soccer, too—and I know she hated it. And then we played music, and she'd say she didn't like something, and then when I said I did, she said she did, too. It was . . . weird. And sort of creepy."

"My other daughter Kristen is the one who told me the truth," Cross said, "and then I had that talk with Jenny. The night after, Jenny called back and said she'd spoken with Amanda, that she was upset because she didn't realize she'd done anything wrong, but she understands. And that was the end of it."

"She never called me again," Maddie said.

CHAPTER THIRTY-THREE

Max sat with Austin on a bench while Grace escorted Jenny down the hall.

"I don't feel any better," Austin said.

"You will. Lying only helps in the short term, to keep you out of immediate trouble."

"I wasn't trying to protect me."

"You were protecting Tommy. I understand, but eventually, the truth comes out. It always does."

"If I never wrote that damn letter for Tommy, none of this would have happened."

"Maybe. Maybe not. Someone killed your sister."

"It could have been an accident. If I had told the truth from the beginning, they wouldn't have thought she was murdered by anyone."

"You could be right. But the specialists I brought in believe that she was pushed. And Thursday morning someone shot and killed Travis Whitman."

Austin jumped. "Travis? Like, shot with a gun? Why?"

"We don't know."

"Because of Ivy?"

"Austin!"

Both Max and Austin turned toward the entrance.

Paula Wallace stood there with an attractive man in a suit who Max presumed was her husband Bill. He resembled his engagement photo from the newspaper, just older.

Austin jumped up. "Why are you here?"

"Because Bill's son is in trouble," Paula said.

Austin looked at Max. "Is that true?"

"No," Max said. "Detective Martin is straightening it out."

"Get away from my son, Ms. Revere," Paula said.

"Stop, please," Austin pleaded. "This isn't Max's fault."

Bill said, "Ms. Revere, I'm Bill Wallace. It seems your presence is disturbing my wife and son. If you could step into another area, that would be for the best."

Max turned to him and straightened her spine. "And you're the diplomat?"

He stared at her, his eyes hard even though his expression was mild. She saw the lawyer beneath the pleasant demeanor.

She didn't budge. Bill Wallace was everything she hated. A liar. A cheat. Destructive and selfish and manipulative. Just like her uncle Brooks. Just like so many men that came in and out of her mother's life. For years, she'd dealt with men like Brooks and Bill, and she was not giving any of them one single inch.

How did women fall for selfish pricks like this? Did they think they could change their man, that he cheated for some reason other than he was a selfish adulterer? Why didn't Paula fear Bill was cheating on her? Did she even care?

"Austin!" Paula exclaimed. "Come here now."

The desk sergeant approached. "If you can't keep it down, I'm going to have to ask you all to leave the facility."

"Let's take this outside," Bill Wallace said to Max.

"No," Max said.

"I should tell you that my lawyers are drawing up a lawsuit as we speak regarding your libelous show," he said.

"Libel? Do you know the definition?"

He bristled.

Max said, "You must not have seen the segment. If you had, you wouldn't even mention the L word." Max kept her voice quiet. "You're just angry because you have no idea what's going on in the lives of your children."

"I will not have my family exploited. You have no idea who I am."

"Don't worry, I think I've got your number," Max said with confidence.

"Just who the hell do you think you are?" he shouted, his composure cracking. Good, she wanted him to snap.

"You'll have to leave," the officer approached again. "Now."

Max turned and walked away from Bill Wallace. She had so much she wanted to say. Ten years ago she would have verbally gone after him. Hell, six *months* ago she would have skewered him. Without much effort, she could tear anyone down. All those years growing up in a large extended family who could quietly and with great class insult anyone.

But David had gotten through to her, and now she was closely watching Austin. For better or worse, these were his parents. If Max humiliated them—which they richly deserved—Austin would witness their downfall. And would that make Max any better than their daughter who had basked in the popularity of embarrassing her peers?

"Paula," Bill said, "take Austin home. I'll handle this situation with Tommy."

"I'm not leaving," Austin said.

"You will do as I say or you'll be grounded."

"Austin, listen to your father."

"He's not my father!"

"Don't do this here, Austin. Not in public."

Grace Martin walked briskly down the hall toward them. Jenny and Tommy were behind her. Jenny had been crying and Tommy looked thoroughly upset. When he saw his father standing in the lobby of the police station, he froze.

Jenny did not. She brushed past Grace and came straight at her ex. But she addressed Paula. "It wasn't enough that you had to steal my family, but you had to make my son feel like he was garbage."

"Jenny, now is not the time," Bill said.

"It's never the time! You're a big hotshot lawyer, but you avoid confrontation with the people who matter. Tommy *matters!* A restraining order? Really?"

"That's not settled. As I told you over the phone, we'll sit down on Monday and work things out."

"Why didn't you just move to Seattle? It would be better for Tommy and Amanda to have a father they see twice a year than a father who lives two miles away and never wants them around."

"That's not true and you know it."

Grace used her fingers to whistle. "Time out. We have more serious matters to attend to than your dysfunctional family. Mrs. Wallace—" Both Paula and Jenny looked at her. "Jenny," Grace corrected, "you will go with Officer Blanchard and write out your statement as we discussed, then you and Tommy are free to leave."

Tommy stood on the edge of the group. He said quietly, "I'm not going home."

"Of course you are, sweetheart," said Jenny. "The nice detective said it's okay."

"Don't talk to me like I'm stupid. I'm not stupid!"

"Of course you aren't. Don't say that."

"You lied. I don't—I can't—just leave me alone."

"Honey—"

Tommy brushed off her hand and moved away from her. By the look on Jenny's face, it was the first time he'd done such a thing.

Grace said, "Let's get the statement signed first. Jenny?"

Jenny looked thoroughly confused and upset when her son turned his back on her. Half in a daze, she followed an officer to a desk in the middle of the bullpen.

Grace turned to Bill Wallace. "Sir, do you still own a nine millimeter handgun?"

"What's this about?"

"Answer the question, please."

Another detective approached them and whispered in Grace's ear. She nodded, then made introductions. "This is Detective Juan Jimenez. He's assisting my investigation into the murder of Travis Whitman. I'd like you both to come with us so we can ask you a few questions."

Bill said, "Questions about what?"

"Your gun and where it is."

Paula put her hand to her mouth. "Oh, my God. That's what this is. That's why Jenny called you. Tommy stole your gun and shot Travis."

Grace stared at her. If she said half of what Max wanted to say, she'd probably be fired.

"Let me handle this, Paula," Bill said, clearly angry with Paula for her outburst as well as with the detective for the question. "Detective Martin, you may call my attorney and he will arrange a time and place for us to discuss this matter."

Max's phone was vibrating. She glanced at it quickly. David. She'd call him right back—she wanted to hear more about this gun.

It appeared the Wallaces' gun might have been used to shoot Travis Whitman.

Jimenez, an attractive detective who looked like a taller, skinnier, younger Ricky Martin, said, "We found a nine millimeter gun at the scene of Travis Whitman's homicide that at first we believed was unregistered, but upon further examination, the last serial number was misread by the technician. We confirmed that it is registered to William E. Wallace of Corte Madera. Ballistics just came back that confirms the gun was used to shoot and kill Travis Whitman. You're welcome to bring in your attorney, but we would like to ask you some questions right now."

"My gun is locked and secure in my home," said Bill.

"When was the last time you laid eyes on your firearm?"

Bill didn't answer. He'd been thrown for a loop. But it didn't take him long to recover. "I need to know exactly what you think and what you're trying to learn. *If* it was my firearm, then it was stolen."

"And you didn't report the theft?"

"I didn't know about the theft until now."

"Who has access to your gun?"

"I see what you're trying to do. You can talk to my attorney, I am not answering any more questions. Paula, Austin, we're leaving."

Grace said, "No."

"You cannot detain us."

"I can detain Austin. He just gave me a statement related to your daughter's murder, and I need him to read and sign it."

"He's a minor. You may not interview him without my consent or his attorney present," said Bill. "Anything he said to you is inadmissible in court."

A civilian staff member approached Jimenez and handed him a file folder, then turned his back to the others and spoke to the detective in a low voice. Everyone watched as Jimenez opened the folder, flipped through two pages, closed it and handed it back. "Go to the DA and get a warrant immediately for the chat room logs and identity."

Grace glanced at him. He said, "We processed Travis Whitman's phone records. We don't have access to the comments, but Travis engaged in a conversation through the ChatMe app. He downloaded the app Tuesday, but his account was created over a year ago."

"What does any of this have to do with us?" Paula said.

"Let's discuss this privately," Grace said.

"I'm not talking without my lawyer," said Bill.

"This isn't an interview. I need to give you information, and if you don't mind everyone here knowing your business, then I'm happy to talk about it here. Your gun was used to kill a high school student. I would think we all want answers."

Paula drew in her breath. Bill was skeptical. "If I believe that the conversation is veering off into another direction, I will end it."

"Fair enough," Grace said.

Max was impressed with Grace's control.

Grace said to Austin, "Sit over there with your brother."

"Tommy is not his brother," Paula said.

Austin glared at his mother with such a deep hatred, Max didn't know how they were going to ever come back from this.

Paula either didn't care or didn't notice her son's reaction. She said, "I'm filing a restraining order against Tommy Wallace. I don't want him anywhere near my son."

Grace said to the desk sergeant, "Keep an eye on the boys."

Bill looked at Max. "She's not coming with us."

Grace glanced at Max and gave her a slight shake. Max

hadn't expected to be allowed into the room, but if they hadn't said anything, she would have followed.

When the four of them went up the stairs, she turned to Tommy and Austin. "Tommy, I know you're upset, but you need to forgive your mother and Austin. They love you."

"They *lied* to me. Because they think I hurt Ivy. And maybe I did."

"I didn't lie to you!" Austin said. "And you didn't do anything wrong."

Max was thinking about the gun. She didn't think Bill Wallace would have killed Travis, and if he had, why would he use his own gun and then leave it at the scene? Bill was an asshole, but he wasn't stupid.

Paula? She was definitely not as bright as her husband, but certainly would know not to leave a weapon at the scene of the crime. And what would her motive be to kill Travis? That she thought he killed her daughter? Except she'd made it clear that she thought Tommy had done it. Maybe she thought she could frame Tommy. But that seemed . . . unlikely.

Austin would have had access to the gun. Where was he early Thursday morning? He made a habit of disappearing and sneaking out of the house. It wouldn't take much for a prosecutor to go after him for murder. Travis had left his house before dawn. He'd been killed before school. Austin could have lured him to the marsh and killed him . . . maybe because of what Travis knew about Ivy's death that he'd been holding back from the police and from Max.

She squatted in front of the boys. Tommy refused to look at Austin. Max put her hand on Austin's knee and said, "Look me in the eye."

He did. He was defiant, but he was also frightened.

Why? Because of the gun or because Tommy wouldn't talk to him?

"Did you take your father's gun?"

He looked thoroughly confused. "No. Why would I? Oh, God, you think I killed Travis."

"Did you give the gun to anyone else?"

"No—I don't even know the code to his lockbox. And I wouldn't take it. Do you really think I'd do something like that?"

"No, but I wanted you to say it."

"But they're going to think it's Tommy. They're going to blame Tommy."

"No, they're not. Austin, pull yourself together. You're mature, but you're still a kid. Do not talk to the police about this without a lawyer."

"I didn't take the damn gun."

"I believe you. But you need a lawyer to protect your rights. Trust me. You should have had one when you told Grace about Ivy cutting herself. David and I told you last night—"

"I know what you said, I just want this to be over with. And I don't want some lawyer that Bill controls. I don't want anything from him. I hate him!"

Tommy flinched, but didn't say anything.

"I can find you a lawyer if you want," Max said.

Austin didn't say anything. Max wasn't certain what the laws were related to minors and lawyers. She knew that they had a right to an attorney in any criminal investigation or questioning, but did they have a right to hire someone separate from whom their parents wanted?

"I'm going to make some calls and find out what your options are. From here on out, Austin, tell the truth. Only the truth. Half-truths and omissions are considered lies at this point, got it?"

He nodded.

Max turned to Tommy and squeezed his knee. "It's going to get better, Tommy."

He looked at her with sad eyes and her heart broke.

"My mom wants to move far away," he said in a whisper. "I don't want to go."

"I'm sorry, Tommy. Let's get through this, and maybe things will change."

"My mom thinks I killed Ivy."

"No, she doesn't."

"Then why didn't she tell the truth about my sleepwalking that night?"

"People do the wrong things for the right reasons."

"She said she wanted to protect me, but that means she thinks I did it. Else she wouldn't need to protect me."

"I think it's more complicated than that," Max said, but didn't know how to explain it. She stood up and her knees cracked from squatting for so long. "Sit tight. I'll be right back."

Max went over to the desk sergeant. Before she could even ask him to watch the boys, he nodded.

She went outside and returned David's call.

"I was in the police station. Did you talk to Madison?"

"Did Grace Martin ever interview Amanda about the night Ivy died?"

Max wasn't expecting that question. She thought back. "No, her name wasn't on any of the lists."

"It's a long story, but ultimately, Amanda stalked Madison Cross after she moved away. Calls, texts, e-mails. The weekend before Ivy died, Amanda showed up at their house for a sleepover. Stephen Cross had a talk with Jenny and told her that the plans for the sleepover were all in Amanda's head, that they hadn't made this arrangement, then showed her thousands of text messages and e-mails that Amanda had been sending over the months since

Madison moved. According to Stephen, Jenny talked to Amanda and he said she hasn't contacted Madison again."

"Maybe I haven't had enough coffee, but how does this relate to Ivy?"

"Amanda blamed Ivy for her friend Madison moving away. Amanda had an unhealthy relationship with Madison. Madison realized it after she moved and tried to cut ties, to the point of changing her phone number and e-mail. I have a copy of everything Amanda sent. I haven't read it all, but some texts are disturbing. And one thing is clear: she thinks her father traded her and Tommy for Ivy and Austin."

"Why on earth—" Max's stomach fell. "Because of what her mother told her?"

"I think Jenny Wallace's rage and sorrow over the affair and divorce impacted Amanda in an unpredictable way. I'm no psychiatrist, but Ullman would probably be able to read through these messages and see that Amanda has a warped view of her family and her place in it."

"Travis Whitman was killed with Bill Wallace's gun," Max said. "What does Travis have to do with this?"

"Travis was dating Ivy at the time she exposed Madison's cutting—which was the impetus for the Cross family to move. Maybe Amanda blamed him as well as Ivy. You said that Travis was holding back—maybe he knew something about Amanda. Maybe they conspired to kill Ivy together."

Max could see it. The details were still elusive, but she could see two people working together to lure Ivy to the preserve and push her off the cliff. The tweet that came after one in the morning would give Travis an alibi. And when Max came to town and started asking questions, Travis panicked. But why would he run to Bailey? Was Bailey also part of this conspiracy?

"Max, are you listening to me?"

"Yes, sorry."

"I said, Amanda Wallace is dangerous. Especially if she shot Travis Whitman—she has to know that it'll come back to her."

"She's trying to frame Austin."

"How?"

"She knows he sneaks out all the time. Like her, he would have access to Bill's gun. The new time of death for Ivy—Austin wasn't on his computer. Remember, he didn't log in until closer to eleven thirty. He has no real alibi, he was the last person who saw Ivy. And before six in the morning on Thursday? Would Paula be able to prove he was home that morning? His house is only a couple of miles from where Travis was killed."

"Amanda Wallace is volatile. Something happened and she snapped."

Max thought. "Travis thought all along that he was talking to Bailey Fairstein."

"You lost me."

"Travis accused Bailey of putting a phone in his locker. Grace said that Travis had communicated with someone via a ChatMe app, and they're working on tracing those communications. But why did he think his friend Brian wanted to run Thursday morning?"

"They go to the same school. Amanda could have known he ran with the guy. She could have texted him saying that she was Brian."

David cleared his throat. "The police will need to get a warrant for her computer and phone."

"With Ivy's death unsolved, she wasn't concerned. Then I come to town, stir things up, Travis panics—what if Travis really thought Ivy's death was an accident, but thought he'd get in trouble because he played some part in getting Ivy up to the preserve? Maybe he thought he was planning with Bailey—he didn't normally talk to her, wouldn't know she was out of town. Neither would Amanda."

"And when the truth came out about the time of death, he got suspicious."

"It made him a suspect, and he didn't have an alibi. Him or Austin. Except, he was killed before the TOD was narrowed down."

"It was a good frame job . . . but has holes."

"Amanda's sixteen," Max said. "She's in self-preservation mode. I don't know what she might do."

Amanda thought her father traded her and Tommy for Austin and Ivy . . .

Bella. Where was the little girl?

"David, I need to give Grace this information. When will you be back?"

"Ten minutes or less."

"I'm still at the police station. But I'll call you if that changes." Max hung up.

After Max went outside, Austin glanced over at Tommy. He didn't know what was going to happen to any of them. He just wanted his brother back.

Sitting straight up, his hands clasped tightly in his lap, Tommy stared straight ahead. His face was damp and flushed. He'd been crying, but he hadn't looked at Austin since Max left. Austin's lip trembled.

They may not be related by blood, but Austin had thought of Tommy as his brother from the first day they'd met. Austin had been five, Tommy ten. He was bigger than most ten-year-olds, but so much friendlier. He played with Austin for hours. Whatever Austin wanted to do. Ride bikes? Tommy was game. Play cards? Anytime. Play with little green army men? Tommy loved it. Austin had more fun creating elaborate military campaigns in the backyard with Tommy than anything else in his childhood. They'd played for hours, until dark, and sometimes in the summer even after dark. They brought flashlights outside and set them up like spotlights. Or pretended the flashlights were helicopters flying overhead trying to find the sniper. When Austin played baseball for a couple years, Tommy was the one who played catch with him, watched his practice, and came to almost every game. Tommy didn't catch too good, but he never said no, he didn't want to do something. Austin didn't know that before they were brothers, Tommy wanted to play baseball. He tried for one year, but the kids weren't nice and the coach yelled at Tommy when he missed a fly ball during a game. Tommy's sister told him that.

"Tommy wants to be normal, but he's not," Amanda said. *"I hate those kids who were mean to him. He loves baseball but he won't play again, no matter what I say to him. And Mom just let him quit. She doesn't like people teasing him, but she thinks that ice cream solves all problems."*

"It's going to be okay, Tommy," Austin said.

Tommy didn't move from his spot on the bench. He would not look at Austin. His frown made his entire face sag.

"I'm sorry. I'm so, so, so sorry. I didn't mean for any of this to happen."

"You lied to me. That night Ivy died, you promised you wouldn't re-re-re—" he stuttered, unable to think of the word.

"Retaliate."

"You promised. But you did. Then she died."

"What I did had nothing to do with what happened to Ivy."

"You broke your promise."

"She was mean to you!"

"And you were mean to Ivy. You're just the same."

"I'm not!"

"You're worse." Tears fell from Tommy's face. "You pretend to be my friend. You tell me we're brothers."

"We are brothers. I love you, Tommy."

Tommy got up and walked away.

Austin called after him, but Tommy wouldn't look back.

Tommy was never going to forgive him.

Austin jumped up and ran out of the station, ignoring the desk sergeant who was shouting after him. He pushed Max as she came in through the doors.

Why did he think he could fix anything? He was just a dumb kid. He picked up speed and ran as fast and as long as he could.

In his pocket, Austin's phone was vibrating. As soon as he was clear of the police station, he read the text message. The number wasn't familiar.

I know who killed Ivy.

Who's this?

I know who killed her and can prove it. But I can't go to the police, I don't want to get in trouble. I'll leave the evidence on your dad's boat.

My dad? You mean Bill?

But there was no reply.

CHAPTER THIRTY-FOUR

Austin didn't stop or slow down as Max called after him. She ran into the station and nearly collided with the desk sergeant.

"Officer, I need to talk to Grace Martin right now. It's a matter of life and death."

He looked at her, skeptical.

"I don't say that lightly. I'm a reporter. My partner learned something that has a direct bearing on the murders of both Ivy Lake and Travis Whitman. Austin Lake is in danger right now."

Whether he believed her or knew that she and Grace had been working together, Max didn't know, but he said, "She's upstairs in the main conference room. I'll call and tell her you're coming."

Looking around, Max didn't see Tommy on the bench.

"He's with his mother," the desk sergeant said as he picked up the phone. He motioned to the bullpen. Tommy stood stiffly behind his mother while she spoke to the officer taking her statement.

Max walked briskly down the hall and up the stairs. She didn't know which was the main conference room, but found it on the second try. Sitting at a table with

Detective Jimenez and the Wallaces, Grace was just hanging up the phone. She looked angry, but Max didn't care if it was directed at her.

"Grace, David just learned some disturbing information about Amanda Wallace, and we need to find her."

Bill Wallace jumped up. "I've had enough of this attack on my family!"

"Sit down!" Max and Grace ordered simultaneously. Grace shot Max an irritated glance.

Bill was stunned into silence but didn't sit.

Max said to Grace, "David's returning with evidence, but did you interview Amanda after Ivy died?"

"No. I didn't have a need to. Her mother said she and Tommy were home all night."

"But we now know that Jenny found the alarm off and thought Tommy was sleepwalking. Want to bet that Amanda turned it off so she could get back in undetected?"

"I need something more, Max."

"David has thousands of e-mails and text messages sent to her childhood friend Madison Cross."

"Maddie?" Bill said. "Maddie and Amanda have been best friends since kindergarten."

"She moved before Ivy was killed," Max told Grace. "Ivy had exposed her as a cutter, then humiliated her by revealing she was on antidepressants and seeing a shrink. Her father relocated the family so his daughter could start fresh. Amanda had developed an obsessive relationship with her, until Madison's father put an end to it—the weekend before Ivy was killed."

Grace nodded. "You have my interest."

Bill said, "I don't believe this nonsense. You're talking about my daughter—she's sixteen years old. She's not a killer! She's a straight A student."

Grace pointed out, "She had access to your gun."

"My gun is locked in a box."

"Your gun is in police evidence," Jimenez said. Max had almost forgotten he was in the room.

"We need to find Amanda," said Max. "If she shot Travis Whitman, she knows we'll be able to connect the gun to her father."

Grace nodded. "Mr. and Mrs. Wallace, go home. We'll find Amanda and figure this out."

Bill shook his head. "I'm going to help. I'm certain this is another exaggeration by the media, which has exaggerated and lied about everything since this woman came to town."

Max didn't inform him that all the fabrications came from homegrown reporter Lance Lorenzo.

Max said, "Austin ran out of the station. I don't know why, but he wouldn't stop when I called after him."

Paula sucked in her breath. "My son? What happened? What did you say to him?"

"We'll find him," Grace said. "Go home."

They all went down the stairs. The police station was far busier now than an hour ago when Max first came in. Grace ordered two uniforms to go to Jenny Wallace's house and bring Amanda to the station.

Jenny heard Amanda's name. "What's going on?" She stood.

Grace approached. "We need to talk to Amanda about her father's gun."

"What?" Jenny said, still confused.

"It's your kids," Paula said to Jenny with a sneer. "They're to blame. We should never have moved here. Bill, we have to find Austin. He's in trouble."

"They're my kids, too," Bill said to his wife. "Go home, Paula. I'll fix this."

Paula looked like she'd been slapped. Her mouth

opened, closed, then tears fell. She turned and ran out of the police station.

"It's about time you realized you had two other children," Jenny said.

"I've never forgotten. You turned Amanda against me with your lies."

"I never lied about what an asshole you are."

"Enough!" Grace said. "Where would Amanda go if she were in trouble?"

Neither Jenny nor Bill had any idea.

"I have two officers going to your house, Jenny. And two more on their way to your house, Bill. Where else? Friends, family?"

"Tanya," Jenny said. "Tanya Donnelly. I have her number and address on my phone." She pulled her phone out with trembling fingers.

"She has a car," Bill said. "I bought it for her sixteenth birthday."

"I need the plates, make, and model." She handed Bill a notepad.

Max liked Grace's focus and efficiency.

"Anyone else?"

"My parents," Bill said. "They live in Larkspur. Not even a mile from here."

"Call them," Grace said. "Ask if Amanda has come by or if they know where she is."

Max looked around. "Where's Tommy?" she asked.

"The bathroom," Jenny said. "This whole thing has been so upsetting to him."

"How long ago?"

Before Jenny answered, Grace ordered a male officer to check the restrooms. He came back a minute later. "He's not there."

"Search the station. Find out if he left and if he left on foot or a vehicle."

"His bike," Jenny said. "He has his bike."

Max ran out to the front where the bike rack was located. There were four bikes locked up.

None of them belonged to Tommy Wallace.

Amanda took a deep breath and put a smile on her face even though she was nervous.

She walked into her grandmother's house. It smelled like bread—banana maybe, or raisin bread.

"Grandma?"

"Mandy? Is that you?" Her grandma came out of the kitchen wiping her hands on an apron. She smiled. "What a nice surprise."

"I went to Dad's house and no one was there. I thought they might be here."

"Just Bella. Your dad dropped her by last night for a sleepover. He said he'd pick her up at noon. She sure keeps me on my toes!"

"Oh, I had a question for my dad. Where's Bella?"

"With your grandpa. She has him watching this silly little show, 'My Little Pony.' Something like that. She has him wrapped around her little finger. I just took carrot muffins out of the oven, would you like one?"

"Yum, thanks." Amanda didn't want a muffin, but she had to act normal. "I thought I smelled banana bread."

"I made banana bread earlier this morning. The church is having a bake sale after the service tomorrow. I have banana bread, carrot muffins, and I'm just mixing up some chocolate chip cookie dough for cookies."

Her grandparents were so . . . *normal*. The kind you read about in books. They were a lot older than most of her friend's grandparents because her dad was a late baby. Her grandmother had told her often that she was told she couldn't have kids, then when she was thirty-five she got pregnant. She was eighty-four now and her grandpa was eighty-six. Her grandpa seemed much older than her grandmother though. And he was forgetful.

She was counting on it.

She followed her grandmother into the kitchen and took a muffin. She ate it, even though she wanted to throw up. Not because it didn't taste good—she couldn't taste anything right now, her stomach was tied up in knots.

She chatted about school until she thought enough time had passed that she'd done her due diligence. Then she said, "I'm going to say hi to grandpa and Bella."

Her grandmother handed her two muffins. "Bring these to them," she said. "Bella loves the carrot muffins. But don't tell her there are carrots in them! She won't eat it then."

Amanda plastered a smile on her face and hoped it looked natural. She walked down the hall to the living room. It seemed to take forever. She saw her grandfather sleeping in his recliner while Bella was watching "My Little Pony" with wide eyes.

"Hi, Bella," she said.

Bella said, "Shh!"

"Grandma has a muffin for you."

Bella turned around, eyes wide. "Before lunch? Yeah!" She jumped up and took the muffins from Amanda's hands. "Grandpa!"

"He's sleeping," Amanda said quietly.

"He's always sleeping."

"That's what old people do."

Bella wrinkled her nose. "I don't want to get old. I don't like going to bed."

Good. Because you're not going to get old.

Bella loved dogs more than anything. Paula was allergic—or so she said—and they couldn't have pets. Amanda said, "Mr. and Mrs. Fremont got a new puppy next door. Want to go see it?"

"Yes! I'll tell Grandma!"

Amanda took her hand. "I already told her. Let's go."

"What kind of puppy? What's its name? One puppy or a litter? A litter is a lot of puppies that come out of the mommy doggy all at the same time. Like twins!"

The phone started ringing in the house and Amanda's heart skipped a beat. But she kept hold of Bella's hand and let the little girl rattle on.

Bella kept talking, and that distracted her all the way through the back door and out to the dock. This was where her dad kept his boat, right on the bay. When Amanda was little, before her dad took off, he used to take her and Tommy on the water all the time. Tommy loved boats, but was kind of scared because he couldn't swim. Amanda loved boats, too. Or she used to.

When Amanda was born, her dad had gotten a boat and called it *Amanda*. She was so proud of a boat being named after her. Now that boat was in dry storage because it had damage from a storm. Her father had a new boat. A bigger, better boat.

He'd named it *Bella*.

Amanda hated it.

"Why are we getting in the boat? I wanna see the puppy!"

"Come on."

"I wanna see the puppy!"

"I have chocolate."

"You're mean!"

"You're a brat."

"I'm telling Mommy you said that!"

Amanda handed Bella what looked like a chocolate candy. Bella glared at her and took it and ate it, like Amanda knew she would.

"Yuck! My tongue! It stings!"

Thank you, jalapeño chocolate.

Amanda handed her a water bottle. Bella guzzled it, crying.

Almost immediately, her eyes got droopy.

Sleeping pills will do that.

She hoped she hadn't put too much in the water. But maybe it would be easier that way.

Amanda picked up groggy Bella from the dock and carried her onto the boat. She laid her out on the deck and prepared to take *Bella* out on the bay.

"Amanda," Tommy said.

She turned around. "You got my message. Let's go."

Amanda saw her grandmother at the back door look out at them, her hand shielding her eyes from the sun now that the fog had burned off.

Tommy hesitated. She was going to have to leave him.

"Goodbye, Tommy."

She pulled in the lines and started the motor.

Tommy saw Bella in the corner, looking like she was sleeping. At the last minute as Amanda pulled away from the dock, he jumped on board.

CHAPTER THIRTY-FIVE

Upon reentering the police station, Max found there was twice as much commotion as five minutes ago. Bill and Jenny stood like a buck and doe caught in headlights.

"Call the Coast Guard," Grace ordered the desk sergeant. "I need every available unit on call."

Grace glanced at Max. "Amanda took Bella from their grandparents' house and onto a boat docked on the river. They're heading out to the bay. Tommy jumped on board at the last minute."

"I don't know what's going on," Jenny said. "What's happening?"

Bill put his arm around her shoulders and said, "We'll bring them home safe."

"I'm meeting the Coast Guard in five minutes," Grace said. "Jimenez, you're with me."

"Let me go," Max said. "Tommy trusts me."

"Trusts?" Jenny cried. "Haven't you done enough?"

Max ignored her. "Grace, I'm the only person who hasn't lied to Tommy. I don't know why he jumped on the boat, but he isn't part of Amanda's plan."

Grace nodded. "Bill, Jenny, you'll stay at the docks

with an officer. You'll be kept informed. Max, with me and Jimenez."

They walked out just as David pulled up. Max didn't have to say anything, and Grace just sighed and nodded. Max and David slid into the back of Grace's sedan and Max filled him in on what happened. The main boat landing was less than a half mile away and they were there in minutes.

The Coast Guard was already prepping the boat to go, and as soon as the four of them were on board, they left in search of *Bella*. Amanda had headed out less than fifteen minutes ago. Based on where she started and the speed of the boat, the Coast Guard had already determined the area they would most likely be found.

As they moved from the pier, David handed Grace all the information he had collected about Amanda from Stephen Cross. Grace scanned the records, but it was Jimenez who noticed the same name on several e-mails as the name that had conversed with Travis on the ChatMe app.

"ChatMe one-oh-one," Jimenez said. "We don't have the transcript, and we likely won't get it unless we obtain one of the phones or computers that was used with the app, but it's the same screen name."

"Send the information to the DA," Grace told him. "Let's get a warrant. For the ChatMe app, for Amanda's computers and phone records, for Travis's records. His parents are cooperating, but we do everything by the book. There has to be a record of their conversations somewhere."

"On it," Jimenez said.

Captain Guzman approached Grace. "We have the *Bella* in line of sight, Detective. It's near Paradise Cay."

"That's a distance."

"I've called in a smaller boat to assist. Their ETA is fifteen minutes." He checked that they were all wearing vests, then escorted them to the main deck. He handed Grace a pair of binoculars, then pointed her in the right direction.

"Shit," she muttered. "She's being reckless."

"Yes, ma'am," said Captain Guzman. "We had reports from a private craft that the *Bella* came within twenty feet and created a hazard."

"Can you call her?" Jimenez asked.

"We've attempted to reach the *Bella* by radio, but no one answers the call. We've determined that she's well exceeding the speed limit for the channel. As soon as she passes the cay and into the main waters, the current will get even rougher."

"You can catch up with her though," Max said.

"Yes, but she has a head start. We're gaining, and expect to intercept before she reaches Angel Island."

A seaman came down to brief him. "Captain, we can identify three individuals on the boat."

"Tommy, Amanda, and Bella," Grace said.

"No sign of the little girl, ma'am. Two boys and a girl."

Max took the binoculars from Grace and focused.

"It's Austin," she said. "He's bleeding."

Austin sat in a corner of the deck, his head aching, mouth bleeding. He pretended he was more dazed than he was.

He'd heard everything Amanda had just told Tommy. Amanda had killed Ivy. She'd killed Travis Whitman. And now she was going to kill him and Bella.

Tommy stared blankly at his sister. It was like he'd gone into total stasis, not seeing or hearing anything.

"Tommy," Amanda said, "understand me! We weren't good enough for Dad. He traded us in for Ivy and Austin. Perfect kids," she said snidely. "I messed up. Travis was going to find out it wasn't Bailey texting him." She switched topics, acting all nutty. "Tommy, why do you love Austin more than me? Why go over there all the time? They didn't want you!"

Amanda turned to Austin and kicked him. "You stole my brother! You brought the reporter and now nothing is right! It was going to be fine. I had it planned. I just had to wait a while . . ." She shook her head. "Ivy took everything from me! My best friend, my daddy, my *life*. And then you"—she kicked Austin again—"you took my brother."

She didn't have a gun. At least he didn't see one. But she had a small knife in her hand. Austin might be able to wrestle the knife away from her, but Bella was starting to wake up in the corner. For the longest time, Austin thought she was dead. He stared at her, as did Tommy. She shifted a little, and her little chest moved up and down. She was cold, pulled in on herself, because she wore shorts and a T-shirt. It was a lot colder on the bay than on shore.

Austin tried to get up but Amanda kicked him down. Tommy yelped as if he was the one who'd been kicked.

"Stay!" Amanda told Austin. "Just stay put." She looked around. Austin followed her eyes. There was a Coast Guard boat coming up to them.

"No, no, no!"

Over a bullhorn, a booming voice said, "Turn off the engine and stay where you are. Prepare to be boarded."

Amanda ran back to the wheel and sped up the boat. Austin took the opportunity to crawl over to Bella. She was trying to get up.

"Aust . . ." Bella's voice was drowsy.

"Shh, it's okay, honey. It'll be okay. Tommy's here."

"Tommy?" She almost smiled. "I miss my Tommy."

Austin looked at Tommy. "Tommy, Bella misses you."

Austin took off his hoodie and put it on his sister. She shivered.

She coughed. "I don't feel good."

"Tommy, get me a life vest. They're in the box right next to you."

Tommy blinked. "Austin. You're hurt. Did Amanda do that to you?"

"I need the life vest for Bella. Please, Tommy. I need you to listen."

"Life vest."

The speedboat went faster. Tommy slipped as he opened the box.

Amanda glanced back and screamed, "Get away from her!"

Austin didn't move. "Bella has never done anything to you," he said. He was shaking from fear more than the cold salt air.

"She's a spoiled brat. She's going to turn out just like Ivy. You know it."

Tommy reached for the life vest. He was shaking, too. His lips were turning blue. He wasn't dressed for the bay. Where was his backpack? He carried his backpack everywhere.

"Mandy," Tommy said. "Mandy, you're going too fast." His voice cracked.

She was steering the boat toward a Coast Guard ship that was coming right at them. "They'll move," she said.

"Don't, Mandy. Please. Please, please, please."

Tommy had the life vest in his grasp. His knuckles were white as he clenched it. Tommy was terrified of the water because he couldn't swim. But even the best swimmers would have trouble out here in the bay. Not only was the water cold, the waves were high and choppy.

Austin said, "Give it to me. Then get a vest for yourself."

Tommy nodded and slid the vest to Austin.

Austin quickly put the vest on Bella. She could barely raise her arms. Her eyes were droopy. "I'm c-c-cold, Aussie," she chattered.

"Shh," he said.

The boat started to slow. Tommy was clutching a life vest to his chest.

"Put it on," Austin told him. "Tommy, please."

"I wanna go home," Tommy said.

"Aussie," Bella said, "I wanna go home, too."

Amanda cut the engine. "How did they know?" she cried.

Tommy said, "Mr. Kane talked to Maddie."

Amanda froze. "Maddie? Maddie Cross?"

Tommy nodded. "Austin, I'm sorry—I should have told someone where I was going."

"It's okay, Tommy. She tricked me, too."

"You're too smart to be tricked."

"Sometimes I'm not. I'm sorry, Tommy. You'll always be my brother. Put on the life vest, Tommy. Do it now."

Tommy nodded.

"No!" Amanda said. "Tommy, he's not your brother! He's one of them. An imposter. A liar. He's just like Ivy. Dad replaced you with him. Don't you see? We weren't good enough. Rewind, redo. Mom cries every night because of him. It's not fair!"

The boat drifted. Austin glanced up. There were three Coast Guard boats nearing. They were halfway between Angel Island and Alcatraz. The waves made the boat rock up and down.

"Aussie, I'm sick," Bella said, clutching him.

"It's okay. It's going to be okay."

"Yeah, right," cracked Amanda.

The guy with the bullhorn said, "Prepare to be boarded."

Amanda screamed. "It's not fair. Because of him!" She pointed to Austin. "You used my brother."

"Amanda, it's over. The Coast Guard is here. They're coming."

"It's not. It's not over!"

Amanda rushed Austin. He shielded Bella, but Amanda cut him with the knife she held and pushed him aside. She picked up the small girl and threw her over the edge of the boat.

Tommy screamed. "No! No!" He ran to the rail and looked for her. "Bella!"

The sirens on the Coast Guard ships shrilled.

"Get away from the edge!" Amanda screamed.

Tommy hadn't secured his life vest. It was too small to go around his chest. But either he didn't notice or didn't care.

Bella popped up, her bright orange life vest visible in the murky green water as she rolled up and down with waves that were taller than her. She was pale and terrified and coughing.

Tommy jumped into the water after Bella.

"No!" Austin screamed. Tommy couldn't swim.

Amanda ran to the edge of the boat. "Tommy, why? Why?"

Austin opened the box and found a life preserver ring tied to a rope. He secured the rope to the rear pole and held it while he looked for Tommy.

Tommy hadn't surfaced.

Two Coast Guard skiffs sped up to the *Bella*. Austin almost didn't notice them. "There!" He threw the ring to where he saw a bright orange spot.

It was Tommy's life vest. It had slipped off him.

Amanda pushed Austin. He slipped and fell and hit his head on the deck. "It's your fault," she snarled. "You and your sister. Tommy is *my* brother. *Mine!*"

Her arm came down and he put his arms up to protect himself. Searing pain throbbed through his arm as the knife sliced. Once. Twice. Austin braced for another when suddenly Amanda's weight was off him.

He opened his eyes. Amanda was fighting and kicking as two Coast Guard officers pulled her off him and took away the knife.

Austin crawled to the edge as another officer knelt next to him. "My brother and sister—"

He looked over the edge. Bella was being wrapped in a blanket on one of the skiffs. "Where's Tommy? Please, he can't swim."

The officer didn't say anything, but wrapped a blanket around Austin. There were divers in the water and two of them pulled up Tommy. He wasn't moving. His eyes were closed and his mouth open.

The Coast Guard moved fast. They put Tommy on a different boat from Bella, and there were people there to help him.

"He's okay, right? He's going to be okay, right?"

"Son, you're bleeding, let's get you taken care of."

"Tell me!"

"I don't know, son."

On the main Coast Guard boat, Jimenez took a sullen Amanda Wallace into custody and separated her from the others. Max had watched little Bella wrapped up and carried below deck by a seaman. She was shaking but alive. Then Max watched as they lifted Tommy up on a stretcher. He had an oxygen mask on his face. They'd performed CPR in the skiff. "Is he okay?" she asked one of the medics as they brought him up.

"He's breathing."

They took Tommy below deck. A whole crew of medics were on the boat and they would take care of him.

Bloodied and bruised, Austin was the last on board.

Max had watched the entire scene play out through binoculars, until their boat was close enough that she didn't need them. Now she went up to Austin and hugged him. He was shaking, but he clutched at her. "Tommy," he said.

"He's alive."

Austin started to cry.

"Shh. It's okay. You saved Bella's life, Austin. Putting that life vest on her saved her life."

The medic said, "We need to check him out, miss."

"I'd like to go with him."

Everyone was protective of Tommy, Max realized—even she had been. Because he was needy. And sweet. And slow. But Austin was a thirteen-year-old boy who was practically raising himself with an absentee father, an absentee stepfather, and a disinterested mother. Who was taking care of him? Who was going to protect Austin?

Max felt a sudden kinship with him. They had one thing in common: selfish mothers who didn't give a damn.

Maybe two things in common. The overwhelming need to protect those who couldn't protect themselves.

"I'm proud of you, Austin," Max said as they followed the medics below deck. She caught David's eye. David wasn't expressive as a rule, but right now he looked both relieved and pained. What they'd witnessed would haunt them both for a long time.

CHAPTER THIRTY-SIX

At the hospital, Bill and Paula Wallace sat across from Jenny Wallace in a private waiting room. They weren't arguing, but they weren't talking, either. Grace arrived to inform them that after having been taken into custody, Amanda Wallace was now secured in a juvenile wing of a psychiatric hospital and under suicide watch.

"We're still piecing together exactly what happened," she said, "but Amanda confessed to Austin that she killed Ivy and Travis. Travis helped to lure Ivy to the preserve because he thought he was helping Bailey teach Ivy a lesson. But it was Amanda who tricked him. Your attorney has requested that she be evaluated by a psychiatrist, and that will happen quickly."

When the three Wallaces didn't say anything, Grace continued. "By text, Amanda tricked Austin into coming to the boat. He didn't know it was she who sent him the message. When he got there, Amanda hit him over the head. He has a concussion. He'll be in the hospital tonight. He also was cut up pretty badly when he tried to stop Amanda from throwing Bella overboard. If it weren't for him and Tommy, Bella wouldn't have made it. The Coast Guard said the life vest that Austin put on her while

Amanda was distracted saved her life. Tommy slipped out of his life vest when he jumped into the bay after Amanda threw Bella overboard. He almost didn't make it."

Grace looked from Jenny to Bill, then settled on Paula. "You have two good boys—two young men—who care a lot about each other. Two boys who risked their lives to save their little sister. I sincerely hope the three of you get some family counseling and learn to live with one another because Tommy and Austin showed a hell of a lot more maturity and heroism than any of you."

She didn't wait for a response before walking away.

Austin woke up, startled. It took him a second to remember where he was.

He looked around in the dim hospital light and saw Tommy in the bed next to him. Tommy was sleeping, his mouth open, snoring lightly. Like Austin, he had an IV in his arm.

But he was alive.

Austin thought he'd died. What had Tommy been thinking, jumping in the water? He couldn't swim. But he did it because he loved Bella.

Careful not to make any noise, Austin climbed out of bed. He maneuvered his IV around so he could walk, then went down the hall in search of Bella.

He found his mother sitting in the chair next to Bella's bed. She was half asleep, but when Austin came in she woke up.

"Austin. Hello, sweetheart."

He didn't say anything. He had nothing left inside, not for his mother. When the Coast Guard was bandaging his arm, Max had told him to forgive. He'd flat-out asked Max if she had forgiven her mother for abandoning her. She hadn't answered.

Max had promised at the beginning that she would

never lie to them, and she didn't start then. Austin appreciated it.

Maybe it wasn't all his mother's fault, but she hadn't stopped Ivy from being mean. But mostly, she'd hurt Tommy. She thought he wasn't a good influence, that there was something wrong with him. That he was broken. Imperfect. Was she going to change her opinion overnight? Austin didn't think so.

He walked over to Bella.

"Let her sleep," his mother said.

Austin sat on the edge of Bella's bed. She was so little, so pale. He loved her. He didn't want her to grow up to be like Ivy. But she wouldn't—because she had him and Tommy to make sure of it.

Bella opened her eyes. She saw Austin and smiled. "Hi, Austin."

"Hey, squirt."

She tried to sit up. "Where's Tommy?"

"He's sleeping."

"I wanna see him. We can play cards. Tommy loves cards."

"Okay."

Their mother looked pained. "I think Bella should rest."

"I'm fine, Mommy. I slept a lot. The nice Coast Guard gave me a warm blanket. And a pin. Where's my pin?" She looked around.

Austin saw it on the nightstand and handed it to her.

She beamed. "See? It says 'United States Coast Guard.' I want to be in the Coast Guard. I want to learn how to swim and drive a boat and dive in the water and he said they have helicopters. I can fly a helicopter. Do you want to fly a helicopter, Austin?"

"That would be fun."

Bella was back to her old self. Twelve hours ago she

was floating in the middle of the San Francisco Bay, and now she was happy and talking.

"Let's go see Tommy."

Austin turned to his mother, defiant. Tommy deserved to see Bella. Tommy had tried to save her life. He shouldn't have to say it. He wouldn't say it. If his mother didn't know, didn't believe that now, she never would.

Paula looked worried, like she was about to lose something important. She already had.

Austin said, "I'll bring her back in thirty minutes."

They walked down the hall to the room Austin shared with Tommy.

"Why can't I be in your room, Austin?"

"You're a girl."

"That shouldn't matter."

"Boys have their own room and girls have their own room."

She stuck out her tongue.

Austin pushed open the door and they walked over to Tommy. He was still sleeping.

Bella climbed onto Tommy's bed and picked up his hand. "Tommy. Tommy. Tommy. Wake up, Tommy."

His eyes opened. He stared at Bella as if he didn't recognize her.

"I don't want to get in trouble," he said, his voice scratchy.

"Silly, you're not going to get in trouble! We're going to play cards. Mommy said I could. Right, Austin?"

"Right, Bella."

"I don't feel so good," Tommy said.

Bella climbed up and laid down next to Tommy. "We don't have to play cards. We can watch cartoons. You like cartoons."

"Okay."

Austin turned on the television and sat in the chair next

to Tommy and Bella. Bella put her arm around Tommy. "I love you."

"I love you, too, Bella."

Tommy looked at Austin with wide eyes. "Am I dreaming?"

Austin shook his head. "No, you're not dreaming."

The next time Austin looked over, Bella and Tommy were sound asleep.

CHAPTER THIRTY-SEVEN

"Why are you blaming yourself?"

"You can't read my mind, David. As well as you might know me, you really don't."

He stared at her, not saying anything.

"I don't regret it," she said. "It was lies that created this mess, and lies that propagated it. I just wish . . . there could have been another way."

"Sometimes only the hard way works."

"And where are Tommy and Austin in all of this? Austin had his own agenda, but Tommy was innocent. All he wanted was to be part of his family again. To belong." She paused. "Maybe that's what's wrong with me. I've never really belonged to any family."

"For all her faults, your grandmother loves you greatly," David said.

"Yes, but you don't understand what I mean." Max took a deep breath. She'd always been open and blunt about her mother and her lack of paternity. She'd always *thought* she'd been open about her feelings on the matter. But family was complex. It was messy and emotional.

"After being forced to face some things that happened with my mother," she said, choosing her words carefully.

David was still touchy about the subject of what had happened in June. Touchy wasn't the right word. He was angry, at himself and at the situation. Nothing she'd said had helped. He'd been hired to protect her, and she'd still gotten hurt. That it wasn't his fault didn't register in his brain, and Max had tried to let time fix it.

"I realized," Max continued, "that part of my drive stems from the fact that I'm searching for answers for others because I have no answers for myself. I see that, I recognize it. I always knew it deep down, because I made everyone's tragedies *my* tragedy. I picked cases I felt I could solve, and even when they weren't easy, I didn't let go. I couldn't. Because if I couldn't solve the problem, it would remind me that I can't solve my own problems.

"And one of those problems is that I don't belong. I force myself into situations, I dominate people, I push and push for answers until people simply give up fighting me. But that still doesn't give me a place. I used to think that was okay. A one-woman wrecking ball."

"That is certainly not how you view yourself, Max," David said.

"Maybe I want to belong somewhere," she said. "I don't know anymore. I never thought it mattered, but now . . . that's all Tommy wanted. A simple enough wish. Something that should have been easy for those who loved him to give. There's no doubt in my mind that Jenny loves her son. But she didn't see he was in pain because she was in her own pain. There's no doubt that Austin loves his stepbrother, but Austin was so angry with the world he didn't know how to be at peace. But Tommy's love was pure. It was real. It only wanted a place to belong, a family to love him back. To protect him. And they all failed him."

"Austin is strong."

"He is." Max remembered what she'd thought on the

boat. "He's like me. A survivor. He raised himself. He looks out for everyone else."

"Were you that angry as a child?"

"No, not like Austin. Not angry. But I was cynical. I still am."

"You're worried."

"They claim they're going to get counseling, that they want to be better parents for their children, but I wonder how long that's going to last." Max remained skeptical.

"You solved Ivy's murder. You can't fix the Wallace family overnight," David said.

"Maybe I did more harm than good."

"You don't believe that."

She honestly didn't know. She tried to imagine *not* solving the case and it pained her . . . not knowing was worse. Yet . . . what if she had picked another case to focus on and not this one?

"Maxine Revere," David said sternly, "I'm not a religious man, but I believe in God. I believe that everything happens for a reason. You cannot possibly know what would have happened if you never came to Marin County."

She arched her eyebrows. "Maybe you really can read my mind."

He grunted. "Consider this—Amanda Wallace is a disturbed young woman. If you hadn't come to town, she would still have been a disturbed young woman and no one knows who else she may have hurt. She had a bigger plan than killing Ivy. She stalked Madison Cross. She killed Travis Whitman, shot him three times—once in the head when he was already dead. She moved his body to delay authorities finding him. She lured her brother to the boat so he could watch her toss his sister overboard. What else might she have done? She needs help. Now she can get it, and Bella and Austin are safe. The family promised to get help, and you can't do any more for them now. You have to let it go."

David dreaded seeing Brittney. But it was Emma's birthday. For Emma, he would withstand what he expected would be a bitter verbal attack.

He rang the doorbell. Her house was small but in a nice neighborhood in Mill Valley, on the Corte Madera border. It was only a few blocks from Brittney's parents, and a couple of miles from David's dad's house. Emma was a good kid. She had grandparents who loved her, a mother who—even though flawed—loved her. She was doing well in school, she had a strong sense of right and wrong, and she helped others. He couldn't be more proud of her.

He would do anything for his daughter.

Brittney answered the door. She stared at him as she always did, with a mixture of hatred and pain.

"May I come in?"

"Emma's not here."

He mentally counted to three. He had to control his temper.

"We'd talked about—"

"I changed my mind. You violated the custody agreement."

"Not intentionally."

"You didn't even inform me. Neither did Emma. You had her lie for you."

"I never told Emma to lie."

"She didn't tell me you were at her school."

"Did she lie about it?"

"Lie of omission. Same thing." She narrowed her eyes. "You know about that, don't you? You lied to me all the time."

"I have apologized repeatedly."

"That woman is not a good influence on Emma."

It took David a moment to realize Brittney was talking about Max.

"She doesn't see Max often," David said. "May I come in?"

Still Brittney didn't let him in. "I've decided that you can take Emma to dinner tonight, but not if that woman joins you. I don't like her, I don't trust her, and I don't want my daughter around her."

David wanted to argue. He wanted to defend Max. But he had no rights. Every hour Brittney allowed him to be with Emma was at her discretion. Their custody agreement could be changed by court order, and there was no doubt Brittney could find a judge to give her anything she wanted, if she wanted it badly enough.

Max would be disappointed, but she would understand. *No, she won't understand.*

He would have to explain it to her. And in the end, if Max didn't understand, maybe there was no getting through to her. But she would have to accept that Emma came first, last, and always.

"All right," he said.

"Just like that?"

"I hope you'll change your mind because you're wrong about Max, but I'm not going to risk time with my daughter."

"I'm not wrong about her. You can pick Emma up at my mom's house at five. Bring her back here by nine, it's a school night." She paused. "You know, I don't have to let you see her at all. Your next visit isn't supposed to be until Thanksgiving."

"I know."

She raised an eyebrow.

"Thank you, Brittney."

"You're welcome." She shut the door.

He walked slowly back to the car, hands fisted, controlling every ounce of his raging anger.

It took him time, but he calmed down. Because he would have four hours with his daughter, time he wouldn't have had if he argued with Brittney.

Some things were worth fighting for, but sometimes the fight was internal.

Max had been expecting the visit from Lance Lorenzo all day. He showed up at Scoma's Sunday night while she was dining alone at the restaurant.

"You fucking bitch."

She looked at him coolly. "I warned you."

"You had me fired!"

"You got yourself fired."

He grabbed a chair and sat across from her. The bartender was eyeing the confrontation, but Max wasn't scared of Lorenzo.

"This was my life. You don't need a job. I do!"

She sipped her wine. "You lied in print. You lied about me. And you used kids as pawns." After finding out that Brittney had forbidden Max from seeing Emma, she'd wished she'd done more than get Lorenzo fired. But what more could she have done?

"You're gloating because you were right?" he asked.

"There's nothing to gloat about," she snapped and put her wineglass back on the table. She had nothing inside, not tonight. Not while dining alone in her favorite restaurant while her best friend celebrated his daughter's birthday with his family. She'd told David it was fine, that she was tired, that she would relax after a hectic week. But it wasn't fine. She wasn't angry, which surprised her. She was sad. Over-the-top sad. And she didn't know why.

But now she could let the anger take over. Fuel her.

Because Lance Lorenzo was scum, and he needed to re-alize it. "You are everything I hate in a rotten reporter. You don't care about the truth, you want your story. You used your sister's future in-laws to your advantage. Your disinformation delayed finding the truth about what happened to Ivy Lake. You attributed quotes to me that I did not say. I told you, Lance, first day we met what the terms were. You help me, I help you. You screw with me, I destroy you. You made your bed. I hope you learned something."

He stepped toward her, hands fisted, but she didn't flinch.

"I hate you," he said.

She tilted her chin up and looked him in the eye. "I don't care."

He pushed the table, causing her wineglass to spill. She didn't move. He stormed out.

Immediately, the waiter rushed over and cleaned up the mess. "I would never have let him come over if I'd known—"

"It's okay."

It was and it wasn't. Lorenzo could be a problem for her down the road, but she didn't regret what she'd done. He'd damaged the police investigation and he was a sensational liar. He'd attempted to humilate her. He had no business calling himself a reporter.

But, worse, he'd brought David's family into the mix. He'd jeopardized David's custody agreement. Lance Lorenzo was the reason Max was alone tonight.

Her phone vibrated again; another missed call from Nick. She didn't call him back. She wasn't in the mood. He wanted a one-sided relationship—if he couldn't share about what his ex-wife was doing that upset him and that threatened his time with his son, Max didn't know if she could fully trust him.

It hurt. She cared. Far too much. But she was too emotionally raw from what happened yesterday on the bay, and missing David's family dinner tonight, to play the game with Nick. Maybe next time she was in town.

If there was a next time.

The waiter brought her another glass of wine and asked if she was ready to order.

"I'll just have the crab cakes," she said. "I'm not that hungry."

"You're always hungry," a familiar voice said behind her.

She looked over her shoulder. Nothing could have surprised her more.

Nick.

He bent down and kissed her on the lips, ran a hand along her back, then sat down across from her. "You've been ignoring my calls."

"It's been a busy weekend."

"I know. I called David to find out where you were."

She didn't know how she felt about that.

"You're mad at me," he said.

"I'm too tired to argue."

He frowned. "Do you want me to leave?"

No. Yes. "I'm not great company."

"That's okay. At least, let me treat you to dinner."

Their conversation was superficial. Two adults who had great sex together, but what else? Max didn't know. She should tell Nick to leave until he was willing to talk about his ex-wife with her. She didn't want an off-limits topic between them.

Brittney's machinations today had hurt and angered Max. She blamed David . . . but she didn't at the same time. All he wanted was time with his daughter, and Max was simply his friend and employer. She'd put too much into their friendship. Family always came first. And it should, when you had a family.

"Hey, what's wrong?"

"Nothing," she said with a smile.

"Tell me."

"Tell me what Nancy is doing in court."

Nick looked like she'd slapped him. "Max, I can't. Don't draw the line."

"You drew the line," she said quietly.

He didn't say anything for a long minute. "I care about you, Maxine."

She had nothing to say. What could she say? That she wanted him to trust her? She'd said that before; he hadn't responded. She didn't like repeating herself. She didn't like being ignored.

"I'll go," he said.

"Don't."

He tilted his head, confused.

He would never understand. And maybe it was over. She'd try not to care so much. But right now Max didn't want to be alone.

She stood and took his hand. Pulled him out of his seat. She kissed him. "My flight leaves at eight in the morning. Let's not waste any time."

"We should talk—"

"No. We shouldn't."

"Max—"

"Shh. It's okay for now."

It wasn't, not really, but she could pretend.

At least for tonight.

Read on for an excerpt from

SHATTERED

Allison Brennan's next Maxine Revere thriller, which finds Max teaming up with Lucy Kincaid

Available August 2017 from Minotaur Books

"Andrew? I'm going to put you on speaker. Sean's here."

Rookie FBI Agent Lucy Kincaid Rogan put her cell phone down on the island in the kitchen where she and Sean had been eating a late dinner.

"Stanton?" Sean mouthed. Lucy nodded. Her former brother-in-law had never directly called her before, and she'd known him her entire life. She was both suspicious and curious. Why would the DA of San Diego reach out to her? Family or work? She'd last seen him over a year ago during the Christmas holidays, and that hadn't been under the best of circumstances.

"Hello, Sean," Andrew said.

"Andrew."

"I'm sorry to call so late."

"Nine isn't late for us," Lucy said. "Just tell me that everything's okay."

"Yes—in a manner of speaking. Your family's fine, as far as I know. They don't really talk to me anymore."

Lucy knew why—her sister Nelia was Andrew's ex, and Andrew had cheated on Nelia. There was more—a lot more—but Lucy had been so young when they split up she didn't truly understand the situation. Andrew had always been kind to her, and when she needed his help last Christmas to get information, he'd come through. She respected that.

Andrew continued. "I don't know exactly how to broach this subject, so I'll get to the point. An investigative reporter is looking into Justin's murder. She claims that she has compelling evidence that Justin's death is connected to two or more homicides in the southwest. She'll be in San Diego tomorrow."

That was the last thing Lucy expected Andrew to say. She didn't know how to respond—her nephew Justin's murder had haunted her for nearly twenty years, but she'd put it behind her. She'd been seven. So had Justin. They'd been best friends and had grown up together until Justin was kidnapped and murdered. It had torn the family apart.

"A reporter?" Sean said, his voice edged with anger. "Why are you calling Lucy?"

"I think there might be something to this woman's theory. Lucy, I don't have a right to ask for your help, but the last time I wanted to revisit Justin's murder, I ran up against a brick wall known as the Kincaid family."

That didn't surprise Lucy. Her family never wanted to discuss Justin or his murder. It had been a dark time in the Kincaid family history. Twenty years was a long time to sit unsolved, and most crimes this old were never solved.

"I didn't know you had wanted to reopen Justin's case."

"As an unsolved homicide, it's never been closed. Eight years ago—you'd just left for Georgetown." He paused. "I never told you this, and I don't want to bring up bad memories."

"I'm a big girl, Andrew."

Sean took her hand, lightly kissed it, and held it. She could feel the tension within him—this was nearly as difficult for him as it was for her. The past. *Her* past.

"After your kidnapping—when you came home—I

wanted to be there for you, for your family. Even after everything that has happened, and all the mistakes I've made, I care about you and all the Kincaids. Your parents have always been cordial, but your brothers and sister never forgave me. Especially Connor and Carina, maybe because they still live here and I work with them. They didn't want me around, and I walked away. But I thought maybe—if I could put Justin to rest—they could find peace. Not knowing why someone killed my son . . ." His voice faded away, then he cleared his throat and said, "I approached your father. He was adamant that I stand down. Carina found out I had pulled the case files, and confronted me—it wasn't pretty. At the time, Patrick was still in a coma, I knew your family was suffering, you'd moved cross-country, Dillon—who has always been the diplomat of the family, and the only one who I know forgave me—was living in DC. I didn't have a buffer, so I shelved it."

"I didn't know any of that." It stunned her, truly. She caught Sean's eye. He was listening closely to Andrew.

Sean said, "Why? If you had something new, why would you shelve it?"

"I didn't have anything new—I just wanted to look at the case with fresh eyes, time, new technology. But I couldn't put your family through a new investigation when they had nearly lost you, Lucy, and Patrick's future was so uncertain."

"I understand," Lucy said, and she did. "And the reporter changed your mind."

"Yes. She has. But your family isn't going to want to go through this, and I don't want to hurt them."

"Then why do it at all?" Sean asked.

"Because Maxine Revere is going to investigate whether I want her to or not. And honestly, Sean? I want answers. God, I want to know what happened. For years

I deferred my pain to your family—Nelia's family. When every lead dried up, they put it behind them. Not completely—I know Justin haunts them as much as he haunts me. But Nelia moved to Idaho, and that was it. They wanted no part of me, no part of my ideas or talking about what happened. But I'm a prosecutor—having any crime unsolved bothers me, but my own son? It's finger-nails on the chalkboard, every waking minute. I've looked into this Revere woman. She has a solid track record solving cold cases."

"But what is she going to do after?" Sean asked. He caught Lucy's eye. She knew exactly what he was thinking. "Lucy and I steer clear of reporters."

"She wants my help, and I plan on laying down ground rules. Protecting you is my number-one priority, Lucy."

"I don't need your protection, Andrew." Lucy saw the darkness cross Sean's face. She took his hand. "What do you want from me? Do you want me to talk to my family? Convince them to cooperate? Talk to this reporter?"

"Actually, I want you to listen to what Revere has to say. You're an FBI agent. You have the training and ex-perience to weed through the bullshit and get to the meat. I know you've had a rocky start to your career—but I have friends in high places, Lucy. You have closed some ex-tremely difficult cases."

True, though she wasn't the only agent involved in those complex cases.

Andrew continued. "In hindsight, I don't think anyone understood the pain you went through when Justin died. He was as close as a brother to you, we all knew that, but in his death everyone seemed to forget that you were grieving. They shielded you from the investigation, from the truth of what happened that night because you were only seven years old. You're probably the only Kincaid who doesn't have a preconceived notion as to anything that happened. I think you're the only one who can look at the evidence with an unbiased eye. Who doesn't blame me."

"No one blames you, Andrew."

He laughed, but it was filled with anguish and sorrow. "I wish that were true. Connor said it when the truth came out—when your family found out I was having an affair. He said if I'd been there, at home that night and not in bed with my mistress, Justin would have been alive. A bit more crudely, but that was his message. There's not been a day that has passed that I haven't thought about that, whether it was true. If I am ultimately, even indirectly, to blame." He took a deep breath. "Nell and I have made peace with each other. I talk to her, once a year, on Justin's birthday. We made a lot of mistakes, but Justin wasn't one of them. She's content now. She has Tom, he's been good for her, and while I don't know if she's happy, I know she's at peace. I don't want to hurt her. I will keep her out of this as best I can, but in the end, she may have information that she doesn't know she has. I know that no one, not even Dillon, will discuss it with her. Except you. I think you would do it."

What did that make Lucy? Cruel? Was that what Andrew thought of her, because she had a reputation for being cold?

"Andrew—"

"I don't know that it'll come to that," he said, interrupting her. "I'd just like you to hear what this woman has to say. If you tell me there's nothing, that going down this path will result in no answers and only heartache for your family, I'll do everything in my power to stop her. But if you see what I see, that we might finally get answers as to why Justin died, that we might find out who killed him . . . I don't have anyone else, Lucy."

"A moment, Andrew," Sean said. He put the phone on

mute. "It's your choice, Lucy. Whatever you decide, I'm with you."

The grief Lucy experienced when Justin was killed nearly twenty years ago had been young and immature, but no less painful. She didn't know what had happened to him, not right away. She didn't know why her mother cried all the time, why her sister Nelia wouldn't talk to her, why there were policemen in her house, why Carina needed a lawyer, why no one would let Andrew come over for dinner anymore. All she knew was that Justin, her best friend since they were born, was gone. One day he was there, playing catch with her in the backyard, swimming with her at the community pool, teasing her when she lisped after her two front teeth fell out. Her mother watched Justin during the week because Nelia and Andrew both worked—Lucy spent more waking hours with Justin than any other person her age. They'd even been in the same first-grade class together. And that summer was supposed to be the most fun ever. They were going to go to a sleepover camp for the first time for two whole weeks. It was all Justin could talk about, he was so excited.

But that never happened because he was killed two weeks before they were going to leave.

He was gone. One day there, the next not. She'd been gutted, but she didn't talk to anyone about it because everyone was so sad and talking about Justin seemed to make them sadder.

Maybe that was why she'd always kept her emotions deep inside. Partly because of her own kidnapping and rape when she was eighteen . . . but it had started a long time before then. It had started when she grieved for her best friend and couldn't talk to anyone about it.

Now, while she understood death, she had faced evil, she knew that bad people did horrific things to innocent people—she didn't always know *why*.

Maybe finding out who killed Justin wasn't as important as finding out *why* he was killed.

And if there were other victims of the same killer, did that mean the killer was still out there? After twenty years? Would he kill again? Destroy another family?

"I have to," Lucy whispered to Sean.

He kissed her hand. "I know."

She would have smiled if she wasn't so melancholy. "I love you."

He winked. "I know."

Now she did smile, because if she didn't, she might cry. And tears weren't productive.

She un-muted the phone. "When is this reporter coming?"

"Tomorrow afternoon. I don't have the exact time."

"Text me the details. I'll be there."

Danielle Sullivan didn't like going out with people from work, but it was expected. For every time she declined an invitation, she had to accept one—otherwise people would look at her too closely. She just wanted to do her job and go home, drink a bottle of wine, and try to sleep.

Try being the operative word. Sleep was a rarity for her. When she felt herself being dragged under from exhaustion, she would take a sleeping pill or three. Her body needed the rest, even if her mind couldn't.

There had been a time . . . more than once . . . when she considered taking the entire bottle of prescription sleeping pills, a large glass of wine, and reclining in her bathtub. Just fall asleep. Slip under. Disappear forever.

But would the nightmare end in death? Or would earth's cruel God force her to relive the worst day of her life? Over and over and over . . .

Nina Fieldstone poked her head into the bathroom. "Danielle, are you coming?"

"Just touching up my make-up. Two minutes?"

Nina smiled. She was a pretty woman, and smart. One of the few in the office Danielle felt a rapport with. Nina was technically her supervisor, but had never made Danielle feel stupid or unvalued. Because Nina had been the one to ask her to join the group for their "Wine Wednesday," Danielle had agreed.

"Alright, but remember, happy hour is over at seven, so don't be long."

Danielle turned to the mirror and pretended to put on more mascara. She didn't wear a lot of make-up, but too many sleepless nights required it. She pulled out a tube of concealer and hid the dark circles. Added a little color. Better.

She still felt like a ghost beneath the gloss and glitter.

The bar—called The Gavel because of the proximity to the courthouse—where the legal secretaries hung out every Wednesday night was two blocks from their law office in Glendale. It was a large firm, and anywhere from four to ten women met once a week to let off steam and enjoy company and gossip.

It was the gossip Danielle hated, almost as much as the small talk.

Tonight six of them sat at one of the booths and drank wine. Danielle had to regulate herself. Alone, she would drink an entire bottle. With people, one was all she could handle.

Nina put her hand over Danielle's. "I'm so glad you decided to join us tonight, especially after the victory you helped secure."

"I didn't do anything," Danielle said. "Just my job."

"You caught two huge mistakes that saved our client tens of thousands of dollars, and a major embarrassment for our firm. Your drink's on me tonight."

Danielle didn't want the accolades. Yes, she was good at her job. It was all she had. Work, or dying slowly. Those were her options.

The women all chatted amongst each other. Danielle responded to questions because it was expected. She asked a few of her own—she could play the small-talk game when she had to. Half the women at the table were married—Grace had no kids, Natalie had a teenage daughter, and Nina had a son.

An eight-year-old boy named Kevin.

Danielle didn't want to ask, but she couldn't help herself. As the conversation turned to relationships and children, she said, "Is your husband home with Kevin? Does he watch him every Wednesday?"

It was casual, and fit with the conversation, but one that had been on Danielle's mind a lot lately.

Ever since she saw Tony Fieldstone watching his law partner, Lana Devereaux, at the Christmas party six weeks ago. The way he looked at her. The way he watched her walk. Danielle knew the look.

She knew it well.

Too well.

Nina rolled her eyes. "Sometimes he does—he loves spending time with Kevin, don't get me wrong, but Tony is all work, work, work. And tonight he had a poker game with Judge Carlson and the gang. Third Wednesday of the month. I say, why not Fridays when you don't have to be in court the next morning? But *men*."

Men. Right.

Danielle had worked for Taggert, Fieldstone, Finch and Devereaux for three years. She knew of the poker game, it was common knowledge just like Wine Wednesdays and the monthly Bunco game Grace pushed that she had, thankfully, avoided almost every month. But she wondered how long the game really went. If maybe Tony Fieldstone had someplace else he wanted to be.

A place he wasn't supposed to be.

With a woman he wasn't supposed to be with.

"You okay, Danielle?" Nina asked.

"Sorry—long day. Little headache."

"Another glass of wine? You can Uber home and I'll pick you up in the morning. You don't live too far from me."

"No, I'm fine." She smiled, such a fake smile, but no one knew. "Do you have a regular babysitter for Kevin? He's such a good kid." Nina had brought him into the office a couple of times when there were minimum days in school and she didn't have a sitter. Danielle tried not to pay attention to him, but she couldn't help it. He was a perfect child.

Perfect.

Tony didn't deserve a perfect son like Kevin when he was off screwing another woman.

You don't know that he is having an affair. You only suspect.

She knew. She damn well *knew* and she would prove it. She always did.

"Tony's mom watches him after school—she lives only a couple blocks from his school, walks over and gets him every day. It's nice, Kevin being able to spend some time with his grandmother."

"It is," Danielle agreed.

But you should be picking him up at school. You should be spending the time with him. Instead you're sitting here laughing and drinking wine with a bunch of selfish, arrogant women.

"We have a regular babysitter when we have to work late—Maggie Crutcher."

There was a lawyer named Wayne Crutcher. Maggie

was his daughter. A teenager. Probably brought her boyfriend over to fuck when Kevin went to bed. They all did. They couldn't be trusted.

The talk turned back to the office, and Danielle was relieved. She still needed to get out of here. Forty-five minutes . . . that was long enough, wasn't it? She showed her face, made the small talk, did the dance, she needed to go because she was already on edge.

"You know, I'm really tired after today," Danielle said. She finished her wine and smiled. "I think I'm going to call it a night."

"Do you want to join us Friday for Bunco? It's at Shelly's house in Burbank," Grace said. "You had so much fun last time you came."

Danielle barely remembered the last time—it was six months ago. She had had too much wine, that she was certain.

"I don't know—my mom is having a hard time getting around and I help her on the weekends. Shopping, fixing things around the house, you know."

"You're so good to you mom," Nina said. Danielle had told her all about her mother years ago, mostly to get out of socializing. "To drive all the way up there."

"Where does she live?" Natalie asked.

"Sacramento," Danielle lied. But it was a lie she told often, so it was one that came out smoothly. "It's only five, six hours depending on traffic. I don't mind, put on a book-on-tape or listen to music. But if she doesn't need me, I'll consider Bunco. You know me, I'm not really an extrovert. Too many people makes me antsy." That was the truth.

Nina smiled and patted her hand. "No pressure, but I would love you to come. It's one night a month, a great way to get out and just relax, no work the next day."

"Thanks." She got up, said good-byes—why did it take

so long to just tell people *good-bye*? Why more questions, more small talk, more *nothingness*?

Finally, she was free. She walked back to the parking garage and retrieved her car. She intended to drive home where she could open a bottle of wine and maybe eat something, but she found herself outside Judge Carlson's house.

The judge had a private address, but she'd followed Tony Fieldstone here last month, after she suspected he was screwing Lana Devereaux. She saw Tony's car in the driveway of the opulent house in the Glendale hills.

And Lana's car. Did Nina know that Lana played poker with "the boys"? The only female partner . . . was that how it started? The one night a month . . . turn into something more?

For two hours Danielle watched the house from down the street. Then a car left.

Lana.

Five minutes later a second car left.

Tony.

She followed him.

Tony didn't go home. She knew where he lived, because she'd once gone to Bunco at Nina's house when she first started the job with this law firm. Instead, Tony went to Lana Devereaux's condo in Los Feliz.

Heart racing, she drove past his car as he got out. He didn't pay any attention to her. And her black Honda Accord was common. It didn't stand out. Just like she didn't stand out.

Danielle went straight home. When she pulled into her garage, she turned off the ignition and sat there. Her knuckles were white. Slowly, she peeled her hands off the steering wheel. They were sore from gripping so hard.

She went inside and poured a glass of wine. Drank it quickly, then poured another and picked up her phone.

"Hello," the familiar voice said. A voice that belonged

to a man she had once loved with all her heart and soul . . . and now hated.

"Have you cheated on your wife yet? Because you know you will. You're all the same. All of you. Disgusting."

"Danielle."

"Why did you do it? Why?"

She asked the same question every time she called him. He never had a good answer. Because there wasn't a good answer.

"I was a fool."

"I hate you."

"I know. Is that why you called? To tell me how much you hate me?"

"No." She closed her eyes. "I loved you so much. I loved you so much it hurts. And . . ." Her voice cracked. The pain was real. Still so very real. Time didn't heal all wounds. Whoever said that hadn't lost their entire world.

"I'm sorry, Danielle. I truly am sorry."

"It should have been you. I wish you had died instead."

"So do I, Danielle. But you can't—"

She ended the call, unable to listen to her ex-husband anymore. She threw her half-filled wine glass across the room and screamed as it shattered against the wall. She watched the red liquid run down the plaster for several minutes, her mind blank.

Then she walked back to the kitchen, retrieved another wine glass, and poured more wine. She sat at the table and stared straight ahead as she drank.

Thinking.

Planning.

Hating.

It was so much easier to hate than it was to forgive.

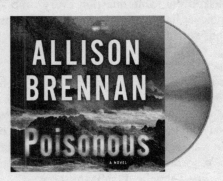

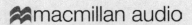